STRIFE &VALOR

REGINA WATTS

PAINTED BLIND
PUBLISHING
LITERARY ALCHEMY

PAINTED BLIND
PUBLISHING
LITERARY ALCHEMY

Burningsoul Saga Book II: Strife & Valor
© 2021 Regina Watts

Text: Regina Watts
Typesetting: M. F. Sullivan
Cover Painting: Vanette Kosman

http://www.hrhdegenetrix.com
http://www.paintedblindpublishing.com
publicity@paintedblindpublishing.com

WELTYR: Now bridle your steed,
Valiant warrior maiden!
A frenzied fight
Is about to be unleashed.
Let Brynhildr storm to battle;
Let her secure victory for the Wotsung!
Let Hunding lie
Where he falls;
He's no good to me in the Valor Hall.
So get ready for war,
Ride fast into battle!

BRYNHILDR: Hojotoho! Hojotoho!
Heiaha! Heiaha!

*—A common tongue translation
of an ancient song for Weltyr,
as interpreted in the time
of Rorke Burningsoul*

BRANWEN'S HERO

BRANWEN'S RESCUE CAME second-nature to me. It would have been that way for anyone I found in peril, but from the first second I glimpsed those familiar gold curls framing her bright green eyes, my body launched into motion. The misshapen bandits around us hissed and drew arms, but Strife was already hot in my hand. I dove into the fray, my as heart gladdened by the sound of Indra's crossbow as by the clinking of Odile's dagger.

And what of Valeria? I wondered about her battle prowess as I ducked a swinging flail. This new angle permitted me to drive the point of my broadsword up into the diabolical centaur's spider abdomen. Just as the ichor of its insides splattered upon the cavern floor, my limbs chilled with the strange kiss of a cool breeze that made no sense in the subterranean Nightlands.

A quick inspection revealed phantom armor had enrobed my body. It appeared as though tendrils of smoke had furled around me to produce a set of plate mail. This armor, despite its semi-transparent appearance, did a better job of protecting me from the dart shot by a nearby bandit than would have my tunic alone. Before I dealt with the shooter, I followed the magical fog that unfurled from my back like the spectral threads of an invisible loom.

The spools from which they unwound were the fingertip of Valeria. The elegant Materna of the durrow people emitted this magical energy from her hands even without the ring she had sacrificed to save my life.

The sight of her naked fingertip irked me. I turned, hefting Strife just in time to parry the scimitar of a scurrying coward who had hoped to overtake me while my gaze was diverted. The fools did not know I had only just done battle with a spirit-thief, the sorcerer Al-listux, and that I was in no mood to trifle with feral thieves of the Nightlands. While the force of Strife's parry snapped the scimitar in twain, the misshapen's eyes widened in horror. The continued force of my blade introduced him to Oppenhir as the greenish vital fluid of the spider-centaur splattered out across the floor. This ichor reminded me, for a flash, of the acidic spirit-thief blood that got me into all this mess. Those squid-headed demons were owed my thanks, in a way, yet I loved them no more for it, I confess.

It was true I had not spent very long in slavery, and that I had consented to it: I had honored the word sworn to Odile and Indra when they revived me from that first battle in the den of the spirit-thieves. But Weltyr— Praise the One True Light!—was the one who guided me to and saw me through those shadows, and brought me out on the other side not just to freedom, but rewards. I had Valeria's love, and Odile and Indra's affection, too.

And now, I had the opportunity to forgive Branwen.

"Rorke," cried the most agonizing of those three party members who betrayed me in the spirit-thief den. The beautiful high elf struggled against the spider webbing in which she'd been encased, going on with a gasp, "Thank Anroa! Oh, I'm so relieved to see you still alive—"

That forgiveness my god challenged me to produce was going to be a tall order. I looked at her somewhat coldly in spite of just how mutual that relief was, then turned to catch the arm of a bandit with Strife's steel edge.

"After the way you left things between us last time," I told Branwen without looking at her, "I never thought I'd hear you say a thing like that."

While the howling bandit stumbled back from the blow and I jerked Strife out of his arm, the elf's great blue eyes filled with tears. Still wiggling in her bonds, she cried out when Odile first hurried to her with the dagger; then, as the dark elf rogue made short work of tearing open the spider-webbing around the captive druid, Branwen's expression of fear faded to one of surprise.

"I'm sorry for what I did to you back in the spirit-thief den," cried Branwen.

By then, I was too busy to respond. I raised my arm and caught a sword's blow against the hard fog of Valeria's spirit armor. As the phantom gauntlet rattled with the energy, I thrust Strife forward and pierced the bandit's humanoid gut. He howled in pain to be disemboweled, falling back upon the earth while Indra at last took down the misshapen who had been blowing cruelly-tipped poison darts to little avail. At the impact of her bolts,

3

the shooter screamed and gripped his wounded arm. His eyes, though lacking pupils as were these eyes of all dark elves, nonetheless still said he finally realized what I had been doing so efficiently to his friends.

By the time Odile finished pulling open the webbing around Branwen, the misshapen had thrown down his blow gun and made a dash to the door. Valeria moved to block his exit. While he skidded to a stop to figure out how to get around her, his spider legs scrambling and skidding across the stones, Indra launched one more projectile of her own and managed to nail the bandit right between his eyes. These now unseeing orbs rolled up into the back of his head and his eight legs collapsed beneath him. The last of the misshapen bandits died upon the floor, leaving myself and the durrow all the more convinced of our ability to work as a team.

Branwen, however, still looked with fear between my companions—as if they were, in any sense, equivalent to those captors who had just held her for ransom or worse.

While Valeria's phantom armor unwound from my shoulders, innocent Indra to the freed captive. "Are you hurt?"

Her delay clearly indicating she belatedly realized the durrow addressed her, Branwen stuttered out, "I—well, yes, a little."

The Materna of the durrow passed me by, saying, "Permit me lay hands on you…you'll feel a bit of heat."

While the other durrow stood aside, Valeria's fine lips moved in a soft healing prayer to her goddess, Roserpine. The dark elf set her glowing hands upon Branwen's unready ones. The high elf gasped softly, her pale face flushing with a sweet pink tinge of astonishment to be healed by a durrow—by a member of the notoriously cruel race of slave-traders. By then, I was less surprised. I may not have worshiped Roserpine or respected her particular teachings, but even I was forced to admit that prayers in the durrow goddess's name had as much tangible effect as any prayer to Weltyr. Before my very eyes, the scratches and bruises across the high elf's pale arms faded to reveal perfect, unbroken flesh.

My hands itched to touch her. Instead, I busied them by wiping clean Strife's enchanted blade and sliding it back home to its sheath.

"How marvelous," commented Branwen, her eyes now tearless but still quite wide while she observed her own healing. "Durrow magic can mend wounds just as well as one of Anroa's healers!"

"Because I'm one of Roserpine's healers," answered the Materna simply, lifting her hands away from Branwen's. As the high elf turned her arms this way and that to investigate how complete the healing process had been, my former mistress stared on. "And you are Branwen. One of the party members who betrayed Rorke in the den of the spirit-thieves."

With no other injury to nurse but a pair of rope-burns, Branwen rubbed her wrists and affected a sullen pout. "I suppose he went about telling the whole city of El'ryh," commented the high elf, her downcast eyes flickering twice toward me. Picking webbing from her hair as she soon was, the high elf was unprepared for Valeria's next comment.

"No," said the woman who was mistress of my heart only, now that my body and mind were once more fully free for Weltyr's command. "He related the story of your betrayal to me once we had made love and his mood grew more gently inclined. Burningsoul is somewhat stoic, otherwise."

Thunder sweeping across her face, Branwen looked between the two of us and said to me in shock, "You and this—durrow, Rorke?"

"*These* durrow," I amended, glancing between the other ladies with a mild clearing of my throat. While, grinning, Indra and Odile waved, I gestured between them. "Branwen, ah—this is Odile Darkstar and Indra of the Nocturna Clan."

"Ho there," said bold Odile, offering her hand for a shake. "No wonder you were so broken-hearted over this wench's betrayal...if only we were permitted to return to El'ryh! She'd make a fine attendant for your baths, Madame."

With a wry chuckle, Valeria explained to the high elf, "I'm afraid you will have to excuse them...Odile is quite forward, and Indra lets herself be pushed around. My name is Valeria of El'ryh, Materna of the City and the representative of Roserpine before the people—and the people before Roserpine."

"When you left me for dead," I said, trying to keep my tone as level as possible, "Odile and Indra here found me. They made me swear that, in exchange for healing, I would come peaceably with them to the city of El'ryh and serve as a slave. Only by virtue Weltyr's grace and Valeria's ill fortune was I able to escape, and now she has freed me...and I should think to find you here as I do now, Branwen, that this has all been timed to the ticking of the All-Father's cosmic clock. I never thought I would see you again, let alone rescue you from brigands like this. How is it you find yourself back down here?"

As if reminded of the increasingly late hour and the need for shelter by the mention of our dispatched foes, Indra and Odile exchanged murmurs. Experienced adventurers that they were, they then set about dragging the vanquished mishappen from the places where they had fallen, patting down the bodies for loot, and organizing them into a semi-tidy row that was easily avoidable. While watching this from the corner of her eye, Branwen found she was out of webbing to pick from her golden hair. Now she simply began worrying a few locks that hung free over her shoulder.

"Anroa haunted me fiercely on our way out of the Nightlands, and once we emerged again at the surface...I don't know how I let Grimalkin talk me into anything like this!"

"So, it was Grimalkin behind the scheme?" The dwarf and I had endured more than one argument between the two of us in our time journeying together. It somehow struck me as wholly unsurprising that he would be responsible, in greater or smaller part, for the treachery that could have easily ended with my death. Unsurprising, and perhaps a bit convenient. I went on, "Clearly those feelings you confessed to me in all the nights of our journey were just part of some greater ploy—"

"No, Rorke!"

One fist clasping at her heart, the druid listed toward me and cried, "Anroa strike me down where I stand if that be true. Each word I said to you, Rorke, I meant."

"Just as you meant that crossbow bolt you would have struck me with." While her delicate jaw clenched in frustration, I scanned the room. "Do you still have the bow?"

"They destroyed it before my very eyes when I was ambushed—I returned here alone, leaving Grimalkin and Hildolfr to do as they pleased with the blasted Scepter of Weltyr and all the reward money. I wanted to find you,

Rorke. I couldn't sleep through the night for thinking I'd abandoned you that way."

"For knowing Valeria as I am now blessed to, I sometimes think it was a good thing that you made such a mistake…and, of course, all our mistakes are guided by the Wanderer."

I withheld my sigh through some miracle of self-control, assessing, as I did, meek Branwen. She had often barely tolerated my spiritual pontification and now seemed no more pleased than usual with such a lecture, but more patient—perhaps knowing its conclusion would be in her favor. I went on, sliding a hand around Valeria's waist to earn a surprised glance from both elf women, dark and light.

"I forgive you, Branwen; in the end, none of us can truly help what we do. Even within the realms of free will, our actions are paradoxically precisely as Weltyr has allotted for."

Her lips briefly pursing, as they would when she was set to accuse me of patronizing her during our religious discussions wherein I would posit to her the teaching that all deities were simply lesser emanations of Weltyr. Valeria, being herself a holy woman, had not taken offense to such a notion when I brought it up; but I have noticed that the less someone understands their own religion, the more inclined they are to take offense when it is challenged. Branwen was a creature of nature, and her goddess, Anroa, was the goddess of Love—that one and only ruler of those who threw themselves into the bosom of life without sparing much thought for what came after. The high elf lived for pleasure…a trait she had in common with her Nightland-dwelling sisters, even if she was not quite as open about it as they were.

But Branwen was not open about many things—

not with the average individual. Still on the defense, she assured me, "If it's true that Weltyr gains any reward from the wills of men, then it is a very mysterious reward, indeed. After all, Hildolfr and Grimalkin have still made off with that Scepter."

My ears perked along with my heart. There was hope! The Holy Order of the Wanderer had sent me on a quest to liberate the relic from the slimy grasp of the spirit-thieves—a task for which I had recruited the one-eyed ranger Hildolfr, the brutish but cunning dwarf Grimalkin, and, of course, sensual and astute Branwen. With my companions having taken the scepter from my grasp, I was unable to be fully confirmed to the Order… and, out of my own personal sense of shame, unable to return to Skythorn, the location of the temple that raised me.

And from the start of my ordeal among the durrow, that had been the most painful thought of all: the possibility that I was doomed to remain in slavery, unable to ever again see Skythorn.

Carefully nursing the potential of completing my quest after all, I asked, "Where have they gone?"

"Grimalkin's plan was to take the Scepter back across the sea and sell it in Rhineland for a hefty reward." While she named the country of the dwarves, I ran my free hand over my jaw. We would stick out like sore thumbs there…and dwarfs were not known for their happy dealings with humans. The high elf went on, "The money didn't tempt me near so much as the thought of your well-being."

Seared as I still was by her betrayal, I wasn't sure I could trust these sweet words to any extent. All the same, the possibility of reclaiming the Scepter enthralled me. Studying Valeria's dark and thoughtful face as though it might hint at the clarity I needed, I swept a few strands of white hair behind the curve of her long ear, then made the Materna a suggestion.

"There are many in the Temple of Weltyr devoted to scrying the locations of lost artifacts. Usually such feats are performed only for Weltyr, but surely the prayers would be equally adept at locating the relics of any god. What say you? We could retrieve the Scepter of Weltyr and, upon its delivery, request the Temple's assistance in locating your ring."

The Materna studied Branwen as though for hints of deception, but had there been any, the elf would have expertly concealed them. Thus, without the ring by which she read the intentions in the hearts of men, Valeria was forced to divine these things from the same body language as the rest of us. Obliged to trust fair Branwen, if only due to my willingness to commit to the same for now, Valeria rested her hand upon my heart.

"If you, Burningsoul, believe such a task will expedite the discovery of Roserpine's ring, I will do it gladly...and, after all I put you through while you were in the Nightlands, perhaps it is the least I could do."

My hand fit to the warm, soft curve of her cheek on instinct. "It was no hardship to serve you, neither as guard nor as lover."

With only the slightest thrill for the thought of jealous Branwen watching us, I bent my head and pressed my kiss to Valeria's sighing lips. The sweetness of her mouth was a nectar on my tongue, and I sighed with pleasure to taste it in the aftermath of that battle. I only lifted my head when Odile dusted off her hands and assessed her work with a sigh.

As my gaze lifted toward her, I happened to note Branwen's unbroken stare of astonishment—and the slightest hint of an embarrassed but fascinated scowl.

"There," announced Odile, hands on her hips. Indra, grimacing, shoved a misshapen corpse into the same nook as the rest of the bodies, then looked down at the ichor on her palms with disgust. Odile, meanwhile, had gone on, "Seems to us that this is good a place as any to wait out the dark…will the elf be staying with us?"

"What do you think, Branwen?" I looked hopefully at her, Valeria's body in my arm pressing all the closer to mine as I addressed my former lover. "Would you care to stay with us, at least until we reach the surface? I would appreciate any information you could give that might ease our pursuit of the traitors."

Her rigid posture relaxing at the invitation, Branwen folded both dainty hands upon her heart and swore, "I'll tell you everything I know, Rorke. Thank you—thank you for saving me."

"Saving you was nothing," I told her, turning to help the ladies bar the den's main door. "Forgiveness, now that's the hard part…and the most important."

JOYOUS REUNIONS

BLUE WISP FIRE burned in the hearth near the back of the den, the smokeless flames dancing together while we huddled around its magic warmth.

We had plundered the chambers of the bandits to great reward. In addition to a vast sum of gold and silver that had surely been raided from the coffers of waylaid merchants, we uncovered many wares. Thick furs from aboveground animals I recognized—dogs of Weltyr, to my sorrow, among the pelts of plains-kings and unmentionable ones—had served as the beddings of the various bandits.

Now they made up our own. A larder turned up bread, salted fish (a hideous, blind breed known only to the Nightlands, with hateful fangs and a thirst for blood), and, most importantly, ale. All this alongside other stores of staples and ingredients that would have required more processing than any of us had interest or experience for.

We ate together in happy relief, glad to have a place to wait out the dark in relative safety.

Maybe even in comfort. When the meal had been eaten it occurred to me that Branwen had been really very quiet throughout most of the conversation. I nudged her, drawing her attention from the bottom of her ale mug, and said merrily, "Now, Branwen, there's no need to look sour—I'm working on forgiving you, remember?"

"And I'm glad. It's only—I suppose I'm just a bit confused about a few things."

While I lifted my eyebrows, Branwen looked between all four of us. Her face soon glowed with blushing contemplation and she said then after a few seconds, "Perhaps I'd ought not to ask."

"Ask away," enthused Odile, swinging her mug in the direction of the high elf. "There'd ought to be no secrets between those who travel together! Especially after what happened between you two before." While Indra softly admonished her friend, Odile laughed and went on, "Well? It's true—she betrayed him. And now, if she betrays him, she's betraying us, too...so it's in everyone's interest that we're all transparent with each other."

Scoffing lightly, Branwen muttered, "As if durrow have any place to talk of morals," before going on. "It's nothing, really, I was just wondering—well, it's very odd, what you said before. Perhaps you didn't understand what I was asking, Rorke, but I think it was settled for me when I saw you kiss Valeria. You two are—companions, yes?"

I glanced between the three dark faces to my right, then Branwen's bright one on my left. "Well," I told her, "I have a great, specific fondness for Valeria, but all three are my companions."

While the durrow made noises of agreement, Branwen rolled her eyes. "You're not understanding what I'm saying," the high elf said—a fine one to talk about patronizing! "When I say 'companions,' I don't mean companions in adventure or travel. I mean—"

"Like this, right?"

With a cheeky grin, Odile set her mug down, leaned across Valeria's lap, and pressed her lips to mine in an eager kiss. I gasped slightly, surprised but far from displeased, and leaned into her affection while the closest servant of Roserpine smiled at shocked Branwen.

"We have what some from the surface would think of as a different way of life, and Rorke here was quite shocked at first…but no man interested in experiencing all that life may hand him minds a bit of well-mannered sharing now and again." While Odile leaned back from me with a wicked grin—then, seeing sweet Indra's lustful look, turned to passionately kiss her friend—Valeria smiled and slid her hand into my lap. "At any rate, he's no more a slave of mine…who could dare call so valiant and bold a paladin as Rorke Burningsoul a slave?"

"None but a god," I assured her, praising Weltyr for the gift of the soft mouth that tipped toward mine. While I embraced Valeria, the scent of her richly floral even after the long bloom and dark of our journey, Branwen observed the proceedings with an amazed expression. Her face was bright red, those eyes of hers wild. Her lips parted softly: pink petals that revealed a glimmer of tongue just beyond.

At last, drawing away from my mouth but staying close against my chest, Valeria turned her head to gaze through lightly tousled hair at my former lover. "Were we to share him with one more, I don't think any of us would be adverse."

Branwen tended to keep a perfectly crafted visage, but just then she was difficult to read for other reasons. It seemed she cycled through several emotions, all of them variations on shock. Desire settled there, but all the same, as Odile and Indra moaned softly beneath one another's caresses, she stood up and cleared her throat.

"Well! Well, since he and I have such a history, I just don't want to make anyone jealous. Maybe I'll go take the first watch."

Looking around, then claiming a scimitar fallen from the hand of one of the exterminated bandits, Branwen smiled uneasily, looked nowhere near us, and said, "I'll be back when I need a bit of rest...I'm certainly wide-awake now!"

She took up the magical lantern that was said to repel monsters, then, and was gone. While the high elf unbarred the door and hurried out to take her chances with the darkness rather than give into her desire to join us in celebration of our freedom—Branwen from her captors, me from slavery, Valeria from a life of tiring solitude as Roserpine's mouthpiece—the durrow watched her go and tried not to laugh.

"All surface elves are alike," commented Odile, resuming the process of getting Indra out of her tight-fitting leather breeches. "You see in their eyes how eager they are to submit to a free way of living, but they all resist...it's the fault of your kind, Burningsoul."

Laughing Valeria gazed into my face while letting her hand rove back and forth in my lap. "Aye," she agreed, "well-said. And, since it's the fault of your kind, Rorke"— my lady shoved me away, giggling cruelly, pushing herself back toward her friends and drawing up her short dress as she did—"you'd ought to go and rid her of these notions that our ways are in any sense profane. As much as she speaks of Anroa, you would think she would prefer to enjoy so much love at once."

While Indra and Odile drew Valeria into their arms to kiss her sensually and rid her of her dress, I stuck around until the scrap of fabric was thrown over my head. While the ladies laughed, I chuckled in good humor, tossed it back at them, and rose with a chivalrous ache. "Very well...you ladies celebrate here, and I'll go see if I can convince Branwen to stay inside with us."

It was not many strides before I found her, in truth. In point of fact, the t-juncture where Branwen was poised stood near enough to the door that, as she was being startled by my approach, the edge of Valeria's husky moan drifted through the door and around the corner of the tunnel. The high elf, who had been lost in thought and pacing about the circumference of the light, whipped around while brandishing her plundered scimitar with dangerous unfamiliarity. The weapon was huge in her delicate hand, and I laughed despite myself. She recognized it was me and grew more at ease, lowering her blade with a scowl.

"What's so funny?"

I stepped forward, catching her trembling hand in mine. "You are," I told her. "Even after what happened before, you make me laugh, Branwen...you're a very brave woman."

Rolling her eyes and staring out into the darkness, Branwen permitted to me to extricate the clumsy blade from her hand. "This is a little too big for you, don't you think? I saw a dagger or two in there....make sure you know which one is suited to you before we move on."

While I leaned the scimitar against the wall, the elf regarded me with a somber sort of longing.

"Wouldn't you rather be in there with them?"

"Now, don't be jealous…I'd rather we were both in there with them, Branwen." While her arms crossed and her gaze darted away again, I assured her, "I know how it might seem to you—"

"Really rather odd," she said tersely, her tone high and mighty. "I *know you were a bit of a cad, Burningsoul, but—*"

The picture of innocence, I asked her, "A cad! Me? Whatever have I done to earn such a lowly status in your eyes?"

At the same time, a fistful of scattered memories blazed through my head. Branwen watching me flirt with the barmaids at alehouses early in our journey, when we were still traveling from location to location trying to find these well-hidden entrances to the Nightlands; that time with the gorgon; defending that working girl in the city of Klexus, which earned particular ire from the high elf because the specimen was another of her species, albeit lowborn. All mankinds have their caste systems, I suppose. I have heard it said that the human race was divided against itself before the existence of all our many brethren in Weltyr's will. Why that is, I do not know, for all men look to be the same shape and color to me—God-like.

Can I help that I find this to be especially so with women?

"You've a roving eye," admonished Branwen, flicking me in the chest while I laughed and caught her small waist in my hands. As she shivered to realize her body was in my grasp—as in so many, still quite recent times—I shifted my embrace and drew her all the more closely against me. She did not pull away, though she still, through heavily lidded eyes, lightly chastised me. "You think you're Anroa's gift to all womankinds."

"Of course not Branwen...I'm Weltyr's gift to to himself."

While she laughed and rolled her eyes, I was pained by the beauty of the gesture and the strange relief it caused me to follow the rolling of her pupil. I had missed her—her eyes, her pretty face. The elegant arch of her brow trembled with the shutting of her eyes. I bent my head over hers to kiss her, exhaling against the instant renewal of passion made all the hotter by her treachery. In fact, while thinking of her firing that bolt at me—betraying me, admitting she had become a victim to the hateful designs of the god of void and money, Oppenhir—I had to have her more urgently than ever before.

And, after my time with the durrow, I had learned a thing or two about what some women seemed to enjoy. When Branwen moaned to be pushed back against the wall, I ran my hand down her waist and beneath the pert curve of a backside that was finely accented by the tight hug of her dark green breeches.

"It's my duty to mete out justice," I assured her when at last she drew back from our kiss to catch her breath, her blue eyes locked on mine with tigerish desire. "Most would not let such treachery go unpunished."

"One week is too long a period of slavery for you," she whispered, gasping while I undid the tie of her breeches and pushed them down her slim hips. She made no protest, only going on to say, "I suppose you expect me to bend to your will now that you've saved me? That I owe you something?"

"Of course not, Branwen...it's all in good fun. But contrition a balm to the soul, don't you think? Why, the Church of Weltyr is very concerned with mortification of the flesh. The All-Father himself is said to have—"

Branwen pressed her fingertip to my lips with a

hushing noise. "Save it for later, Rorke…I think between this and a spanking, I'd rather have a spanking."

Laughing, I fell down upon the protected grounds illuminated by the magic lantern light and dragged Branwen with me. After haphazardly arranging her over my knee, I gripped her by her svelte waist and liberally applied the flat of my hand to her round rear. She squealed right away, squirming and attempting to keep her cries muffled.

"Rorke—oh, Rorke! You've never been so—*forceful*…"

"Yes, and I regret that now. Perhaps, had I not been so patient with your petulant behavior, you would have known it was very unwise to betray me…especially in a matter concerning my god, and my relationship with him."

"I'm sorry, Rorke! Oh—oh, I really am sorry—ah—!"

Despite her playful protests, her back arched more with each swat of that wonderful rump. "Perhaps, if we show you a good enough time, you'll be incentivized not to do it again."

"Oh! Oh! Ah—you expect me to—become one of 'your' women, do you?"

"I don't expect it," I told her, drawing her upright in my arms to run my free hand down her cool thighs, then back up to the heat between, "but I can't deny I'd enjoy it. And, at any rate, I belong to my women just as they belong to me…those durrow would take great offense to the thought of it only going one way."

She moaned, her thighs splaying, her bosom heaving within the confines of her brown leather bodice. "I can't believe you and those durrow—oh! Burningsoul…"

Through the wild curls of her golden hair, Branwen

gazed up into me and yielded the honey of her body at the lightest trailing of my fingertips. "I *have missed you...*"

"You've missed my body," I corrected her, sighing while she reached between us and half-twisted in my lap to free me from my breeches. "And I've missed yours... but I've also missed you, Branwen. I hope you'll realize soon enough that you really did miss me."

Though she glanced up at me upon hearing such a thing, the high elf continued the task of freeing my manhood and straddling my lap.

"I did miss you, Rorke," Branwen crooned, her face arranged with those heavy eyelids and lustful lips that revealed her secret wanton streak. "Truly, I swear it by Anroa...but I will admit, I missed this big thing, too..."

While her hand trailed up and down my length, I drew her mouth down to mine and nearly consumed her. She moaned into me, squirming beneath the pressure of my kiss, then proved unable to resist me even to tease us both. She glanced down and carefully fit herself to the tip of my member, her gasp widening her mouth while she eased down the shaft and lit both our bodies with sparks of pleasure.

"Oh," she cried softly, "Burningsoul!"

A sudden spate of moaning from the durrow orgy in the emptied den made me all the harder within Branwen's familiar core. She gasped, glancing at our point of connection, her hips rippling to the beat of an ecstasy that filled me topfull of desire—and frustration. How had I let her do such a thing to me before? I had to keep her in line this time. Still kissing her, I gripped Branwen's legs to my body and rose easily with her still mounted upon me.

The elf gasped, crying out in sheer delight to be pushed against the wall and held there while I buried myself in her. Her soft hands trailed over the muscles of my arms, hardened with the support of her slight frame. She received every hard stroke with greater joy, the pounding that rattled her dainty body causing her face and throat to redden exquisitely in the light of the lantern. Each thrust rippled through the cleavage of the sumptuous globes bursting from their leather confines: I bent my head to kiss her flesh and breathe the sweet aroma of her sweat.

While her golden eyebrows knit dynamically above her fluttering eyes, Branwen gazed into my face, moaning to watch the man who took her.

"I'm so glad you came back," I told her, my forehead pressing to hers, fire no doubt burning in my eyes for as hot as the embrace of her body made my mind. "Yes, and gladder still that it was the misshapen who found you... had the durrow captured you, you would have been in the heart of El'ryh and made into a slave. You had ought to be grateful, Branwen...by any standard—certainly by the durrow standard—you owe us your life. You were right before...you're a slave to all of us, in a way."

Her body fluttered around me at the notion, wetter at once. She even moaned, her gaze darting toward the shut door and its den of impromptu pleasure. I bent to kiss the ridge of her pointed ear, my tongue darting out against the sensitive flesh to send goosebumps racing down her neck.

"Come along with us, Branwen," I bade her softly, "not just until we reach the surface. Help us win back the Scepter of Weltyr and free your soul of guilt, and in the meantime taste the delights I've come to know in just a short span of time. Weltyr has had concubines beyond counting," I added, lifting my eyebrows while she laughed merrily. The sound was often broken up with little moans of pleasure as I filled her, her thoughts barely able to form.

"That explains why you're such an eager goat of a man...oh! No, no, a bull—oh, Rorke, yes, by Anroa, take me, Rorke, harder, harder, please!"

I braced her back against the stones, the new angle of her pelvis deepening the potential of my thrusts and leaving her speechless. As I worked her rapidly, the delicate elf's features trembled as though she might cry. Her brow furrowed with a kind of consternation and her eyes rolled up.

While her pupils angled toward her brow, nearly crossed, her trembling eyelids and quivering mouth foretold the sudden quake around the dagger I buried in this traitorous wench I nonetheless loved. Branwen moaned my name, her legs tightening about my waist as she climaxed, her brow unfurrowing with the bliss of her body's crescendo. Yet still she seemed unsatisfied, begging me even as she came, "Rorke! Oh, sweet Anroa, yes, by the goddess, let me be your love-slave! Use me as it pleases you, give me to your other women...I will obey you, if it will earn forgiveness. If it will earn your love back, Rorke."

"You already have it back," I assured her, my head light with pleasure that tightened all the muscles in my body. While her voice began again to mount toward its euphoric peak, I nuzzled my lips and nose against hers. "But I'll gladly command the direction of your love until you're comfortable enough to admit you'd like the company of the durrow as much as I do."

"Oh, yes! Yes, Rorke, yes, oh, if there's anyone who can manage such a thing, it's you—yes, Rorke, yes, please, I want to feel you inside me, dripping out of me! Rorke, Rorke, fill me to the brim, go on—"

Groaning, I did as she begged of me and pounded home into her until I saw stars—until those searing stars shot their light into my brain and sped through me into sweet Branwen's belly. She moaned, trembling, her body quivering with a second climax to receive my seed. Her face searched mine and, without having to be begged, I kissed her.

Somehow her mouth seemed to have grown sweeter with the course of our lovemaking. I sighed into her soft lips, drawing from her when the storm had passed, then eased her down upon the stones of the tunnel beneath us. We kissed while I straightened out my clothes, and I found on leaning back that she had gotten her breeches back up. I smiled, about to utter some word of fondness for her.

Something massive scuttled in the darkness at the edge of the lantern and I pushed her behind me, the scimitar in my hands at a second's notice.

3

BITTERSWEET FREEDOM

ADONISIUS HAD A knack for surprising us, it seemed—but I still felt terrible to have more than once drawn arms on the good-natured misshapen. He raised up his hands, in fact, laughing as he took a few more steps into the light and revealed the spider torso that distinguished his race from that of the durrow.

"I wondered if that was you from a distance, Burningsoul," commented the Nightlands guide, "but now it has to be you! No one else is so quick on the draw."

"Hail, Adonisius! How good it is to see you again. The Nightlands being as they are, I expected our paths unlikely to cross again…at least, not so soon."

"My kinfolk live this way," he explained to the immediate sinking of my intuition. "It's funnier that I should find *you* here! I thought for sure that spirit-thief would make quick work of you…I guess I was wrong."

Trying not to let my ego be bruised by this well-meaning but backhanded praise, I instead struggled to think of how I would tell this misshapen the unfortunate truth about his kin. It seemed to me that, unless this area formed a complex of misshapen dens, (and, considering the structure of El'ryh and its strange hivelike arrangement, that might have been the case), the odds were more than good that I had slain most if not all of Adonisius's family members.

Unsure as I was on how to proceed, I was almost relieved when Branwen said with a quick look of shock at the spider-centaur's lower half, "You're a misshapen, too! Like one of the bandits Rorke saved me from."

Adonisius's mouth opened in fright. "Bandits? Oh, no—"

Looking shocked, then, slowly, horrified, the misshapen removed the helmet Valeria had given him. His pupiless gaze darted between myself and the high elf still half-hidden behind my shoulder.

When next he spoke, Adonisius's voice was soft.

"Why is it that you're here, Burningsoul?"

"I heard the screams of my friend," I told him, trying to walk the fine line between solemnity and condescending insincerity. "And I had to help her. I'm sorry, Adonisius."

As the gentle man's eyes filled with tears, I reached out to lay a hand upon his arm. He took a step back and I admonished myself for the sting this caused in my spirit. What right had I to feel any sort of bruise? What obligation had he to tolerate comfort from the same hand that had dispatched his relatives but an hour or two before?

"Please," Adonisius said, covering his eyes with his free hand. "Don't—oh, don't. You killed them?"

"Yes," I said, glancing at the floor, feeling the abashment of a child before a parent. "It is my oath, Adonisius. I must defend the defenseless. She was defenseless; they were not."

"I'm sure," said the weeping misshapen, turning to study the shut door around the corner from where we stood. "No, I'm sure you did what was right. They were *vile men.*"

Adonisius at last forced himself to look upon me, a curious tone to his voice. As though he begged me to understand that, "I've been kept as a hostage—forced to pay my room and board and serve as their maid while they rob and kill defenseless passers through. In some way, some awful way, I am almost glad to think them gone…but they were my family, Burningsoul. My only kin."

"Had I known that, Adonisius, I might have done things differently."

"It's no use speculating or wishing things were different," lamented the man, wiping the back of his hand definitively against the high peak of his cheekbone and then replacing the helmet to somewhat obscure the sorrow in his face. "No, no use. And for the best, perhaps, that they are gone and I'm now free…but I am honor-bound to shun you now at best, Paladin. At worst—I dare not even dream of avenging the violence commissioned against my kin. Not as concerns one such as you."

Looking pained, the misshapen lowered his head and said, "I suppose you and the others will be putting up in there for the dark?"

"We planned on it, Adonisius, but—"

"Then stay as my guests," he said. "It's my property now. Stay as my guests to permit me to thank you for my inheritance. And then, kindly leave at bloom's first light."

27

Thinking of the misshapen's intimate familiarity with the tunnels of the Nightlands, I dared ask, "Perhaps you might be good enough to take us some way that would hasten our leaving?"

The gamble paid off. He looked reluctant but nodded in the end, saying, "Yes, I can show you an expedient way back to the surface, though it is a taxing climb at some points. Let it be my final payment to you, then let us do business no more. Life down here is dangerous enough... the last thing I wish is to be haunted by the specters of my ancestors, not just for failing to avenge them but for too often helping the man who took their lives."

I will admit—in those days (or blooms, if you are reading this, greatest love of all my loves), I had rarely spared deep thought to the lives I took in battle outside of prescribed. It was the nature of my station to pray each morning and night for my own welfare, for the souls of my ancestors, for the salvation of the lives I had taken in battle, and for the manifestation of Weltyr's will upon the planet through my works. Therefore one would think me used to slaying my enemies...but that was just the problem.

I *was* used to it.

After a lifetime of prayers, I had been hypnotized into not thinking with any great depth on the lives Weltyr ended through Strife; through me. I had not before been confronted face-to-face with the family of any creatures, criminals, or monsters I had slain. Indeed, I had seen these vanquished foes as little more than obstacles between myself and Weltyr's will. It had not yet fully dawned on me that the Day Bringer could easily have allotted me the same fate.

However...in that moment I could not help but see, at least in small part, the pain I was capable of causing.

Though I had never thought the taking of a life was a small thing, I realized in that moment that I had never been in touch with death. Not really. I turned entirely away from Oppenhir, whose awful void-realm was the black pit to which I sent those heathens and opponents to Weltyr who were, sadly, beyond repentance. In failing to contemplate the nature of this death, I felt somehow I had done both it and myself a strange disservice.

Certainly I felt I had done Adonisius a great disservice—even in my freeing him from his proverbial shackles. Before I could say anything to this effect, however, the misshapen bent his head and retreated into the dark.

"I'll come meet you all here at tomorrow's bloom. The journey will be a few blooms and darks. You'll have to forgive me if I keep to myself."

"I understand."

Though he hesitated, perhaps wishing to say more, Adonisius at last turned away. He went off into the tunnels of the Nightlands to spend time in contemplation for his dead relations, however complicated that relationship had been. I felt oddly chastened...not by Adonisius, but by that great inspirer of all magnificent things both good and bad. I felt my god had, as they say, "called me on the carpet" in some way, though I was not yet sure of the specific lesson he wished me to learn.

"You'd think he'd be relieved," said bratty Branwen under her breath, perhaps only projecting her own joy at being rescued. "Those brigands were abysmal creatures."

"That may be so...but what family is without its controversy?" With a lift of my brows at Branwen, I shook off the interaction with the misshapen as best I could and gestured the high elf back toward the door of the appropriated den. "After you."

"I'm nervous to walk in on them...oh, I'm afraid I embarrassed myself."

"Not at all. I'm sure they're used to an adjustment period when it comes to those who live aboveground."

To my disappointment but Branwen's sure relief, whatever had occurred in my absence had left all three dark elves entangled and content. When we found them, their bodies at relative rest save for the petting of an indolent hand along a miscellaneous limb.

"Did we hear you speaking out there?" Valeria's innocent question, her eyes lit with a mischief I had not enjoyed knowing in her while she was captive to her city.

"I'm afraid these weren't just any band of misshapen brigands," I told them, kneeling down to kiss Valeria upon the mouth, then Indra and Odile upon their cheeks. "These were the kinfolk of our guide from before. Adonisius."

While the veteran adventurers did not look particularly moved by this appeal, Valeria—softer-hearted than any of us after a lifetime of living in the Palace of Roserpine and caring for all the citizens of El'ryh—appeared shocked. Her lips tightened into a thin line while she looked away from me, toward the poorly covered row of bodies that would soon be covered in mushrooms and picked apart by insects.

"He has agreed to show us an expedient route to the surface, but warned me that it may take some effort. For the most part, he just asked we leave him be."

"He'd ought to thank us," said Odile.

Branwen, quick to relate to the most selfish member of our merry band, nodded vigorously. "That was what I said, more or less—Rorke is a hero, so far as I'm concerned."

"Heroes can only be so heroic to certain types of

people." Sitting up slightly from the pile of flesh, Valeria reached for a nearby loose fur and said, "If we're to take advantage of Adonisius's offer without falling behind or otherwise earning his greater impatience on this journey, then we had ought to sleep soon, and well."

"I know I will," said stretching Odile, pinching Indra's hindquarter while sitting up to set the magic lantern by the door. "And, from the sounds of it, so will our new friend."

"Well—well"—Branwen was red to the tips of her ears, and I had to turn away to keep her from seeing my barely contained laughter as I undressed—"*well*, if you really must hear about it—"

"Lighten up, surface girl! I was only kidding." Checking the bar of the front door and dragging over a set of shelves for an added precaution, Odile satisfied herself that the den was secure and pranced back to the furs to bundle up against Indra. "Who can keep a man like this one around and not put him to good use? Or be put to good use by him—eh, Indra?"

"Don't tease me, Odile! You know I'm sensitive when I'm tired…"

While Indra and Odile settled in together as was their custom, Valeria sat up on the edge of our pile of furs. Undressed, I stretched out and invited her, with the extension of my arm, down into my embrace by the flickering blue flames of the hearth. The displaced queen of the dark elves took my offered caress, melting against my body, her white hair falling in waves across my face and neck.

"Is this what adventuring is always like?"

Her pale eyes searched mine. Fingers running through those silken tresses, I pushed aside the curtain before Valeria's face and confessed to her, "It did not seem as such to me until I met you...I'm starting to think that, despite the rumors otherwise, Roserpine is far more gentle a goddess than Weltyr is a god."

With a light scoff and a little laugh, Valeria's nose brushed against mine and she patted my chest in a manner that was genuinely fond. So intimate it seemed as though we had known one another for years, yet so fresh it excited me to new thoughts of love in an instant.

"That's what I've been trying to tell you," she said, her tone one of playful remonstration. "Good dark, Paladin of Weltyr."

"Good dark, Materna of Roserpine," I said against her ear while she turned away from me. She settled in with her round backside pressed against my hip and her face to the room, away from me, where I could not see if she was asleep or awake with restless thoughts of danger, of future, of what she had lost and perhaps would never regain.

Then, there was Branwen. Branwen, who understandably did not seem inclined to get out of her armor or clothes. The truth was, however, that this would be our last opportunity for some days to divest ourselves of such things and sleep behind the relative safety of a door. I pitied her for missing the chance to be comfortable for even a few moments. I glanced down at my free arm, then looked hopefully at her.

"I've two arms, Branwen."

With a skittish, embarrassed glance at Indra and Odile curled together, then another at Valeria to my right, Branwen took off her boots and rested beside me.

How familiarly she settled in my arm! I thrilled. But what man wouldn't to have a woman in each arm, plus two more sleeping near his feet! Weltyr's kindness was unmatched, truly.

Hot-and-cold as always, Branwen looked wryly at me even in my arm.

"I'll bet you're pretty pleased with yourself right now, aren't you, Rorke?"

"Wouldn't you be?"

With a scoff and a roll of her eyes, (as Odile produced a short "Ha!" while drifting off to sleep), the high elf tried to hide her crooked smirk by laying her face against my heart. "Good night, Rorke."

"Good dark, Branwen...sweet dreams."

ABOVEGROUND

THERE ARE THINGS in accounts such as this that, as a reader, I tend to skip. Ahead of me lay two such narrative traps: the recounting of a dream, and a long journey from one place to another with little to no action. The first, I must share because Weltyr commands it, and because it will become important later. The second, I may compress in order to sooner discuss those things that happened on the surface—but, rest assured, it was an arduous task for myself and my companions to follow the misshapen along his shorter route out of the Nightlands.

And all the way there, I found myself bleakly revisiting the dream I had the dark after we rescued Branwen.

I was not sure it could rightly be called a dream. Dreams, after all, were perceived as gifts from gods—containers for divine information and inspiration that could not be received by the human mind in another fashion, whether direct or obscure.

As was taught in the Church of Weltyr and the Temple where I was raised, the information in dreams was concealed in their symbolism. Even a dream that seemed forthright tended to contain a second or even third meaning, and the challenge was to plumb the depths of those meanings for the concealed message. Dreams with prophetic content—of the sort Valeria experienced and attributed to her goddess, Roserpine—were the dubious pleasure of only a few, and by and large considered undesirable. It was burdensome to become the waking—or in this case, dreaming—tool of Weltyr, and those who experienced such things did well to be afraid.

Then there were dreams that were not messages from gods, but instead transmissions from something else.

A red organ throbbed like a palpating heart in the shadows of a flooded chamber. In the way of dreams I knew without having to be informed that this chamber stood in a distant land and was very, very old...but not half so old as its contents. Red tissues kept the mass of unidentified muscle clinging to the stone walls, and I knew the texture of these stringy, vein-filled nettings in the same manner that one knows their hand is made of flesh.

You are being lied to, Eradicator.

The hivemind of the spirit-thieves throbbed a message through my brain, the knowledge of its words flying in as though they were my own thoughts.

Your history, your Church—all of it is full of lies.

A bubble expelled from an orifice in the shapeless red hivemind, rising with a few companions to the surface of the dark chamber.

I could tell you the truth now...but it would disturb you too much.

The floor above the hivemind rattled with the footsteps of its approaching keeper.

Instead, I simply encourage you: pay attention. Pay close attention. Ask questions. Learn to look around yourself. You know your problem with your god, don't you, Eradicator?

A trap door opened over the fiend and a square of light shone in.

He only has one eye.

"Supper's on," said an old man whose voice sounded very much like my own, or, at least, as it would be once Time had stuck a hand down it.

I snapped awake and safe, in reality, myself. Surrounded by splendid women, and changed from the man I was before this sojourn into the Nightlands to do the will of Weltyr—but, all the same, myself.

Why should the dream have greatly disturbed me? Because it was so clear, for one. Yes, it was possible that it really was just some dream. That it might have referred to both my battle with Al-listux and the portal through which he leapt, which contained a man I could only describe as a far older version of myself.

But the sharp, deliberate nature of the information was what gave me pause. Dreams have a certain appearance in the memory—hazy and drained. But this vision was as crisp and clear as any other recalled event in which I had participated while waking.

Was this transmission because of Al-listux, I wondered on our long journey to the surface? Thanks to the intervention of Valeria's guard, the spirit-thief did not long have its tentacles in me. At the time I saw a pulsing flash of that awful hivemind, but I then thought no more on the matter because I had been preoccupied by escaping El'ryh and hunting Valeria's would-be assassin. This second time, however, I recognized it straightaway—and sensed that, even with so little exposure to the direct control of the spirit-thief, the hivemind of those hateful squid-headed beings now had some insight into my consciousness.

In the time it took us to emerge from the Nightlands, I managed to tell myself all number of things—that I was being paranoid, absurd. That I was ascribing to a far simpler dream the will and intercession of an interloper when I had no real evidence that such things were possible. What did I know of magic, though? I had met many magic-users of many different kinds, but only those whose spells were related to prayer made any real sense to me. I had no head for arts described in grimoires, and in fact I confess I then maintained a certain suspicion of such crafts. Even Valeria's prayers to Roserpine were, strictly speaking, heathen magic that was engaged without the permission of the Church...but, as previously mentioned, I have never taken offense to the veneration of lesser gods. Their worship did not empower them; certainly not enough to mitigate Weltyr's glory.

Similarly, there was a part of me that did not wish to ascribe any power at all to the despised enemy of sentient life on Urde, the hateful spirit-thieves. It were as though, in admitting to myself that brief contact with Al-listux had done something to me without leaving behavioral evidence behind, I would be the bearer of some black mark. Some unlucky and uncomfortable brand many more times more painful than the one upon the back of my shoulder, now healed and scarred over in record time thanks to the potion the ladies gave to revive me for a second time.

We arrived at the surface after two blooms and two darks, and in that time precious little was discussed for fear of drawing monsters to us. We had no wish to test the limits of the lantern's kindly ward; and, as we journeyed farther from El'ryh, that became an increasing possibility.

"There are all sorts of hideous things through here," our guide deigned to tell us, his hushed voice all the lower for the obvious fear he had of this subject. "You'd think things would be more dangerous the deeper you went, but in my experience it's the other way 'round. Closer to the surface is where you find creatures of the types that prey on lowly adventurers without the expertise to make it too far down."

"When I was coming down here by myself this time," said Branwen, arms folded while she walked as part of the column formation I tailed, "I saw a thing or two that was very strange...one awful thing, a creature that was just a mass of flesh dotted with gibbering mouths. Like something from a nightmare."

I arched my brow. "And the other thing?"

"Oh," she said, "only these funny little creatures like gnomes, or so I thought...but I happened to see them from nearby while I was in hiding to let them pass without trouble. They looked like little dragon-men!"

"The gimlets," said our guide with the most genuine levity he'd shown in our whole journey. I suppose that, because Branwen was not an aggressor in the extermination of his family, he felt more comfortable with her. I can't say I blame him, but it was certainly good to hear him laugh for once. He continued, "Ah, I love them!

What merry little fellows. Not very well-organized, and a bit skittish—always on the defense—but in spite of this, really rather charming. Once they get to trusting you, they're exceedingly loyal."

"Like dogs," muttered Odile, drawing a sharp look from Adonisius and a displeased little sniff as he turned his head away again. "What? It's true...there's something of a dog about them, you can't deny."

"I suppose, if you must. Perhaps you find them that way because of their voices...they don't have the vocal range to speak the common tongue, nor any other known to mankinds, so there will always be a language barrier to overcome. But there are other means than speech to communicate in this world...decency is universal."

This, I am sure, is the only reason why Adonisius did not lead us to our deaths. Over those two days we gradually climbed to the surface by way of inclining tunnels, claustrophobic crevices, and sometimes frightful cliff-faces that Valeria in particular struggled to scale. We were tired, aggravated, and uncomfortable. Thanks to the food taken from the bandit den, we were not famished.

We only once ran into difficulties with monsters, the magic lantern keeping at bay all things but a slime creature that Indra wanted to show us. She recognized it with great excitement spread out on a wall and dashed off to poke it with one of our pilfered scimitars.

While explaining a bit about it—like, for instance, its nature as a dormant mold until it was touched, at which point it sought out and consumed all organic materials it could absorb—Indra scurried away like a girl for the security of the lantern's halo. As she giggled, the brainless beast formed itself into a great cube and slowly oozed after her. I admit, I was quite astonished to see its like!

It was then that we learned another valuable lesson—that the light of the lantern had no more sway over brainless entities than over highly intelligent evils. The sweating cube wriggled into the light and kept coming for us, its digestive body dirty with the filth of the Nightlands and visibly full of matted fur along with dissolving bones. Strife, much to my dismay, merely severed the cube in twain and produced two writhing, shivering jelly creatures. Indra suggested lighting a fire.

"Maybe that will scare it off," she cried, her crossbow raised out of habit rather than effect while Valeria began conjuring her wisp flame.

"It's the only way to kill one of these things," agreed Adonisius while backing along the tunnel down which the cube lurched. "Fire, lightning, some kind of elemental spell."

"Good idea," called Branwen, pushing past me with one fine hand braced upon my shoulder. The other outstretched toward the beast. The air around the druid seemed to glow; it certainly gathered a thick charge of static. She had braided her hair into comely twin plaits that draped over her shoulders, but this summoning of nature's lightning revealed that in the time of our journey many little hairs had come undone. They floated, even her very braids levitating as light leapt from her fingertips and jolted down the tunnel to burn the malicious slime.

The durrow all cried out and covered their sensitive eyes. A terrible wet spurting noise, like the tearing of organ meat, flopped fluidly through the tunnel. The cubes, reduced in size and no longer capable of maintaining definite shape, reformed into one quivering mass and retreated back down the tunnel to let us go along our way.

Aside from that, we encountered nothing else. No

giant spiders, no gibbering sacks of flesh, no curious gimlets—just a long, exhausting hike during which I had time to think of two things incessantly. That dream, and what we were going to do once we were on the surface.

That one flash of lightning from the tips of Branwen's fingers made me consider an important point. Durrow eyes were extraordinarily sensitive. Once aboveground we would have to travel mostly at night. In fact, even if we managed to lay hands on some dwarfish welding goggles or colored scholar glasses effective enough to protect their eyes, night would still be the most prudent time to travel for social reasons.

I had seen men and women of all colors and creeds in my time growing up of the surface of Urde. There were countless travelers from all countries who came through Skythorn on business or pleasure. Humans aside, dwarves and gnomes and elves and even sometimes half-orcs had come to the Temple to be baptized or to simply observe a ceremony. I had met all manner of people on the surface of Urde.

But I had never seen a durrow until I ventured into the belly of the Nightlands.

Now, of course, I understood some reasons for their secrecy. I also understood that this scarcity of their race aboveground would draw attention to us…and not always desirable attention by any means. Yet, to Valeria, the risk seemed worth it—and, at any rate, she trusted I would find a solution for her in one way or another.

To the former Materna of Roserpine, I must have seemed a fairy tale savior. If she was to be believed—and to look at her, I could not help but see honesty in her features—she had dreamed of me since she was a girl. Dreamed that I would free her from El'ryh. Dreamed that I would show her to the surface.

And here we were.

I am not sure how I knew we were near the surface. Perhaps I picked up on some change in the dirt or some alteration of echo that my conscious mind did not catch. There is part of me, though, that suspects I knew we reached the end of our subterranean hike not because of the echo or the air current, but because of Valeria's trembling. She quivered while we drew higher, drew nearer to release. When I brushed her hand, she jolted as though she had seen another monster like the shivering cube.

Valeria looked at me then, her delicate features an intermingling of fear and excitement. As I held the Materna's hand I felt Branwen's blue eye on us, and I hoped she knew I would have done the same for her had she needed me to.

At last, once we had clambered up the sharp edge of another cliff, the misshapen for whom such things were much less taxing watched us help each other to our feet.

"This is where I leave you," said our guide, once again speaking primarily to Branwen. "I am not welcome on the surface. The end of this tunnel opens to a mountainside cave in Cascadia. If you descend, you should easily enough find the highway, or so I am told… you can follow that to a small village, Soot. Although, which way one might go to find it, I am not sure."

I nodded, knowing he would not accept the shake of my hand and leaving it at a slight bow of my waist. "Thank you for assisting us, Adonisius, even after all we've done against you."

"You've done plenty for me, as well as against me." After tapping the helmet Valeria traded him in exchange for guiding us to the garden of the mysterious Nightlands shape-changer, he admitted, "I'm not so sure I will be able to return to that home and sleep again, but I may be able to make use of the property in some way."

He turned to leave, but Weltyr urged me onward. I reached out and touched his arm, pained to think of the perception this good and quiet man should have of me after what I had done to his kin. He winced, deepening the sorrow I felt, but as our eyes met he clearly saw there was no malice for him in me.

"Whenever you offer Hamsunt libations or gold or whatever other gifts you devote to him," I bade the Nightlands guide, "pray for my forgiveness, please, Adonisius. Even if you are unable to forgive me, pray that your god will."

Though somewhat taken aback, the misshapen turned this over in his mind. As I released him, he nodded earnestly. "I will. I will do that, Rorke Burningsoul, Paladin of Weltyr. I'll pray for all of you—for your wellness, and safe travels. Be careful…I've heard it said that there are stranger and more terrible things on the surface than any I have met in the Nightlands."

And, with one more brief genuflection of his spider legs, Adonisius scaled back down the tunnel system through which he had guided us.

"Onward," I said, my hand resting upon Strife's pommel while I led the way to the surface.

The final passage of our journey was a long and dark one. Now I could definitely tell we were close to the surface just by the smell of the air. To describe the Nightlands as foul or even stuffy would be perhaps inaccurate— surely these effects were psychological. I am a tall man and broad-shouldered, and confined spaces have always left me somewhat ill-at-ease. To have a cavernous roof over my head rather than sky therefore produced in me a certain psychological tension; an oppressive dreariness that came on so steadily I had not even noticed its insidious arrival until, with proximity to the surface, it lifted. Free of this shroud, my step hastened just slightly, and my heart sped with anticipation to breathe the fresh air of Urde.

My companions, meanwhile, seemed to experience similar invigorating effects. The journey had been tedious and, with grim Adonisius leading the way, sometimes uncomfortable. We had not been able to discuss much more than harmless matters of small-talk—the flora and fauna of the Nightlands, the food of El'ryh, and the prior adventures of Indra and Odile were our main matters of discourse until our guide left us. Now, in a straightforward exit of the tunnel system with little in the way of danger, my elfin companions chattered away in delight and relief.

"I've never been to the surface, Odile!" Indra in particular burst with excitement, her words bubbling out of her with girlish glee. "What will it be like?"

"Bright, mostly…but beautiful."

I glanced back at that. "What did the people of your colony do to protect their eyes when traveling on the surface during the day, Odile?"

"They didn't. Mostly we went about our business in the nighttime, and a few sympathetic humans or other surface-dwelling people helped us with what we needed during the day. There was a man in my village, a musician, who managed to spend more time on the surface than any of the rest of us. He used colored glasses to protect his eyes from the light…but not even those were sufficient, and after quite a few years of doing this, he ended up almost blind."

With a grimace of sympathetic pain, I said, "Perhaps we'll travel at night until we come up with a solution, then…lucky us, it seems like it must be nighttime now."

It was, indeed—perhaps even later than I had anticipated, the lack of sunlight being disorienting as it was to my sense of time. In fact, the night was already so black that I did not realize I was looking at the end of the tunnel until Valeria's breath seized in her lungs. In a move so sudden and therefore uncharacteristic it almost startled me, she bolted past me. She somehow even found the energy to sprint down the tunnel. I called after her, as did Indra; after glancing back over my shoulder at the other ladies, I took off at a jog to catch up to her. Branwen, Indra and Odile ran after me, each wondering in her heart what it was Valeria could have seen. At long last, we broke free of the tunnel and skidded to a halt in open air.

Indra and Odile gasped; Branwen and I cried with delight.

Valeria, eyes full of tears, stood with one hand over her mouth and her face turned toward the stars.

"I can't see them," she whispered, laughing, blinking, the soft white plumes of her hair blowing wild in the night breeze of that cold mountainside.

"What's that, Valeria?"

I placed my hand on her shoulder and she laughed all the harder. She shut her eyes, tears streaming down her cheeks, and flung her trembling body into my arms. While I pressed her to my heart, she gasped out, "The stars, Rorke—I've waited so long to see them, and now after all this time I can't see them because I'm crying too much."

I laughed very gently, my hand keeping her fragrant head against the throbbing rhythm of my heart. "There we are, my queen, good Materna of Roserpine—there are your stars, Valeria. They'll be there still when your tears have dried, I promise."

"Not if I cry all dark." Laughing, Valeria wiped a finger beneath her eye. Then, clasping my hands, she gazed up at the sky and smiled to herself in awe.

Indra managed the same feat without weeping— though, to my great surprise, the same was not true of Odile. The seasoned rogue glanced up at the stars, stared for a handful of seconds, then turned her face away, to the base of the mountain, with a guarded sweep of her hand over the curve of her cheek.

I pitied her immensely just then. She had told me once of the terror of her colony's extermination at the hands of the Order of Weltyr...the very same protectors of the Temple who raised me, and the establishment of knights I was on this journey to join. Just to think of them, the odious dream-vision from our stay in the den returned to me again.

You are being lied to, Eradicator.

The voice pulsed in my brain, once more taking the same paths intuition took within my consciousness. I gritted my teeth and let my heart fill with a prayer to Weltyr—an expression of my gratitude to be led out of the dark terrors of the Nightlands. To show my thanks to the watchful god, I looked around the world he made and took in everything I could.

Adjusted as my eyes were by then to the darkness of the subterranean Nightlands, I had little difficulty making out the state of the terrain around us. Not beneath that densely starry sky. If I had to hazard a guess, this entrance was one utilized by travelers and merchants from the town Adonisius had called Soot. This village's soft lamps glowed through the night in the distance to the north, natural gold rather than the blue wisps that hovered about the durrow to keep them warm.

Valeria's own floating faerie light had dropped near

her feet so she might see the sky without its interference. The tips of her fingers resting upon the edge of her lower lip, her eyes trailed wildly over the sky. She marveled, "There are so many more colors than I was told...bursts of purple and blue and red...and *so* many stars!"

"They have names...some of them make pictures or even stories. I couldn't tell you the first thing about any of them. Oh! Well—wait, that fellow there, do you see those three? That's Urio, the hunter. He's supposed to be fighting a bull somewhere around here...who knows where *that is.*"

While Valeria laughed along with my poor description, I smiled over at Branwen. The high elf, looking quite relieved, herself, looked away from the stars that had been helping her get her bearings.

Her attention caught, I asked, "Could you show our friends a few basic constellations, Branwen? Help them orient themselves?"

"Oh," she said, pleasantly surprised and somehow pleased to have been called upon to teach the durrow anything at all. "Well, sure—first, you find the North Star..."

As she pointed up and the dark elves gathered around her to follow her explanation, I looked around the area. Trees were not abundant at this altitude, but they were around, and a small cluster of pines marked the curve of a workable path down the edge of the mountain. How long it would take that path trod by merchants and wanderers to develop into more harrowing terrain, I was not sure. I thought it good to explore the issue somewhat.

Though I was concerned the fallen branch I collected from the base of that micro-grove was perhaps too damp to serve as a torch, the magical light of Valeria's fire took to it generously. While the torch burned in my hand, I told the companions who paused mid-lecture, "I'm going to go down a ways and see if the path holds up. If it looks bad, I'll come back—if it's fine, I'll call up."

"You should let someone come with you," Branwen told me, looking ready to volunteer. I shook my head, gesturing with the torch toward the tunnel.

"Even with the wisp lights, it's too cold for us to be standing around unprotected unless we're going to be on the way from one place to another. Stay by the mouth of the cave and let me determine whether it's safe."

Valeria touched my hand. "Be careful, Rorke."

After a returned squeeze of her soft knuckles, I made my way down the side of the mountain with my blue torch lifted high.

My first note was that the path from the mountainside cave was well-trod, indeed. In fact, the more I thought on it, the more I found it odd that an entrance so treacherous and so far from the city of El'ryh would be a popular means of merchants bringing wares into the Nightlands. With all the cliffs we had been forced to scale, or all the claustrophobic passages through which Adonisius navigated us, how could a merchant burdened by goods possibly make their way to the city by such a route?

I tried to imagine doing it with just that burden Odile and Indra had forced me to haul from the spirit-thieves' so-called temple. Any way I thought of it, the task was impossible. But who would be using a path in and out of the Nightlands enough to tamp it down—and perhaps even deliberately maintain it—to such a degree as this?

Soon enough, I had my answer.

To my surprise, I found a juncture. It gave me pause and I considered using this marker to call up to the women, who were quite far away by now but surely still within calling distance thanks to their sensitive elf ears. Then, however, I found myself alerted by a curious sound: a yelp like that of an animal.

Unfamiliar with what beasts might be found on the mountainside aside from rams, I thought perhaps we could have a meal to restore some energy to our weary bones. Making my way along the right path, the path of the juncture winding around in the direction of that noise, I drew Strife and journeyed on.

And around a tight corner, I was surprised by a meeting with my first gimlet.

The little lizard man let out a yelp identical to the first I'd heard and backpedaled a few steps. All the time it looked rapidly at me and then, with more surprise, at my torch. I was quite surprised, myself. Despite Branwen's imagery, I had not expected a kind of small bipedal dragon. Nor one so—well, oddly charming. It did, somehow, bear some resemblance to a dog, and not just in voice.

I could not put my finger on it—perhaps its muzzle's general shape, or the little tuft of tawny fur between its horns—before the whelp sprang up and, quite unexpectedly, snatched the torch out of my unready hand.

"Hey," I called, dashing after the thief who literally turned tail and ran. "Get back here!"

The gimlet giggled maniacally at that, knowing I had no leverage to make it turn around. It was quick, darting at an angle just when I managed to find myself in grabbing distance. The hyperventilation of its tiny lungs was clear, and I almost thought that I might outrun it based on sheer endurance. Then, to my frustration, it darted off the path entirely and scaled down the rocks

STRIFE & VALOR

It was not my best decision, but I needed that torch: without it, I was going to be stranded on the mountainside until my party found me, or until the coming of the dawn. Therefore, I hurried to keep up with the gimlet, trying to gauge its path before the light disappeared. This quickly proved treacherous, with smaller stones slipping out from beneath my feet and larger ones seeming as though to spring from the dark. Even when the terrain leveled out, I was amazed to discover just how rocky the area was—and how ornamented.

When I realized the gimlet had come to a stop, I also skidded to a halt. Cautious, Strife still raised, I made my slow way toward the little beast. The plateau where it had led me was very strange, indeed. A pit lay in its center, and around this pit had been arranged all manner of precious objects. Dead flowers and fruits stood vigil with little statues carved of bones and even small piles of golden objects.

There was a nearly limitless selection of items arranged around the mouth of the pit beside which the gimlet stood, and it seemed the fellow intended to add the torch to this assortment. He barked, pushing the base of the torch into the gravelly terrain and propping it upright with a nearby golden bowl of fruit that had been frozen by the altitude.

"Now, I know a sacred site when I see one..." Slowly, carefully, I lowered Strife, my grip on the blade nonetheless tight after seeing the surprising strength that had allowed the gimlet to wrench my torch from my hand. "I don't wish to disturb anything here, friend...but I need that light if I'm to leave you alone, eh?"

The gimlet barked, its scaled tail lashing back and forth. I took a step closer and did not hear the rocks beneath my feet groaning in protest.

"Now," I was too busy saying, "let's have the torch..."

Strong enough for a gimlet's small size, the rocks making up the hallow plateau were not strong enough for a human man. With a cataclysmic, certainly panicking rumble, the rocks gave way beneath my feet. I cursed, attempting to catch myself on the edge of the stone before me and instead simply knocking it out of place. The gimlet gasped, then laughed madly to see my dilemma. Even as the stars rang in my head and my body rattled with the pain of the landing, the little cretin leaned over the edge of the hole to enjoy the sight of my suffering.

"Weltyr's beard, you little rat—come down here and see how long you laugh."

Uncomprehending or uncaring, the gimlet's giggling head disappeared and its light footfalls knocked away enough rocks to let me know it was on its way back to the path.

Groaning, head aching, I wondered to myself if the fall would have been worse or better with armor on. I was going to have to figure out how to get my hands on a new set when we were in Soot...once I had gotten out of that pit.

And once I had done something about the exquisite woman I found unconscious within it.

5

ROUSING THE MOUNTAIN WITCH

SHE WAS THE first thing I noticed when I sat up: the only thing there was to notice, aside from the dessicated skeletons of a few unfortunate gimlets.

I had fallen into some kind of sepulcher. An apparently fresh body had been lain upon a bed of stone, and I was quite amazed to see it in one piece. It were as if this woman had died that very day, yet such thing was impossible. The offerings circling the tomb's rotunda had been so vast in number that I was certain they'd gathered for years. All the same, she for whom the offerings were apparently meant surely had to be a recent addition. Perhaps an offering herself. I kept a hand upon Strife and was aware at all times of my surroundings, but the pit was enclosed and bore no signs of animal life.

Alert, I edged nearer. The blue light of the torch at the lip of the sepulcher illuminated the darkness. By virtue of this friendly flame I absorbed, in awe, the stern features of a deathly goddess. Her pale face was artfully decorated in smudges of kohl as black as raven's feathers—as black as the hair that plumed around her pallid features to form pillow and shroud in one. The body, interned beneath what I now realized was not a natural plateau but a deliberate cairn, was without the least hint of breath, yet I swore she still possessed the tension of life and the strength of a woman as healthy as my companions. Animal furs enfolded her flesh, but the muscles of one slender, spry leg left exposed by the position of the furs made her good health on death clear enough.

And oh, what pain! What terrible pain swept over my heart to see such a beautiful woman left dead. Had the gimlets committed this crime against one of Weltyr's finest creations? Perhaps Branwen had been right to chastise me for my love of women, but my love of women was really only my love of Weltyr and the fine world he had made for all of us to live in. When I saw that sacred creation profaned, it wounded me—and there was nothing more profane than the annihilation of life from a creature so sacred that I almost feared looking up her face.

The dark lines arcing around her orbitals and over her lips, this latter the tip of an arrow pointing up from her delicate chin, somehow only made her more exquisite. I averted my eyes, unable to bear my own mournful thoughts, intending to find a way out of the pit by climbing a wall or some such.

To my surprise, my investigation yielded not a way out, but a sort of instruction manual. I might have been almost grateful to the gimlet, had its theft of the torch that lit the images not been the reason I'd become trapped in the first place. In such incidents lie Weltyr's higher plans. I saw evidence of this in the rudimentary pictures painted on the wall beside the sleeping demi-goddess.

How old these images were! I could not have guessed, but I was sure the depictions were well and truly ancient. The shapes were so rudimentary it took several minutes in the dimly lit darkness before I could fully discern what they were intended to represent. A feminine figure, distinguished by long hair: doing battle, I thought, or perhaps hunting. At any rate, a great deal of creatures surrounded her, some of them—little lizard-like humanoids included—being grabbed or otherwise poised before her hands. Another of the same figure with some kind of power emanating from her. The figure arranged in her mausoleum.

Two faces pressed together, followed by an illustration that looked like a blossomed flower.

This last image gave me pause. I looked at it for a few long moments, along with all the others, and tried to discern a clearer meaning. There was none.

Slowly, still as uncertain as I have ever been, I turned back to the unconscious woman and reached down to touch her cheek. I have seen ghouls and zombies and heard terrible tales of undead magicians who had spent eternity as immortal sorcerers called "dirges;" I had even had my share of encounters with skeletons by that time in my short adventuring career. Among all these undead, not one of them produced any body heat when close enough to touch.

Yet the woman, unconscious, unbreathing, was warm to the touch. Warm and soft as any I had known.

With one more reluctant glance at the images upon the wall, I leaned down and pressed my tenderest kiss to the woman's soft mouth. The mark on her underlip trailing down her jaw, I was amazed to find, was a tattoo; and her lively mouth was soon as awake as mine. As the flower petals concealing her tongue parted, I was beset by the urge to recoil in fear. At her soft, sleepy moan, however, I urged myself onward. Soon my tongue was invited in to slide against her cool one, and another, longer sigh of pleasure rattled up from the base of her unpracticed lungs.

When at last I lifted my head she had begun to nuzzle eagerly against me, her hand lifting to caress my chest.

"Sweet moon," she gasped, sitting up beyond me, her senses sliding into full awareness from the thickness of her enchanted sleep, "good shadows! What sacred night to look upon again—who is this hero who disturbed my slumber? Let me look upon your face—"

She turned to see me. As her hibernating eyes found focus, they widened with a kind of shock. I told her, "I am Rorke Burningsoul, Paladin of Weltyr. And I get the feeling that you have been here, asleep in the mountains, for a very long time."

The woman laughed heartily in the way of warriors and witches. "Somehow I do get the sense that King Hundil of Iltraxia has no more qualm with me...I'll travel the world freely again, how good it'll be!"

Her accent was thick with a brogue I'd not heard, and neither the monarch nor the nation were familiar to me. I made a mental note of it all and asked, "So, you can remember names of cities and monarchs—I assume that you remember your own?"

"What a pity that Gundrygia the Sorceress should

go unrecognized by sight! One look at me once inspired cold fear deep in the hearts of the bravest men."

"I assure you, Madame, that fear is still among the plethora of feelings you inspire…but only by the humbling point of your poison-tipped beauty, rather than any reputation."

The wild woman threw back her head in another mighty laugh, her lips peeling back from teeth that seemed somehow fanglike. "What a thing to say to me, hero! What god sent you? "Weltyr," you called him?" She thought for but a second, then looked at me with fiendish eyes that glowed in the darkness. I wanted to make love to her then and there, her petulant sneer somehow leaving me all the more eager to feel her body in my arms.

"Yes," said the barbarous witch, shimmying off her slab and twirling away from me, "I know that god…he was called something different in my time, and something else long before that. Praise be to you, wanderer! It feels so good to move about and stretch…and awful, too."

Gundrygia doubled over to touch her toes and shake out her hair, her body dancing through her furs: bright white shimmers of light glowing through the ink of night to reveal strange dreams like the shapes of the dwarvish toy sometimes called "a magic lantern." A funny thing, with moving pictures that often told a story. What a story, Gundrygia's body!

I tried not to be too distracted…or not to sound as such, at any rate. "What was my Father called before his name was Weltyr?"

"It's secret, wanderer. Secret as the place to which his other eye flew when he tore it from his own skull in sacrifice."

"So you *do* know my god. A sorceress, you called yourself?"

"The very chieftess of all who would call themselves magicians, rest assured." Her movements, at first stretching, slowly became literal dancing. That body of hers swayed within her primitive garb in what I assumed to be some celebration…or, perhaps, invitation. "But I am not interested in myself just this moment…who are you that awoke me? Rorke Burningsoul, this is your name, but whence hail you?"

"The city of Skythorn is my home," I answered her, allowing myself to openly appreciate the roving of her hands over her splendid breasts. "And I go now to pursue the Scepter of Weltyr—a precious relic stolen by my old companions, Grimalkin and Hildolfr. My being here is but by the grace of my Lord."

A smile crossed her face. When I asked her the matter, the sensual woman shook her head and turned her swaying, arching back to me, her hips rolling within the artfully split confines of her furs to show sometimes this leg, sometimes that one, now a bright and beautiful flash of lunar skin that vanished as quickly as it extended. "You are a man of few words, and yet in those words you say very much. Rorke Burningsoul, Rorke, Rorke…"

The words rolled from her in the growl of a big cat, each iteration another ten degrees of temperature in my blood. I almost had to clutch the slab to keep myself seated upon its edge. Around this time, it occurred to me that her dance might not be meaningless after all—neither meant to celebrate, nor seduce, but instead to cast a literal spell. I also realized in that moment that I did not care. I basked in the slide of a hand down the long white column of an arm.

"You are a man of god, Burningsoul. That much is clear."

"Before anything, I am Weltyr's son. All other

58

things in the world that are sweet to me—for instance, being private audience to a dancing enchantress—are gifts from my god for performing his will."

"Enchantress! What a flirt you are…"

While she uttered that high, wild laugh, I my heart raced with delight and dread. Struck with the immense craving to know more about her, I begged, "Whence do you hail, Gundrygia, and how came you to find yourself here?"

"You really did find your way here by accident, eh? I suppose most have forgotten me by now. I'll find my father—he'll tell me the time."

"And where is your father?"

"Across the sea from here," she told me. "Far away, north of Rhineland."

Ah! Now that was a country I knew. "That's where Grimalkin hails! Rhineland—but how is it that you're here, Gundrygia?"

"I won't tell you that easily. I'd just as soon not think about it at all."

The music of her presence was overwhelming to me, and I could not discern what enchantment she had put upon my person. Perhaps it was simply an assurance that my love for her would burn wildly, savagely, from those first moments of our meeting—even once everything was said and done.

"What will it take to get you to tell me?" I asked, still poised upon the edge of the slab and barely containing myself. "A woman like you is the sort that a man has to know everything about."

As her bright teeth flashed with her laughter, Gundrygia lowered her furs from her shoulders and let them gather at her bare feet. "Then fight me for it, warrior…let's wrestle awhile and see who pins whom."

Exhaling, I considered her nude state and the shining glory of her exposed body, the high globes of her swollen breasts round like the wonderful flesh of her backside. The dark thicket upon the delta of her womanhood drew my eye as I said, "To wrestle a woman is a different matter entirely. I might upset you if I prove too rough."

The arrowhead tattooed upon her chin and lower lip produced the effect of a constant pout that was, in that moment, accentuated by a real one. Her hands ran back up her waist and over her breasts again, the lovely pink peaks of her nipples stiff with my attention. "You think you'd need to take it easy on me, do you? I assure you, Paladin, I'm a worthier foe than all that."

"If you are to prove a worthier foe than I would suppose without the assistance of your magic, then I would demand worthier prizes. What is the name of your father?"

"That fee is simpler, because his name will mean so little to you...I'll give it for another kiss, Paladin."

Somehow, I still found myself frozen beneath the fixating power of her gorgeous face and body. The witch closed the distance between us, lean muscles rippling beneath her soft white flesh. Gundrygia poured herself against me, her white arms enfolding my neck, her graceful mouth offered to mine like the mouth of a flower.

How gladly I pressed my lips to the petal of that rose! I held her by the shoulders at first, but soon one hand found its way into the wild mane of rich black hair that so elegantly framed her face. She moaned softly as my other palm slid down the curve of her spine to settle in the small of her back, that flesh as agonizingly smooth as I had expected it to be. Even through my tunic, her nude body was warmer than those of the other women whose company I had begun to regularly enjoy. She yearned for me, this much was evident, and her embrace of me tightened to permit her to slide upon my knee. There she slowly rocked herself, her fingertips tickling through my hair while at last she drew her mouth away.

"My father's name is Clinschor," she whispered, gazing into my face, her hands traveling over my chest while I sighed with pleasure to study her features. "And if my name is forgotten, his is sure to be."

"I struggle to believe anyone could forget a woman like you."

"All things are forgotten amid the march of time, Paladin...Burningsoul. Handsome, proud"—her long fingers at last reached my breeches, those tantalizing lips brushing mine while she slowly untied them and unleashed my gasping desire for her—"night's hair and smouldering eyes...what is your breeding, Burningsoul?"

Exhaling as she explored my anatomy, I trailed my hands over her curves and confessed to her, "I don't know."

Her smile grew wicked and inspired a throb of mad pleasure. "Would you like to?"

My lips parted in shock. Gundrygia laughed at once, delighted by my astonishment. As the high spate of madwoman's laughter cracked like a peal of thunder, another sound reached my ears.

Branwen's voice, calling, "Rorke! Ror-ke!"

I still do not know how I got up out of that pit. I still do not know what happened to that pit. One second I was grabbing Gundrygia's wrist to detain her for further questions, the time for games having suddenly passed us by. The next, I lay upon my back surrounded by those offerings the gimlets left the sleeping woman, the torch's blue glow illuminating the plateau where once had been a hole—and where now I rested, supine upon flat ground. Disoriented by the transition as I was, I still had faculty enough to answer Branwen's repetition of, "Ror-ke!"

"Here," I called back, unmoving, my head for some reason aching. This, I thought, might have had something to do with finding myself so suddenly in another place. Soon footsteps hurried to my location. The search party made up of Branwen and Indra found me where I'd awoken.

"Rorke!" Branwen gasped, hurrying off the gimlets' road and down to their site of strange worship. "Are you all right?"

"Seems like I'm always waking up to beautiful women," I said while the pair helped me up, Indra frowning while she kindly dusted me off. "But this time, I was the one who did the waking…I thought I did, at any rate."

The warmth of her body in my hands, the taste of her on my lips—no.

It could not have been a dream. It was not a dream. The taste of her was *still* on my lips. I touched them in dreamy delirium before looking up to ask my rescuers, "How is it you found me?"

"You were gone on the trails at least an hour—far longer than any of us expected. Then we heard a noise like a rock slide. I decided I'd better track it down." Looking me over for cuts or bruises, Branwen asked with curiosity, "What is this about a woman?"

"A mountain witch of some kind…under this plateau here. There was a sepulcher. Its rotunda was thin before, collapsed right beneath my feet, and…"

I looked between them, then down at myself. All three of us stood atop the same place I had fallen through. The ground beneath our feet showed not the slightest evidence of instability.

"Maybe I did dream her," I said softly, baffled.

"Perhaps you tripped and hit your head?" Indra, concerned, leaned upon her toes to check through my hair and along my scalp. "We didn't see anyone on the trail."

"Not even a gimlet? I remember, now...yes, a gimlet stole my torch and brought it here. But why were they worshiping this woman? Gundrygia..."

While I fell into a state of almost trancelike rumination on the subject, Branwen and Indra shared a look of concern.

"Come on," said Branwen, "let's get you back to the fork...we'll call up and see if Odile and Valeria can meet us there. If not, I'll go fetch them."

6

THE TOWN OF SOOT

PRAISE BE TO Weltyr for sparing our precious time! Valeria and Odile were able to hear us without issue. They met us at the fork and, together, we made our long way down the mountain.

Though not nearly so grueling downhill as it had been up through claustrophobic caverns for blooms on end, our descent to Soot proved a long hike and an appropriately belabored denouement to our journey through the Nightlands. Even now I remain awash with gratitude that Odile's lantern and the warmth of the dancing wisp flames made it an easier task to navigate than one might have otherwise expected.

Except, of course, for watching out for Valeria, whose face so frequently darted toward the stars that I feared she would trip and slide down any number of the steep switchbacks we navigated in a slow and steady line. I slid my hand into her splendid, soft elbow to keep her upright. She smiled at me, and I smiled back, though I confess my thoughts were elsewhere.

Upon touching her, my hand crackled with the memory of touching Gundrygia.

Had I really tripped and fallen? For some reason the events in that hidden sepulcher were hazy to my mind when I pictured them, leading me too easily to believe them to interlinked dreams. Yet some pieces of definite sense-memory fell through the cracks. Then there was the frightful question of my missing time: subjective in the slash through my perception as I suddenly found myself flat on my back upon the rocks; and, more alarmingly, objective in the length of time I had been absent from my friends.

I had walked down that hill perhaps twenty minutes; chased the gimlet for five, and spoken with Gundrygia for surely no more than ten minutes more including the time I woke her. Branwen declared I had been gone an hour even before she and Indra set off to search for me— mean that, for almost an hour, I could not account for my own whereabouts.

The thought numbed me into a kind of maddening dread, as you may well imagine, but I suspected this amnesia was linked to whatever magic Gundrygia wove over me. Of course, I had no proof. No proof that she had enchanted me. No proof that she had even existed. I had no proof of anything at all, save for the mysterious taste of woman upon my lips—and, of course, my memory.

Ah! What good was memory to any but his master, Weltyr? He flew away just as soon as you set eyes on him. Memory served no purpose in matters of legal testimony, and in religious testimony it was even less useful without those accompanying miracles sent to us as signs of confirmation.

Rather than dwell on my memories of Gundrygia, therefore, I thought of her words. Of what she had teased me with. Knowledge about myself—knowledge about why she was there.

Pay attention. Pay close attention. Ask questions.

"Rorke." Valeria drew me from my thoughts, her soft voice gilded with concern. "Are you all right?"

"Just feeling somewhat scattered after falling," I said, adding truthfully, "and a bit embarrassed I let that little scoundrel make off with my torch for even a temporary span of time."

"You've been off in your own thoughts longer than that, though." Regarding me carefully, Valeria suggested, "I don't know what it is, but you've seemed—different somehow since the bandits. Pensive, I suppose."

"I'll tell you about it when I've figured it out." Owing to a reflexive glance toward the back of Branwen's golden head, my attention was drawn eastward across the graying sky. I was seeing rather well: dawn was nearly upon us. "How are your eyes? It looks like Weltyr's shown us his favor and sent a cloudy morning. We should be able to make it to Soot and get a roof over our heads before the sun breaks through, assuming it does. Cascadia is a notoriously overcast region."

"That's good...I'm not bothered yet. Frankly, I wouldn't care if I *were* bothered. I want to watch the sun rise, oh—Rorke." Her hand tightened around mine and she insisted, "I've never seen a thing like this. I wish I might do it with eyes that weren't so sensitive."

"We'll find a solution," I swore to her, my heart leaping as my sentence was punctuated by the cry of an early raven.

We were nearing the ground. I had endured a few hikes in my time, but of them all this had been by far the most arduous. The sentiment was likely held by my companions, who stumbled into Soot with me while its markets were still opening. There were therefore not many people to gawk at the paladin and his retinue of fine elves from both above and below Urde's surface, but in a village the meager size of Soot, all it takes is one or two prying eyes to spread news like wildfire.

The innkeeper, for instance, had no discretion, but probably made his best living by being indiscreet unless paid. We knocked on the front door of his establishment, the tavern entry labeled with the name *The Weeping Willow*. I recall thinking it a dreary moniker for a place of relief and revelry when at last our knocking was answered, and the man—ruddy and mustached as I suspected all innkeepers were required to be—cracked open the door with a tired, somewhat sour look to see who it was so early.

He saw, all right.

"Cor," said the man, his eyebrows traveling halfway up his bald head to see my companions. "It's finally happened. I died in my sleep. You lovely lot must be Selectrices, here to whisk me to Weltyr's castle in the sky."

I couldn't help myself but to laugh, unconvinced he had even noticed me.

"Oh good," said Branwen, looking tired from the hike and unamused by the innkeeper's (in my opinion) quite innocently meant appreciation of my companions' good looks. "You two will get along, sounds like."

Maintaining an earnest expression, I bowed to the innkeeper and told him, "Good morning, sir. I cannot deny we were sent by Weltyr, but I also cannot promise you these companions of mine will be your guides to the Hall of Valor. We're but weary travelers in search of a place to stay."

"Oh, aye, well, you're in luck when it comes to that. We just had two rooms vacated by another couple of adventurers...not near so comely as this lot. Never in all my days did I expect to see a durrow aboveground! They're twice as beautiful as I'd imagined."

Clearing my throat, sympathetic to his distraction but no less tired or in need of rest, I urged him gently, "They are, indeed, and would be all the moreso if given a little time to rest their after the long journey. Two rooms, you said?"

"That's right, just turned over yesterday. I'll give 'em both away and throw in meals for"—his eyes scanned our number and his head buzzed with calculations—"an ounce of silver a head a night, how's that."

"We'll take them," I said. Even Odile couldn't complain at that price; at her nod, Indra opened the party's purse, its weight surely handsome after being filled in the bandits' house. I carried on asking the fellow, "And would you happen to know a smithy here?"

"Sure enough! There's Regin down the ways a bit. Just follow the clanging sound anytime the sun's up...I'd mind who goes with you, though, if you see what I'm saying." While accepting the coins from Indra's hand and smiling fondly at her, he inspected the silver, dropped the disks into his apron, then stepped aside to let us into the yet-closed front of the house. "In fact, you ladies might want to spend a good deal of your time in your rooms, and exit out the back door I'll show you if you need to leave at some point during daylight hours...people round these parts are strange when it comes to durrow. Sometimes even just elves. Rural folk!"

While Branwen, aggrieved and exhausted, rolled her reddened eyes, Valeria nodded. "We'll keep it in mind," she said. "We won't cause you any problems—yet I can't help but notice you don't seem to be strange toward us, yourself."

"Well! I didn't say their strangeness made sense to me, did I? Me, I'm a man of the world! Been to Draston and Massadua, as far north as Perodule. And all the women I've seen in all those places have qualities to commend them...I were only just talking to one of the last fellows about Rhineland, as it happens. Now there's a splendid place! Don't know much about the women from it since they won't give a human man the time of day—but the food? Well, let's just say there's a reason most dwarves are twice as wide as they are tall!"

The jolly man, fairly round, himself, broke into laughter and patted his stomach though his apron. By this point, though, Branwen and I had already exchanged a glance.

"Excuse me, sir," she said, managing to work from her tired voice an especially feminine lilt that always served her well. Indeed, the innkeeper turned his bright eyes upon her, expectant and clearly eager to answer her least question. "These other adventurers—was one of them a dwarf, by chance?"

Glad she had seemingly read my mind on this issue, I pressed, "And the other one a tall man, a bit older than you—missing an eye?"

"Well now!" Laughing, stroking his mustache, the loudmouthed innkeeper looked between us and enthused, "Aren't the two of you astute! Friends of yours?"

"Yes," said Branwen without missing a beat, her lips arranged a sweet, even smile. "We were separated, you see."

"Is that so! They didn't mention anything about you...can't believe they'd leave out a lovely group of elves wandering with a warrior."

"A Paladin of Weltyr," I told him, earning a lift of his eyebrows. The expression of new interest in me remained as I went on, "And it's true, they probably did not mention anything about us. These three were not with us then." I gestured to the durrow and the man followed my motion, thinking on it with a hum. "As it was, at the time, just myself and Branwen here they expected, I don't think they would have felt us extraordinary enough to mention."

"I suppose not! We'll, they'll be in for quite a surprise when you lot meet back up in Skythorn."

My blood ran cold at the thought of showing my face in the city without the scepter in hand. "They went along to Skythorn already?"

"Oh, aye, to catch the airship to Rhineland! Poor sods just missed the last one a day or so before coming to stay with us. Leaves once a fortnight, and costs a bit of a fortune to fly on. You lot going across the sea with them?"

"If we can catch them in time," I told him, feeling somewhat guilty for telling these half-truths. I was at least secure in knowing that Weltyr himself was fond of such verbal games, and that all this was, as always, in his service. Our helpful host, at any rate, did not notice the slight tint I had given reality. He went on without hesitation.

"Well, if you need horses, I think the Dardrie family in the ranch south of town always has a handful for sale. Breed 'em for farmwork. Not exactly fit for a paladin, but they'll take you where you need to go, and if you'd prefer to rent them awhile I'm sure the Dardrie boy would be glad for an excuse to ride to Skythorn and lead 'em back up after you've departed on your flight. Come on up here! Let me show you the rooms."

The Weeping Willow had six guest rooms circling above the tavern, arranged along a hallway open like a balcony. Ours were the two on the farthest end, quite cozy little chambers with surprisingly soft beds and well-kept furniture.

"I'm Erdwud, by the way," he told us at last, watching with a pleased smile as we inspected the rooms. "If you need anything at all, myself and my wife, Lively, are always somewheres around. Ask one of the maids for us and tell 'em your room numbers."

"We will," I said, shaking his hand. "Thank you so much for accommodating us, Erdwud. Oh, and—if anyone does come asking after my companions"—I produced a few coins from my own small bag, meriting a corresponding glint in his eye—"would you keep things quiet for us?"

"With pleasure, sire, with pleasure. Weltyr himself could not pry the mystery from my lips. I'll let you get settled in now and tell Lively to run up with breakfast."

Bowing, scraping, casting a few more appreciative glances at my companions, Erdwud made himself scarce and let us retire to the solitude of our rooms. Convening in the one at the farthest end, we shut the door and, sighing en mass, divested ourselves of weapons, armor, and the burdensome equipment we had carried with us out of the Nightlands.

"By Roserpine"—Odile kicked off her boots and dropped upon the foot of a bed wide enough for three if we were lucky—"are all surface men that impudent?"

"Things here are very different from the way they are in El'ryh," I warned not just Odile but all three durrow. "He's a friendly old man, and men of his sort tend to show their friendliness in a very forward way. Let's count our blessings he's well-tempered and not inclined to spread idle gossip as long as we keep him paid."

"We'll see about that," said Odile with a snort, draping her hand over her eyes. "Oh! Darkness. That feels delicious. I'm going to fall right to sleep."

"How can anyone sleep?" Buzzing with excitement, Valeria hurried to the window and peered through the curtains at the small town square beneath us. Girlish delight that seemed almost unknown to her glowed in her face, and she looked delightedly between me and the vision of sleepy townsfolk waking up to go about their days. "How wonderful this is! It reminds me of illustrations I've seen...why, what's that, what's that woman leading there? That's a horse, isn't it?"

I peered out past her, swallowing back a light laugh. "Yes, it is most certainly a horse—you mean, you've never seen one!"

"Of course not. Where am I going to have seen a horse in El'ryh outside of a book?"

"By Weltyr...then I suppose it's useless hoping you already know how to ride, right?" At her somewhat blank look, I exchanged with Branwen the silent realization that we had quite a task ahead of us. "Do *any* of you know how to ride a horse?"

"I was sat on one as a girl a couple of times," said Odile. "Fewer times than I was invited to the surface, even...but I don't really know how to ride, no."

"I can ride a spider," Indra offered, loosening her hair from the long plait that held it.

"He didn't ask if you can ride a spider, Indra," the terser of the two rogues said. "He asked about horses."

Blanching quite adorably, Indra scoffed. "Well! It's a similar principle, I'm sure."

We would see about that…for now, I tugged open the tie of the leather purse at my hip and considered the coins within. There would be enough for a suit of armor in there, with some negotiation, maybe. But for a suit of armor and the rooms? The horses? New equipment for Branwen, for whom the plunder from the bandits proved inadequate?

I was not quite sure how we would manage it. There was no doubt that, one way or another, Weltyr would allocate his riches to help us acquire what we needed, no matter how different what we truly needed was from what we thought we needed…but the murkiness of our monetary future kept my busy mind all the busier while I put my gold away at the knock upon the door.

Lively, I should not have been surprised, appeared about twenty years older than her husband and was certainly a great deal more pleasing to my eye. She glanced shyly about the room, a towel over her shoulder and a washbasin in her hands. All the while, she smiled, the expression cutting early wrinkles into her tan features with the kind of pretty effect such mirthful lines often had on a woman who took care of herself. "Hello, hello— my goodness, it's a crowd in here!"

"We'll separate ourselves out into reasonable groups soon enough, ma'am," I told her, thanking her for the basin she set upon the nightstand. While Valeria hurried to make immediate use of it for her hands and face, Lively set her towel down with a wave of her hand.

"Oh, it's no trouble at all. You've no neighbors on this side, so if you're going to be chatting at this hour, it's best to do it here."

"You're both too kind to see to us so well," I told her, meriting another wave of a hand she then reflexively wiped upon her apron.

"Happy to do it, happy to do it. It's not often we get elves of any sort coming 'round!"

Not wanting to risk more annoyance of any kind from Branwen, I stayed on the point. "Would you do me a favor, Madame"—Lively glowed at the appellation, but not near as much as she did when I placed a casual hand upon her shoulder and gestured with the other toward the window—"and point me toward the smithy where Rigan works?"

"Of course! You're going there right *now?* Cor, you lot look so tired! I'm surprised you were even awake to answer me knock, I was ready to leave the washbin at the door for you."

"As the temple priests used to tell me, there'll be time to rest when I'm dead."

Lively laughed in sympathy, patting my hand, as charmed by me as her husband was by my companions. "Sure enough, my mother used to say that, too. We'll be lucky if we even get the chance to rest *then,* so far as I can see it! All right, come on...let me show you where Rigan's at. Erdwud's so terrible with directions..."

Bless her, Lively was much clearer than her husband had been, and far less brimming with nosy curiosity about just what our business together was. All number of questions had been bubbling under the man's mustache, but if Lively was curious about anything, it was durrow fashion. "Aren't you cold in that short little dress, love?"

Valeria looked down at herself with a shake of her head. "No," she said, studying the dark legs left bare by the golden party dress she had not had a chance to change out of since our escape from El'ryh. "It doesn't bother me any—if anything, it's quite warm up here compared to my home."

"Well, you just let me know if you need something

to go about in. I might have an old dress that'll fit you, if you don't mind a moth hole or two..."

Yes—clothes for Valeria, now there was another cost to consider. Finding myself biting back a sigh, I thanked the innkeeper's wife for her directions and said to my comrades, "I'm going to speak with that smith and see if he'll be willing to work with me on a new set of armor."

This may well have been the only combination of words that could have gotten Odile to sit up just then. "A whole new set! Are you mad? I thought you wanted—that we were going to catch up with your friends," she corrected with a glance at Lively.

How grateful I was for that kind woman! She made Odile helpless to stop me when I said, "Yes, which is why I've got to get him started on my commission now...but if you ladies are going to learn horseback riding, well, the soonest we'll be able to leave here is a couple of days from now. I won't have you breaking your backs because we were in a rush to leave..."

A fine thing coming from me just then! I may not have been in a rush to leave Soot, but I was certainly in a rush to leave that inn. The outdoors called to me. After my time in the Nightlands, to go without a roof or any cover at all over my head seemed like a blessing beyond compare. I stepped outside, Strife once more on my hip, and took a breath of the heavenly mountain air that I had not truly appreciated before my near-death experiences and my long journey through the dark.

All around me, Soot teemed with life, the village square through which I passed populating with artisans eager to sell their fruits and vegetables. I stopped off for a handful of blueberries and, after even my short period of slavery, the use of money was its own delight. It made me remember what it was like to be a young boy getting his first experiences of the world—that was how fresh I felt beneath that cloudy sky.

Strange to think this town had, only a few days before, played unknowing host to Hildolfr and Grimalkin! It was bold of them to take the Scepter through Skythorn to bring it to Rhineland, if Erdwud's information was accurate. The city traffic was tightly monitored and guards had been known to search through the bags of untrustworthy looking individuals. Would boldness protect them from scrutiny? I somehow doubted it…but then again, as bold as Hildolfr was, I should have known better. That boldness had lost him his eye in the fashion of my god. Appropriately, like Weltyr himself, Hildolfr's decisions were often surprising to me.

As Erdwud had promised, the rhythmic clatter of Rigan's anvil reached my ears before I ever saw his home and the outdoor forge where he worked beneath little more than a roof to protect him from rainfall. A raven croaked throatily, laughing at my discovery. My mind filled with visions of Nibel, the berich dwarf whose form Al-listux had adopted to assassinate Valeria. Here, however, as I rounded the corner and saw over the waist-high fence to the man working within, I found myself faced with a human almost Hildolfr's age.

"Hail, Rigan, Smith of Soot." The hammering ceased. Rigan turned to see who addressed him, a pair of hard eyes the blue of clear water fixing me to the spot. "Erdwurd and his wife, Lively, sent me out your way today."

"Don't recognize you. What's it you want?"

"I was wondering if it would be possible to talk to you about a suit of plate mail. It may seem out of my price range to look on me now"—I laughed down at myself, dirty yet from the journey to the surface—"but I can negotiate, and at any rate we have a few things yet to sell from the Nightlands."

"Nightlands?" Muttering in an old man sort of way that reminded me of a certain Temple bookkeeper, Rigan turned upon his seat once he had set his hammer down completely. Peering at me through those somehow surprisingly bright eyes, he asked, "You wouldn't be Rorke Burningsoul, would you?"

Shocked, I looked about as though in anticipation of an ambush. The town's only discernible noise was clearly little more than the bubbling daily mirth from the market.

"I am," I told him cautiously, regarding him straight on and trying to discern if he were perhaps some disguised monster along the lines of the spirit-thieves. "Were you told to expect me?"

"Sure I was. You don't need t'worry about paying me nothing more, your friend covered the cost up-front...but it's not quite half done yet. You'll need to wait another week if you want the full suit."

I looked at him a moment, trying to discern his meaning. Annoyed, the old man snapped, "What's that stare for, boy?"

"Oh, uh—it's nothing, nothing at all. Only...I'm a bit confused."

"You look it." With a wave of his hand, the old man hobbled back around on his stool and picked up the hammer again. Without another word on the matter, he went back to work and left me standing there.

I found I could not move. My mind reeled with strange thoughts. I knew already which friend had paid for a bespoke suit of armor tailored to my needs, yet all the same I still felt the need to confirm.

"When you say—"

The beleaguered old craftsman slammed his hammer down and looked at me, nearly cross-eyed with annoyance to have his morning so interrupted. I smiled meekly, wishing all people would succumb to my charms as easily as Lively.

"When you say 'friend,'" I continued, nonplussed, keeping my tone as simple and pleasant as I could, "I don't suppose he gave you his name, did he?"

"Tall fellow," Rigan said. "One eye. I'm no good with names. I only remember yours because he told me to swear I'd remember it."

I nodded, thanked him, and left in an uncanny daze.

DEEPENING BONDS

SOMEHOW, IT WAS unsurprising that Hildolfr had done such a thing for me. He had a strong sense of honor and might have felt obligated to restore the armor lost in the spirit-thief den. Moreover, he might have felt it unfair for us to stand at odds when I had nothing more to my name than Strife, however much a boon the blade was.

Yet that only begged more questions. How was it, for instance, that Hildolfr would have known I was still alive? How would he have known I would escape the Nightlands and come through Soot? Unless my geography was off, Soot was quite a ways south from Klexus. This elfin region of towering trees and wild forests was where we met Branwen and Grimalkin, and where we entered the Nightlands together. Hildolfr would have had to return there to collect his boarded horse.

Therefore, it seemed to me that in order to arrive at Soot and commission this set of armor for me, he would have had to make a specific detour for it. There were faster highways between Klexus and Skythorn: I confirmed it in a map in the registrar's office on my way back to the inn.

It seemed to me almost that Hildolfr had known by some occult means that I would arrive where and when I arrived, yet I could not account for this. To the best of my knowledge the ranger had no such magic. Certainly nothing like Gungdrygia and her thieving of my time.

Another mystery! Ah, Gundrygia. Just the thought of that name made my blood burn with desire. Yet this unfulfilled lust was very nearly welcome. Otherwise, my mind was too at odds with itself: too bogged down with its countless unanswered questions. Hildolfr, Gundrygia, the hateful hivemind of the spirit-thieves…and, of course, the most pressing and disturbing matter. The old man through the portal, whose face resembled mine.

How tired I was! My body was drained by the journey, my mind was drained by questions; yet still I could not rest. First I took to the town bathhouses, quiet that early in the day. Then I made south, to the Dardrie Ranch. The family was very kind when it came to the matter of loaning out their horses to a total stranger, although the deposit was quite a sum and practically emptied the leather pouch at my hip.

No matter. The most important tasks seen to, I returned to the inn, ate an early lunch in the corner of the tavern, then climbed the stairs to rest my aching body.

This also proved somewhat challenging at the outset. I had a decision to make—Indra and Odile, or Branwen and Valeria? I paused by the first door. By the density of Odile's snores, it would have been as fatal to wake her as to wake any dragon taking a well-earned, post-rampage rest.

In the other room, then. I eased softly into where Branwen and Valeria slept, or pretended to amid a whirl of thoughts as strange as mine.

The women slept in a fashion that was the polar opposite of how Indra and Odile always seemed to intertwine when at rest. Their backs to one another, Valeria and Branwen each slept on her own edge of the mattress. I did not take this as a general sign of mistrust in one another so much as an unfamiliarity, but I have to admit I thought it something of a shame I didn't walk into the room to find them already embraced in sleep as lovers. A man can dream that things should run so smoothly, anyway!

Just inside the room, I undressed and found as I did that Branwen, facing the door, peered sleepily at me. "Did you get our horses?"

"Yes, Branwen," I whispered, coming into the bed and forcing her to wiggle nearer Valeria. Thanks to the small mattress, their bodies pressed together and the dark elf stirred in her hefty sleep. "I got our horses."

"'Zah," she murmured, her eyes closing. That smooth elfin brow of hers furrowed, though, as I slid an arm around her and she got a whiff of my skin. "You're clean!"

"Never would I have expected you to find *that* objectionable, Branwen."

"Where did you get *clean!* Of course it's objectionable, I'm blind with jealousy."

"Well…lucky for you, I like a dirty girl."

Valeria's laugh revealed her to be awake. She rolled over to see us, telling Branwen, "You'd ought to tell him to sleep on the floor, Branwen. It's the only way for a man to learn when his impudence is getting him into trouble. I've been close to making him do it once or twice, myself."

Pouting in a way that was maddeningly sexy even in my physically exhausted state, Branwen said to Valeria, "I can't. In fact, it's just the opposite…I promised him I'd respect his leadership, and yours."

My fingers ran through the high elf's golden hair and trailed down her neck while she shivered. "She's lucky she wasn't made a slave in El'ryh, or a servant to the misshapen."

"Yes, very lucky." Valeria was fast in these games of seduction and slid her arm around Branwen's waist, the elf gasping to be touched by the nude dark elf. "A high elf in particular would prove quite valuable for all number of purposes…and you might even come to enjoy those purposes of your own volition, after a time of servitude."

Moaning, glancing over to feel me against her back and rear, Branwen bit her lip and rolled her soft blue eyes toward Valeria. The dark elf's hand shifted lower beneath the blanket, caressing down her pale sister's stomach and along a slowly moving thigh.

"This all feels so embarrassing," the high elf whimpered, gasping as Valeria's exploring hand softly delivered more deliberate pleasure. Red-faced, Branwen moaned, her eyes darting sometimes shyly my direction.

"Nothing is embarrassing about ecstasy," said Valeria, watching her face, then glancing at me as I leaned down to kiss Branwen's throat and sweeten the tones of her gasps. "Pleasure is a sacred experience from Roserpine. Our birthright, and part of why we are on Urde instead of floating about in the Wyrd beyond space and time with other non-corporeal entities. Have you ever made love with a woman, Branwen?"

Her cheeks and lips and throat rosier than ever I'd

seen on her, Branwen shook her head. With the briefest glance at me, Valeria drew the high elf into her dark arms and lowered her mouth for a sensual kiss. Then another, and another. Branwen gasped beneath the ministrations of Valeria's hidden hand, their tongues mingling in secretive pink shimmers between their shifting lips. Eventually, the high elf's shocked hand lifted to the durrow's breast and carefully caressed, her eyelids fluttering with pleasure.

I had seen Valeria with quite a number of women during my time with her in El'ryh, but suffice it to say nothing had been so sweet to my eyes as the vision unfurling before me in that little inn of Soot. The two women whom I loved, their limbs contrasting in more ways than simply color. Both were well-shaped and feminine in all the best ways, but Branwen had a layer of muscle that Valeria's indolent lifestyle as the Materna did not necessarily permit. The women moaned together amid a tangle of caresses. Soon, much as Valeria's fingers worked beneath the blanket that slipped slowly farther down, so too did Branwen's hand go searching for a more efficient way to stimulate her companion's nerves. Valeria gasped, nuzzling against Branwen's ear and whispering something there at a volume so soft only an elf could have heard it.

Whatever it was, Branwen laughed and kissed her.

How my head and body swam, drunk with more desire than exhaustion! Yet I did not wish to interrupt the scene, this moment of Branwen's experimentation. The novelty certainly seemed to have an impact on her: between the softness of Valeria's feminine caress and the invigorating effects of my observation, Branwen reached a surprisingly fast climax and seemed as though to nearly wince with the power of it.

Certainly her leg twitched up, holding Valeria's wrist

there, and her eyes fluttered along with the contortions of her brow.

"Oh yes," she gasped, "oh yes, oh yes, oh, Valeria—"

"Would you mind if I rode him first?" Brushing her damp lips over Branwen's pink mouth, Valeria smiled as she murmured, "I've wished to use him for quite some time…but it was more important to me in the bandit den that he go put himself to use on you."

Shocked, Branwen searched her face and asked, "Why?"

Valeria didn't look like she understood the question. Knowing how loose the mores of the durrow could be in matters of jealousy, she probably didn't.

"You surface beings really are very repressed," Valeria said with an aristocratic titter, nuzzling Branwen before pressing her body into my arm. "Here, Paladin… hold her while I ride you, help me pleasure her before she takes her turn."

Though I was no longer Valeria's slave, there were some commands a man didn't mind taking. My arm sliding around Branwen, I caught her jaw in my other hand and drew her honeysuckle mouth to mine. Her sweet, breathless moans only sharpened as Valeria drew the sheet away from me to reveal how excited I had been by the exhibition beside me. With an admiring groan, the durrow leaned her head down and ran her tongue along my throbbing length.

A vision of Gundrygia rolled through my mind.

Why that phantom appeared just then, or why she rattled me so, I could not explain. Perhaps it was because Gundrygia had excited me so sharply in sepulcher…or perhaps it was something else. I tried not to ponder what that could have been and committed myself to kissing and caressing Branwen.

My hands followed the familiar smooth curves of her body to tickle along her backside, down her thighs, in between her legs. While Brawen moaned, I made more than one noise of my own pleasure—first beneath the unearned suckling of Valeria's lips, and then the slight weight of her body as she mounted me with a rolling groan of my name.

"Oh, Branwen! Isn't he such a fine man..." Taking to the rhythm of riding me at once, Valeria slithered in my lap and smiled as the sight of my cock piercing dark labia made Branwen moan. "Yes, oh, why, he's such a gorgeous stud that the sight of him fucking someone else is nearly as exciting as being fucked by him. Let me watch him spill his seed in you, high elf...oh, I can think of few visions as sweet as that."

Branwen's body grew soaked beneath my fingers at that plea. "How could you want to watch a thing like that? Don't you feel jealous at all? Oh, Anroa, I'll be so exposed..."

"That will make it all the sweeter, to have the coupling witnessed. Oh, yes! Yes, Burningsoul...Rorke, this sword of yours, oh, by Roserpine, I could fill myself with it all day..."

The dark elf leaned back to work her hips up and down upon my throbbing shaft. I groaned, the sight of my hard manhood sliding in and out of her dusky flesh and that valley of pink in between enough to make my head swim with bliss. Branwen also seemed quite taken with the sight, crying out as my fingers slid inside to work her over properly. She offered her mouth to me, her cherry blossom lips falling open, her tongue coaxing into action the eager playing of my own. My fingers moved faster as her body tightened. Seeing this, Valeria hastened the pace of her riding, her body tipping into an ecstatic orgasm that tightened her core and made her flutter wildly around my length.

"Yes," she moaned, her hands tangling in her long plumes of white hair, "yes, yes, oh, Burningsoul, yes, yes! Soon you have to fill me with that seed of yours, Paladin…yes, oh, soon I want to feel your cum dripping out of me again! But for now…"

The dark elf dismounted me and smiled as I bobbed with yet more desire. "Go on," she urged, caressing my cheek. "I want so terribly to watch."

Happy to oblige her, I turned to see Branwen's face and found her every feature ablaze with lust. Seeking to cool her with my kisses only worsened her fever, and, moaning into my mouth, the high elf soon sprawled upon her back to offer me total use of her body. I slid between her widely splayed legs and drew her hips toward me, a pillow fitting beneath to provide an extra bit of leverage. Then, with Valeria watching intently and my eyes often roving over to hers, I aligned myself to the sweet pink ripples of Branwen's oozing ocean and, one inch at a time, pushed home into her.

"Oh! Rorke! Rorke—oh, Anroa, you always feel so big, but especially at first. And, now—"

Her scarlet blush had reached the tips of her high pointed ears. She glanced through streams of blonde hair at our bedmate, who watched with one cheek propped upon her fist. Valeria's other hand slid down to hold Branwen's, and somehow this sight was erotic to me in its own right.

"There, now, I know you can take it, Branwen…I see how much potential you have to be an eager little slut for Rorke, for me…if only you'd let yourself."

"Ah! Ah! Ah! Oh, I can't believe—this is all so strange—"

While I drew her thigh a little higher to pound her all the more deeply, Branwen nearly wept with pleasure and gripped the headboard in her free hand. As I gave it to her, still thinking reflexively as I did of her face at the moment of her betrayal, Valeria lowered her head to kiss and nuzzle and occasionally run her tongue along the edge of Branwen's surely sensitive ear.

"It only feels strange because it's new, friend, rest assured...why, soon I'd wager you'll be comfortable with Indra and Odile playing along, as well. Just wait until you see how hard Odile likes it! Oh, it's almost frightening...I love to see it."

Branwen gasped abruptly, her body contorting up toward mine. "Rorke!"

The tone of her voice, the sight of the women nuzzling against one another, the way they held hands while I laid claim to Branwen—it was all such a peak of stimulation after Gundrygia's teasing and the rest of our journey into town that I groaned, giving into the rapid squeezing of the high elf's tight body as her orgasm attempted to inspire one of my own. Pleasure bolted through me like lighting, racing from my groin to my skull and through every inch of my suddenly electrified body. Branwen gasped to receive my seed; Valeria moaned just to see such a thing. Everything slowed and, for a few sweet seconds, my mind was at perfect ease. Indeed, my mind was no mind at all.

And then, nearly soon as it came, the climax faded. I gasped myself to consciousness. Branwen still shivered beneath me; I admired her face somewhat blearily while she was wracked with her own pleasure. When her body finished this celebration of joy, I kissed her, then drew myself from her flooded valley.

"Isn't it lovely to feel him inside you even now?"

Valeria's tone, though sleepy, was sensual even still. Shyly blushing, Branwen bit her lip.

"It is a rather exciting sensation," the high elf allotted stiffly while I, chuckling, stretched out along the side of the bed nearest to the door. "I'd ought not to, since if he were to give me a child my adventuring days would surely be at an end…but it's such an intoxicating feeling, and oh, I love to have him so deep inside me…ah!"

Valeria had sat up. Now, to Branwen's surprise but not quite so much to my own, the dark elf drew apart her surface cousin's thighs and examined the shining flesh beneath. "You really are so frightfully shy, Branwen…but you like to be looked at, don't you."

Whining, writhing, the high elf gasped while Valeria lowered a fingertip to that sensitive nodule of feminine desire. After a few little passes, the durrow's fingers caressed lower, lower, and soon slid just within Branwen's tight body. While the high elf moaned, so did the durrow, enthusing, "Ah, Branwen! How sweet, I can still feel his semen in you…how wet you are with it!"

Laughing, Valeria drew her fingers from Branwen's quim and admired the contrast of my white seed upon them. Then, working this into the supple skin of Branwen's pubic mound, Valeria continued teasing her clitoris until the druid erupted in a new, far sharper orgasm.

"I know you just love his cum," Valeria said approvingly, settling down between the two of us with a look of nearly feline contentment. "So do I…and I don't mind sharing if you don't, Branwen."

Now that was the real trick!

8

GUNDRYGIA'S FIELD

THE CAREFREE SELECTRICES attending Weltyr have never slept half so well as I did following that little bit of celebration. After our escape from El'ryh, our battle with Al-listux, our rescue of Branwen and our treacherous journey through the Nightlands, I was simply happy to be alive. Happier, still to have the affection of so many beautiful women. Happiest of all that I dreamt no more terrible visions. In fact, even Valeria seemed unplagued by her usual troublesome nightmares.

Yet still she was a very sensitive woman. Branwen sprang out of bed a few hours before nightfall, shaking me awake to demand directions to the bathhouse.

"Why don't you go ask old Erdwud," I teased her. "I'm sure he'd like to think of that."

She slapped me in the side of the face with a pillow

and demanded the directions again. Once I yielded the information, she sprang out of bed and was gone, leaving me alone with Valeria. The displaced Materna had been awoken by the good-natured quarrel between myself and the high elf. When we were alone, she turned over to face me, her body stretching along mine.

"Good bloom to you, Burningsoul," she said in husky tone that fired my blood anew.

"Good morning," I told her, glancing at the curtains. "Or evening, rather."

How soft, those privileged fingertips! She had well and truly never worked a day in her life, Valeria; not with her hands. I exhaled and drew them to my mouth from where they trailed along my chest, their fragrant skin like silk against my lips.

"There is certainly something different about you," she perceived softly. "I can't divine what it is…"

"Strange dreams," I confessed to her. "Tonight was the first night in some time that I have slept well and not been plagued by a disturbing vision of one sort or another. First upon waking once Al-listux escaped, then while we slept in the bandit's den."

"Perhaps that was the fault of the Nightlands… it must be disruptive to your mind to have the cycle of glorious sunlight taken from you. Oh! Burningsoul, even with the curtains filtering it, it's so bright…how can you stand it?"

"Just made for it," I told her, my hand trailing over her cheek. "I want to find a solution for your eyes… maybe when I go bother that smith again—ah!"

The dregs of sleep drifted away to leave, with sharp clarity, all the memories of yesterday. I sat up slightly, telling Valeria, "Hildolfr—he paid for a suit of armor for me."

Her lips parted in confusion, Valeria had to actively parse my words before understanding them. "The old man? But why would he do that after leaving you for dead?"

"I don't know," I told her. "I don't understand it. It seems like some gesture…of what, I'm just not sure."

Invoking Hildolfr so suddenly brought to mind the first strange dream—one I had nearly forgotten in all the hustle of our journey out of the Nightlands. Hildolfr fishing by a stream; the nightmarish eight-legged stallion rearing to reveal its writhing mess of legs.

Wait, a stream? No—no, it had been much wider and more dramatic than a stream. That much was clear in my memory. Not a stream, then. A river. What river, I wondered?

I glanced at Valeria, who was far more expert in these matters than I. "How do you tell a precognitive dream from a vision—for that matter, from a regular dream?"

"All dreams have the capacity for certain degrees of prescience," she explained thoughtfully. "I do not know whether that is because they are derived from the gods or because, having seen the symbol in sleep, our minds seek it out in waking life. So far as prescient dreams heralding actual events are concerned, they are often very vivid, but ultimately the cruel joke is that it is impossible to tell a prescient dream from a more common one until the event in question."

"Naturally…" Sighing, I shook my head and told her, "These matters are cryptic to me. The Church of Weltyr teaches that every dream sign contains messages from the All-Father, but I admit they are not always the clearest to me. The priests at the Temple do more interpretation than any other duty."

"Few durrow are as in-touch with the contents of their dreams," Valeria confessed. "Perhaps if they were the Nightlands would be at greater peace with aboveground societies."

"Perhaps...but the same could be said of us up here. I can't speak of elves, but most humans don't think twice about the contents of their dreams. The only reason why the priests have a pool of so many people coming to request their interpretations is because there are so many people, worshipers of Weltyr especially, living in Skythorn. Ah..."

My hand slid over her arm and my gaze drifted toward the covered window, where the supple golden glow of evening light eased through the curtains to enchant the room. "I am not eager to return there empty-handed, Valeria...if we are to ask the priests to divine the location of the ring for us, they're going to want to know why I am pursuing an artifact unrelated to Weltyr and the task for which they sent me from the city in the first place."

"But with the ring we could surely reach the scepter with greater ease. It increases my perceptive abilities and grants me many magical powers I do not have otherwise. Without it, I'm precious more than a healer. With it, I can do far more."

Yes, perhaps that was true—but I still could not shake the feeling that, whatever Roserpine's ring bestowed upon Valeria, the last thing the Temple wanted to hear was that I was working with a heathen to retrieve one of her goddess's artifacts. I kissed the top of her head and drew her ear to my chest, where there we lay until Lively knocked upon the door to deliver a meal. Valeria hurried to cover herself and I drew on a pair of breeches before answering with my finest smile.

"Hello, dear!" With a smile of her own, Lively pretended not to ogle my chest by instead looking down at the broad and surely hefty tray of sausage, grits, and other breakfast foodstuffs she had been kind enough to put together despite the evening hour. "Here's breakfast for ya. Delivered it to your neighbors already. Shall I leave it in the hall?"

"No," I told her, gesturing, standing aside from the door. "The table there is fine."

"You'll have to pardon the small oranges," she told me, shining her smile upon Valeria while placing her tray down upon the corner table. "We get them from down south, of course, but lately it's been hard to get a delivery of anything from that way. The gimlets have been intercepting just about one out of every three shipments, I'd wager...haven't killed anyone yet, thank the Wanderer."

"That certainly is a blessing," I told her. "I didn't realize the gimlets were a problem for you here...I had a run-in with one myself while we were coming down the mountainside." I was almost tempted to ask her if she knew anything about Gundrygia, but she was already going on and I was not sure how to broach the subject without sounding insane.

"Yes, well, they've been a problem for Soot just as long as the town's been around...at least since my grandmother's time, and before. Since they're very poor hunters, they make their living scavenging. Mind you lot stick to groups if and when you leave the town—they're not liable to start a fight they're not confident they can win."

Then, wiping off her hands, the kindly woman said, "Oh, and I've one other thing for you—I hope it'll fit, hang on a tic..."

Fluttering back into the hallway, Lively returned in a matter of seconds with a package tied in twine. "Here's that old dress I was telling you about," she said brightly, setting it on the nightstand beside smiling Valeria. "You let me know if it doesn't fit or you don't want it, but I think it'd ought to suit you. I'd have tried to scrounge up more for your friends, but none of 'em seem the dress wearing type."

"Your generosity is truly without parallel, Madame," said Valeria, smiling softly. Of the mind that all her well-behaved guest were good as family, Lively patted the elf's hand without a second thought for the fact that she wore nothing but a blanket.

"It's nothing, dearie! Every man had ought to treat all strangers with at least this much kindness…never know when a guest might be an angel in disguise, or one of the gods themselves."

Then, she was gone again. Valeria investigated the contents of the package as I smeared a bit of long-missed butter, that greatest of luxuries, upon one of the supplied pieces of toast. "How long this thing is! It must be quite difficult to move about in…I'll save it for tomorrow, once I'm more used to riding."

Translation: the Materna was too famished to delay breakfast by figuring out how to dress in these new garbs. I moved the tray upon the foot of the bed and we feasted together there, nearly every bite punctuated with a cry of Valeria's delight at the freshness of foods like eggs and even the small oranges that were quite literally rarer than gold in the Nightlands. Halfway through, Indra and Odile drifted over. The evening wore on into night and I explained a little something of horseback ridings' general principles until Branwen joined us, looking flushed and relieved to have bathed at last.

"It feels good to take a walk under an open sky, doesn't it? Though—we seem to have caused a stir." Branwen laughed, shutting the door and dropping into a creaky old chair at the table in the corner.

Valeria looked at me carefully. "That won't be a problem, will it?"

"We'll have to see," I told them. "Let's just try to keep our heads down and avoid any fuss."

"That's sounding pretty impossible by now," said the high elf. "The manager of the bathhouse approached me and asked if I were the elf traveling around with the durrow...I denied it at first, because I wasn't sure what her intentions were, but she convinced me she was friendly after a minute or two of talking. She told me that if you three need to use her facilities after hours tonight, you should go knock on the door of the little house behind the main building."

The durrows' voices arose in pleased tones while I said, "We're lucky the citizens here have a friendly curiosity, rather than a dangerous one. Regardless of who already knows what, we would do well to proceed with caution."

How hard it was to avoid detection, though! We would inevitably draw attention by moving about the town at night—especially by engaging in horseback lessons at such hours. It seemed to me that it would behoove us (ahem) to engage in such activities as far away from the town itself as we could. So, while the durrow bathed, I took one of the two stallions out for a ride around the perimeter of the village and a few of its surrounding ranches.

The land of the region was well-maintained and populated, and it became apparent soon that the only reasonable location for such lessons would be near the woods at the base of the mountain. From that distance we would neither have to worry about prying eyes nor making noise, and the terrain forbade farming. No neighbors, then. We would be able to conduct a few lessons in peace for several nights in a row, then take off for Skythorn as soon as my armor was ready.

Of course…just who would be taking off with me still remained to be confirmed. When I returned to the stables attached to the inn, the well-trained but energetic stallion pleased to have been given a bit of exercise after a day of inactivity, I was just thinking about trying the other when I found Branwen already there, patting and whispering to a champagne-colored mare.

"She's a gentle one," Branwen told me, a faint smile on her lips as she gestured toward the stabled horse. I nodded, guiding the stallion into the empty space beside them.

"They all seem very well-bred—a testament to the family who loaned them to us. Would we had a bit more in the way of gold! I'd leave them a tip for their fine expertise."

"We could have more gold, you know."

"Branwen."

I knew what she was getting at right away and hoped the stern tone of my voice would ward her off from the subject, but she continued nonetheless with her eyes wide and her tone emphatic.

"You think those durrow aren't planning something much the same with us, Rorke? You think they won't just use you to acquire that ring you all keep talking about, then leave you behind—or, worse, enslave you again?"

"They would have a hard time enslaving me up here, with me the picture of health and El'ryh farther away all the time."

"Who knows what spells or potions these cunning dark elves could produce. You can't trust them, Rorke. They live beneath Urde and away from the light of the sun for a reason."

"What an absurd thought! You don't know the first thing about them, Branwen. The durrow are just like you—surely you can see that by now, especially after last night."

"The people of Klexus have nothing to do with slavery," she said tersely. "Nor do we engage in breeding programs, nor do we consort with chthonic deities. We are happy, healthy people, well-balanced and fair-minded."

"So fair-minded that you would write these women off based on nothing more than the failings of their cultural environment. The ways of the durrow as a species may be distasteful to us aboveground, but our friends are not to be held accountable for the sins of their people."

"Really? None of them? Not the queen who ruled them, or the slavers who sold you to her?"

Very well! So she had a point—but I was still by no means ready to concede that ethical failings such as the tacit support of slavery signified anything about their individual inner nature. "Had they been born in another place and time, they would abide by different standards. Not a one of them knows anything truly different. Slavery and all the unfortunate problems that come with it are normal to them."

"Normal! "Unfortunate problems." You mean like beating and murdering and raping slaves? Those kinds of unfortunate problems?"

While my nostrils flared, my back against the proverbial wall, Branwen folded her arms.

"The durrow are different from us. They can't be

trusted, Rorke, no matter how seductive they are—in trusting them, we hamper ourselves by being forced to travel at night. We're risking our necks for some ring when all you want is the scepter."

"You're a fine one to speak of trust!"

Realizing the volume of my voice, I forced it to lower while I told the elf, "You shot at me with a crossbow. Then you left me for dead just as much as Hildolfr and Grimalkin did. The durrow, meanwhile, have done nothing against me that was not quickly resolved or clearly ordained by Weltyr."

"Oh, yes…very convenient that Weltyr ordains you to do whatever you please, up to and including keeping a harem of women around."

"We keep telling you, durrow culture is different— are you *jealous?*" Her expression transfigured at my question and I almost laughed, catching myself at the last second lest my mirth bring her rising rage to the surface. "You are, aren't you? You know, Branwen, these durrow are exceedingly reasonable. They are not the least bit jealous of you. Did you not enjoy yourself with Valeria last night? Did she show you any ill will or unkindness? For that matter, have any of them?"

"Well." Branwen fell back upon one foot, her weight shifting with the stance to make her appear somewhat off-balance. "Well, no."

"That's right. It would seem to me that they've treated you as one of their own—whatever the normal standards of their culture would be. The fact is, Branwen, they are not among their own culture anymore. They left it. If they were the types of women who truly fit in there, don't you think they would have stayed?"

Her nose and ears pink with a combination of frustration and embarrassment, Branwen said nothing.

My tone gentler now, I advised her, "I am disappointed to see that you have yet to change, Branwen, and I hope that you will soon. You know you don't have a valid argument against these women, which is why you can't say anything to their faces. Instead you would rather run away with me; risk facing Hildolfr and Grimalkin without their help. Perhaps you ought to investigate in your heart why such danger is preferable to you."

A footfall alerted us both. We turned to find, shielding their eyes from the torchlight positioned upon the outer walls of the stables, the subjects of our current discussion.

"Ho, Burningsoul!" Odile's hair was drawn up in a bun that left her neck and collarbone attractively exposed within the confines of her light leather armor. "We were just looking for you. Ready to give us our first lesson?"

"Certainly, if you three don't mind a walk. Come along, let me show you how to introduce yourselves to the horses, first...Branwen?" I looked at her in as genuine a welcome as I could muster in that moment. "Would you care to come with us to the base of the mountain?"

"I think I'm still feeling a bit tired tonight." Baring teeth in a forced smile of her own, Branwen passed me, then the durrow on her way from the stables. "Perhaps next time."

While she disappeared, the durrow paid her no mind. Only I looked after her. Instead my lingering companions hurried into the stables with a series of delighted noises to be surrounded by animals that were to them so very strange.

"Phew! They're awfully smelly." Indra laughed and wrinkled her nose while Valeria delicately sneezed.

"That's only the stables," I assured them, drawn out of my reverie by the charming sound of the Materna's allergy. "Once we're out in open air, you'll hardly notice."

That much was true…if only because there was so much more to focus on when one was learning the art of horseback riding for the very first time. Somehow I didn't realize how much there would be to explain until I found myself out there at the base of the mountain, demonstrating the mechanics of saddling, mounting, and riding the beasts. In the Temple I had been responsible, after a certain age, for helping teach new students the basics of sword-fighting, so I was not a terrible teacher—and Odile, praise Weltyr, was delighted by how quickly her vague familiarity with the act of riding returned to her in the blue light of the wisps arranged around our field. She proved a competent assistant to me after the first hour.

Valeria and Indra, however, were not quite so fast when it came to learning. I soon found myself cursing Branwen for her refusal to come along. Such an absence meant that, until we were all comfortable with the idea of more independent and unsupervised riding, the two most unseasoned trainees would be forced to take turns and thereby extend the lessons. Nevertheless, it was exhilarating to see the delight on the women's faces as they gradually grew adapted to the act of climbing astride the beasts; glorious to see the bounding of Valeria's flowing white hair as she urged her horse into a canter about the field.

Were it not for the bat—for Gundrygia—it would have been a fine night, indeed.

It may have been a plurality of bats, actually. I still to this day am not sure. All I knew then was at one moment, when Indra was taking her turn practicing a canter, something swooped down upon her from the dark. Crying out, Indra ducked her head while looking up, her whole body cringing and her heels digging into the flank of her mare. The horse whinnied and, at this familiar command, tore off at a gallop while Indra cried in surprise.

Odile cried out after her friend, frightened by the sight of the mare's charge into the brushes and through the high boulders. Trees grew plentifully throughout much of the mountain's lower quadrant. If I did not move fast, Indra could easily have found herself lost—at the mercy of the horse and its familiarity with the region.

"Stay here," I commanded Odile and Valeria, urging the second stallion into motion in pursuit of the unpracticed rider. The beast, obedient to my command, galloped off into those same brushes, around the same boulder, and far off from Valeria and Odile in a matter of seconds. I was confident that catching up with Indra was a matter of choosing the right path through the trees.

What a fool I was to still dream that anything could be so simple!

The light reached my eyes a second before the forms did—regular torchlight, not the blueish tinted kind produced by my comrades' inborn magic. I attempted to slow the horse, but too late. A pair of gimlets leapt from the darkness and, with a surprisingly practiced arm, lassoed the beast about the neck to provoke its fearful rearing. I was only barely able to hang on and keep myself from being thrown to the ground. By the time its hooves were again upon the dirt, a few more baleful little imps had leapt from the darkness to jab at me with the tips of primitive flint spears.

"Enough," called a woman's voice. "Enough! Leave him alone."

Much to my surprise, the yipping lizard-men around me glanced in the direction of the sound and hastened to obey. I looked around myself, seeking Indra and her horse anywhere within in the torchlight.

Instead, I only found Gundrygia.

The wild sorceress slunk from the dark when her worshipers had settled down and my mount had followed suit. My fury with my captors and fear for Indra leveled into shock to see Gundrygia's approach. Her furs had been abandoned and exchanged for gauzy garments, semi-transparent things that had been perhaps crafted by magic and were, in the end, no more substantial than those textures we feel in dreams. Still, so far as my eyes were concerned, the fabric was as real as the curves to which it clung. As real as the decolletage whose cut it emphasized, or the leg that peered through its pale pink drapery.

Gone was the eye make-up from before, and the tattoos along with it—but for all the civilizing effect these things had, Gundrygia's hair still seemed an indisputable tell of her wild nature. A crown of bright red poppy flowers adorned hair that, though pulled up and back, was still as unkempt as a feral creature's pelt. Her crooked smile, too, reminded me of beasts, and the stare of her eyes was that of a madwoman, albeit one who had been driven to such dire straits by the insurmountable task of spending her life so painfully beautiful. In her hands were all number of flowers, one of which she dropped at her feet before selecting another.

"Let him down," she said, drawing the white petals of a lily across her lips and down the curve of her neck. "Don't let his stallion wander off."

"What have you done with Indra?"

Gundrygia's chin tipped up and back. She laughed, shaking her head, then disappeared beyond the torchlight at the slow pace of her swaying, slithering gait.

Gritting my teeth, I dismounted the horse and offered it but brief comfort. "Don't harm a hair on this animal's head," I told them tersely, looking between the lizard faces and finding perhaps more understanding than I had expected to. With another reluctant glance around, glad I was in the custom of bringing Strife wherever I went, I rested a hand upon the pommel of the blade and walked into the darkness after Gundrygia.

The trail of flowers dropped one by one marked her path through the darkness. I followed the lilies and the lilacs and the daffodils, each comfortable upon the bed of moss over which I trod with no hesitation. The farther I grew from the torches, the thicker that darkness became. Where had she gone, damn it? What had she done with Indra? It didn't seem possible that I should have been able to make it this far into the trees without meeting the dark elf or her startled horse. Where, then, were the both of them?

A soft light gradually edged into my awareness, revealed by the increasing color of the flowers at my feet. In total darkness, they had appeared variations of the same blacks or grays. Now, flower by flower, each was more colorful. So was the mossy eart upon which these flowers lay. I looked up and found the trees through which I'd been walking opened up ahead of me, their space permitting me to step into a clearing that reminded me somehow of the sepulcher into which I'd fallen.

Yet this space was the polar opposite of that ancient chamber of stone and death. The exquisite clearing, where Gundrygia had arranged her body back upon a bed of moss, teemed with the sweet sounds and aromas of life. Crickets chirped and fireflies glowed softly in the air, calling their lovers to them while similarly hopeful frogs croaked in the pond beside Gundrygia. Seeing me, the hand that had been resting against her cheek trailed over her breast. Her dark gaze slid over my body, my face, and then rested with anticipatory pleasure upon my eyes.

"Hail, Rorke Burningsoul, Paladin of Weltyr...the hero who woke me from my slumber."

"Yet here you seem to have thrust me into one of my own."

"This is no dream," she assured me, one knee bending to permit the slide of a silken hem along her thigh. I struggled to maintain eye contact while the exquisite witch told me, "Though I suppose it's true enough to say this space does not exist. Not in the conventional sense of existing."

"I don't care about that. Where's Indra?"

"Back in the real world," she said, laughing at me, her impudence incensing my desire. "Yes, by now she should be out of the trees...maybe even with a better grasp of riding. You're welcome."

My hand tightened around Strife's grip. "So you lured me here. Why?"

Another mocking laugh peeled past her lips, though more softly. The hand that had trailed over her bosom continued its journey and, at her hip, steadily gathered the fabric of her gown. Higher, higher still, the hem of that garment rose along her thigh.

"Why do you think?"

Her question was a whisper, a smirk quirking her lips just barely up past her teeth. I inhaled over my shoulder at the exit of the evidently enchanted grove. Seeing my hesitance, Gundrygia clambered upright upon her knees and threw herself forward. Before I could move she clung to my waist, her earnest yet mad eyes plastered upon mine between fronds of her wild hair.

"Would you deny me, Paladin? Would you look

around this space I've made just for us and refuse me the satisfaction of my lust?"

"Why me?"

Her smile widened. Kissing my stomach through the fabric of my tunic, she told me, "Because it was you who woke me, of course."

"No," I told her, catching her by the hair and yielding a gasp, "that's not why. Tell me the truth, Gundrygia."

But I had already made a mistake more fatal than following her into that grove in the first place. No matter what touch was lain upon her, Gundrygia perceived only pleasure. Soon I would learn there was nothing with which I could dissuade her from my seduction.

"Oh, yes"—she gasped as I tugged her by the hair away from me, heavy lids revealing eyes amorously aglow—"yes, Rorke, pull my hair…oh, treat me roughly, discipline me for my wicked ways. Turn me toward your god, Burningsoul! Win me for Weltyr with the raging flame of your passion."

"Who are you?"

She produced another infuriating cackle at the question. I shoved her away from me entirely, ignoring her drama-laden cry as she caught herself upright upon the flower bed where I'd tossed her.

"So cross with me, Rorke! Whatever have I done to earn such rage?"

"Using my friends as tools in whatever game of yours this is supposed to be," I told her, my hands forming fists when I found that the path into the clearing had disappeared. "And mocking me with this secret knowledge you have of my heritage."

"Mocking you!"

Springing upright, the wild woman threw her arms around my neck and caressed my face. I stared coldly as she shook her head, her devious expression a pantomime of cajoling tenderness.

"No, no, Paladin," she insisted, her body fitting so perfectly to mine that I had to repress a groan of agonized desire. "No, I would not dare to mock one so mighty. One meant for such great things."

"How can a man think on the great tasks of his future when the past is a stranger to him? Speak, Gundrygia, or let me go free—but do not continue in this taunting, this lording of your knowledge over me."

"What knowledge lies in me that does not already fill your heart? What mother could beget such a great hero as thou, Burningsoul? What father's seed could engender a savior of Urde?"

"Damn your riddles!" Frustrated, I caught her by the arms and shook her. She laughed, moaned, showed her teeth in a terrible grin while those eyes clapped upon mine. "Tell me what I want to know. How is it that you know all this? Where was I born, whose son am I?"

Her eyebrows lifted toward her hairline, knitting her smooth brow with cruel humor. "Art thou not the son of Weltyr, Paladin?"

What was it about Gundrygia that so erased my sense? I struggled to contain the emotions she inspired through her arrogant manner and the cruel retention of knowledge I had pondered for a lifetime. All the childhood nights spent in the dark, wondering why I wasn't good enough for my parents—wondering if they were nobles or serfs, kind or cruel. Imagine young boy wondering all of that for years on end, before he finally gave up and decided the issue was better uncontemplated. The inferiority. The isolation. The helpless decades of frustration.

It was that young boy, still so much a part of me at

that age, that guided my hand in the impulsive slap I will forever regret.

I had never hit a woman before—outside of an actual battle, of course. Weltyr willing, I never again will lift a hand to any creature of his making outside of the proscribed circumstances. But in that grove, so soon after the argument with Branwen and now infuriated to find Gundrygia had endangered my friend, lured me here, and told me nothing, I could not withstand the impulse. My hand cracked across Gundrygia's face, the sound blotting out her gasp.

Instead all I heard was the moan that followed it, so sensual it were as though I had caressed her. Her wild eyes all the more ablaze, the witch threw her arms around my neck and pressed her lips to mine in a savage kiss.

She smelled like lavender and honey. Like the hands of the pretty and kind older girls who worked in the kitchens at the Temple; who told beautiful fairy tales and sang funny songs when the priests weren't around to chide them for it. But she also smelled like a woman—rich and acrid, somehow chalky. Cruel. I can't explain it.

She was wise, and she whispered to me profane magical secrets.

She knows things, Gundrygia.

She frightened me. In my fright, like a captive animal, I sought to annihilate her body with mine. And all the while she moaned and laughed, and whispered to me things that made my heart race. She told me some strange and horrific truth. With my body inside hers, Gundrygia told me things I had never known. All the secrets of the world. All the answers to all the things I could possibly ask.

And why, friend, do I not repeat them here, now, at this very moment?

Because I did not remember them once she released me from her embrace.

That was the most terrifying revelation of all. On later inspection, I remembered plunging into the forest after her, and finding her in that clearing. I remembered the early snippets of our conversation as I have related them to you. But as I try to picture the hours when our clothes were off and we rutted like animals in the wild of that strange magical artifice, Gundrygia screaming with ecstasy in my embrace, the memory becomes fragmented somehow.

That was why it was like a dream, I suppose. In dreams, we are given so much information that we forget all of it, or nearly all of it, unless we are trained or interested in such matters as the recollection of dreams. In the space Gundrygia created for us to be together, I sank into a pool of hedonistic bliss and was given a crystal clear look into the absolute nature of reality: and because I was so unready for the experience of that absolute nature, because I took to trembling in *her arms as her secret-whispering went on and on, my mind did not, could not, would not retain it.*

To describe the time as entirely missing, or my state as a black-out one, would be to refuse responsibility for my poor decision early on in the experience as much as it would be an inaccurate picture of how I continue to perceive the event in my memory. When Weltyr's most sentimental servant comes to sit upon my heart, I recall that first time with Gundrygia not as a gap in my consciousness, but as a chill.

I, Rorke Burningsoul, Paladin of Weltyr, am chilled.

And that is why I will end this event's account here.

9

WELCOME TO SKYTHORN

GUNDRYGIA HAD HER way with me and took my seed, and when the trauma of her secret-telling passed over me, she said, "Don't worry, Rorke, don't worry—you'll leave this place and you won't recall a thing."

As I have already told you, that is not quite true. After all! I remembered her telling me that. But it was true in a wildly important sense, and when I suddenly found myself with the horse's reins in my hand and dawn creeping across the valley, I remembered two things only: the immense, feral pleasure of the witch's embrace, and the shame I felt at having struck her.

I resolved to be a better man. After looking around to find I stood as though having just stepped from a small grove of trees—one into which I could not possibly have chased Indra, might I add—I knelt to pray.

There are many prayers to Weltyr, some involving the use of his runes. I prayed only for his forgiveness, along with the strength to be a better man in my dealings with my fellow creatures in the world.

It was not just having struck Gundrygia that distressed me about myself. It was what I had done to the bandits—the bandits, whom all throughout these pages I ought to have been calling "the kin of Adonisius." I was not an executioner or inquisitor. It was not my place to slay for just any reason. For all I knew, one of the misshapen in that den was not a worshiper of not Roserpine, but Weltyr. Unlikely, I know, but who was to say?

Above my head, a croaking caught my attention. Drawn from prayer, I looked up. A great raven sat high in the cedar above me, its black feathers bristled widely and its black eye fixed on me.

Very strangely, I wept a little. Perhaps it was my introspection, or an aftereffect of whatever Gundrygia had done to me. I finished up my prayers and, once the raven flew off in the direction of Soot, mounted the horse to follow. Through the hills and dales of the valley, we traveled together from the edge of the mountain and into the heart of the town.

People gasped in delight and waved at me while in the middle of setting up their market stalls or walking their children to Soot's small village temple. I waved back, thinking only that they were being quite pleasant. Then, feeling similarly pleasant after whatever had transpired between myself and Gundrygia—no matter how eerie I sensed it all had been—I put the horse back in the stables among his comrades, strolled merrily into the front door of the inn's tavern, and was almost startled into drawing Strife by Lively's delighted cry across the room.

"Oh! Burningsoul, welcome back!" Wiping her hands and hurrying to me, Lively enthused, "I just fetched your ladies their breakfasts and it seems like they're all awake. Oh, they'll be glad to see you! Been a lot of long faces up in those rooms."

"Is that so?"

In a hushed, conspiratorial tone, Lively covered the side of her mouth with one hand and leaned into me. "Oh aye, well, can't rightly say I blame 'em. Six days is an awful long time to wait for word for any friend, let alone one's as close as you lot seem to be."

Six days!

The words passed over me in a great shock that had only just begun to settle when Lively asked, "So, d'ja find it?"

"What's that, Lively?"

"Whatever that thingie is you're lookin' for...oh, what was it"—on the other side of the tavern, in the hallway poised above the bar, Branwen stepped out of the room at the end of the hall; her face widened in shock and relief and a strong hint of anger before she dashed toward the stairs—"some kind of, um, oh, a staff, or a—"

"Scepter," I told Lively absently, my gaze following Branwen and my body turning toward her as she charged down the stairs.

Without saying a word, the high elf threw herself into my arms. Her face pressed against my shoulder and, with a shaky inhalation, she tried not to cry while I held her close to me.

Moved and a little flustered at the sight, Lively looked between the two of us with a motherly smile and said to me, "Just let us know if you need anything while you're settling back in."

"I will, of course. Thank you so much."

While Lively walked off, Branwen looked up at me through red-rimmed eyes and hissed, "We thought you were *dead.*"

"At moments it felt like I might have been…I think I need to talk to you four."

"Yes, you certainly do. Oh! You're so lucky Valeria is—Valeria." I realized with an odd jolt that Branwen had now spent about as much time with the durrow as I had—more, strictly speaking, with Indra and Odile. "We were talking about going to try to find the scepter without you, but Valeria convinced us to wait. Well—she convinced us to put it to a vote, at least."

"And which way did you vote?"

With a pouty look and a roll of her eyes, Branwen didn't answer. She just grabbed my hand and said, "Come on, Rorke—oh! Rorke. I'm glad you're here. I'm really—so glad you're here."

To my astonishment, Branwen said such a thing and I actually believed it. After all…she was still there. With me thought dead by my companions and the town at large under the impression that I was simply out on an errand to another location—either to save a murder investigation or protect their rights to the other horses—Branwen had absolutely nothing binding her to the durrow. If she really wanted to slip free and go her own way, she would have done it while I was gone.

Yet, she did not. She remained, and I felt happy relief to know that her heart was a great deal more stalwart than her business sense tempted it to be. Regardless of whether her staying on was due to latent guilt, (I had, after all, disappeared when she and I had just had something of a row and she had refused to come horseback riding with us), she had stayed on, and the durrow had, too.

Pushing open the door to the room on the end of

the hall, Branwen called inside with a grin she couldn't banish, "Okay—I have great news. But don't scream."

From within the room, Odile brusquely asked, "What," while a chair screeched across the floor. Branwen pushed open the door and I found Valeria had already risen to her feet, her face expectant, her garb—surprising.

The embroidered square neckline of her white blouse crisp against her dark skin, Valeria stood before me in a loose bodice and a skirt that was, for her, something close to chaste. She had modified the long blue garment so that it was no longer quite so long and now was cut closer to the cloth of her priestess's garb, but modest enough that she could fit in a little better among the denizens of the surface world.

"I knew it," she whispered. The Materna dashed across the floor to touch my face, then my hands, a literal sigh of relief heaving from her bosom on contact. "Rorke, Rorke—I knew you would be back."

"Well," said Odile, tossing down the cards in her hand and leaning forward. "This sure is a surprise! All right, I know when to admit I was wrong—"

Indra, too, bore features wide with delight while slapping her friend on the arm. "I told you," she bragged in spite of her friend's attempt to respectfully eat crow, as the saying goes. "Yes! I told you, Odile! There was no way anything could have happened to Rorke. He's much too great a warrior."

I hardly had time to be flattered before Valeria drew me down into an intense kiss, her tongue lashing mine. Groaning at the taste of her love, I chuckled as I lifted my head for a breath.

"I'll have to be abducted by strange witches more often," I said, earning a laugh from Odile and surprised looks from the others.

The rogues and druid, I noticed, were also dressed in fresh clothes—and, notably, a pair of goggles were poised atop Odile's head. She adjusted them slightly while leaning forward, asking, "What's this about witches? Do tell."

Indra's eyes had widened with shock. Sitting up all the straighter, she asked, "Is this like that woman you found? The one in the mountainside?"

"The very same," I told them, removing Strife's scabbard from my belt and sitting upon the edge of the bed. "Let me tell you some things that happened..."

Starting with the gimlet who stole my torch, I related to all my companions as fully as I could the neglected story of Gundrygia and her awakening. The women listened with intense interest and varying degrees of concern. Odile, for instance, took the story like a man listening to his friend relate a conquest. Indra looked concerned, then vaguely guilty when I mentioned her disappearance into the trees—though I impressed upon them all that this had been caused by Gundrygia, and not by some mistake of Indra's.

Of them all, Valeria and Branwen appeared the most concerned. In her usual fashion, Valeria did not mind my extracurricular excursions but, seated beside me upon the edge of the bed, focused on that element that also troubled me: "You remember nothing after making love to her?"

"It would be wrong to say I don't remember anything...but I don't remember all or even most of what was done and discussed. I remember asking her many questions, and—I do remember her answering me, but... ah!" Irritated, I rubbed my forehead and assured them, "I've been rolling it around in my mind all the way back to The Weeping Willow. I can remember the questions I would have asked—questions I'm sure I did ask—but for the life of me I have no concrete memory of asking them, nor of the witch's responses."

"Not even this information she claimed to have about your birthright?" Branwen asked this from the window where she stood, her arms folded and her countenance grave.

I shook my head.

"Maybe she was some kind of hidden person."

My brow arched. "Some kind of what?"

"You really are a city boy, aren't you...you know. The good neighbors. "Faeries," they call them sometimes in the common tongue around here. Watch this—if we ask Lively about local faerie legends, we'll probably hear something interesting."

While Branwen stuck her head from the room to call for the manager, Odile said, "Sounds like you didn't have it so bad, Paladin. You got us worried...we thought we were going to have to cut and run to avoid paying for a dead horse."

"Glad you were worried about me as well as money, Odile...what are those goggles, though?"

"Oh, these? Indra and I just can't keep sleeping during the bloom—er, the day, so I asked Erdwud to go down to the forgemaster here and sell a couple of old welding goggles. He only had two to part with, though, so Madame here keeps one and Indra and I trade off with the other."

Indra nodded, having listened to all this quite guiltily and saying with a look down at her hands, "Not that I've been able to sleep anyway. I'm so sorry, Rorke! I didn't mean—"

"It's all right, Indra. Whatever happened, it's true that I feel I had...mostly a good time. I think."

Still looking grim as Indra was, I crossed to her side and knelt to take her hand. Holding it between both of mine, I looked into her somewhat surprised, certainly flushed face and told her warmly, "Did you work on your riding while I was gone?"

Snapped a bit from her malaise, Indra earnestly told me, "Well—yes, of course we did."

"One of the other reasons for the goggles," said Odile. The high elf re-entered the room just in time for the elder rogue to continue, "Branwen taught us."

"Did she!" Pleased, I smiled at the moody druid and got a roll of her eyes along with a spate of deep blushing.

"Well! Someone was going to have to do it if we ever had a prayer of leaving Soot...looking around for you was good practice."

While I stood, Lively knocked upon the door and let herself in. Her eyes bright, her hair up in a blonde ponytail that bobbed as she looked around, the inn's manager said, "Don't we all seem in better spirits already! You needed something, dearies?"

"Actually, yes." Glancing at me, Branwen gestured and said, "While traveling, Rorke heard something about some kind of faerie legends around Soot. We were just wondering if you knew anything about them."

"Oh, aye! You lot certainly *are* adventurers, aren't you...well"—waving her hand, looking pleased for a few seconds away from her work, Lively looked almost conspiratorially at Branwen—"people say it's bad fortune to be talkin' about the hillfolk without their explicit permission, but I don't go in for all that, so I'll run me mouth a bit. It's all about them gimlets, see, up in the mountains."

Everyone in the room was now fully interested, with even Odile turning eyes toward Lively and her story.

"I've told you all about the little buggers, always causin' us problems. Well, I think it's said they used to have a queen? I don't know, there are different versions to these things all the time...she was either the creator of the race, or a human woman who eventually became their queen after she was spirited away to serve the gimlet colony.

"At any rate, all kinds of different people have seen them with her over the years. They say she sleeps long hours—whole seasons, depending on who you ask—and that people who go missing in the hills are taken by her."

Thumb worrying against the edge of her lip, Branwen asked, "Why does she take people in these stories?"

"Oh, who knows! All kinds of reasons. Fools that go lookin' at her, I think. That's the most popular one, anyway, but I've heard causes range from simple trespassing to accidentally waking her up." While I mulled this over, Lively said with a light laugh, "I don't know if it's worth you lot taking your valuable time to look for her, but if you were to relieve our gimlet problem a bit, I'm sure no one would complain."

"We'll keep it in mind," said Valeria with a polite smile. "Thank you, Lively."

"You're all welcome. Let me go finish that breakfast for you...I'm sure you're famished after your long trip home."

With the door again between us and Lively, I told my companions, "It's true I woke her up when I found her on the mountainside, but that was also when she told me one or two things I do remember. She told me she came from north of Rhineland, and that her father is named—Clinschor, I think."

"Interesting." Folding her arms, Branwen asked,

119

"Could she have been making it up? Faeries do that sort of thing all the time."

"I don't know...aren't faeries supposed to be small and winged?"

"No," Branwen answered, "those are pixies—crude little pests, tiny goblins with wings. Faeries could pass as human, or something close to it...they don't care for human cities, but they mingle freely with elves and otherwise live in their own pocket dimensions parallel to Urde. Just like the place where Gundrygia lured you."

Given how similar the two experiences were, I found myself wondering if perhaps there wasn't some truth in this suggestion—yet I thought back to Gundrygia's answers to my questions and decided after a moment of contemplation, "Whatever she be, faefolk or human witch, I believe what she said about not being from around here. As to what all this means, and how she should know anything of me, I can't say. Do faeries tend to possess powers of telepathy, Branwen?"

The elf shook her head. "Not specifically that I know of, though they keep many secrets. And it's hard to say, too, what a faerie would be doing consorting with gimlets."

"Maybe they found her there and thought she was some kind of goddess," I suggested, still feeling this, too, was wrong. Nevertheless, I persisted. "Whatever the case may be, Gundrygia certainly seemed to have confident control over them. Never once did they buck a command or show anything but eagerness in pleasing her, and of course there were all those offerings they had arranged upon her burial mound."

"Faeries come and go out of mounds," Branwen informed me.

"If he has been marked somehow by this creature"—

Valeria leaned forward, her expression tense—"do you think she will come back for him again?"

"It's possible. Yes," decided Branwen more confidently after another second of reflection. "It's certainly possible. I would even go so far as to say that moving on to Skythorn would be in our best interests, if only to keep Rorke safe."

This discussion of Skythorn brought a frightening notion to mind. "Have we missed the airship to Rhineland?"

"Erdwud said it goes out in five days," said Branwen. "If we push the horses, we can make it to Skythorn and still have a few days to find Hildolfr and Grimalkin...but if we arrive too close to departure—as in, the day of—we'll have to assume they've already boarded and hope there are still unbooked tickets."

"Last minute is better than late," I told her, looking between the women, "but I've always preferred arriving early. Are you all ready to set out right away?"

Looking somewhat dubious, Valeria asked, "Are you?"

"I'm tired, but after a meal and perhaps an hour to close my eyes, I'll be right as rain. Ah...and I do have one more thing to do before we leave town."

That errand, I attended after I'd rested a bit. While Branwen talked to Lively and Erdwurd about whether or not they knew anyplace in Skythorn willing to board durrow, I made my way across town to Rigan's smithy. As he had last time, the old man hammered away. This time, he looked up at my approach. Rigan raised his face mask to reveal his white-stubbled face and grumbled a bit before producing audible words.

"Paladin," he said, placing down his hammer, "Burningsoul. About time you showed up."

Unable to help my chuckle at the crotchety smith's ways, I confessed to him, "That's me…early or late, never just right."

"Sure seems to be that way with you. Come on in."

Rigan pushed open his property's short gate for me, waving me thereafter into a front door that was open to permit the cool spring breeze through his cabin. The main room was cluttered, and so was the second room where he brought me—but the weapons displayed around the old man's private armory were immaculate.

Unlike the rest of his house, these items must have been carefully dusted every day and polished regularly. The man had good reason to take pride in his work. A few mannequins held different styles of armor, all of them artful and in some cases even elaborately decorated, and I wondered if I had seen anything half so quality as his swords displayed around the burning forge of Roserpine's palace. The newest pieces—of rather more utilitarian design compared to those that had been embossed with a snarling gold plains-king or marked with shapes upon the back like raptor wings, but certainly no less beautiful— shone from their place on the stand nearest the door.

"There you are." Rigan gestured as he made his slow way over to unbuckle the breastplate and help me into it. While I tried the helmet on, he asked, "How'd I do? Your friend was vague with the details of your size, but I think I got a sense of you once you came to visit me."

"This is perfect, Rigan. I can't begin to thank you!"

"What for? I was paid for it, wasn't I? Don't thank *me*. Thank your friend…"

"He didn't ask you to pass anything along when he commissioned these pieces for me, did he? Indicate anything, say anything?"

"Only thing he said was that I could expect you

sometime soon. Other than that, he just paid, explained what he wanted, and left. Gave me extra to get it done in a rush...I hate rushing."

Tell me about it! I could certainly appreciate that, being now in a rush as I was. We were going to be in for quite a trip.

Assuming our travel went smoothly and we could make it there before the airship departed, we might not need to worry at all about buying a ticket. It would instead be a matter of finding Grimalkin and Hildolfr... which, in the city of Skythorn, seemed a tall order.

That, however, was what divination was made for, among other things...and if Weltyr's blessings were with us, we might not even need that.

Erdwud and his wife were sorry to see us go, and not just because of the money we brought in. Lively had developed a fondness for the ladies and regarded them as friends of a sort. She seemed particularly moved to know we were on our way and did quite a bit of blinking while hugging us good-bye. For his part, Erdwud was also disappointed, but wasted no time in handing me a sealed note of which he declared, "This'll get you a nice, cozy little room in an inn called The Poisoned Mongoose, assumin' you don't mind a bit of hollarin' in the night. Things can get a little rowdy there...but it's me friend's establishment. Like a brother to me, Sharp is! He'll see to it that you lot are well looked-after."

I thanked him for his generosity again and shook his hand warmly, keeping it held in mine while asking for directions. As I occupied him, the women filed out through the tavern's back door before the lewd old innkeeper could take too much advantage of the opportunity to hug them good-bye. Then, delaying only to explain to the Dardries where and when they could come collect their horses, we paid a fee for the extension of their rental leases and headed south to Skythorn.

Having spent much of my life in the Temple's properties, I had not been prepared for how beautiful the trip out of the city would be. Heading back down to it, the journey seemed doubly so. Farms and orchards marked most of the route, and Valeria in particular was breathless to look upon sights that were mundane to most. She and I saw them in similar lights—for Valeria, these rural plots were novelties. For me, they were examples of the intricate beauty by means of which Weltyr's world functioned. Joy filled me to see every rice paddy, every artichoke field, all the trees full of nuts and fruit swaying softly in the wind. I had appreciated the landscape when on my way to the Nightlands, but had no idea how much I would appreciate them after my return.

All the time, Valeria—and, to a lesser extent, Indra—demanded to know the names of all number of things. Fruits they had not seen, crops they did not recognize; birds and beasts of burden that were unrecorded in durrow encyclopedias due to lack of interest, context, or relevance; the dog of Weltyr that seemed to follow us on our journey, each night lurking some distance outside our lantern but evident to the sensitive eyes of the subterranean elves. Twice Valeria stopped us to pick and learn the names of flowers, and the absolute ecstasy in her tearful eyes to see so many fields of verdant plants made me think nothing of the delay; and even Odile gasped with girlish delight, shielding her goggled eyes with one hand and pointing up with another, as an airship from the far Eastern nation of Pulnoma meandered across the cool blue sky ahead of us to the Skythorn airport.

There was nothing that escaped their amazed eyes. Branwen and I felt like teachers; the guides of aliens who had literally come from a different world. That was certainly how it felt when, at night, the durrow taught us deeper pleasures than we had previously enjoyed upon the surface. It would seem that, in her week with the durrow, Branwen had become slightly less protesting. Beneath Valeria's radiant stars, the women would take turns with me, each watching the others enjoy her pleasure while in turn pleasuring one another. Branwen and I rarely had a moment alone to talk, but in our nights of witnessed passion I felt a certain powerful intimacy. Arguing with me, losing me, and being forced to grow accustomed to the durrow without me seemed to have changed her. Perhaps she learned, as I had been learning, to think of the consequences of her actions, and to remember how easily existence was taken for granted.

This journey was a relief compared to the one out of the Nightlands. Protected by the magic lantern while tucked in a grove of trees that would further dissuade the attention of bandits—or any other brand of marauder who would be undeterred by the light, unlike the great wild dog to whom I tossed a few scraps each night by way of peace offering—we rested well, and beneath the light of the sun traveled safely south.

My only concern was related to the durrow. With but two pairs of goggles, Indra and Odile continued to trade off as they had mentioned to me. Valeria offered hers up multiple times, but, loyal to their culture's royalty, they refused to deny her the protection and instead wore cloaks with thick hoods. They pulled these hoods down low before their faces whenever required, and though I remained concerned that the protection was insufficient, the women nonetheless insisted they were fine. How much of this was show for Valeria's sake, I'm not sure; but I'm sure they also felt, like I did, that once we were safely at The Poisoned Mongoose we wouldn't have quite so much to worry about.

Those hoods were important in other ways, too. Skythorn was a place of mingling, as I described it to Valeria. Men and women, upper class and lower, mankinds of all varieties met and worked in the city as casually as you pleased. Humans of every creed and color passed through the city walls.

But never, not once, had I or anyone else that I knew of seen a durrow come through.

To Skythorn citizens, dark elves were as good as faeries. Most only knew them as far-away creatures living below the surface of Urde, a kind of anti-elf renown for sadistic inclinations and their penchant for slavery. They were sometimes used as the villains of fairy tales, or as a way to get children to behave at bedtime. "If you don't go to sleep right this instant, your mother and I will sell you to the dark elves..." (Did I miss that much by not having parents? When speaking to those allegedly more fortunate than I, I always wondered.)

In other words, durrow were as uncommon as it got. I was therefore far more concerned about traveling through the streets of Skythorn than I had been about moving through Soot. There was nothing necessarily illegal about their presence in the city, but between Odile's recollection of her colony's destruction and the general bigotry that mankinds could show one another, I could not shake my worry.

However...much to my relief, no one we encountered on the highway seemed to give the women a second glance outside of the sort men tended to give women as painfully beautiful as my companions. I admit, I felt rather prideful to have them all by my side. What I had done to deserve such companionship, I was not sure—

but I was also very thankful for their beauty, because it provided a natural glamor in the magical sense of the word. Those who looked upon them were so taken by their radiant looks that it was hard to notice details, like the slight disfigurement of the fabric of their hoods or the slightly exaggerated facial features that marked them as elves rather than human. Accordingly, when we reached the busy gates of Skythorn, there was no problem other than the wait to get in.

The city's namesake, not unlike the tower at the heart of El'ryh, was a citadel swirling toward the clouds and punctuating in a sharp black spire. The heart-warming structure had been visible for some leagues by then, but when we rose up the final hill overlooking the city, my heart throbbed with fierce pride at the durrows' gasps.

For the first time they took full stock of the sprawling scale, a single city comparable in size to some smaller countries.

From our new vantage the city seemed to go on forever in all directions, an extraordinary sea of buildings whose greatest towers could not amount to one half the central landmark's height. Millions of people navigated its streets and, that day, at least a hundred were trying to get in ahead of us.

Indeed, I would almost go so far as to call Skythorn its own city-state, save for that it fell under the legal jurisdiction of Cascadia and owed its taxes to the king of the land just as much as any other town.

But that was where the similarities between Skythorn and any other town had a way of stopping. The line of merchants, travelers, entertainers and others seeking entry to the city was astonishing, and dwarfed by far even that entry line to El'ryh. Unlike the guards of El'ryh, who appeared to primarily act in the name of preventing slave escapes, the purpose of the guards here was to filter out known terrorists and occasionally sort through a merchant's goods to prevent the smuggling of contraband, foreign seeds, dwarvish pistols, or anything else verboten in the city—a very small list of items, truth be told, when compared to how freely the citizens came and went. Most who were not merchants never had to worry about such scrutiny, and in the end, though the line was vast, we took only an hour to reach the front.

All my anxiety was for nothing. The guard took one look at the tattoo of Weltyr's sigil upon my neck, asked if the women were with me, and let us through without much more than a brisk glance at my face.

Then, as though I were coming to the end of a dream—or deeper in the midst of one than ever—our horses set hoof upon the paving stones of Skythorn.

"And I thought El'ryh was crowded!" Laughing, Valeria stared around the noisy city and pushed her hood back enough that her view was obstructed by nothing more than the rims of the welding goggles. "Why, I've never *seen* so many people...certainly not so many men."

"This is all a little surreal," agreed Odile, peering from the low beak of her hood. "Boy, look at that one—he'd be excellent in agriculture! It's probably what he does here. Why don't we lure men down to the Nightlands anymore?"

"Because there isn't any need," Valeria said, spreading her hands. "So many of our slaves our bred now."

"I guess that's true...boy, and that one!"

Odile's fascination for the existence of free men was funny in some ways, disturbing in others. It was very strange to know someone for whom basic liberties were foreign notions. What would it take, I wondered, to change the culture of the Nightlands?

As much as it would take to change the culture of Skythorn, I'm sure.

One develops blind spots for the shortcomings of one's only home. Much as the durrow were not used to living in a culture where all those who worked were (ostensibly, at least) paid fair wages, I was not prepared for what our time in Skythorn would reveal to me about the city—and, sadly enough, the Temple—where I was raised.

"Let's find this tavern Erdwud recommended to us," I said, glancing at the letter peering from the edge of the saddlebag. "While you ladies rest, I'll consult the Temple as to the location of Grimalkin and Hildolfr...Skythorn is a vast city, an easy place to become lost."

Lips parted in amazement as she peered through the protective glass of her occluded goggles, Valeria indicated the citadel in the center of it all. "And this is the Temple?"

"It is...it is, indeed. Which city inspired which, of course, I cannot say for certain."

Valeria, not given to so quickly scoffing at me, spoke in a dubious tone. "El'ryh has been the hub of durrow existence for well over 150,000 years."

"No one knows how old the Skythorn is," I told her, "nor the city around it. The priests have documents with information on the subject, but they are extremely rare and cannot be shared with great ease. One of their most important duties is to maintain this information by rewriting it in new manuscripts."

"Have you no printing presses in Skythorn?"

"These histories, I have been told, contain things that ought not to be printed for the common man." I explained this as our horses made their ways down the busy street, pedestrians going to and fro on either side of us and thankfully thinning as we plodded through this heavily-trafficked corner of the city. "It is for the priests to interpret the holy books of Weltyr, and to communicate their contents to laymen. The information is too mentally devastating to the individual."

"Roserpine's relationship with her worshipers is a personal one," she responded.

"As is Weltyr's, if the individual should will it…but, in a personal relationship, one person does not tell the other everything all of the time. Not when the relationship is between a master and his slave, for instance."

With a faint sniff, Valeria moved her horse along a little faster and cut ahead of me on the street. I peered up beyond the sullen priestess, at the tip of the Temple vanishing into the clouds.

The Mongoose was not difficult to find, although I should not have been particularly surprised, going by its name, to find it where we did. When I confirmed Erdwud's (as usual, poor) directions to it, the guard who answered me glanced at my companions with a wiggle of his mustache.

"You sure that's the spot you're looking for?"

Never a good sign to hear that when one is after lodgings, but we were only going to be staying a night or two if I had my druthers. In fact, Weltyr willing, we might not even have to deal with that much. If I could speak to Father Fortisto—in my mind, foremost among Weltyr's Temple priests—I might get the information I sought without receiving much remonstration for failing at my first attempt to retrieve the Scepter. There were those among the brotherhood who would have had more than a few harsh words for me, and a few who would have even taken the task from my hands altogether. That would have been a disaster. I was not interested in having to choose between my duty to the Church and my affection for the women whom I had agreed to help, and to whom I now had a responsibility as their escort outside of the Nightlands.

I could not help but notice how protective I had become of them. They did not need protection, of course— had any man attempted to interfere with them, he would have walked away, at best, with a broken hand or nose. But I nonetheless marveled at my own internal protective urge: as if I walked with Elishta-bet, a certain childhood friend of mine. Wild animals in the countryside were of no concern to me, nor were nighttime monsters. The ladies could all handle themselves. Yet, I suppose because I wanted them to think well of humans and of Skythorn, I was on such high alert and so poised for something to happen that the last problem I expected to have was with the innkeeper, Sharp.

The Poisoned Mongoose was aptly-named. The working class quarter where it was located was full of ash and smoke and other artifacts of manufacture that were no doubt responsible for rotting the lungs and temperaments of all the people about it. We found the inn and its dingy tavern squeezed between a cobbler and a fish market, and the scent was so foul that Odile looked up at the sign with a curled lip.

"Are you sure there isn't somewhere better we can stay? I'll pay for it from my own purse."

"It'll be fairly quick…and anyplace so ill-managed in appearance should be liable to have some empty rooms for us."

With the inn located, we hitched our horses at the nearest (and most trustworthy-looking) paid stables, made our way back through the busy streets to the Mongoose, and soon enough interrupted the gaunt innkeeper in the middle of counting his money behind the bar.

"Welcome to the Mongoose," he said without looking up from the coins he stacked. "What'll it be for you?"

"Are you the friend of Erdwud of Soot? Sharp?"

He glanced up at me briefly from the coin sorting, his pale eyes then drawn away and, as was inevitable, to the elves with their heads covered. Sharp's attention lowered coolly to his till again, his hand resuming its motion. "What's it to you?"

Politely as I could manage, I set the sealed letter on the counter and slid it across to the weaselly man. "I was told you could provide us fair and discreet lodgings."

Sniffing lightly, the man set down the remaining handful of his coins, wiggled his mustache, and tore open the letter without bothering to look too closely at the seal. He unfolded the vellum within, his eyes darting back and forth across the lines of text. I leaned against the counter, hands patiently at rest. He continued on. I had just caught myself wondering how versed he was in the task of reading when he folded the letter up again, tucked it into his apron and nodded in the direction of the women.

"You some kind of pimp?"

With a light, quite shocked laugh, I glanced back toward the women and found that, luckily, the durrow weren't familiar with the term. Praise Weltyr! Branwen's face, however, was bright red with hateful displeasure, and she narrowed her eyes at the man. A haughty scowl contorted her lovely features into something that exuded utter loathing.

"I will have you know that I am the descendant of Klexian nobility," she told him coolly, earning little more than a brisk glance. "You'd ought not to make such crude presumptions about someone you have never met."

"Twelve ounces of silver a night per room," he said, adding, "and we don't do food."

With a scoff of outrage, Odile pushed back her hood to look the man in the eyes. "Twelve, with*out* food! Erdwud gave us room and board for—"

But she stopped. The innkeeper had recoiled a step and looked at me with dark shock.

"Bloody durrow," said the man. "Now I understand what that letter meant about safe haven. What's your game? Slavers? Spies?"

His motions so quick I did not have time to draw Strife before he had reached beneath the bar, the innkeeper drew a dwarvish pistol and clicked back the hammer.

"Whatever it is you're angling for, you'll have to find it someplace other than Skythorn."

10

THE TEMPLE OF WELTYR

I WAS BEGINNING to regret following Erdwud's advice, but the experience of meeting Sharp was ultimately invaluable. It showed the durrow the importance of concealing their identities in surface cities, for instance. While Odile looked wide-eyed with shock, not so much at the gun as at the realization of what she had done by failing to think in a moment of irritation, I stepped between the innkeeper and the women with my hands patiently raised.

"Now, sir, there's no need for any of that—I assure you, we're not slavers or spies. I am a humble servant of Weltyr"—I gestured toward the tattoo upon my neck, and to Sharp's credit his arm began to relax—"and these fine ladies are my companions in my mission to acquire a lost artifact for the Temple. However, since they cannot all stay as guests of the Temple, I thought it best we find an inn somewhere. Erdwud suggested here, but if it's too much of a problem, we can look elsewhere."

Sternly studying me, his eyes darting behind me a few more times, Sharp lowered his pistol all the way. "You ain't under some curse, is you?"

"No, friend, nothing like that. We're hoping we won't be in Skythorn more than one night. These women have been a great boon in the task I perform on behalf of my Temple."

Relaxing somewhat further, the man set the pistol down even if he did not put it away. It rested by the money he resumed counting, saying as he did, "Don't believe in the gods. Believe in gold and silver and copper."

"There's a god for those, too," I assured him, earning a brisk glance back up and a hefty sigh.

"Seven silver pieces a night a room," he said. "My best offer. You won't find nowhere more discreet in the whole of the manufacturing district."

And that is the story of how we ended up once again divided across two rooms, albeit ones that were of far lesser quality than the pair at The Weeping Willow. Indra and Odile careened over from theirs, having locked their equipment safely within and divested themselves of their cloaks.

"What a *price!*" Odile pressed her hand to her forehead, grimacing. "And what a fool I was. You just don't think about your body language in the heat of the moment."

"These things happen, Odile." I patted her sympathetically upon the shoulder and chuckled as she slunk past me to throw herself upon the bed where Valeria and Branwen already reclined. "We'll make our business here as quick as possible to avoid incurring another fee, then we'll get onto the task of searching for Roserpine's ring. It's all a mater of talking to the priests, so I'd ought to go now."

"We'll stay here and rest," agreed Branwen.

"And guard our equipment," muttered Odile, glancing at the wall as though through it. "This place isn't nearly as nice as the one in Soot."

True enough. The Mongoose was dirty, our room's bed was barely made, and I was quite certain I heard a rat scrambling through the wall. Nevertheless, it was good to have a place where, no matter the personal distaste of the innkeeper, we were with someone for whom our privacy was their best interest—if only to save a friendship with Erdwud.

"Gather your strength," I told them all on my way out the door. "But remain alert in case something happens or I return for your assistance in hunting the traitors."

On my way out, Sharp's eyes burned into the back of my skull. I ignored him, interested in only one thing at just that moment: retrieving the Scepter of Weltyr.

Though, I do confess…free for the moment of the women I adored, who took so much of my attention because I loved their company, I was at last fully able to steep my senses in what it meant to have returned to Skythorn. Even considering how ardent I was in my beliefs concerning that great god of Light, I was still perpetually amazed by the things he did for me: by the sorrows he allowed me to evade, and the trials he permitted me to conquer, and the women who emerged from the world before me like flowers in the meadow of life. And, to top it all off, I had been permitted this chance to return to my home.

How full the city was that day! How long it seemed

to take me, that march down the slope to the center of the northernmost district and the Temple situated there. However, unlike the pattern of El'ryh, as I drew closer to the eponymous structure of Skythorn the traffic began to lighten. Soon it had evaporated altogether. Centers of all forms of commerce were scattered around the many quarters of the city. Those citizens who had any brand of wealth at all tended to live as close as they could to the central structure—not just out of religious belief, but out of a general sense of security.

Areas near the Temple were kept free of loiterers and well-patrolled by guards. As one traversed these quieter neighborhoods, one found all manner of stylish gardens and splendid homes. When there was no room for a garden, there was almost always a window box— but more than likely many such structures had rooftop gardens, or their own small plot in a back yard. Birds twittered with pleasure and, with evening's approach, the air had begun to cool. I felt a great yearning pain for the days when I was a young man, barely even a trainee, and these streets had not yet been laden with any nostalgic sentiment because they were simply the world to me. Now the Temple and the area around it was only the orientation point—the center of a great circle of reality that I had already come to find was more infinitely varied and wildly rewarding than I ever could have anticipated.

Where would my children, Weltyr willing, call the center of the world? With so many women in my intimate company, I could not help but turn my thoughts to these matters as I never before had. It was entirely possible I had left a few heiresses behind in El'ryh—I was still not certain of the mechanics that permitted the durrow species to be a race of only females, and that permitted them to still seem so purely durrow despite being begot by typically human fathers. Still, if any daughters of mine remained in the Nightlands, I considered that they may well go on to live there for the sum total of their lives. I would never know them.

And for the children I would someday know, whom I would call my own? I was somehow not quite sure where they would see their realities as being rooted. When I was a boy, I had taken it for granted that I would fall in love with a woman from Skythorn and raise my family there. That no longer seemed realistic. Perhaps it was a certain concern that was brought to the forefront of my mind by our troubled interaction with the inn keeper. Whatever the reason, the question plaguing me was: Where could a durrow live on the surface without fear of persecution?

After a certain point I became so consumed by this question that I barely noticed I approached the Temple until I passed through its open gate. Suddenly I blinked awake upon the stone path that spiraled over the lawns. It had not been the gate that stirred my awareness, though, nor the proximity of the holy house itself—rather, it was the splendid woman who swept the walk, long waves of chestnut hair hanging around her face while she minded her work.

No face was required to place her in a crowd. The pattern of her body was unmistakable, and the patchouli scent of her flesh on the wind overcame me with joy. Even the blue cloak hanging from her shoulders seemed somehow well-suited to her, though I had no specific memories of her wearing such a garment. I simply knew her ways, and recognized her at the glimpse from the farthest distance.

Elishta-bet!

I had expected to see at least one or two fellow orphans from the old days, but Elishta and I had been thick as thieves until she was sent off to a convent as was the custom with unmarried, unadopted young ladies who fell into Weltyr's service but showed no interest in the more dynamic clerical activities of serving as paladin.

"Elishta!"

Invested in her work as she was, Elishta didn't recognize my voice. Perhaps she was not expecting me back so soon, or even at all. Her head lifted from her sweeping and she looked past me before looking at me. Eyes widening, she very nearly dropped the broom—certainly she looked twice at it in her hands, as if wondering what she was doing sweeping walking paths when I had returned to Skythorn. Leaning it against the nearby column, Elishta emerged from the breezeway around the quiet Temple entrance and threw her arms about my neck.

"Rorke," she exclaimed, her face aglow with joy, "oh, Rorke! Welcome home!"

"Elishta! What a welcome face! Perhaps this visit will go smoothly after all."

That joyful expression fell as she leaned back upon her heels. "Only a visit? You mean you're not staying?"

"My quest isn't over," I told my old friend, taking her hands in mine while admiring the disappointed contortions of her coppery face. "I've come back to ask Father Fortisto to help me find two vagabonds...they may have information on the location of the Scepter."

Her hazel eyes quite wide at that, Elishta said, "Really! You're on its track? When you wrote me about embarking on your quest, I thought for sure—well, I thought at least you would be side-tracked by some pretty lady and settle down a hundred leagues from here."

Thinking of all the pretty ladies waiting for me at the Mongoose who were, so far as I could tell, not particularly interested in conventional forms of settling down, I couldn't help but laugh at Elishta's concern.

"Of course not, Eli...you know that my heart is Weltyr's before anything or anyone's. That reminds me"—I touched her elbow and her whole body tensed as though she needed to brace herself against my touch for reasons I didn't understand—"just what are you doing back from the convent?"

"Oh—well..."

Blushing, Elishta wrung her hands and glanced bashfully to the side.

"It's nothing, really. I just—I'm not very suited to the nunnery, I think. You know how my imagination is! My head in the clouds all the time. I just can't live so rigidly. You and I didn't even get up so early when we were children!"

"Contemplation takes a long time...but it also takes a willing heart. There's no sense in forcing a woman into the convent if she can't take to its ways."

Nodding, Elishta told me, "Father Fortisto's been very kind, though...he let me come back here to work and says I'm welcome to teach when I feel the urge."

"Now, that does sound a mite more pleasant than spending the rest of your life in a convent! Will you tell me, Elishta, where Father Fortisto is at the moment?"

"I suppose he's in the rectory hall...let me walk there with you, Rorke." The suggestion uttered from her lips like a sort of plea. As her hand landed upon mine, her complex eyes searched my face. "I've missed you. How worried I've been!"

Leaving her broom behind, we made our way into the anteroom just within the main entrance. "Worried? Now, whatever for?"

"The thought of you traveling abroad, looking

for that relic with nobody to help you but whatever mercenaries the Temple let you hire—it sounded to me like a wild goose chase, and dangerous."

"Dangerous, perhaps, but all in the name of the All-Father."

Our voices softened to see the chapel doors were open. Carefully walking upon the carpet rather than the metal floor beneath to keep our sound down, we glanced within at the trio of priests who planned services near the back of the pews. The warm scent of incense embraced me as a son while the soft murmuring of the old men filled the dimly lit, richly-ornamented space like the sound of a brook.

One of them, seeing my tattoo peering from beneath the plates of my armor, nodded at me with great respect. I felt a boyish flutter to remember that, by all appearances, I was a fully ordained and consecrated Paladin of Weltyr—a member of the Order, rather than a mere initiate. We continued beyond the doors and I resumed to her, "At any rate, I haven't been alone. I've joined with a handful of fellow travelers. With them at my side, I'd venture a guess that I'm a fair bit safer than most sent on quests for the Temple."

"Servants of Weltyr, these travelers?"

"No," I admitted to her, bending and lowering my voice all the more. "Heathen worshipers of Roserpine, and one of Anroa—but I believe Weltyr desires I should work with them, so work with them, I do."

Though Elishta-bet appeared somewhat scandalized, it was only in the way of those who delighted in scandal. "'Roserpine!' I've never heard of that one."

"She's a goddess of darkness, among other things. So far as I can tell, all durrow in the Nightlands are taught to praise her above the Bright God…but one can't rightly blame them, given they cannot see the sun and therefore don't have any means or incentive by which to contemplate its mysteries."

"How sad!"

"Perhaps, yes, perhaps it is…but I have no doubt that, should Weltyr wish to present himself and the knowledge of his salvation to the durrow, he would find a way. It's their slave trade that keeps them from his favor, I would think, but such speculations aren't my place."

"Nor any man's," agreed Elishta, mounting the stairs that curled through the heights of the Temple. "As you said…when the time has come for them, surely their priests will be made ready for the knowledge."

"Priestesses, actually." She glanced over, and I explained, "They have only priestesses, Roserpine's people—the durrow are an exclusively female race."

How Elishta's eyes widened! She put together one or two things a mite more quickly than I would have liked. Her face redder by the second, my old friend stuttered, "O—oh! *Oh!* Goodness! All of them?"

"Yes," I said, lifting my eyebrows, unable to help the glint in my eye, "every last one."

"Oh," repeated Elishta. Scrutinizing me more closely now, she said, "So that means your companions—"

"Are women, yes."

"I—I see. I see."

Laughing, I jostled my old friend by the shoulders. "Come now! Surely you aren't jealous, Elishta."

"Of course not," Elishta hastened to answer, her gaze averted, her blushing face nonetheless gravely sad.

All at once Elishta gave me pause in a way she never truly had before. Was I reading into my oldest friend's concern for me? Making some embarrassing misinterpretation of her tone?

Or was there something more than a yearning for friendship behind those downcast eyes?

"Elishta—"

A delighted bellow from the landing above interrupted us.

"Rorke Burningsoul!"

My gaze was drawn to Father Fortisto, a ragged and moth-eaten but kindly old man who for the last four or so years had adopted a way of quivering when excited by some activity or bit of news. Looking between myself and his feet, he waved a trembling hand and eventually rested it upon the rail of the spiraling metal staircase. "Weltyr's eye, how blessed I am to see you again!"

"Not near so blessed as I am," I said, adding, "wait there, please," as I turned to Elishta. "My task here is urgent, and I may not be able to linger long once Fortisto has divined for me. Is there a way, perhaps, that you could meet me at the inn where we stay? Ah—but the neighborhood forbids it, so perhaps—"

"Which one?"

Her eyes were dangerously bright. Not wishing to give her an inroad into getting herself hurt, I neglected the name of the place and instead simply told her, "Let me speak to Fortisto and take care of a few things while I'm in town. If it all goes well, we'll spend at least an afternoon catching up and celebrating before I have to hurry on again."

"All right, Rorke." With a faint smile, pained but not wholly joyless, she pushed her hair from her face and stepped back from me. "Will you promise?"

"I promise."

Then, though it pained me to leave Elishta behind, I strode quickly up the stairs to embrace Father Fortisto.

"Ah!" The little man laughed and patted me a few

fond times, observing on his release that, "You've got new armor! Fancy stuff." He rapped a knuckle against the breastplate I'd not even thought of taking off for as quickly as I'd been moving from Point A to Point B. "The Order Magistrate will complain that it's not to regulation, but we can get you a new, official set before our induction ceremony...did you bring the Scepter, my boy?"

"That's what I wanted to talk to you about, Father. Could we sit in your office for a few moments?"

His merry features rearranging to concern, Fortisto ran a hand over his patchy gray beard and said with a wave toward the hall, "Of course, of course. Let's sit down and have a talk...but, about what?"

"About thieves," I told him, my voice lowered as we made our way to his office. Each floor of the Temple was a little different than the last; and each, in my opinion, provided jarring contrast to the strange black metal of the hallways and exterior. The level commonly called "the rectory hall" was expansive and elegant, floored not in metal but wood and plush red carpet. Paintings adorned the damask walls, and, somewhere unseen, a fountain bubbled on the other side of someone's open office door.

Fortisto had left his own empty office open. He ushered me inside, sealing us together. The walls were cramped but the high ceiling permitted some impressive bookshelves, all of which the disorganized priest had filled to the brim.

As a consequence, his desk overflowed with poorly sorted stacks of books and paperwork. Among this difficult to interpret collection of objects I counted no fewer than three pairs of reading glasses. Knowing Fortisto, I suspect that he was only really aware of two. I repressed my fond smile as the eccentric priest sat across his desk from me.

"Now," said Fortisto grimly, hands folded, "what is this about thieves?"

My warm feelings to be home faded into the pressing matter that had brought me here to begin with. Posture mirroring his, I rested my forearms upon the edge of his desk and told him as quickly as I could the story of how I came to be stranded in the Nightlands. For some reason, when imagining this moment, I had imagined massaging the truth somehow, or perhaps outright lying to save face—but I could not look Father Fortisto in the eyes and do such a thing, no more than I could lie to anyone and still think of Weltyr without shame or fear.

Besides...Father Fortisto was among the most gentle-hearted of the priests in the Temple, and, I would wager, the most gentle-hearted of the priests in Weltyr's entire church. He listened to me with an open heart and mind, no trace of judgement in his face as I described my time of slavery (sparing certain details, of course, such as my willingness, and the particular uses my mistress had for me) and my flight out of the Nightlands. As I went on, though, attempting to explain about Branwen, he paused.

"What was it you were saying about that ring?"

"Some trinket," I assured him. "An idol. Magical, perhaps, but ultimately the ring's importance is as a kind of tribal fetish by which the durrow choose their next queen. I must get it back for the woman helping me with all of this, as she sacrificed it to protect my life—but only once the matter of the Scepter is seen to."

Stroking his beard again, the old man waved his free hand and said, "Continue."

I did—after explaining Branwen and our time in Soot, I summed it all up. "Hildolfr and Grimalkin must have come here if they are headed to Rhineland with the

146

Scepter. I aim to stop them before they can get anywhere close, but if they board the airship, I'll be in real trouble."

"Don't want to end up in the brig for starting a fight on the ship," he agreed thoughtfully, his eyes distant. "Do you know to whom they intend to sell the artifact? Did the girl, Branwen, say anything about it?"

I shook my head 'no.' "That doesn't mean she doesn't know...she's tight-lipped, Branwen. Seeing as she betrayed me once, I wouldn't put it past her to withhold information or lie to me again. But..."

For a moment I thought of telling him about Gundrygia and the week I lost to a few hours of her passion, but the clock of my soul ticked steadily on. Unable to soften the gravity of my voice, I told him firmly, "The simplest solution is to catch them before they can board, and get the scepter from them by hook or by crook."

"I agree wholeheartedly," said the old man, nodding. "Well, come on—let's see what we can find with the runes. Sometimes, that's all we need, but if we have to go deeper I can always see about consulting the Wyrd."

Fortisto pushed himself from the desk and made his slow way around it, stopping by a board set in the corner nearest the door. After rifling through a collection of maps poorly filed in a nearby rack, he came up with a map of Skythorn that he smoothed into place in the board. To contain all of the city the map was less than detailed, but it would serve our purpose for divination. I rose from my seat to watch as he picked from a shelf above his head the bone container that had captivated me as a young man. He it twisted open, his hand sliding within to rifle through the carved pieces.

"This isn't a time for use of the seidr?"

"No, my boy...the seidr is used for drawing forth the

future. Divining the present is another matter entirely, and far less extraordinary. Excuse me."

The priest knelt before the board, the container pressed to his forehead. I stepped back to give him space, deliberately turning the attention of my ears away from the contents of his prayer. The Temple Fathers were good men, and good teachers—but, as I had been taught in the battle lessons of the Order, not every method of connection to the Wandering God was meant for every man. Still fewer women. Certain extraordinarily ascetic nuns and women who died in the name of the faith had been granted powers acknowledged to be from Weltyr, but such powers had occurred to them only at peaks of great suffering, and only without their full comprehension.

Yet there was Valeria with her dreams, and that ring with its capacity for extraordinarily perceptive insights among other powers unknown to me—all said to be from Roserpine.

Fortisto threw the runes across the map of Skythorn. As he pondered with the tip of a wand he used to probe them about, I asked, "Is it possible, sire, that Weltyr's lesser emanations may transmit valid divinatory information in the same way as the All-Father in his purest form?"

Pausing his contemplation, wand frozen mid-prod, kindly Fortisto looked up at me with surprise but twinkling, almost mischievous interest. "Well, now that is a very interesting question! One that not many members of the Order think to ask...or many priests, for that matter."

"You don't seem ill-disposed to it, Father."

"I'm not, of course...in fact, I should think that most of the priests who dwell here in the rectory hall are rather more open to the notion that other gods are, as you say, lesser emanations of Weltyr."

"I would have thought it to be the opposite case."

"Only those closest to the master may understand how much his property encompasses. There are two ways to look at the gods revered by heathens in our world. One is controversial. The purpose of the Order, as you were taught, is to stamp out seditious and heretical behavior, and to complete tasks abroad in the name of the Lord. Most members of the Order of Weltyr, therefore—along with most clergy not blessed with interest or insight— believe that all other gods are inherently false, dangerous constructions that must be destroyed. I, personally, do not always believe that to be the case."

Fortisto resumed studying the cryptic messages of the runes. While he read, he spoke absently. My attention wandered to the sound of a raven's hoarse croaking upon the balcony of some office on the other side of the hall. "Some gods are sacred messengers," the priest was saying, "yes, and deliver good news and secrets in dreams at Weltyr's behest just as he would. Some have even had Church-confirmed blessings attributed to them—though, of course, one again, these are recognized as being derived from Weltyr, who works through lesser manifestations of his might."

"Of course," I said, my ear still caught by external noise. Now not by a raven's croak, but by a slight scuffle that rang oddly soft. Shaking it off, I struggled to hone my attention in on Fortisto, who continued.

"Some heathen gods have even been known to bless artifacts on behalf of Weltyr...there are three in particular that spring to mind, items as coveted as the Scepter of our Lord. The Ring of Roserpine"—a horn in the courtyard indicated the time to be 1700, its brass announcement braying five times while Fortisto thought out loud as much as contemplated the runes and responded to my question—"the Lantern of Hamsunt...and the Casket of Oppenhir."

"Wait," I said, struggling to focus above all these noises and, most of all, the rising commotion in the hall outside. "Did you just say the Lantern of—"

"Let *go* of me, Zweiding!"

Elishta's voice wrenched my attention out to the hall entirely. Now knowing it was her, her tone had me moving quick as a flash. I threw open the door, Strife drawn by the time I stepped into the hallway. Indeed, I was assailed by the sight of Order Commander Zweiding, his powerful frame filling the hall and Elishta's narrow wrist clenched in his fist.

"You heard the lady," I told him. Having been long enough absented from the Temple and since educated in the value of impudence, I did not think twice about threatening a man fundamental in my training and status within the Order—a man who could, by rights, have ordered me to do nearly anything so long as it be in Weltyr's name.

But I had never thought twice about defending Elishta from cruel teachers when we were children. Now, shocked to be addressed in such a way, Zweiding released her. Elishta-bet scrambled away with her long skirts held around her ankles.

"Why," he said, a dark laugh on his sneering lips, "Burningsoul! Back at last—with the Scepter, I presume?"

"Not yet." Seeing as, unarmed, Zweiding wore his black Temple garb, I sheathed Strife and studied Elishta as she rubbed her wrist. "Are you hurt?"

"Oh, please. She's not made of spun sugar, Burningsoul. The little witch was eavesdropping on your meeting with Father Fortisto...you had ought to thank me, then profusely apologize for your mistake."

"While it may be out of line to point my weapon at a superior officer, I only heard a woman protest—and, seeing as I did not know the context, I thought it better that I should intervene first and worry about the details later on."

"Well, now…travel has changed you at least a little, hasn't it! What happened to the boy who wandered off to find the Scepter? A man now…still empty-handed, though."

I had never liked Zweiding on a personal level, and after my time abroad he seemed more unpleasant than ever. At the very least, he did no honor to the mark upon his neck.

"Not for long," I told him. "You remember the report I sent you?"

"Ah, yes—something about the Nightlands, correct? Seeking the Scepter there, in a den of spirit-thieves. How did that go for you?"

"I was captured by some durrow, but—"

"Durrow!" With a noise that was something of a crossbreed between a scoff and a laugh of derision, the steel-haired officer folded his arms. "You were captured by a bunch of *elves*, you mean?"

"I went with them honorably," I corrected him, maintaining as calm a tone as I could in the circumstances. "They agreed to heal an otherwise mortal wound if I would consent to come with them as a slave and not to trouble them about it."

Zweiding's shock only grew. "And you *did* it? Surely not."

"It was the honorable thing," I repeated, though this seemed to mean next to nothing to him. No more than it did, infuriatingly, when I pointed out, "I sensed it was Weltyr's will that I should obey. Sure enough, look how soon I was liberated from the bonds of—"

But he had stopped listening and, in fact, had been laughing for some time. "What a fool you are! How less than a man you are, permitting yourself to be captured by a bunch of women…it's true, isn't it, that they're all females? Weltyr's beard! All this time I'd been worried that you would return home and prove a problem between myself and my intended—but what concern have I that a wretch so unmanly might usurp my right?"

I, baffled, could only help but ask before he carried on, "How do you mean?"

"Ah! You didn't tell him, Elishta?" His laughter fading, that arrogant sneer returning in full, the Commander glanced at my old friend. Elishta had been cowed into thin-lipped, shame-faced silence. She stared at her feet while Zweiding informed me, "Elishta here is my intended."

Mouth open, I looked between the two of them and saw very clearly that Elishta-bet had no part in such a decision. "How could that be? Did you not just call her a witch?"

"And I meant it. You are one, aren't you, Elishta?"

My heart was pained while my friend clenched her hands in fists of impotent rage. Now I could feel Fortisto in the doorway behind me, wondering perhaps if he had ought to intervene. I silently willed him to stay out of it while Zweiding went on in a mocking tone, "This wretched girl was thrown out of the convent for practicing profane magical arts not permitted to members of the Church. She's lucky she wasn't killed! But, owing to her ties to the Temple, we have deigned to reform her. In such a case as this, part of the reformation process involves the engagement of the witch in as many sacraments as possible…Matrimony and Extreme Unction being foremost among them. Seeing as I have always found Elishta-bet to be incredibly lovely, I volunteered for the former. Hopefully it will not yet come to the latter."

Trembling, Elishta burst into the motion of a startled bird. I nearly cried out as she darted between me and Zweiding on her way back down the passage to the curling stairs. Fury burning in my breast, I told my Commander, "Can't you see she wants no part in this?"

"The pairing has already been approved by the administrative board."

"But surely, Commander, you could examine your conscience and—"

"My conscience tells me that the world has no room for another dangerous heretic driven mad by magical powers she has not earned...and that, if I want to see such danger stamped out, I had ought to commit to the task of her reformation. If you were any suitable fit to the Order, you would agree with me—just as you, rather than consenting to come along with them as their chattel, you would have eradicated the durrow who helped you for their own benefit."

You are being lied to, Eradicator.

My eyes squeezed shut.

"I won't let you do this," I told him, pushing to the back of my mind all the consequences that surely awaited me for this.

A scoff rose from Zweiding's chest. He now looked at me not with derision but stern displeasure. "Oh?"

"I can't stand idly by and permit even you, Commander, to force a woman into a marriage against her will." My stomach tightened as I went on, but I had no choice. "Not even if the Church says that is what is necessary. Weltyr himself would consider such a union a woeful sin—I'm sure of it."

Speaking as though unable to control my tongue, (and certainly not able to hear the priest behind me, who softly uttered my name as though to plead that I stop), I placed my hand upon Strife's pommel.

"Commander Zweiding, I challenge you to a duel for the sake of Elishta-bet."

Expression all the darker, Zweiding hooked his thumbs in his silver belt. "Do you, now?"

"If I win, you must release Elishta-bet from her obligation to marry you."

"And if you lose?"

"Then I will never set eyes on her again. I will mind my own business and say nothing of the union, which must, in the case of my loss, be for the benefit of Weltyr… but I do not believe that will prove to be the case."

The raven from before hacked out a laugh that carried through the rectory. Ignoring it, Zweiding responded coolly.

"That will be the very least of your forfeits. A place in the Order will be among them, Burningsoul. Are you sure you wish to challenge me?"

I had the feeling my place in the Order would be dubious regardless of whether I won or lost. Certainly, unless I acquired the Scepter soon, it already was.

"Yes," I told him, knowing only the deep fury that filled me to think of Elishta-bet conscripted into this loathsome arrangement. "The challenge stands. Choose the time and place and you will find me there."

"You always were a foolhardy boy, Burningsoul. Very well. I'll give you…three full days to come to your senses. Should you still wish to throw your years of training— your whole life—into the gutter for the sake of a heretical woman, I will meet you in the gardens before our Temple on the dawn of the fourth day."

"Then you will see me there, Commander," I told him. "And I pray to Weltyr that you will not bear the burden of ill feelings if the All-Father should prove my cause more just than yours."

With a snort, Zweiding looked hard into my face and, saying nothing, exited in the same direction as Elishta-bet. I struggled to avoid following him. Thankfully, Fortisto was there to place his hand upon my shoulder.

"I hope you know what you're doing, Rorke," said the old man, his expression grim. "I dislike the idea of Elishta's reformation as much as you, but—"

Outraged, I said, "I've never heard of such a thing! How could the clergy ordain practice so barbaric?"

"Order recruits and young Church members alike are shielded from such nuances of the faith," he confessed, shaking his head sadly. "Generally, once a paladin learns of them, he's already been confirmed and battle-proven, and he is much too devoted to the protection of the Church to think twice...therefore, it never changes. The practice is traditional, extending back many centuries to, oh, several wars, when concubines taken amid the spoils required education in the ways of their new faith."

My jaw hung open only wider. "Is this not the very practice of slavery for which we people of the surface claim to despise the durrow? For which our Church has called the whole species heretical?"

Still quite grim-faced, Fortisto said, "That is, I should say, only the foremost reason why the dark elves are so despised by the Order...but, populated as it is by brutes worse than Zweiding, I must admit your branch of the faith has no particular love for anything but itself. It has no patience for other faiths, species, or thoughts. We share the same roof, and our god bears the same name...

but there are times when I wonder if we are, in any sense, part of the same organization."

I overflowed with questions about such a disturbing revelation from which my childhood had shielded me, but the old priest was already heading back into his office. As I followed him, he adjusted the reading glasses he'd put on to study the runes.

"Now—if I'm reading our Lord's will correctly, it seems you'll find what you seek in this area, or thereabouts..."

Of all districts, he pointed to the one where we stayed.

My heart leapt with hope and I caught his shoulder in enthusiasm. While Fortisto laughed merrily as I told him, "Of course, the slums—Grimalkin hates to spend money even more than Odile."

"Odile?"

"A friend." I hesitated, guarding the truth only because of my conversation with Zweiding. "Someone from the Nightlands. Surely—surely, Father, it was the right thing to stand by my honor and do as Weltyr commanded me?"

"It was, of course. You know the culture of the Order...you've never been suited to it. If you were not such a superb fighter I would tell you to join the brotherhood of priests—but then, you are as much a wanderer as Weltyr himself! And when he commands us to wander where we are not comfortable, we must swallow our fears for his sake."

I nodded, somewhat more vindicated, and looked over the runes with curiosity. "So, Father—where might I find the men called Grimalkin and Hildolfr?"

"Hard to say..." Humming, looking over the runes, Fortisto said, "There's so much...feminine energy here.

And…money…one of these traitors wasn't a woman, was it?"

"She was, but she has since repented for her crimes and agreed to assist me in reclaiming the Scepter."

"What a good time you seem like you're having! Making so many friends. Well…hm, then I don't know what all this female energy is amid these messages…"

Yes, it was strange. Of all the men I'd ever known, Grimalkin was perhaps the least feminine by far. In fact, I'd heard it said the whole race of dwarves knew nothing of femininity—that even their women had been seen wearing beards. Whether this was true, I couldn't say: all the female dwarves I'd known were smooth-faced. Whatever the case, Grimalkin tended to love women of other races…and he did love them. Women were the one matter on which we agreed—until, of course, our final conflict.

We'll all be dying eventually anyway. Might as well die rich, fat, and well-laid.

"A brothel," I said suddenly, crying out in delight to realize my own foolishness. "Of course! Where else would Grimalkin be? His last nights in Skythorn… naturally, he'll be spending them in one of our brothels."

"Good show, Burningsoul!" Excited to have been whisked even peripherally into the quest upon which I'd been sent, Fortisto slapped his hand to his fist and said, "That's the way Weltyr's sight works…through us, my boy. Through our knowledge."

"So it is, Father." My attention caught by the arrangement of runes upon the map, I indicated one that had fallen at the very edge of the board. A blank rune sat just outside the city boundary. "What does this one indicate, sire?"

"Ah—Weltyr. There are some priests who believe

that, because the blank rune was incorporated later than the others, it is less valid...but Weltyr would not have inspired the meaning had he thought it inappropriate. All runes have some purpose, some definition, as much as the letters of the alphabet are defined by their sounds. I would take this to mean"—he prodded the blank rune just north of the map—"that Weltyr is watching over you very closely, Burningsoul...very closely indeed."

"What a gratifying thought that is." My hand pressing to my heart through the plates of my armor, I nodded at Fortisto. "Thank you, Father, for your time and service. Now it's a question of discerning just which house of ill repute he's chosen to visit! There can't be that many, can there?"

11

GRIMALKIN AND THE SINGING NIXIE

HOW NAIVE I was! Looking back, I laugh at my relative innocence. Not having ventured far from the Temple until that far-venturing took me away from Skythorn altogether, I had not explored the more derelict districts of my own city and was therefore out of touch with them until we took rooms in the Mongoose. I therefore did not understand how desperate the poorer citizens were for any form of entertainment, be that an old-fashioned tavern brawl or the embrace of a woman paid for a few minutes of tenderness.

After bidding Fortisto good evening, (and assuring him more than once that, whatever the outcome of my duel with Zweiding, I accepted it was the doing of Weltyr), I exited the Temple. All the time, I looked for

Elishta. Finding no sign of her, I resolved to check in on her the next day but then sadly had to rearrange my priorities away from concern for my friend. The most pressing issue was, in my opinion, the matter of finding Grimalkin. If I didn't catch him soon, it would be some trick to subdue him in either the airship or Rhineland.

Therefore, my heart with Elishta, I hurried through Skythorn and headed again to the outer districts. As the air thickened with putrid chemicals, I slowed to more carefully assess my surroundings.

Amazing. When one wasn't looking for them, they blended in completely...but, when the eye searched the crowd for a working woman, the fast-acting mind could pick them out in droves. Amid the artisans and hard-working laborers of the factory and production districts, a woman scanned the crowd on nearly every block.

Now realizing this process might have been a mite more challenging than previously anticipated, I regretted not having brought at least one of the women along to approach the prostitutes on my behalf. The truth of the matter was that, to a Skythorn woman looking for clientele—whether she was independent or affiliated with a brothel—the tattoo on my neck and the armor I wore was the ultimate sign of authority. The Temple had legal power as well as religious power, and the city guards were trained as part of the Order before being disseminated to cause trouble for already very troubled people.

Add to that Strife at my hip, and I appeared to be an extremely unsubtle officer of the law looking to harass the working poor.

Therefore—thanking my good looks and even pausing by the window of a nearby leather-worker to fix my hair—I approached a ragged but motherly-looking older woman poised in an alcove where she intently scanned the faces of passers-by.

"Excuse me," I said, trying to soften my tone further when she cringed at my coming and turned toward me with hard eyes that defied me to arrest her.

Speak from the heart, said a spirit inside me. Another of Weltyr's messengers: intuition.

"Do you have a moment to answer a question in the name of Weltyr?"

Her expression changed into one of mystified amusement. Looking me up and down, beginning to relax, she asked, "You some kind of missionary?"

"Yes, in fact." Seeing her heavily made-up eyes lingered upon Strife, I gestured to its pommel and told her casually, "For self-defense."

"Uh-huh." The woman looked harder into my face. Her hair had been bleached blonde with queer concoctions enough times that it had started to thin, and it moved stiffly in her hand as she pushed it from her eyes. "You don't seem the type of fellow to be talking to a lady like me."

"Well, you see, I've lost track of a friend of mine. I think he's probably spending some time with one of you lovely ladies somewhere around here."

"A friend, huh?"

"One of my best," I said with a smile that couldn't help its own crookedness. She laughed at my unveiled irony, her posture relaxing more fully, her gaze turning from me and across the crowd again. "Lucky for me, he's quite recognizable. A dwarf"—I gestured and her attention returned to me—"about yea tall, reddish beard usually adorned with runes, can't seem to remember if he happened to have a weapon today..."

Rubbing her jaw, the woman drifted into thought

before saying, "I ain't seen anybody like that come through today. But you just go down these blocks here and try a few of my friends. If you have problems, tell 'em Kuldi said they can talk to you. You don't seem too bad...I can tell a real bastard when I see one."

I laughed, assuring her, "If that's the case, you would have remembered my friend."

While Kuldi threw her head back with a witch's cackle and a light slap of my arm, I smiled, bade her good evening, and set out again.

You may imagine, friend, that this process was repeated many, many times...with some variations. A few of the ladies I approached tried very hard to earn my patronage, and though I admit I have never had anything against prostitution, I certainly didn't have a need for affection what with my companions waiting at the Mongoose.

Therefore, politely as I could, I kept it short and sweet, inquiring whether anyone on the street had seen Grimalkin. At last, slowly, my blind dousing yielded a trickle of information.

A pair of girls were able to tell me that someone fitting his description had walked by earlier, perhaps an hour or so before. Someone else said they saw him walking with So-And-So. And where did *she* work? Oh, the girl I asked wasn't sure...but maybe if I checked with What's-Her-Name at the end of the next block over, she could remember it.

Finally, I got a chance ask Miss What's where Miss And-So happened to work. Thanks to my ability to invoke the names of Kuldi, Veria, Quorana and Ishtrina, (as well as a few ounces of copper), the information was yielded: So-And-So was an elf named Cloyenda, and she worked at an establishment called The Singing Nixie.

The very sign for the place seemed, to my sometimes naive eye, quite risqué for something visible from the street...but what did I know about such things? It had surprised me how readily the women tried to push me into employing them. Things were very forthright in those hard-working quarters of the city, and it was simultaneously amusing and disorienting.

Particularly disorienting was the mingling of professionalism and sexuality. As I had been instructed, I went to the side of the building (for, like many such lightly disguised operations, the front was an apothecary) and knocked upon the employee entrance there. A slot slid open and a woman's rustic voice demanded after a few seconds, "Who sent you, Paladin?"

"My god," I told the darkness of the brothel, "and Kuldi."

With a light snort, the madame informed me, "Kuldi's our competition. Why would she send you to us?"

"Because I'm not looking for company. I'm looking for a customer."

A hesitation. Consideration. Finally: "If I let you in here, what cause have our customers to trust us again?"

"The customer isn't from here, and knows no one to tell about all this. You needn't tell anybody any details. It's rooms men buy in these establishments, correct? Not women. Therefore"—I held up a few gold coins and swore I saw points of light in the darkness of the slot—"all anyone need know is that I came to buy a high-priced room for a few hours, and things got out of hand."

The slot slammed shut. After a second or two, the door protested its way open. A severe-looking woman with tight gray hair and a dress of red velvet appeared on the threshold. Her hand extended without remark.

I set the coins in her palm and she tested their weight, sought the impressions of her teeth, then slid them into her slightly stained pinafore before she stood aside to let me in.

"If you intend to cause any kind of trouble, cause it outside."

"Thank you," I told her, trying to make myself seem as small and harmless as I could in the lounge dotted with faded furniture and dying plants. "I swear to you, madame, I will mind my business…but, theoretically, if a red-bearded dwarf did come through here—say, with a Cloyenda—what room would you have rented to him?"

She gestured, heading through a beaded curtain to put her money away. "That hallway, past the parlor, third door on the left once you're up the stairs. Don't let me hear a commotion."

With that, the madame of the house vanished from my sight. I set a hand upon Strife's pommel and made my way upstairs as quietly as my armor and size would allow…and although the thunder of my usual stride was softened by my intent, it was by no means muted.

There was also the small matter of getting into the room. I therefore stopped by the parlor before the stairs, hoping to find someone who might assist me in this scheme. At once my eyes filled with a wealth of silk, lace, and floral flesh.

It was fair to say that not every woman there was of exceeding beauty, but it was true that each had her charms, and most were, at best, half-dressed. They perked to see me fill the doorway. After taking in my face, a fair few looked a way I can only describe as hopeful. Preening, smiling, batting eyelashes, these interested saleswomen leaned forward or recrossed their legs to fix the hem of their skirt a bit higher.

Only one, however, spoke up to me: a splendid redhead, a woman perhaps fifteen years my senior who was as beautiful as Weltyr's bride ever made her chambermaids. With a foxy smile fluttering past her crimson lips, the woman looked me over and said from where she leaned beside the hearth, "Are you looking for a room, soldier?"

"And someone to take me to it, yes. You look like you might be willing to help."

"Oh, for a visitor like you? Always."

With a sly wink at the disappointed ladies who sank back into their couches and resumed their conversations at a more subdued murmur than before, the redhead pushed herself upright and smoothed the fabric of her long slip. The extraordinary sky blue of her thin gown was one of the things that drew my eye to her (aside from her many other natural qualities, of course) and, as she slunk past me, she smelled of rosewater and myrrh. I took a liking to her instantly: whatever her profession, the aroma of her hair and body reminded me of church. This seemed to me as fine a sign as any that I had made the right choice.

Indeed, I discerned she may well have been pious. In the hallway into which she led me, she asked, "Are paladins of Weltyr permitted the leisure our rooms afford, sire?"

"Please, miss, 'Rorke' is fine…and, unfortunately, I must confess I am not here on leisure, though if I were I do not think Weltyr would have the least qualm were I to spend leisure time with you. Only priests and monks need to turn their attentions away from women…we paladins are so much of the world already, and so much in tune with Weltyr's dynamic power as the All-Father, that it does us no harm to indulge in other worldly pastimes."

Having paused upon the first landing of the stairs to listen, one foot poised on the step before her and the other still supporting her slight weight, the woman looked at me curiously. "If it is not leisure that brings you, then what?"

"That would be a far longer story than to just give you a few coins to get me into a certain room…a story that might get you into trouble, too, depending how this goes."

With a crooked sort of grin and a twinkling light to her strange green eyes, the prostitute folded her arms over her ribs. "I never get into trouble that I don't cause… believe me."

"Weltyr has sent me here," I decided to say, the coins already rattling in my hand evidently not sufficient to buy the businesswoman's compliance. "I am on a mission from the All-Father to retrieve a missing relic of his. The man in the third room on the left should have information as to its whereabouts."

"What relic would that be, sire?"

"Please, 'Rorke' really is perfectly fine—I don't suppose you'd be wiling to accept that this is a private matter on behalf of the Church?"

"For all I know, you're not a servant of Weltyr at all, 'Rorke.' You could be anyone…a slave to Oppenhir."

"Then this tattoo"—I indicated the black sun upon my neck—"would have faded; and this sword would have broken, no longer serving any purpose in my master's name."

"I suppose that's true…" Considering me thoughtfully, the woman at last extended her hand for the coins. I filled her palm and let her count before, smiling, the prostitute crooked a finger and continued up the stairs. "Very well, Paladin. Come along, follow me…

let me give a moment to get my colleague out of the room. You said he was staying third on the left? With Cloyenda?"

"I believe that's just the case."

"I saw him come in…a dwarf, was he? Red hair?"

"The very man."

"Well, be careful…he brought an axe with him, much as you brought along your sword."

I had been counting on that—that some altercation would occur regardless of whether or not Gimalkin was armed—but I don't think I anticipated the struggle that awaited me. The greatest problems had previously been the matter of how to get into the room, and how to get the prostitute named Cloyenda out before any collateral damage could be done to her person.

The woman I hired solved that for me, both matters simple with her at the task. I walked softly with her and, at her gesture, waited against the wall. She paused before the door and rapped lightly upon it, calling, "Cloyenda?"

A bit of muttering was audible from within the room. Footsteps creaked along the wood and the door cracked open. My guide through the house smiled at her colleague, asking, "Could you come out here please, Cloyenda?"

Brushing a few blonde locks behind her elfin ears, Cloyenda stepped into the hall with her arms folded over her robe. She left the door unlatched but closed it nearly all the way. From her periphery, she caught a glimpse of me and turned to face me, her breath almost hitching, her eyes certainly wider. Her mouth opened but, before she could speak, my guide pressed a fingertip her lips and shook her head. Glancing between us, the elf then looked with reluctance at the door to her room. My guide slid her hand into Cloyenda's and led her away, the elf going without argument but with a few more furtive studies of my admittedly looming person.

Alone in the hall, I gripped Strife in its scabbard and approached the open door.

Luckily, if Grimalkin could discern a shift in the footsteps of the woman he was with, he did not stop to think why that might have been the case.

"There you are," he groused, sitting on the edge of the tangled bed while beard-deep in a mug of some ale that was no doubt sixteen times the price one could expect to pay at a more straightforward establishment. "Now, what the hell was all that about?" Not very professional."

"You're a fine one to speak of professionalism," I told him. As his back and shoulders sharply tensed (somewhat difficult to discern beneath the coating of red hair almost comically dispersed over the dwarf's back), I shut the door behind me. "When most do not feel they are being paid enough by their employers, Grimalkin, they lodge a personal complaint or find a new job. They don't betray them at the very task that they were hired for."

"So you came for your money? That's just fine…I've plenty here, it's no trouble to give you what you're owed."

"Don't play games with me, Grimalkin." While I spoke, he set the mug upon the nightstand. All the time, Grimalkin was still facing the wall. I took a step toward him and found the room so small that a mere four strides would find me at the foot of the bed. "I came for the Scepter, and I won't leave you to your own devices until it's in my hand."

"Then you'd best be looking elsewhere," the dwarf told me, slowly rising from the edge of the bed and stooping to pull his trousers up. "I don't have the bloody thing."

I completed my approach. "Lying again, Grimalkin? Don't you think I deserve better than that after you left me for—"

His motions were quick, but the act of pulling the axe from under the bed was too involved for him to arm himself and face me before Strife was in my hand. The sword's blade rang sharply against the axe: the power of dwarven steel was a reasonable match against the enchanted metal of Strife. Both weapons bounced sharply apart and Grimalkin, owing to his stature, backpedaled a few steps and slammed into the nightstand. The mug's contents upended over him, leaving the surly dwarf sputtering with outrage. He took a wild swing with the axe and missed—but, stepping back as I was, I unfortunately gave Grimalkin room enough to leap upon the bed and spring off from the other side.

The chase was on. I was surprised to find the dwarf so fast, considering how short his legs were But, between the encumbering weight of my armor and his desperation to escape retribution, Grimalkin might as well have been a racehorse. He tore through the hall and leapt down the stairs while I trundled along behind him, human height soon to prove a disadvantage in more ways than one.

Rather than taking the anticipated route through the alley entrance I had used, Grimalkin made a sharp left and cut through the parlor.

While women shrieked and scattered like birds, the dwarf led with his axe and used his speed to propel the blade straight through the single window of the room. The old glass shattered so thoroughly that few shards remained. After briskly clearing the pane with the blade of his weapon, Grimalkin launched through the opening and out upon the street.

Gritting my teeth, clearly unable to fit through the

window, I looked wildly about to find my way through the hallways to the tavern entrance.

"Hojotoho! Hojotoho!"

The warrior's call, raised in a woman's voice, caught my attention. I lumbered in its direction and recognized the prostitute who had guided me up to Grimalkin's room. She was now down a side hall, vigorously indicating, "This way, Burningsoul!"

I dashed down the hall toward the sound of her voice. Two rooms from the parlor, she held the kitchen door for me.

My heart throbbed with such relief to see this exit that I would not realize I had not given this strange woman my surname until much later.

Just then, I had no room in my consciousness for such details. As was the plains-king for its unlucky prey, I was driven toward my goal—toward the capture of Grimalkin. Dodging past a baffled and bored looking cook, I hurried through the kitchen and out into the alley around whose corner Grimalkin disappeared right away. In hot pursuit, I swept down the alley and around the same corner past which his hairy shoulder had just disappeared. The dwarf was ducking between people and generally using his short height in ways I couldn't...but he did not know Skythorn as well as I knew Skythorn, nor did he have a god on his side. Not one as powerful as Weltyr, at any rate—nor one so well-regarded in the city.

Seeing how crowded the district was at that time of evening, I ran in the street rather than on the walkway and sometimes darted along the gutter. This was not easy either, as tired men and women alike sat upon the curbs to have a few minutes of whatever counted for peace in their exhausting lives. To my left rolled the tires of carts and mule-driven taxis. I kept an eye out for something helpful—and, praise Weltyr, I struck gold just as Grimalkin turned the corner to make his fast way down a somewhat less central street.

A tired-looking man had guided his horse to the curb and seemed about to unload the contents of his covered cart into a nearby building. I placed my hand upon his shoulder and, when he stiffly turned to see whomever it was Weltyr had sent to challenge him now, I gestured toward my neck. The fellow's eyes, taking in the tattoo of the Order, widened with disbelief. While he looked me in the face, I told him, "I need to borrow your horse, please, friend—I'll see to it that he's returned to you within the hour, or my service to Weltyr means nothing."

Exhaling heavily, then nodding, the man turned and hurriedly freed his stallion from the cart. I sat astride the beast in a heartbeat, my heels digging in to send it flying in the direction Grimalkin had headed. The horse seemed glad to have a reason to gallop and in fact proved quite adept at ducking through the traffic between us and our quarry. When the road cleared for a spell, it was faster than ever: a bolt of white lightning that claimed the street for its own and permitted me to overtake Grimalkin before he could make himself scarce down another alley. My mount pulled up before the dwarf with a whinny.

A few seconds later, Strife was a few inches from Grimalkin's nose.

"Let's return you to The Singing Nixie," I told him while he lowered his axe in defeat. "Get you dried off and in your clothes before I question you...you deserve more dignity than you afforded me in the Nightlands. Not to mention the ladies of the Nixie, who deserve payment for a new window."

Soon enough, (and a long conversation with a very angry madame later, my advocate from before sadly nowhere to be seen), I stood with Grimalkin's axe in my folded arms and my back to the door of Cloyenda's tiny room. His expression sour not just due to his capture but to the fact that I made him dress in front of me to assure myself he had no concealed weapons, Grimalkin looked at the head of his axe but only very seldom forced himself to peer into my face.

Upon eyeing the equipment he dragged from beneath the bed to don while we spoke, I could not help but note, "So you at least told the truth—the Scepter isn't here."

"Aye, and I'd think you'd be relieved to know the precious relic of your god isn't sitting under an elvish whore's dusty bed."

"It has less to do with her heritage or her profession than the dust, truth be told…and the general disrespect. You look at the most sacred artifacts and see only money."

"And you look at money and mistake it for nothing."

"Far from it…all property, all things, are Weltyr's alone. When he chooses to allocate such gifts to his servants, the wise servant should be grateful. He most certainly should not take more than he is given. Such a betrayal against one's master is sure to be punished in time."

"Weltyr's no master of mine," grumbled the dwarf.

"Those who deny him are but his blindest slaves. But come, Grimalkin, hurry and dress so you can take me to the Scepter."

"I'll dress as fast or slow as suits me, human…but no matter how fast or slow I go, it won't help you get what you're after. I don't know where the blasted Scepter is."

I searched his face for a hint of falsity and found there nothing deeper than the same dislike he always displayed when we discussed anything of any nature. "What do you mean, you don't know where the Scepter of Weltyr is?"

"I mean just that, you oaf! I mean that the Scepter is with Hildolfr...and Hildolfr and I have parted ways, in case you couldn't guess."

Mouth widening somewhat, I glanced down at myself and the suit of armor for which the old man had paid. "Parted ways, did you? But I thought you had a buyer in Rhineland."

"Aye, I did...the government of Rhineland would have paid handsomely for it, as they do for all such relics of magical inclination."

"But you weren't sent here specifically for the theft?"

"By someone else, no...but an earth-spirit sent me a dream that great fortune awaited me in Cascadia, so off I flew." While my ears perked at mention of a prophetic dream, the dwarf continued, "I bumped into Branwen, and we into you...you know the rest of the story."

"Yet, I don't. What caused you and Hildolfr to split up?"

"That blasted Scepter, I should think!" Straightening up from fitting his feet into his boots, Grimalkin, now mostly dressed, rested against the edge of the bed. I enjoyed a rare moment wherein he deigned to make eye contact, and in the depths of his dark eyes there blazed a very real fever. "There's an enchantment on that thing—no, a curse—that drives men mad with jealousy! There must be. I've never seen someone grow more unreasonable than Hildolfr when he had that thing in his hand. Frosted over at once, and kept dead bloody silent until we were on the surface again."

Rubbing my jaw, I offered, "Hildolfr is always a very quiet man."

"Not this way, though. He waited until we were out of the Nightlands to announce that he was taking the Scepter and there wasn't a bloody thing we could do about it. He said we could come with him and reap rewards or go our ways and perish."

Shock washed through me to hear this claim. I had suspected something was the matter with Branwen's story about her change of heart...now, I understood that she had been outraged by this turn of events, and had descended back into the Nightlands to see if I still lived in order to court me to her scheme of revenge.

Ignoring the bitter emotions such a notion caused and tucking the matter away for later, I asked the dwarf before me, "What did Hildolfr intend to do with the Scepter?"

"I traveled with him a few days while we picked up his horse. Then we spent a night in an inn in some dead-end little town north of here. By the time I awoke, the bastard had vacated his room and left in the night."

"Is that so?"

"It is, though I can't tell you anything that'll convince you it is. That's up to you...I suppose you could take the gold as proof, assuming you believe me when I say it came from him."

A familiar anecdote was then told to me. Grimalkin awoke at The Weeping Willow the next morning to find Hildolfr had gone on without him to whatever destination Hildolfr had in mind.

He had also found, however, that Hildolfr had paid for both their rooms—and left behind, in the empty room, a small purse of gold that Grimalkin had not before noticed on the old man's person. The whole thing so recalled the strange gift of the highly priced armor that I was stunned into silence. Grimalkin saw the eerie feeling reflected in my face.

"Strange, innit?" Shutting the heavy leather parcel and shrugging while affixing it to his belt again, the dwarf went on, "Reckon he thought he owed me for cheating me out of the cost of procuring the Scepter. That, or he was giving me a reward for not trying to take it by force...but, as I always say, the surest way to stay alive is to recognize a losing fight before it's started."

My mouth shut in a frown of concern, I offered him his axe. Grimalkin nodded appreciatively and slid it into its holster upon his back as I asked, "And he didn't tell you anything about what he wanted to do with it?"

The dwarf shook his head. "I asked him plenty enough times, but he never answered...would only say things like, 'It's mine; why should it concern you what I choose to do with my property?'"

Scoffing at the ranger's audacity, I shook my head and said, "He never seemed so unreasonable when we were journeying together."

"Aye, and that's why I'm telling you that scepter is bloody cursed. He got it in his hand and changed at once. That, or he had no more need to pretend to be the man he seemed while on our way to the Nightlands."

Though the latter seemed the more likely scenario to me, I made a mental note to ask Father Fortisto what the powers of the Scepter were purported to be. For now, Grimalkin was getting edgy. Shifting upon his feet, looking regularly toward the door, the dwarf seemed unprepared for me to offer my hand in a shake and delayed somewhat in taking it.

"You were wise to avoid confrontation with Hildolfr...he's a warrior skilled like few I've seen."

"Like I said…no sense in getting myself killed over a bit of gold."

"Will you be going back to Rhineland on the airship?"

"Oh aye, next flight out. Was just trying to have a good time before leaving town…we don't have many elves in the dwarven cities."

"Their constitutions are too delicate for all the factory smoke, I'm sure…even your poor Cloyenda looked a bit bedraggled just from working in this neighborhood."

Laughing, Grimalkin made his way past. "Paladin, she's far from 'my' Cloyenda…and at her prices, I don't think I'd want her to be!"

12

A CALL FOR RESCUE

HOW LOW MY spirits were as I made my way back to the Mongoose! I ought not to have been, but somehow I was shocked by my conversation with Grimalkin.

Perhaps it was because, when I imagined myself confronting the dwarf, I had always pictured walking away from that confrontation with the Scepter of Weltyr in my hands. I was always like that in those days—prone to anticipating that the hardest task would arrange itself into some easy pattern for me. That perhaps Weltyr would somehow intervene in my work on his behalf and see to it that my accomplishments were natural and smooth.

But, of course, if Weltyr were inclined to intervene in these matters, what need would I have to work on his behalf? I tried to remember that all the way to the inn…just as I tried to remember that I ought not to have expected any grand change of heart in Branwen.

How sad it was to know for certain that she had not returned to the Nightlands out of unselfish concern for me! Instead, she had wound up down there simply because she had no other way to claim and pawn the Scepter.

No, it was not a surprise. She had disappointed me so sharply with her initial betrayal that, even after I and my companions saved her life from the bandits, I was still not able to fully trust her story. Yet I made myself agree to it without deeper inquiry, even if only to keep peace with our new companion while on our way to the surface.

And, in making myself agree to it, my heart forgot the sharp sting she dealt it in the den of the spirit-thieves.

My love for her had renewed itself more swiftly than I ever could have anticipated—and, now that she had spent a week with the durrow while I was in the enchanted arms of Gundrygia, she had become ensconced in our group as naturally as any one of the rest of us.

I had to hope that her time staying with the durrow while I was away had truly affected the change I had already believed she experienced. But, in spite of this reminder to hope, I could not help the bitter displeasure that arose in me at the thought of seeing her in our room in the Mongoose.

Lucky for me—for a certain definition of the word 'luck'—I was soon to find myself and everyone else distracted from the matter.

The Mongoose's tavern was packed by the time I returned from my errands, workers having vacated their posts and come in for a drink or twelve at the end of the day. Barmaids scurried from table to table and a new man stood behind the bar.

Though a mite more pleasant-looking, he still eyed me until I made my way upstairs with the confidence of any inn guest. After finding our room, I tried the knob and found it locked.

I knocked on the door and waited.

Indra's lovely face filled the gap that cracked open.

Though I smiled at first, when she looked up at me with uncharacteristic grimness I let the expression fall.

"What is it, Indra?"

"We were just wondering when you would come back...Rorke's here," she said, pushing the door wide while looking over her shoulder at someone. "Tell him everything."

While the door eased open, I stepped within and found myself amazed by what I found—or whom. The Mongoose's innkeeper stood with a dark expression, his arms crossed over his thin chest. Valeria had adopted a similar posture, leaning against the unsteady dresser on the bed's other side.

The mattress itself was host to Branwen and Odile— each of whom flanked none other than Lively of Soot.

I almost did not recognize Erdwud's wife for as reddened as her face had grown beneath the onslaught of tears, beneath the dirt of her journey, beneath the ashes of her home. To see me standing there, she ceased her weeping for only a few seconds—then another wave came on, stronger than ever, and she threw herself into my arms.

"Burningsoul," she cried, "sire! Please—Soot— help—"

"The gimlets," said Odile, glancing over at Branwen. "I told you they were bad news."

"They raided Soot—oh, the very day you lot left, they attacked the village in broad daylight and ransacked every building. Erdwud, oh! He tried to—he tried—Erduwd!"

With a violent sob, Lively pressed her tear-stained face to my breastplate and wept in a way that caused convulsions. My heart sinking into a great bog of remorse to think of Erdwud losing his life in such a sorry way—not to mention, to do so the same day I had left the town—I eased Lively gently upon the edge of the bed once again.

Kneeling before her, I took her hands in mine and told her, "It's all right to cry, Lively…I am so sorry."

While Lively dissolved into tears, the Mongoose's innkeeper—and, of course, Erdwud's friend—at last spoke up.

"She said they had a woman with 'em."

Remorse deepening, I looked at Sharp before turning my questioning gaze upon Valeria.

"Yes," agreed the Materna of the durrow, assessing me expectantly. "She was looking for you."

"Screaming and screaming and screaming," said Lively with a shudder, her hands lifting to either side of her forehead. Her eyes squeezed shut. ""Where's Burningsoul? Who's hiding the paladin? Bring me the slave of Weltyr!' On and on and on, every time she found a new person to scream at."

"And did you tell her?"

Nodding, Lively said, "When I heard her in our inn and Erdwud was cornered, I came downstairs. I said, 'He's not here! He's not here, he's gone to Skythorn!'"

"Did she believe you?"

"I think. But it didn't matter. This is my punishment, I know that it is! I ought not to have told you about her. She told me she'd keep Erdwud—all of Soot!—hostage to the gimlets until you came to meet her."

Relieved to hear that, at the very least, Erdwud may still have been alive, I patted Lively's hands.

"And so I shall—"

"Rorke!" Her eyes ringed with terror, Branwen leaned forward and said, "You can't! If this woman really is a faerie—"

"If she really is a faerie, then she'll be able to find me wherever I go…if that's what she really is, and what she wants is me, then it seems to me she's capable of far worse than what she's already accomplished in the name of opening a dialogue."

The embrace of Gundrygia's hot arms; the whispers that shook me, even without my clear recollection. It all rushed back while I knelt before Lively.

I confess to you and you alone, my friend: my heart was full of dread in that moment. I had been so glad to leave Soot behind! Not only because it meant that we were truly free of the shackles of the Nightlands.

In truth, I was glad to be away from Soot because I was frightened of Gundrygia. I was frightened of her knowledge; I was frightened of her power; I was frightened by my own yearning for her, which I had failed to recognize as such until the very moment I learned that I needed to see her again.

And Weltyr, finding my heart emptied by this fear, filled it up again with courage. Valeria, my prize from the underworld I escaped, knelt with me before Lively.

"I can promise you, Lively—if there is one man in all Urde capable of ridding Soot of its captor and liberating your husband, it is Rorke Burningsoul."

"He saved me, remember," said Branwen, who might have been ill-positioned with me in that moment but nonetheless received an appreciative nod in exchange for her vote of confidence.

"Yeah," agreed Odile. "As far as people who talk about religion all the time go, he's very dependable in battle."

Indra, clasping Lively's hands, added with a nod, "And kind! I'm sure he'll be happy to help you."

"Of course I will be," I told her, eliciting a few more tears of gratitude and a kindly little sob. "Yes, I will certainly be happy to help—but please, you all must be very careful in the city without me."

"You must let us come with you," Valeria insisted, her slim hand sliding along my shoulder.

Branwen nodded. "After last time, if she takes you away it could be forever."

"Someone has to stay here and be of comfort to you," I told Lively.

Odile, looking relieved to hear me say such a thing, suggested, "Aye, and someone has to buy those airship tickets."

"The airship is out," I told them, eliciting four sharp glances in my direction. "I'll explain it when I can—but to some of you, that may not be for a couple of days. I have to ride to Soot. Indra and Odile, why don't you two stay here with Lively. Valeria and Branwen, you two come with me."

While rising, I patted Lively's hand one last time. "You didn't walk here, surely, Lively?"

"I think she aimed to make me, but I walked to the Dardrie ranch and stole a horse. They didn't seem to be needing it, what with their being brought into town and made captive with the rest of us. Think the gimlets were planning to eat the horses…"

Watering eyes fixed upon me beneath her furrowed brow, Lively said, "What could they want, sire? Why would the gimlets attack after all this time?"

Leaning forward in her seat, she asked in a hoarse whisper, "What does she want with you, Master Rorke?"

How I wondered!

Yes, how I wondered. I wondered it in between all the other things I wondered. There got to be so much wondering flying about my head that I seemed to think of nothing at all. Instead I numbly washed my face and hands while Branwen packed up for us. Valeria, examining my stern countenance, pushed upon my shoulders until I sat at the edge of the bed. With Odile and Indra getting Lively settled down to sleep in their room, Valeria perched upon my knee and tenderly took the rag from me. After dipping it in the water and sponging my brow, she remarked, "This is quite some life you have brought me into, Burningsoul."

I chuckled softly, shutting my eyes as her delicate hand soothed my overheated skin. The armor lay to the side, at last removed for the time being. While Valeria's cooling cloth was guided down my neck and into my tunic, I assured her, "Before I went down to the Nightlands, nothing ever seemed to happen quite so fast…certainly not so—well, *busily*. Nor so dangerously. And that's not all—"

I was about to mention the duel when, amid little more than a brisk knock at the door, Odile let herself in with Indra upon her heel. "Out like a candle flame after a cave-in, the poor woman. She's exhausted."

I shook my head. "It sounds like she's lucky to be alive after her ordeal."

"No kidding." Folding her arms beneath her round breasts, Odile looked me over and asked with an arched brow, "Now—what's all this about not needing the airship anymore? I thought that was half of why we came here, or something."

185

"The information was only partly correct," I told them. "Grimalkin and Hildolfr stayed at the inn together, but they didn't really leave at the same time...and only one of them has the Scepter."

"Not the one you found, I imagine?" Odile rolled her eyes and rested her head back against the wall. "We're never going to get the ring back, are we?"

"Be patient, Odile," admonished the Materna, lifting my tunic and moving the cloth over the planes of my stomach. Her lovely eyes fixed upon me, Valeria said in a tone of adoration, "We must take these things one step at a time...though, *did you have an opportunity to ask after Roserpine's Ring, my love?*"

I shook my head and confessed, "Amid the trappings of Weltyr, I was focused on the Scepter only...and, well—I saw an old friend. I might have remembered to ask about it after, had it not been that I stepped into an altercation she was having..."

Pausing her soothing caresses to see the tense expression on my face, I explained, "She is being treated in a way that—well. It doesn't matter. It won't be an issue once I've defeated the Commander. We have a duel set for four days hence; I must return by then."

"My brave warrior," cooed Valeria. The rest of the women produced shocked noises ranging from worried to annoyed.

Indra leaned forward, her hand upon her heart. "A duel! Aren't you afraid, Rorke?"

"I'm only afraid for Elishta-bet if I don't make good on my challenge. She's being forced into an unjust marriage. I do not and cannot believe Weltyr will allow such a thing—especially not in his Church."

Odile tapped her foot. "So what will we do after this duel? Surely dueling isn't legal."

"Not conventionally," I said. "But within the confines of the Order, it is an acknowledged tradition. However...you are right to wonder what will happen after it's all over. I wonder, too. I do not think, given the stature man I have challenged, that I will be welcome into the Order one way or the other. In fact, it might very well take reclaiming the Scepter to earn anything approaching forgiveness."

"And if the trip to Soot takes longer, Rorke?" Branwen studied me with concern. "If we can't make it back here by the duel?"

I spread my hands. "We must. I suppose, if the gimlets haven't eaten the rest of the horses, we could trade off at Soot. Ride ours all night and all day save for small breaks, get there in 36 hours or so to deal with Gundrygia, and then switch out and ride back."

Scoffing, Branwen asked, "And what kind of condition will that leave you in for a fight?"

"If my victory be Weltyr's will," I told her, "then I will be in condition to win...whatever condition that is. As it happens, after I challenged Commander Zweiding to the duel, I found Grimalkin...and he had more to say than "

"O-oh?" Flush-faced at once, Branwen turned away to secure the strap of her pack. "And what did he say?"

"That he and Hildolfr had a disagreement, and Hildolfr walked away with the Scepter because Grimalkin wasn't interested in a fight...and he was willing to be bribed."

Odile, trying not to sound annoyed, asked, "So this Hildolfr is the one who has it?"

"It would seem so. Where he intends to take it, I don't know...but I also have no evidence or indication that he came here to Skythorn."

"Fantastic," sad Odile. "In other words, we're running in circles."

"Not so. If I win, the duel will be the perfect time for me to consult Father Fortisto again. He can guide me to Hildolfr and Roserpine's ring; it was his expertise in reading Weltyr's messages that led me to find Grimalkin."

After another dip of the rag in the bowl, Valeria pressed her breasts to my chest and repeated the operation of washing—now, under the back of my tunic. The scent of her hair and weight of her body produced a primitive ache that thrilled me beyond all reckoning. My hands slid over her thighs of their own volition while she told me, "When it be Roserpine's will that we find the ring, that is when we will find it...I am patient in these matters, and so is she."

"With all due respect, Your Holiness"—Odile leered at the scene developing before her, her hand sliding up the door jamb to hit the lock—"it seems to me like you didn't actually enjoy being the Materna anymore, and that you're just having fun running around with your boytoy...some of us had actual lives we'd like to get back to somebloom."

With a chuckle, Valeria enfolded me in her arms and slowly ground her body in my lap. I exhaled while, smiling into my face, she suggested, "And you will, of course, return to the Nightlands when it's the right time...but why not take advantage of the opportunities provided? These gifts from our gods...one must seize pleasures while they remain available."

I could not help my sigh. My hand slid up beneath the fabric of her dress and over the smooth, supple flesh of her rump. Tilting her head, Valeria kissed the corner of my mouth, the burning flesh of my cheek, the curve of my ear. The heat of her body inflamed mine and, while

Indra and Odile looked hungrily on, Valeria rocked to pleasure herself upon the aching protuberance yearning for freedom in my lap.

"That might be wise...you two, come here—surely you'll miss me when I'm gone..."

Though she snorted in a jovial fashion, Odile nonetheless strode forward and bent over me and Valeria. Her lips brushed mine and she said, "I don't know about missing you, Paladin...but I'll pray for your safe return."

I sighed with pleasure as Valeria pushed my tunic up and away. By the time my vision was once more unobstructed, smiling Indra had appeared to my right. She took her turn for a kiss while the Materna and Odile, each with their hands roving over me, glanced over at Branwen.

"Well?" Odile arched a brow expectantly. "You in, or out?"

For just a flash I wasn't sure if I even wanted her involved—not that the options of cuckolding or rejecting her were any better—but the bite of her supple pink underlip and the desire filling her eyes overwhelmed me. How dear she was to me! Amazing to think that Branwen was, strictly speaking, at least twice my age: she was selfish in the way children were selfish. Thoughtlessly, without malice. Somehow this notion made me pity her, and while she vacillated between the scene unfurling and the door to the room, I extended my hand.

"Come, Branwen...for all we know, this will be the last time I'll be able to hold you before a wicked faerie queen whisks me off to another world."

Savagely rolling her eyes, Branwen kicked off her boots and climbed upon the small bed with us. Her lips struggled against a smirk until they drooped over me. Then, they parted for a kiss.

I obliged with joy, reaching up to caress her face and the long blond locks that tumbled around me when Valeria let down Branwen's elegant mane. Soon she moaned softly against my mouth, her pleasure produced not just by our kiss: Odile and Indra lifted hands from me to caress her, and a look of the most delicious embarrassment crossed her reddening face.

She was only able to look reluctant for a few seconds. While the durrow undressed Branwen amid sensual caresses, Odile caught the point of her chin and drew her close for a consuming kiss. I watched with unabashed satisfaction, knowing my observation heightened her embarrassment and subsequently her pleasure. When she glimpsed me in the middle of turning to kiss Indra, it were as though she checked to make sure I still watched.

The thought of such a thing made me all the more hungry for her and the other women around me—for Valeria in my lap, who rose only to help me remove my boots and breeches before sliding out of her own clothes. The sumptuous globes of her dark breasts, already struggling to be contained in Lively's old dress, burst from their confines. Her nipples were beaded with excitement, and while her eyes flickered often to the scene with Branwen behind me, she climbed upon my lap and let the soft flesh of her sex brush my exposed nerves.

How wet she was! Valeria's performative nature thrilled me as much as her generous heart. She pushed me down gently upon the bed, that treasure at the apex of her thighs poised to tease the organ of my lust while together we watched as Branwen was pleasured by the rogues.

Odile, by kisses and caresses, guided Branwen down upon the pillows and with Indra's help divested the high elf of her underthings. When naked, Branwen gasped and attempted to lay hands between all our hungry eyes and the rosy tips of her breasts or the patch of fuzz crowning the cleft between her legs. She did not try very hard to keep them there and in fact seemed thrilled when Odile and Indra each caught a hand and exposed her to our eyes. Indra, squeezing between her pale legs, sighed with pleasure up at her friend.

"Oh, Odile! She's dripping. Look"—the younger durrow spread Branwen's labia for her friend—"she loves to be watched almost as much as the Materna!"

"I'd think a thing like that to be impossible," commented Odile, reaching down with her free hand and experimentally tickling her fingers along the displayed flower of bright pink petals and shimmering dew. The durrow's eyes widened and she laughed, saying, "Why! Maybe you're right, Indra."

"Please," whimpered Branwen, "please, oh, it's so embarrassing—"

"But you like being embarrassed, don't you..." Chuckling evilly, Odile slowly worked Branwen's clitoris beneath the tip of her finger. The high elf moaned to be so indulged. "Sure you do...you want to be used by all of us. Watched by Rorke as we get you nice and excited for him."

Gasping, moaning, Branwen made a feeble protest while Odile slipped a pair of fingers slowly into the hot heart of her femininity. While the high elf's bare toes curled with delight, one foot twisted out toward me. I caught it in my hand and kissed the delicate arch, yielding a sharper moan of surprise from her as I caressed my way down to her toes. Valeria, meanwhile, worked her wet vulva slowly over my length, teasing back and forth but not yet taking me into her. Occasionally her hand would lower to press my head just to her quivering entrance, and she would pump me against herself before reaching down to tickle my testicles.

Together we marveled at the sight of Odile's dark fingers working steadily in and out of pale pink Branwen, each of us more inspired by the second. When those fingers were removed and Indra bent down to her apply her mouth to the task, Valeria at last lowered herself upon my aching cock.

While my fingers sank into her thighs we moaned as one, the pleasure that rushed through the both of us no doubt equal in its sublimity. As much as it relieved me to find her soft body so tight and wet around me, it paradoxically served, as always, to deepen the ache. One hand lifting from her thigh to again press Branwen's dainty toes to my mouth, I watched how this sweetened the high elf's pleasure and couldn't help but count her lucky. With Indra's tender kisses between her legs, Odile suckling at her nipples and caressing her breasts, and my mouth at work upon her foot while the woman who rode me moaned in approval, Branwen was no doubt in a state of ecstasy.

Indeed, she thrashed wildly—but, for as enraptured as she was, she never looked away from the sight of Valeria writhing upon my prick, her dark body working up and down and her magnificent breasts bouncing with every self-impalement along my length. So far as I could tell, Branwen's eyes themselves were an outlet of pleasure equal to, or perhaps exceeding, all the others. The longer she took in the sight of me fucking another woman, the greater her pleasure grew until it overflowed from her with a cataclysmic cry of bliss.

Odile playfully hushed her, saying, "Remember Lively next door now, friend..."

"Oh," gasped Branwen, the sight of whose orgasm had inspired Valeria's sudden clamping and shuddering around me, "oh—yes, of course, I'm sorry—"

"Never apologize for pleasure," moaned Valeria, her own climax washing over her in a series of waves that left her nearly stuttering. "Ah! Oh, Burningsoul, you are hard tonight…"

"I had to go to a brothel to find Grimalkin today… you wouldn't believe the ladies that were there."

"And yet you saved all that rich, hot seed of yours for us…all the pleasures of this cock. What a good man you are, Rorke." Laughing, Valeria pushed her streams of white hair back over her shoulder and dismounted me with a shudder, a strand of her liquid pleasure connecting us until it broke. "Go on…put it to use on pretty Branwen."

As if snapped from a trance by her orgasm, Branwen began to sit up while saying, "Oh! No—that's all right, I really should go get some food for the trip—"

Odile pushed Branwen back down, face contorted in a wicked grin. While Branwen gasped and gazed upon her with a crimson face, she tried to gently extricate herself from the dark elf's grasp. She was quickly unsuccessful, as, given her strength, Odile had no trouble wrangling the high elf's hand and pinning it by the forearm beneath one thick leg. Even slender Indra had no trouble subduing Branwen's other arm, however, or holding wide her legs to display her sex for my hungry eye.

"Don't be shy, Branwen," encouraged Odile. "You've watched him fuck all of us…but only Valeria's gotten to see you get fucked by him."

"You told them about that!" Blushing furiously, Branwen bit her lip and whined, squirmed, keened with pleasure just to have her free leg touched by Valeria's hand. The Materna, chuckling, finding only desire in Branwen's eyes amid her faux protests, drew wide this other leg and teased the flesh of Branwen's pretty thigh.

"There are those, Branwen, for whom inhibitions are so powerful that their most heartfelt desire is to have their barriers broken down as if against their will. I know how it must excite you to think of me sharing stories about your body…just as it excites you to be offered for Rorke's use. Go on, Burningsoul."

I must admit: with the three durrow holding her down and keeping her spread-eagle in offering to me, Branwen looked more erotic, more gorgeous, and more aroused than I'd ever seen her. A few locks of blonde hair fell across her blushing cheek, her lower lip hidden behind her topmost row of teeth as she gazed into my face. While I sat up, Valeria's free hand gently spread Branwen's labia to display her.

"Come, Paladin…fill this pretty little high elf with cum for us."

Such a suggestion would have been impossible to resist even if I'd wanted to do such a thing, rest assured! Finding Branwen's face shone with anticipation and hope, I knelt before the offered altar of Anroa's passion. Weltyr's gift to the world—that rose whose loveliness possessed the capacity to make me overlook, from the heights of passion, any flaw or wickedness in any woman, so long as her body was beautiful, and her embrace, eager.

And Branwen certainly possessed both those qualities. With the durrow kissed and caressed us, still with Branwen's limbs held apart, I buried myself inside of her and felt her body flood from the first penetration. She moaned, obviously humiliated to be so excited by this exhibitionism, and lowered her eyes from me. Odile, who was an expert in the use of cruelty to sweeten pleasure, caught the high elf by the hair and forced her head back to ensure that her eyes had nowhere to rest but upon us.

We fought well as a team; it was only fitting that we should love well as a team. While Branwen squirmed beneath us, the durrow and I pleasured her from stem to stern. I plowed deeper into her tight embrace by the thrust; and while her eyelids fluttered to feel my flesh slap against hers with each complete penetration, the durrow kissed her, me, one another, all the time cajoling and caressing. Branwen particularly responded to their blandishments, each teasing admonishment from Odile and every appreciative compliment from Indra coaxing a flutter out of the sheath that squeezed my blade.

Each thrust seemed to leave her wetter, tighter. By the time she was enjoying her second orgasm, she had once again forgotten all about poor Lively next door and screamed my name with abandon. Her body arched up to mine and I took her hard, my prick—having been covered first in Valeria's arousal and now in lovely Branwen's—leaving her with a far more powerful orgasm than anything she'd had from Indra's tongue. The divine creature trembled on the bed while we all enjoyed the sight together, her breasts heaving with the panting rhythm of her breath.

"What a nymph she is," cried Odile with approval and delight. "A real sylph…I could look at her all day. No wonder you've been able to see past her bad behavior!"

"Well," I confessed with a wink as I withdrew to take into my arms Indra, who hurried into my embrace for a turn. "I did give her something of a spanking back in the Nightlands…"

Tickled with wicked hilarity, all three durrow laughed in delight.

"Did you *really?*" Valeria asked this of me with a

twinkle in her eyes. I couldn't help my smirk while traitorous but irresistible Branwen sputtered in embarrassment.

"I did indeed," I said, helping Indra out of her bustier and then her leather breeches. "How is it you think I got over her indiscretion in the first place? Not that she didn't enjoy it..."

"Oh, well!" Quite thrilled, Odile sat against the headboard of the bed and dragged Branwen over with little effort. I laughed, bending to kiss Indra while the elder of the two rogues pulled the high elf over her lap so her pert, white rear was exposed in the air.

"You should have said something sooner, Rorke," chided Odile, shifting her leg over both of Branwen's so the high elf's knees were pinned between the dark one's thighs. Her hand caressed Branwen's rump and the high elf moaned at the contact. "I love to give a naughty elf-girl a spanking...reminds me of home! You'd make such a fine slave, Branwen."

"Oh," was all Branwen could say as Odile's hand struck sharply to work. While the round cheek's flesh bounced beneath Odile's hand and the high elf to which it was attached squealed away, Valeria wiggled over to land a few swats of her own. I grinned and continued my caresses of Indra, making myself comfortable in her body just as Odile said, "Hey, Burningsoul—remember to save some strength for me."

13

SOOT, AGAIN

IT'S TRUE THAT, when a man puts so much energy into the satisfaction of four exquisite, sensual women, he doesn't have much energy left for anything else—but there would be time for me to doze in the saddle of my horse. I closed my eyes for all of two hours when our bodies were worn by the richness of our love, willing to wait to leave until the darkness was thick and easy on Valeria's eyes.

But that same Materna of the durrow, already given to hyper-vigilant bouts of sleeplessness due to her long history of narrowly avoiding assassination, was awake to caress my chest and face when the time was right. Her damp lips trailed over my ear, sensuality second-nature to her even in the most serious of moments. The soft whisper of her voice was a balsam carried on a sweet, damp wind, and it caressed me awake amid the warm bodies that slept around me.

"It's time to go, Burningsoul, my love."

I wished nothing more than to shut my eyes and bask forever in the cool indulgence of her whisper, but she was right. There was no more time to waste. Now that night had fallen heftily upon Skythorn, we needed to leave at once.

Valeria tugged my hand and drew me from the bed. I blinked myself from sleep to find her already dressed. She had arranged my clothes upon a nearby chair and, with eyes perfectly accustomed to the darkness of the room, the Materna of El'ryh set about dressing me.

There was a kindness to Valeria—a nurturing quality that, I suppose, had made her such a caring and hands-on ruler of her people. No doubt she had not truly been required, per se, to hold court with her subjects. She could just as easily have hired a magician or sorcerer with talents similar to the perceptive qualities of Roserpine's Ring and permitted them to handle the matter of slave appraisal.

Instead she had been interested in their lives as sentient beings. Instead, she had been looking for me.

When at last I was dressed, I bent to embrace her. She paused in surprise before melting into my arms.

"I'm glad you've come to the surface with me, Valeria," I told her so softly I could barely perceive my own words. Her sensitive ears caught every last syllable and her breath hitched in her emotion. "I have to admit... I'm not looking forward to finding your ring."

Her face pressed against my tunic. Her head lowered a few degrees. She said nothing, but her grip around me tightened. I felt a great pain, a great fear, that I tried to push way until Branwen stirred and did it for me.

"Oh," she murmured with a mighty sigh, "is it time to leave?"

Soon we were, all three of us, leaving Skythorn in the dark of night. Our horses, having no doubt taken better advantage of their rest hours than we did, seemed ready to get on the road and out of the poorly maintained rental facility. Odile had resentfully awoken just to present us with her lantern, and I was so bedraggled for want of sleep that I did not remember to ask her if she knew anything about this "Lantern of Hamsunt" before we left. However, I consoled myself. Surely she knew nothing; perhaps less than that. It had been Kyrie the wadjita who sold her the lantern, after all. Where Kyrie had gotten it remained unclear, but I had the feeling it was not, as the durrow had been told, a matter of scavenging. That spirit-thief, Al-listux, seemed to have something to do with it...but what?

More useless wondering.

The darkness was muddled with lamplight and torches of all kinds throughout the city, but once we were outside of it, the night sky was a deep velvet tapestry. Valeria rode our first mile with her chin craned so high that I worried she might fall backward off the horse—but, oh, her mystified smile as she admired the ocean of constellations! By Weltyr, it was a more beautiful sight than any distant nebula.

Branwen's countenance was much more stoic after a certain point. She had been light-hearted owing to the successful distraction of our fun time in the Mongoose's bed, but as we drew farther from the city the happy memory faded into angst.

"You really don't know any reason why this woman might want your audience, Rorke?"

I glanced over at the high elf's question, shaking my head. "Not the slightest. If it's desire, then I can assure you both this is a woman so beautiful she, like either of you, could lay claim to any man in all the land. I do not think looks have any bearing on it."

"Is it because you woke her up?"

My hands spread nearly of their own accord. "Perhaps. I truly couldn't say...she is a cruel woman, exceptionally cruel. If it is my love she wants, I can't imagine giving it to her of my own free will. Not even in the confines of slavery."

Of course, having already seen how quickly my ire could flip over to love with Branwen, I ought not to have made this statement with quite so much confidence. Simply speaking of Gundrygia evoked the feeling of her body in my arms—ah, the soft aroma of her flesh!

Yes, I did indeed feel as though I had been enchanted. Even then, riding toward her, I seemed in the throes of an action not of my free will. Rather, going to her was something into which I had been tricked...or, more aptly, forced. For, my first duty being to Weltyr, I had no choice but defend innocents in his name when they came to me for help. Though I did so with a warm heart, I could not shake the chilling sense of awe that gripped me when I thought of doing battle with the powerful sorceress.

So I thought, instead, of Weltyr. Of the Scepter, out there somewhere in Hildolfr's possession. How was I to go about the business of finding it? My Father's world was vast beyond all measure. Those that called it small had simply lost their sense of scale amid the synchronistic meetings and connections they had observed over time. The truth was that there were nearly infinite places for a man to go...especially a man in possession of a relic as valuable as the Scepter.

But it was not a mere thing of gold and gems. It was no mere totem or magical artifact. It was more than that, I was quite certain. Like Valeria's ring, it held some power that I had not yet detected—that, perhaps, only a few had ever detected. I glanced down at the lantern, pondering its ability to repel lesser monsters and unintelligent animals of the surface.

"Branwen," I said, "do you know anything about magical relics?"

"Hm…well, a thing or two, I guess. What do you want to know?"

"I've been wondering about Valeria's ring. And, of course, the Scepter…especially after talking to Grimakin. He claimed it inspired greed in Hildolfr—that the old man got it into his possession and was changed at once."

"He did seem very different once we left you behind," Branwen confessed. "I thought it was because he regretted what we did to you. We all did, I think, but…"

Her eyes fell away and I glanced forward, suddenly unable to look her straight-on. "Yes, well, what's done is done. Perhaps he regretted what happened, or perhaps he was driven blind with greed by the Scepter…perhaps you all were, even before setting hand on it. What was it Grimalkin was petitioning you for when I met you two, exactly?"

"Oh," she said with an absent wave of her hand, "he wanted me to help him find work. Some silly nonsense about dreams promising him riches…imagine doing something like flying all the way across the world just because a dream told you to!"

Valeria and I exchanged a glance at that.

"I don't know," I said, maintaining a casual tone. "I think that prophetic dreams are more common than most would have them. I've had an odd one recently, myself."

Looking at me all the more sharply to hear such a thing, Valeria asked, "Have you?"

I nodded. "While we were all still in the Nightlands,

I had the strangest experience. There was a dream where I was viewing the hivemind of the spirit-thieves. Where it was located, I couldn't rightly say. It looked like some kind of heinous tumor submerged in a flooded chamber. Someone opened a door to feed it."

I considered mentioning that the voice of the caretaker had noticeably resembled my own, but I neither wanted to alarm them nor encourage them to write it all off as a mere assemblage of the day's stresses and the morrow's worries. Therefore, I refrained from additional details except to say, "The hivemind urged me to be more critical of the institutions around me...though I must confess that, when I consider the source, my kneejerk reaction is to close my eyes and ears and be less critical than ever before."

"Have you ever had a dream like this before?" Valeria studied me closely, adding, "Or since?"

"Not that I can recall...and I think I would recall something this vivid, this strange. No...it was the only time. I suspect it has something to do with Al-listux. Back in your palace chambers, Valeria, when your guard came to my aid, the spirit-thief was attempting to enlist me to its baleful service. It had just begun the process of zombifying me—"

Ears perking with renewed interest, Branwen asked, "What's that?"

"Zombies," answered Valeria, "are the personality-less servants of spirit-thieves. Empty vessels. Any being whose mind is invaded by spirit-thieves can become a zombie. They roam around doing the bidding of the demon who made them, completely oblivious and unconscious, generally responsible for only the most basic tasks like guarding a location or collecting brains for their masters' suppers. Once someone has been changed by a spirit-thief, they are effectively dead...there is no bringing them back without very advanced magic, and even then they may never be quite right."

With a shudder, Branwen shook her head. "I'd rather be a slave in El'ryh for a thousand years than a spirit-thief's zombie, I think."

"We would make it very fun for a slave as cute as you," said Valeria in a teasing tone that faded quickly back to serious concern for her appraisal of my vision. "It is very possible, yes, that this is some side effect of the spirit-thief's assault...though, I admit I have not heard of such a thing before."

"Well, most who have a close enough encounter to get a tentacle in the ear don't manage to get away. I was lucky Fiora was there to help me—I hope she isn't in too much trouble back in the Nightlands."

Valeria stared grimly forward to think of the guard who submitted her armor at the Materna's command. Shaking her head, the leader of the durrow said, "I must find that ring as soon as I can," and did not see how the mere thought, spoken aloud, was as painful as any arrow through my heart.

I understood her dilemma. Her duty was first and foremost to her people, for without her to act as a figurehead they may well have already begun to lose their sense of unity. Surely El'ryh as a whole was thrown into chaos to think its leader had disappeared. I hated the thought of all the people there suffering...but, selfishly, I hated even more the thought of losing Valeria.

And Branwen, too. Now that I had spoken to Grimalkin and learned what he claimed to be the truth, I thought about prodding her on why she had really come back to me...but would it have done any good? Further—whatever reason Branwen thought she had returned to me, did that matter when the true reason was Weltyr's will? Her behavior was selfish, yes, it was true. But the longer we journeyed together, the more she opened her heart to me. That heart would change, or not, (or already had, I hoped) in accordance with Weltyr's designs.

I did not question Branwen, then, lest I sour the mood or give her too much to think about. I wanted her prime for a battle and, most importantly, on my side. She had acquired a new crossbow in my absence with Gundrygia, and, when she practiced with it during our few breaks along that long trip back the way we had come, I couldn't help but notice her aim was on something of a hot streak.

It was a true relief to know I had with me someone who could, if nothing else, hit a target when I needed her to. Valeria was good in a support role, but I wasn't exactly keen to test her skills in combat anytime soon. My exchange for access to her healing and empowering magics would be keeping an eye on her for the duration of any conflict…and that was a potentially steep cost, however worthwhile.

The highway from Soot to Skythorn and back again was one that would have been treacherous were it not so well-maintained. In fact, even with this maintenance in mind, I am sure many still lost their lives—and yet it was still, is still, the most beautiful region through which my travels have borne me. Our first time, Valeria had not been able to appreciate the sights around her. We had passed through during the daytime hours and, as a result, the most beautiful parts of the trip were those when she had been forced to keep her eyes shaded by her hood and a pair of welding goggles.

Now, however, as we passed from the long stretches of farmland north of Skythorn and into the superlative mountains of the Cascadian wilderness, we did so in the evening hours of our journey's second day. Her face filled with wonder, Valeria dared risk her eyes to behold the mountains of Weltyr's careful sculpting. Glorious works crafted over time, with weather and fire and the interference of mankinds: all those tools with which the All-Father artfully coaxes the emergence of eternity from temporal existence. The mountains through which we followed long highways, with little rest for our poor horses or ourselves, were well worth the harrowing reason for our journey back through them.

Although, I must admit, my heart was still filled with fear to see Valeria drawing back her hood when even a twinkling of Weltyr's light still tinged the sky. And, in a paradox, the opposite feeling rose up at once: pleasure seized me to see her in sunlight for the first time, even if heavily filtered. Every rich hint of obsidion, almost bluish undertone to her flesh was evident against the turquoise-pink sky that melted into orange fire between the mountains. Those splendid hills, awash in seas of emerald fir trees, formed a sensual bed for the encroaching night. Their soft frame loaned a reassuring quality to the glittering darkness that promised, as always, to swallow the landscape.

But the loveliest color of all was that which I found in Valeria's eyes. Squinting at first in the low light of evening through which we rode, soon they managed to relax into the vision surrounding us. To my astonishment, I found that durrow did indeed have both irises and pupils. Against the pale lilac of her eyes, I marveled to recognize a white disk and, within that, a pupil roughly the same hue as her sclera. The effect was so subtle I wondered if it always appeared as such to the sensitive subterranean elves. I worried, too, that its appearance was the sign of some damage, and remembered Odile's story of the blind durrow bard with grim concern. Valeria reassured me.

"My pupils? Of course they're always there, Paladin. Your eyes are too poor! Just like your ears. Who knows what else you're missing in the world?"

"That may be so…but what are we going to do if you go blind?"

"Once, in light like this, won't hurt me…and Roserpine will heal anything she desires to be healed. To see a thing like this is my reward for following her will… you understand that, I'm sure."

I did, indeed, understand that. Valeria was part of my own reward for following the divine commands that ordained my path. I could not help but feel, therefore, a certain impulse to protect her from her own decisions. Of course I knew that she was not some object to be carefully withheld from the world…

But, given what we were coming up against, I could hardly help my concern for her wellbeing.

There was no telling what would happen once we reached Soot, nor what state it would be in. Lively had precious little information on the subject since she was tossed out at the height of the gimlet invasion. With nothing to go on, we had to keep our eyes open some miles from the town. We were not far from Dardrie Ranch when the signs of devastation began to take hold.

Tucked as it was amid the mountains, Soot was frequently foggy for long hours. However, as the horses dutifully carried us into the mountains cloaked in night, the cool and fresh mountain air was soon stained by the hard-edged scent of fire. When Valeria commented on the lack of stars, it occurred to me that the problem was not fog, but smoke; and, as we rounded the turn of a pass and saw Soot as a small scatter of lights off in the distance, Valeria gasped in horror to see what Branwen and I could not.

"The fields! Oh, Rorke—I think they've been scorched—"

With her own sharp intake of breath to hear such a horror, Branwen listed forward on her exhausted mare. "Is that what we've been smelling all this time? I thought I was dreaming it."

I shook my head. "I've smelled it, too. I guess we'd better hope Dardrie Ranch is still standing."

Praise Weltyr, it was. We left our horses tied in a thicket of trees about two miles south of the ranch and let them take a well-earned rest in relative safety. With them obscured in the trees and further protected by a fence of brambles that sprang from the ground on our druid's command, we turned Odile's lantern down to the bare minimum required for Branwen and I to see. Then, together, we three made our slow way to Dardrie Ranch.

Until we were near enough to see lights glowing in the windows of the ranch house, the value of Valeria's sensitive eyes had not fully occurred to me. Her arm extended out across my chest and stopped me in place. With a sharp hush, she peered into the darkness and whispered in a tone so quiet I strained to hear it, "Those must be your gimlets."

Amazed that she could see them, I shut the lantern off entirely and asked, "Where are they?"

"Running about, doing something—wood," she discerned at last. "A few are scurrying back and forth with logs of wood. Carrying them into the house."

"Trying to burn it down? The fiends!" I drew Strife at once, outraged and horrified to think of the poor Dardries. Like most of the citizens of Soot, they were simple folk who made an honest living and, so far as I could tell, bore ill will to none. They had been very lenient to us, we strangers, when renting horses, even given Erdwud's good word; and they had asked no questions, nor shown any negative inclination toward the rumors of the durrow ladies allegedly in my company.

I made my way to the property with my sword drawn. A kneejerk reaction—based, I see in retrospect, on emotion. At the time, bedraggled by our long travel, a seemingly endless chain of conflicts, and the fears Lively related to us about her husband and the people of Soot, I was not in any mood to patiently wait and see how things developed. Valeria whispered in a sharp tone after me, "There's surely more than just the two I've seen rushing in and out!"

"Then let me lead," I told her, moving at a semi-crouch through the darkness and around the perimeter of the ranch's burned property.

Though Weltyr did not bless humanity with the sensitive dark vision of the durrow, he did see fit to allow gradual adaptation to the night. Therefore, in the absence of the enchanted lantern, I (and, I would imagine, Branwen) saw more of the property by the second. Shapes distinguished themselves from the darkness, aided by illumination in windows and something that I discerned quickly to be the stable's stalls outlined in the structure of an outbuilding.

Behind it all, the town still a mile off glowed as it never did so late at night. While I feared a fire yet burned there, my priority was preventing a new one.

Luckily, we would be able to get from one place to another fairly quickly. We made it to the stable building undetected and crouched behind it on the side opposite the house. The horses had not been slaughtered yet, it seemed, and could be heard softly snorting and occasionally pawing the earth as they settled in for the night. While I wondered how it was that the terrain could be so scorched while the buildings remained untouched along with their animal inhabitants, another noise from within the stable made us all tense up.

The yelp of a gimlet, chittering away as though laughing.

With a hard look back at Branwen and Valeria, I nodded. Lifting her crossbow, Branwen nodded at me in return, then toward the open door of the softly lit stables. I indicated for Valeria to remain where she was.

Strife raised, I swiftly rounded the doorway—

And startled the gimlet who, poised upon a stool, giggled to himself while petting the nose of one of the Dardrie horses.

The little fellow shrieked and fell from the seat that had boosted him up to the mare. While the horse whinnied with its own surprise, I faltered in the doorway and looked with open-mouthed surprise at the finding. Branwen, who had been about to hurry in behind me, bumped into my back and fell upon her heel.

"What's the problem?" She peered around me and lifted her crossbow, but I raised a hand to halt her.

"Wait, you didn't see him. Look! They haven't hurt a single horse!"

"So?"

"I think he was petting that mare over there—hey, sh. It's all right, my friend."

Seeing how the quivering gimlet had scrambled to his knees and clasped his hands for mercy, I sheathed my blade and showed my empty hands. The pupils of his watery lizard eyes grew more prominent, his fear fading to relief but his hands still clasped—now, to his heart. A terrible guilt washed over me for having charged in; I thanked Weltyr for giving me time and insight enough to spare the life of the creature who did not seem ill-disposed to life. The Bright God had truly answered my prayer for his help in dealing rightly with other beings. At least, he had begun to.

"There," I said, "now...I'm sorry to have surprised you, friend. Can you understand me? Do you understand the common tongue?"

The gimlet nodded. I must confess I marveled a little at that, having expected to go through the process of some difficult interpretation to make communication even a remote possibility. What a relief to know that was not the case! I sighed aloud, in fact, and gestured toward the house.

"Are those your friends in there?"

Again, the gimlet nodded.

"What's your name?"

The creature yelped.

I grimaced back at Branwen.

Lightly clearing my throat, said as politely as I could, "Well, "Yelp""—Yelp laughed at my approximation of his name, and I think we both felt somewhat more at ease with one another from then on—"my name is Rorke Burningsoul, and—"

But Yelp's eyes grew wide in disbelief. The little gimlet, barely tall enough to reach my chest, scurried up to grab my hand—all while jabbering so excitedly in his doglike voice that the horses grew uneasy and shifted in their stalls. While Branwen soothed the nearest one with a practiced hand and a loving whisper, the gimlet led me outside and pointed with his free hand at the glowing town.

"What about Soot, friend?"

Yelp pointed at his chest, then at me. Mid-gesture

toward the town, he grew startled by motion in the dark. The gimlet leapt between me and Valeria, a short growl on his muzzle. I tried not to laugh, but Valeria did so openly.

"You make friends very quickly, Burningsoul…it is your finest quality."

"I'd be inclined to agree with you, were the same not true of enemies…it's all right, Yelp. Valeria is—my mate." My choice of label earned a sizzling glance from the durrow while I happened to note Branwen's profile in the darkness of the stable. "One of them, anyway."

"A*ha*," the gimlet hilariously enthused, elbowing me with a wiggle of the crests above his eyes. He barked and yelped out a few more chains of laugh-like syllables before waving toward the town with both little lizard paws again.

Finally, I gathered. "You want us to go with you?"

Yelp nodded, tapping the tip of his nose, then pointing again to the town. I rubbed my jaw and asked him, "Why?"

Now it was his turn to look rather thoughtful. Tapping his chin with one finger, the little lizard-dog-man then gestured toward the ranch house. He cocked his head questioningly. I nodded.

"We did intend to go in there, yes. You and your friends can't stay in the Dardrie house."

With a hefty sigh, the gimlet nodded as if to say he had known that all along, but that it had been a good time while it lasted. Gesturing with his hands that I stay behind, Yelp turned and took some steps toward the house.

I followed.

Hearing the steps I took, in part due to the plate mail, the gimlet stopped and turned with a bark. Perhaps he expected me to stop. I continued on. Yelp uttered another noise, a shocked little mewl somehow closer to a cat than a dog. He hurried up to me and tugged on my arm, unable to stay me by gripping me and digging in his heels. When he saw my companions following us, he panicked and hurried up to the open back door of the house.

Owing to last time, I did not draw Strife, and I was glad I didn't.

Were I not concerned about the welfare of the Dardrie family, I would have found the scene somewhat charming—even comical. As it stood, I couldn't help but find the sight of these gimlets pretending they were citizens of Soot to be somehow very morbid.

No evidence of the Dardries' actual presence was immediately clear to me. That was a point of great concern when I stepped into the living room and found a pair of gimlets stoking the hearth, yammering before the fire until Yelp successfully interrupted them with a wave of his arms and an urgent series of noises. They looked up—as did the one who, from Mr. Dardrie's armchair, investigated the luminous illustrations of a printing press-quality book that completely swamped the creature's small lap. This gimlet uttered a shriek to see me, the volume falling from its knobby knees. Only after a few iterations of Yelp's frantic patter did they cautiously relax.

One last lizard-creature appeared from the doorway to the kitchen, Mrs. Dardrie's apron trailing around its waist in a fashion closer to an award banner at a village festival than a protective cooking garment. The spoon clutched in its hand dripped brown stew fairly close to the color of its wide eyes: aside from this so-called implement, not one of them was armed...though now

I had to wonder if the brown trousers rolled up around Yelp's knees really were his own.

After moving from tense face to tense face, I looked back at Yelp. "Where is the Dardrie family?"

The gimlets populating the house exchanged a glance. All of them, Yelp included, shook their heads or shrugged in variation.

Exhaling in displeasure, I looked at the one with the spoon and said, "Finish your supper, then get out of this house and leave its animals alone."

The pair who had been seeing to the fire took my command immediately, scurrying past us to stumble out the door and vanish off into the night. Yelp, looking relieved that I was reasonable, said a few hasty things to his friends before hurrying to the door, himself. Rather than passing through, he paused on the threshold and gestured that we should follow him.

This time, we did. We had planned to take the horses, but if the gimlets were open to persuasion and all (or even most) could understand the common tongue as well as the ones in the Dardrie house, coming in on horseback would add an unnecessary element of intimidation. Given how jumpy the creatures were—and how many there must have been to have successfully captured the town and held it for almost five days—anything I could do to reduce the odds of conflict would be a certain boon.

After all...there was going to be enough conflict with their leader.

When the city was, as Elishta-bet sometimes said, a stone's throw away, we were relieved to see that the inundation of light was not from houses that stood ablaze. There did seem to be some wild bonfire burning in the town square if the halo of light arcing in the sky was any indication, but the vast majority of the light we had seen from the distance appeared to be from lamps and lanterns and candles and all manner of other things left burning in the houses.

And inside all these brightly lit houses, moving about as though the properties were theirs and they had done such things for years, were the gimlets.

But they were not just in the houses, we were soon to find. As we penetrated the boundary of Soot with our guide hurrying along the road before us, other gimlets became apparent moving about the streets. They went to and fro much like the ones Valeria reported before the farmhouse.

These, however, carried items other than firewood. In the hands of one, for instance, I noticed a small box from which dangled a necklace fit with a small sapphire—perhaps the only item of value that the true owner of that box would ever possess. Another hurried with a few printed books, and one bore a thick fur coat plundered from someone's closet.

If they noticed us in their single-minded scurrying, they were far less afraid than the gimlets in the Dardrie farmhouse. I suspect their numbers gave them confidence. All around us, more lizard-eyes peered from cobblestone alleys and dusty panes of window glass. The town pulsed with activity due entirely to the little robbers.

And I speculated wildly as to their intentions for us, for the town, for the citizens—until, at last, we emerged in the village square to stand before Gundrygia.

14

THE WANDERER

I DID NOT see her at first. The blaze of the bonfire raging in the square was so bright, so feverish, that it blinded me. And imagine poor Valeria! While the durrow hissed and threw her hands over her wincing face, I struggled to take stock of gimlets numbering fifty or more.

Some playing flutes of bone and drums of animal hide, they danced and skipped and barked in jubilation around their fire—and, my eyes soon allowed me to perceive, a throne produced with pieces of furniture plundered from the cottages of Soot. Tables had been interconnected and chairs overturned so that the central seat rose high before the flames. The gimlet with the jewelry box scrambled expertly up this artificial incline and knelt at the left hand of the throne. There Gundrygia, resplendently arranged in a bright gown she had surely made with magic rather than condescending to steal, reclined like the languid sovereign she certainly was.

"At last! At last—my knight has arrived. Hail, Paladin!" The drumming reduced to a steady beat as, permitting the gimlet to scale her throne and hang the necklace around her pale throat, Gundrygia called, "Hail, Burningsoul. Look, my little treasures! Your brother, Yelp, has brought the finest offering of all."

A few of the lizards howled in delight and ran to embrace Yelp, who wagged his tail like a pleased canine to receive the adulation of his friends. Despite several glances from Branwen, I kept Strife sheathed for now. I am glad to say that, unlike her, Valeria was diplomatic when it came to towns held hostage by strange witches and the lizard people they controlled.

"We understand you called for Rorke," Valeria answered on my behalf, gesturing to me. "That you are holding this town and its innocent people captive to have an audience with him."

"Yes," answered the witch in a droll tone. "With him…not with his companions. But, why, what is that you have there?"

Gundrygia leaned forward in her seat, gesturing toward the lantern that I had begun to suspect was a sacred artifact seeded among our party by forces with ulterior motives. Valeria lifted it and assured the witch, "Only the light by which we've traveled here. It keeps wolves at bay, and worse things, too."

"A pity it won't protect you from my children. Go on! Take the lantern for me."

The time for diplomacy passed that fast; that fast, I brandished Strife. It and I pushed between Valeria and the mob of gimlets that rushed her, but too many came from too many sides for my bluff to count. A few of the scoundrels snatched the lantern from her hand; still others disarmed Branwen and carried her new crossbow off to parts unknown. They knew better than to even look at the sword in my hands.

While the druid cursed them in the name of Anroa, Gundrygia laughed at a high and glimmering pitch.

"How easy it is when you won't attack, Burningsoul… they are dear creatures, aren't they?"

Sweeping the tip of my blade around us to give us some space from the crowd, I let both women press against my back while I told the witch, "They can be, when they act in accordance with Weltyr's laws and not at the behest of a wild pagan woman. What are you to them? Why should they have any call to serve you?"

Her painted lips contorting into a parody of a pout, Gundrygia leaned toward the gimlet hurrying up with the lantern in his hands.

"It's annoying to see how much a man can forget sometimes…but, then again, you were very upset. I created the gimlets, Burningsoul. Gimlets, and many other things besides…none of which, I found, any being of Weltyr's would accept as one of their own. Even Valeria there"—who tensed to be addressed by name—"should know the evidence of my handiwork."

After a steady pause, Valeria looked frankly at her. "The misshapen?"

Her long fingers tickling her servant between his stubby horns, Gundrygia, who had been smiling into the gimlet's little face, looked shocked by Valeria's use of the moniker. "What a sick thing to call them! They are beautiful men. Custom-made for your kind, you know… and you threw them away."

"They proved wickeder than we," Valeria answered, shuddering at the thought of the spider centaurs. "You must indeed be very ancient, Madame, to have such claims as these."

"Your line had not yet been established, Rosewallow," was the witch's curt response while she took the lantern into her hands. Her eyes danced with a merry light of their own as she adjusted its valve and brought it to life. "Durrow history was not being recorded in full at that time. I speak of a time older than you think. In fact, the durrow had barely settled El'ryh...the first berich dwarves, with whom they were doomed to quarrel, were still excavating the city."

This was a common story told of the Nightlands—that its originating settlement, the city-state of Valeria's origin, had been founded with intention for the durrow and berich to rule it in partnership. A failed power grab ended with that tribe of berich dwarves as the first batch of durrow slaves. As these things went, the practice continued...and with slavery grew El'ryh.

Valeria's expression did not shift.

"Your power is indeed very great to have created whole races with magic alone...and, as the Materna of El'ryh, I can sympathize with your desire to see your people thrive. But we are here on the command of divinity." Valeria waved between us, adding with a gesture toward Branwen, "Even the druid is a devotee of Anroa, who would not have guided her this far without a purpose to her being here."

"You certainly are here by the grace of the gods," agreed Gundrygia, leaning back in her throne with her long legs akimbo. She rested the lantern in her lap, one hand caressing its glass surface in a way my eye simply could not avoid. The gimlet had curled at her feet and now rested its cheek against her knee, where it wagged its tail occasionally amid her words.

"Had it been up to me, the paladin would be here alone. How you burn with questions, Rorke...I see all the same old things bursting up in you, and more. So much more. Like the relics."

Branwen shot me a glance I could practically feel through the back of my head. "Should you even be entertaining conversation with her, Rorke?"

Too late—Gundrygia had snapped my attention with that, and my thirst for information from even a questionable source was irresistible. "What can you tell me about the relics Father Fortisto mentioned? Is that the Lantern of Hamsunt?"

With a long, predatory smile, Gundrygia cradled the lamp to her breast with one hand and used the other to pull her hem up around her knees. She rose without help from the servant who scrambled off and, effortlessly picking her way down from the throne, the gimlet queen said, "Once upon a time, things were different in the world. Future gods were then just menfolk. Weltyr had a different name. All this was even before my time...before the durrow broke ties with the berichs. Before, even, the elves separated from them."

The high elf and dark one exchanged a glance of some interest. For Branwen, the expression was one of surprise that I happened to catch when I looked over my shoulder at them. By the time I looked back, the witch had reached the foot of her throne and now slunk toward me. A raven cawed in the distance, and the noise caught my attention only due to the late hour.

"There are many treasures in this world...many things that draw their power from the secret threads making up the tapestry of our reality, that same Wyrd net that we embroidered figures might learn to weave by what is called magic. Most such objects are accounted for. Four of particular importance have been lost to the endless chain of mortal fascination, stolen and traded and gambled and killed for. Weltyr made what is now called the Scepter as the manifestation of his purest will; Roserpine's Ring was crafted to win his love; the Lantern of Hamsunt was said to be Weltyr's punishment for the very disobedient god; and then, ah…the Casket of Oppenhir. The most important treasure of all."

"How can that be when you just mentioned the Scepter of Weltyr was crafted by the All-Father himself?"

"Because though the Scepter may be useful, immortality is not foremost among its gifts. And I do mean immortality…true immortality with no hint of aging for as long as the individual sleeps in the casket. When the user returns to beds, their aging picks up where it left off. One man has had it for years now—years and years, for at least as many as I slumbered before you woke me up."

She looked only at me. Gundrygia still held the lantern in her hands, its light reflecting off the countless gems and chains and bangles and belts of copper and silver and gold with which the gimlets had adorned her. I understood well how it was that she had earned a reputation as some wild faerie queen…but she was not that. I lifted Strife between us knowing that if I could strike her, she would bleed.

The only issue was whether or not I could land the blow. However it would make me feel to have killed a woman, such complex emotion would have all been part of the aftermath.

In the name of defending myself and my companions against her magic, and in protecting the people of Soot, and in obeying the will of Weltyr, I would have stricken her down as readily as any truly dangerous opponent—regardless of sex, race, or beauty, or even my own personal desire.

And this fearful desire stung me with memories of our embrace while she stood before us, the lantern glowing in her hands.

"Tell me what you've done with the people of Soot—then leave, and don't force me to strike you down before your children."

Her smile fell; the wildness of her eyes returned, madness lining her face with the urgency of her petition. "My children are why I've done this," she insisted, the gimlets about her yelping and nodding. While a few darted up to kiss her feet and cling to the hem that had once again fallen down around her ankles, Gundrygia went on. "My creations would not be so foul toward the races of Weltyr if they were accepted. My good gimlets! How sweet they are. Would Yelp hurt you, do you suppose, Paladin?"

"If I made a move to cut you down right where you stand, these servants of yours would certainly throw themselves to the task of defending you."

"Yes, of course. And any human would defend his own home from an attacker. Come now, what a silly thing to say! Look at him."

She gestured to the worried gimlet who led us here—who now looked between us and Gundrygia while wringing his little paws. Clearly the creatures were no fans of conflict. Gundrygia went on sternly, "They were cast out of this blasted village, and every other place where men or elves or any other form of mankind dwell, for hundreds of thousands of years! For countless generations they were rejected rather than accepted into so-called civilized societies...and all because they cannot speak the languages of mankinds. Because they simply look too much the part of animals. But look, Paladin! Look!"

221

She turned the lantern's light up as bright as it could go. The gimlets cooed rather than recoiled.

"Do they shy from the Light of Hamsunt? Are they mere animals? Do they deserve to live hidden in the hills, waiting me to lead them out of their hellish existence? Men will not let them build cities or towns. There are even those in Soot who would kill a gimlet on sight and think nothing more of it than ridding their cellars of a rodent."

Her hard affect softened then. She regarded me tenderly. "But you think of it, Burningsoul...you think of much."

"I think the problems that the gimlets face is no call for doing what's been done here. What have you done with the people of Soot?"

"Nothing they haven't done to themselves."

Gritting my teeth, I shouted, "Speak, you harpy! Give me the lantern and release the town, or face the wrath of Weltyr!"

Tipping her head with a wicked laugh, Gundrygia slithered back into the crowd of gimlets that quickly formed around her. "You barely understand the wrath of Weltyr, Burningsoul...you barely understand yourself."

Behind her, the pile of furniture and gold twitched as though alive.

I'd heard tales of golems—the name most often given to semi-autonomous products of powerful magi with ancient means and cryptic purposes—but I had never seen one for myself.

The towering, broad-shouldered form that rose up from the collection of valuables was something it would have taken most magical artisans weeks, maybe months to create. For Gundrygia, it was nothing: a matter of will and of direction of heart. Soon, non-living things were made alive. It was a perverse mockery of Weltyr's gift, this artificial life bestowed to a pile of objects. It took a thundering step forward while the gimlets went skittering away amid a series of high barks.

Gundrygia made a low-throated snarl of her own. Those gimlets still around us sprang into action at once.

While Yelp cried out in protest, Valeria and Branwen did so in panic. My companions were apprehended while the friendly gimlet looked frantically up at my face, then darted to Gundrygia. He pushed through the crowd of gimlets around her retreating form and tugged on her dress when within reach, whimpering and pointing at my friends.

"Oh, now, poor thing!" Kneeling, Gundrygia tucked the lantern in one arm to caress Yelp's muzzle and pinch his chubby gimlet cheek. "Don't worry, angel...we only want Rorke, don't we? The others will be free to go eventually."

With a laugh, Gundrygia rose again and continued away while swarmed by her attendants. Their absence opened up most of the town square between myself and the raging bonfire.

In that gap now towered the golem, a fourteen-foot monstrosity that stared through heirloom eyes of ruby and displayed a grimacing mouth of valuable crockery. Mentally apologizing to the good people of Soot for destroying their finest belongings, I raised Strife high and charged the monster.

The eerie thing about the golem was that it made no sounds of exertion or pain. I hacked the enchanted broadsword into its thigh and found it did not even seem to react. The golem looked listlessly at the point of contact, where a valuable carpet had formed a kind of skin, and did not even move as a cluster of coins slid out—save that it knocked me aside with the sweep of a hand.

I clenched my teeth, skidding a few feet beneath the force but unharmed thanks to the plates of my armor. The gimlets all laughed—save for Yelp, who looked extremely serious—and my companions screamed. Gundrygia did not laugh or scream, but watched coldly with her arms around the lantern.

Within seconds I had sprung upright and charged my foe again, unsure of my plan but unwilling and unable to let the thing remain animate. Not when Valeria and Branwen were held captive, and the location of the citizens was yet to be determined. Strife's blade smashed part of a china cabinet that made up the giant's hip; the glass front broke and the wooden structure fell in on itself, causing the golem to career a bit. It flailed at me with an arm again and this time I dodged the blow. A good thing. The ground rattled upon the impact of its fist.

Pushing itself upright, the golem stumbled after me when I backed up to gain some ground. I slashed its wrist a few times but found this joint was mostly metal, kitchen pots and pans and old tarnished armor or military shields that occasionally broke open beneath Strife's blows.

The hand itself, however, did an admirable job of staying attached. To make matters worse, I noticed with a grim glance at the thing's hip that the parts making it up were shifting about to repair and maintain the form.

Had it any kind of heart? I struck up to stab it in the chest while it lifted its abused hand in a fist meant for me. Instead Strife plunged into its torso and it careened back beneath the force. The dwarvish grandfather clock making up its lower left leg creaked but ultimately held together as the golem stumbled toward the fire.

Smoke thickened in the air. The golem glanced back at the crackling sound accompanying, then lifted a fist engulfed in flames. I was vaguely aware of mingled noise from the crowd as I realized the obvious solution and regrouped.

It took several seconds for the golem to straighten itself up. By the time it was upright, its hand was a raging fireball. The construct turned upon me with its flaming fist cocked back for a punch. I narrowly avoided the first blow and feinted left, leaving my opponent just to my right. With new space between myself and its flaming left fist, I swept at its legs—

And was promptly grabbed by the metal fingers of the golem's less fiery hand.

Baring my teeth, I shifted my grip on Strife and stabbed rapidly down into the wrist of the hand that clutched me like a child holding a figurine. Without the slightest reaction, the golem continued lifting me toward the blaze. As Valeria and Branwen called my name while struggling against their captors, I hacked away at the thing's wrist as though using Strife to chip ice.

That was what I seemed to have done when the glass vase inside the structure of the wrist met my blade and caused the hand holding me to collapse. While its fingers fell apart, I cried out and dropped ten feet—I had to roll, in fact, to avoid the fire. But when I stood, shattered glass falling from my armored shoulders like crystalline snow, the golem had only one hand to speak of.

The flaming fist was still a threat, but now its use sent the false creation off-balance while its other hand slowly restored itself. As pieces of furniture and hand-carved jewel boxes and long-cherished wine bottles reassembled themselves piece by piece, the golem took another fiery swing at me. I raised Strife and barely deflected its blow, the heat causing my face to break into a sweat as splinters of flaming furniture flew off in either direction. Its fist tore away and I charged again, fully dedicated to immolating the entire structure before its hand could re-form.

Ignoring all reluctance, all possibility of danger, I charged in beneath the golem's arms and hacked wildly at its legs. To the gasps of the gimlets, the construct stumbled back. I slashed on and on, and the creature shambled toward the blaze against which I forced it.

"Go, Rorke," screamed Branwen above Valeria's quiet prayers. "Push it in the fire!"

My slashes turned to high hammer strikes against the golem's torso and pelvis. Each blow rattled through the animated body with greater force, the pieces coming apart, until a final stab left Strife stuck through the artificial torso.

The golem looked down at itself as though surprised, its flaming hand lifting toward my blade. Before it could touch either of us, I braced my foot against that grandfather clock in its leg and used the pressure to pull Strife free. Once the sword was out, the force of my foot sent the golem stumbling back into the bonfire's flames. There it fell apart in an instant and was at once rendered nothing more than fuel for a fire that raged more mightily than ever beneath the sudden inundation of old valuables.

While the gimlet crowd erupted in anguish, Valeria and Branwen were released. The women cried out and hurried to me, embracing me by turns while I caught my breath.

When I looked up, Gundrygia had worked her way through the gimlets. She now stood across the empty plaza from us.

"How carelessly you destroy my creations, Burningsoul. Small wonder Adonisius was so affected by you! You adventurers think nothing of killing innocent creatures trying to live their lives."

"Your creatures aren't all innocent. Those misshapen bandits seemed poised to do worse to Branwen than rob her, if you ask me—and the gimlets may be charming, may be victim to mankinds' unfair judgment and ostracization, but they have still displaced the people of Soot, ransacked their homes, eaten their food and destroyed their belongings. And the fields—"

"*I* burned the fields," said Gundrygia, "and chased the fools from Soot into the hills—just as mankinds burned the fields of all my creatures whenever they endeavored to settle somewhere and begin their own agricultural communities. I used my magic to show them what it's like to lose everything…and now, Wotsung, I think I'll show you."

Never had I heard that word in all my days beneath Weltyr's eye, but there was no time to ponder it. Gundrygia's eyes glowed a hot violet-pink, the air around her shifting to a similar hue. I released my companions, ready to meet an opponent I was not confident I could best—

And a pair of ravens bolted from the dark, their beaks and talons poised for Gundrygia's eyes.

Amazing to think that a woman so terrifying might be afraid of anything in turn! Yet the sharpness of her scream as the ravens descended to tear at her face and scalp was like the wail of a dying banshee. As she howled with fear, the visible evidence of her magic vanished. Instead Gundrygia raised her arms before her eyes and cringed away. Her gimlet servants scattered, the little cowards, and the lantern fell from her hands.

To my awe, one of the ravens caught the lantern's handle and flew off with the hefty relic gripped in its black claws.

While this mighty bird—surely more than twice the size of even the largest raven I had ever seen about the streets of Skythorn—bore the lantern from Soot, its brother continued the vicious assault against Gundrygia. Cringing face filled with terror, the woman cast me a look, grit her teeth, and drew the hem of her dress up over her head.

The twisting fabric transformed in an instant to the plumage of a snowy owl. Shrieking in this new form, Gundrygia flapped silently off with the second raven in close pursuit.

I had to make a choice, and made it in an instant. Without saying a thing to Valeria or Branwen, I tore off after the fast-receding ball of light that marked the raven with the lantern.

The women called after me, but there was no time to waste. I was already far behind the bird and, encumbered as I was by my armor, it flew farther and farther beyond the possibility of my acquisition. The raven soared effortlessly beneath the pale face of the obscured moon, the beating of its widespread wings evident in the lantern's golden light.

Less effortlessly, I pursued it.

On and on: it flying, me running, I thought of nothing but getting Odile's lantern back safe and sound. The treasure was too valuable…and, after it had been identified by Gundrygia as that same relic Fortisto had mentioned, I could not let it go without a fight.

I was just not prepared for the fight I was due.

Focused as I was on the bird, I did not realize how far it had led me outside of Soot's boundaries until the ball of light descended not far from the site of our horseback lesson. Seeing my chance, I paused only for a few short breaths before doubling my pace. Strife bounced in its scabbard to keep the pace of my steps.

Moments later, I stumbled into a quarry of stones and through these high piled stones followed the raven's call.

Its croaking laughter was gradually rendered unnecessary by the glow of the light that led me to itself...and to the old man at whose feet it shone. After all I had been through in the past forty-eight hours, I could hardly believe my eyes.

Thinking my vision failed me, I blinked several rapid times—but Hildolfr was no mirage.

Much as he had when represented by that nameless creature in the secret garden cave of the Nightlands, the ranger sat upon the edge of a great stone. This time, rather than tending to his pipe, the one-eyed old man and last of my traitors sat with one hand upon his knee while the other remained casually draped about the lance forever within his reach. His familiar raven, its feathers glossy in the light, perched upon his left shoulder to casually groom itself.

"Hello, Rorke," said Hildolfr, his tone strangely mingled somewhere between pride and sorrow. "It's good to see you again."

My heart was as stony as his seat. "I wish that I could say the same. Each time Weltyr has deigned to show you to me has proved more painful than the last."

Hildolfr's lips quirked beneath his beard. "Is that so?"

"Indeed, it is. First, a heinous creature of the Nightlands stole your form to address me; next, you appeared to me in a dream. Now you're here: a hallucination brought on by ceaseless, sleepless riding and the fatigue of a hard-fought battle."

"Life would be much simpler for you were I not before you now, Rorke Burningsoul…but it would also be the same as everybody else's life. And you've never been satisfied with the idea of living everybody else's life. Isn't that why you joined the Order?"

"I joined the Order in service to Weltyr, whom I thought you yourself knew nearly as well as I did. Your treachery down in the Nightlands proves otherwise. What have you done with the Scepter?"

"I have taken it out of the hands of those who would misuse it."

With a scoff, I drew Strife. The ranger remained where he sat, unmoving.

"All night," I said, unable to help the frustration in my voice. "I've been asking simple questions and receiving no answer. This night, this journey, my whole life! I'm tired of it. I'll ask you again, you old snake—where is the Scepter? Or is it in the same place you left that missing eye of yours?"

Now Hildolfr laughed, albeit in the dark way of a disbelieving adult to whom a toddler had just spoken crossly. "My missing eye is the one you see through now, Paladin. I cast away my foolishness…now it stands before me."

The second raven croaked in the distance and earned the attention of the first. With a flapping that whipped up a miniature gale, the bird upon Hildolfr's shoulder rocketed into the air and flew to find its cohort. I let it go without looking away from my opponent, saying only, "I can't stand here chatting all night, Hildolfr. There's a madwoman about—"

"Gundrygia fears the very sight of me. She'll be

nowhere near here while my birds are about."

"You always were very coy about your animal companion."

"I was forthright...when you asked me about them, I told you they were out in the world, off doing my business for me. And they were."

"I hope for their sake that they are talented fighters enough to survive Gundrygia's magic. What business do you have knowing that baleful woman's name?"

"What business do you have knowing that baleful woman?"

While I scoffed, somewhat shocked to be evidently reproached for something this man had neither business nor manner of learning, Hildolfr's stoic lips turned up in a crooked smirk. It was a fond, grandfatherly expression that at that moment enraged me for what I perceived as mocking intent.

"You do remind me of myself, Rorke...when I look at you, I remember what it was to be young. Sometimes I even long for it again, but I admit that my spirit is more peaceful without the young man's pursuits."

"What would you know of me, Hildolfr? The past weeks have seen me so changed that I hardly know myself."

"I'm glad you're starting to understand that."

My jaw tight, I brandished Strife and assured him, "Since you understand so much about me and my journey, perhaps you'll manage to make me understand what drove you to such perverse lengths as absconding with the Scepter of Weltyr."

"The Scepter is mine."

"It is the All-Father's property. It belongs in his house."

"It belongs in whomever's hands he sets it in,

Burningsoul. For years, it has been trading owners. Awaiting a worthy champion of Weltyr."

"It awaits its chance to return home to the Temple. You think you know the highest divine will?"

"No," said Hildolfr quickly. "Not even I know those cold machinations without assistance. There are magics so deep and experiences so profound not even the most educated and ancient magician could experience them and live."

I shook my head. "At least you're not completely mad. Grimalkin said you were changed when the Scepter came into your hand...I didn't want to believe it, but this conversation has given me the sense that he might be right."

"Careful, boy." Rising from his perch with his lance in one hand and his good eye upon me, Hildolfr advised, "You know I abide much, but such consistent disrespect is not something I will tolerate."

"Then prepare to yield the Scepter."

Strife's blade gleamed in the light as I charged forward.

"Rorke—"

I had seen Hildolfr's speed in battle, but I had not been faced with it myself. The lance seemed to jump up in his hand. With a grace that was truly second nature, Hildolfr bounced my blows aside and left me wondering what enchantment had been woven over the tight-lipped man's weapon. Runes glowed around the shaft when it was in the midst of battle, but, as with many things, Hildolfr had always managed to change the subject when I inquired about it. He was as crafty with the dagger of his tongue as he was with the point of his spear, and while our weapons clashed, each glance of Strife reverberated through the quarry rocks and off into the distance.

"Give it up, Rorke," said Hildolfr. "I didn't come here to harm you, and I won't—but what will happen instead will seem almost worse to you."

"I'm not afraid of you, old man," I told him, shifting away and swinging Strife in an arc against my opponent.

Hildolfr raised his lance to block the blow.

The top half of Strife glanced away, jarring my hands with the new and lighter weight they gripped.

Like that, I wielded only half my sword.

My stomach turned itself inside out. An infinite number of thoughts flew through my mind—the future duel, the ominous nature of such a sign, the immediate threat to my life in the context of this conflict. But, most of all, the teachings of my Church reared up to my consciousness and shook me from my naive slumber.

The enchantments fused into the metal of the blade were prayers so powerful that they could only be broken by Weltyr.

I could not admit it. It was too much to see him. If I had believed it fully while I stood there, I would have gone mad—terribly mad. I would have shaken with fear as I did later on when I considered what had happened, and what had been happening for the entirety of my journey. For the entirety of my life.

Feeling as if my own numb heart had been struck in two, I regarded the shattered edge of Strife's blade as though from a distance, then tried looking up into Hildolfr's face.

I could not make myself.

Slowly, silently, I genuflected upon the ground, first to lower the broken blade and then to clasp my hands together.

"I am so sorry," I said softly.

"To whom do you owe your fealty?"

My heart hammered in my chest. Face flushed, I knelt there, frozen. Was this how the mouse felt before the cat? I closed my right hand into a fist to place it over my heart. How wet my palm felt with sweat! "To Weltyr, and Weltyr only—Weltyr above all the most coveted material bribes that Urde could dare offer me."

"Your loyalty's not to the Church? To the Order?"

Given pause, I searched for a trap. I glanced up into his face but found that I could not ever again directly behold the eye that was once so friendly to me. Fear filled me to even gaze near it. I had never known myself to be a coward, but I suppose now that only the greatest of fools would persist in bravado when faced with the truth that admonished me then. Glancing down at his boots, I said, "No—only to Weltyr."

"And that is why I am entrusting you with this task."

My mouth dry, my eyes searching for any purchase upon his person and in the end not even able to hold the sight of his boots, I studied the earth beneath them instead. "Please, my Lord—what task is this?"

I am still not convinced that his answer pertained to what he considered my true task, knowing as he did that the information was too overwhelming to be delivered to me then. "You must protect the women who are meant to perpetuate your line," he answered instead, which was also the truth. "You must teach your children to live by my laws and wander far and wide, spreading knowledge of me as neither the Church nor the Order can disseminate."

"Are these institutions not manifestations of your word? Are they not the enforcers of your will upon Urde?"

"No institution can understand the teachings I provide. Only a Wanderer can carry my news about, and only a Wanderer can understand it—but those to whom the Wanderers carry my news are doomed to only understand such things insofar as it suits them."

Lips dry, my gaze still darting about, I asked, "Do you mean to say it is my destiny to leave the Order?"

"All these things will sort themselves in time."

To my astonishment—and, somehow, greater fear—he lowered his lance to the ground and slowly knelt before me. Hildolfr's once-familiar hands fit to my shoulders and I forced myself to keep my eyes open.

"You're wise to humble yourself, Rorke," he said in that same grandfatherly manner from before, "but you, of all men, have little need to fear."

The crown of my skull itched as I looked upon him. This was the aged face of the same friend with which I'd journeyed to the Nightlands—a man with whom I'd ridden horses and sparred while traveling and flirted with women all over Cascadia.

And all this time...all this time.

"Master," I said, my throat parched, "why me? What purpose serves my line?"

I paused, searching his face, afraid to ask more but unable to help myself.

"What is a "Wotsung?""

The smile that crossed his face was one I had rarely seen Hildolfr wear. His good eye crinkled with the appearance of teeth that were bright, white, and perfectly straight, each one gleaming in the light of the lantern.

"You have much to learn, Burningsoul...and your companions are nearly here. Protect them, and love them, and find others who will see the wisdom in your heart."

For some reason, I thought of gentle Elishta-bet— and the duel, for which I now had no weapon. "My sword! Oh, what am I to do about Strife?"

"Never challenge me again," he said, releasing me

and rising while I studied the ground at his feet, "and you will find a sword in your moment of greatest need."

I exhaled, lifting my head to ask him so much more.

Instead of the man who called himself Hildolfr, I found the Scepter of Weltyr.

15

ORDER RESTORED

A GREAT TENSION released upon my sudden solitude. My armor rattled around me while my body collapsed into tremors, the euphoria to be alive mingling with profound fear, respect, and gratitude.

It was impossible to comprehend what had just happened. Impossible to think that I had just been met with (and journeyed with before!) the most powerful of the gods. The Great All-Father, whose far-seeing eye uncloaked the contents of all the world's shadows.

And the evidence of my bond with him had been shattered by his sacred lance.

My heart twisted in pain. The broken sword still lay before me on the ground. Unspeaking, I lifted both pieces of Strife to my heart. How easily I might have met the fate of this sword!

How easily I might (any second, every second) meet the fate of that sword even now.

Overwhelmed by tears, I covered my eyes in one hand and silently wept.

As far as I had already journeyed, as close to death as I had come, as many battles as I had already fought in my then-short life, I did not tangibly awaken to my own personal fear of death until that very moment. It were as though Weltyr had forced me to draw nearer it by steps: first, with the pain of Adonisius for his family and my new regard for the act of killing. Then, by sparing me in spite of my arrogance.

My body screamed with relief to be alive, to know itself—to have its future, its past, itself. Friendly chemicals as I had never felt swept through me…but I had been left with something that I knew from that very moment would never depart me. Aware of Oppenhir's shadow as I suddenly was, feeling its palpable black form cast across my face, (and, worse, understanding that it had always been there, waiting for me to notice), I knew that I had not escaped it. That none, truly, could ever escape it.

None save for those who, by the grace of Weltyr and the gentle hands of his Selectrices, joined the Hall of Valor.

With a glance at the scepter reclining against the rock where Hildolfr sat moments before, I remained kneeling and shut my eyes. With Strife still pressed to my breastplate, I prayed as even I had never prayed before, with my attention focused on whole-heartedly celebrating what it was to be alive. Yes! Just to be alive. To be blessed with a mind and conscious perception and Weltyr's great gift of Reason—one of the greatest powers granted us. To be alive, and to have therefore the conscious basis of reality and all its nuances: the wonders of the sense-organs, the majesty of the sun, the loving arms of a woman, the promises of things unknowable but hoped for and all the adventures of the future.

And yet to be alive so tentatively. To be alive on the face of a vessel circling a ball of fire amid a cold, black ocean. To be one heartbeat away from nothing—nothing. To be one heartbeat away from not even knowing nothing.

As if any man could.

"Rorke!"

Branwen's call seemed only to reinforce the beauty of the All-Father's gifts. How ignorant I had been to scorn her for even a moment! How ridiculous I was to hang the mistakes of anyone over their character and judge them by these flaws. Was I not the most flawed among all men I had known, even if only to myself? How dared I sourly close my heart against fully loving Branwen when her betrayal had been Weltyr's will? How could I help but forgive her when she, hearing my footfall as I rose to call to her, burst into the quarry where I prayed?

"He's here," she called, cupping her hands around her mouth, "he's here, Valeria!"

Branwen's smile turned upon me again—but how her face fell when she saw Strife in my hand!

"Rorke! What's happened?"

Sliding my empty arm around her taut waist, I drew her into my embrace and guided her mouth to mine. Though surprised, she yielded at once, her soft lips fluttering to permit the trailing of her tongue into my mouth. The sweet pitch of her moan fired my blood, a flame whose growth was accelerated by the energy that flooded my body when faced with the divine. When she pulled away for a gasp of air, her face was flushed and her eyes had grown glassy with desire.

"What a place for a kiss like that," chided the elf, who nonetheless bit her lip and looked shyly away. Her eyes widened to cross the Scepter reclining against the stone. "Why—is that—"

"It is," I told her.

"Where did you—how is it *here?*"

I did not have to be told that I could never speak in full to anyone of what had transpired there. No one but you, reader, into whose hands this chronicle will have been placed only once I have retired from the business of being an old man to become a young one again in Weltyr's manor-house. At that time, though, with the event so fresh, I could not even think of it for how mad it made me feel. Able to produce neither lie nor truth, I looked at the Scepter and evasively said, "The raven brought me to it."

"I see the lantern there. How is it possible? Was it some druid, or another witch in disguise?"

I shook my head, unable to speak further on the subject, and was awash with gratitude when Valeria hurried into the clearing amid the stones.

"Ah," she cried with relief, "Rorke, oh, we were so worried she had taken you again—"

"She'll have to pull a trick even craftier to lure me into her false world next time…I've no need of the pleasures she provides with the two of you here, and if she had genuine divine truths to impart she would share them in a way that permits me to recall them. I have no use for her. What of the gimlets in Soot?"

Branwen shook her head. "When you were following the raven, they scattered in all directions. Anroa knows where they've gone."

I rubbed my jaw. "Hopefully not back in those houses…"

What would be the outcome of this harrowing week? The people of Soot would, at best, be furious. At worst, a few of them would be ill or even dead from their time spent living in the hills without supplies. There was also the cost of the ruined fields to consider—and the question of how the future would look long-term for the already troubled relationship between the gimlets and the villagers of Soot.

"I think I have an idea about how we might broker a peace," I told the women, my eyes falling across the scepter while my arm loosened its hold on Branwen's waist. "But I'm not sure how it will go—these things are delicate in the best of times, but…"

Valeria noticed it upon following my gaze. Her pale eyes widened in the sublime mask of her face.

"It can't be—"

"It is," said Branwen while I made a silent approach.

All thought dissolved into nothing but miscellaneous sensory experience as the Scepter of Weltyr drew me in to witness its majesty. Mesmerized, I knelt before it, my forearm draped over my knee and both my hands clasped. Its many gems gleamed with lustrous beauty in the lantern's light. In each one was reflected my own awestruck face. Even the gold, immaculately polished in spite of its long sojourn away from home, bore traces of my phantom.

I had expected to look at it and feel some tremendous impulse to touch it, or to covet it greedily—this was what Grimalkin had implied. But, especially now knowing why Hildolfr had behaved as coldly as he apparently had upon killing me, (It was, after all, he whose weapon mortally wounded me before the durrow came to my aid!), I felt not the least spark of covetous inclination. No desire to sell or barter or trade.

I still did not understand what I was to do with this thing. All I knew at that moment was that it was a symbol of a new covenant between myself and Weltyr—a private one, set apart from the covenant I'd once had with the Church.

The covenant he destroyed with the flick of his lance.

"Pray, Valeria—do you have an extra petticoat under there that I might borrow to wrap this in?"

But the high priestess of the durrow shook her head and, drawing her hem to her knees, knelt upon the rocky ground. "That is not a just manner of transport for such a sacred object…Roserpine would not permit it."

Valeria shut her eyes, her hands clasped before her face. Her lips moved to emit words that were soft and meaningless to me as her breaths, but, for their music, twice as wonderful to hear. The air around her took on the thunderstorm quality of magical weavings, and as the prayer grew on, it took the rhythm of a kind of song.

The prayer was not the only thing to be woven, however. While the song climbed delicately up, spiders scuttled in through the rocks.

As the first few wolf spiders bumbled past and scurried along the scepter to learn its dimensions, I'm embarrassed to say I was more startled than Branwen and recoiled upright from where I knelt. The druid, though surprised, was far more intrigued, and marveled around her as readily as though the little creatures were squirrels or fawns.

"How helpful," she commented with a laugh, offering a more approving and warm-hearted look toward Valeria than I think I had then seen her give. "It takes a spectacular heart to see the creativity of spiders and call on them without fear."

"And Valeria's heart is most certainly spectacular," I agreed while more spiders flooded merrily into the quarry. Fuzzy tarantulas scuttled down from the mountains while trapdoor spiders crawled from their holes and raced to hear news from those comrades who were first to the scene. Jumping spiders sprang out of shadows and even a few plane-shifting spiders the size of large mastiffs vibrated into the visible dimension. Their purple eyes studied me warily until I moved back from the Scepter to let the arachnids do their work. These demi-alien spiders had to be about as careful as I was when it came to avoiding their tiny brethren; but, somehow, their silk threads were no less fine!

The weaving had begun before I even realized it. It was the nighttime hour, I think, coupled with the arresting sight of all the many spiders. One became focused on the arachnids and not necessarily on what they were doing. But what they were doing, I was soon to find, was incredible.

Strand by strand, the spiders created a silk shroud long enough to wrap around the Scepter of Weltyr. It tucked into itself with ease, allowing the concealment of the sacred object's either end. The cloth shimmered in the light nearly as brightly as did its charge. When it was finished, it wafted down into my hands as lightly as would have the veil of a bride.

When the work was finished, the spiders remained only to assure themselves that I understood what to do with their gift. As I approached the relic with the cloth over my arm, they dispersed. Rather than the awesome waves in which they'd come, they left the area in a gradual black trickle as though rejoining the pool of night's darkness. By the time the plane-shifting spiders phased out of the third and fourth dimensions back into whatever one they preferred to spend time in, Valeria's song had reduced to soft chanting. A few wolf spiders remained to watch us finish what they started, and when satisfied that their work was a perfect fit, they scurried off to resume their business.

"I have to hand it to them," I said, stepping back from the wrapped scepter to admire its new cocoon, "they really are capital tailors."

"That was such a beautiful prayer, Valeria," said Branwen, still in that tone of genuine compliment. "I never would have thought of calling on spiders for assistance…we druids tend to favor mammals, but now I feel like it's some kind of prejudice!"

Smiling thinly, visibly tired to call upon so great an act of magic without the aid of Roserpine's ring, Valeria swayed up to her feet and permitted me to take her warm, sweet-smelling body in my arms. "Perhaps it is something like that…but, in the Nightlands, the animals we know best are snakes, bats, and spiders. Roserpine loves all those creatures that move through the darkness."

"Then please pray to her as well as to Weltyr that such love has been shown to the people of Soot. Branwen, take the lantern…"

I paused. My chest grew pained to look on Strife, broken there amid the rocks. If we were met with trouble I would have only my own prayers with which to defend myself. None of those could be said to be directly offensive in nature except, perhaps, for Weltyr's occasional willingness to bring about undead entities through me—always temporary in nature, and usually only something automated like the severed hand of Al-listux. I supposed, in a pinch, I could always lead my enemies back to town and around to Soot's small cemetery.

Luckily, no such thing was necessary. After all—I

had just been told that, in my greatest need, a new sword would be mine for the taking. I trusted I would not require a weapon until then, although my heart still ached while Valeria tenderly took Strife's pieces and, as I had, pressed them to her heart. She looked at me curiously, but did not ask me any questions. That quality of Valeria's— her ability to perceive when it was not yet time to ask a question that seared her with intense curiosity—has always been the one I most appreciated in her.

Then, with the Scepter snugly in its silk wrapper, the women and I set out to find the citizens of Soot. Valeria bore Strife in one hand and the lantern in the other. I, the holy relic. Branwen, meanwhile, carried her reclaimed crossbow.

"Yelp returned it to me when he saw you run off," she explained.

"Do you suppose that fellow's still around the town?"

Branwen shook her head, uncertain.

Together, the three of us took to the hills. The mountain nearest the town of Soot, the very same down which we'd come, was a natural place to look. We had not long wandered toward the base of the mountain and the altitude that was richest in trees when our calls of, "Hello? Hello? Erdwud? Rigan? Mr. and Mrs. Dardrie?" were at last answered by a hopeful response.

"Who's that?"

"Rorke Burningsoul," I shouted into the trees. "Lively called for us."

"Lively!"

Erdwud thundered through the trees and underbrush, bursting out through a pair of trunks and regarding us with wild eyes. In spite of his obviously haggard appearance—malnourished, unwashed and scruffy to say the least—the tavern-keeper looked desperately at us. "Is she all right?"

"She's in perfect health," I assured him. Erdwud wept in relief, his hands clasping before him as he fell back against the support of a tree trunk. I continued, "And she's very brave—she rode all the way to Skythorn to find us. Weltyr must have inspired you to send us to your friend so that she would know where to look."

More of Soot's citizens made themselves known from the trees, guided by the light of the lantern and the sounds of our voices. Rigan, the old blacksmith, appeared next. "Did you slay those little—"

"The gimlets are still around—however, because they value their lives, we don't think they'll be in your homes any longer."

The old man regarded me sourly. "What gives you that idea?"

"Because their queen has fled, pursued by a magical animal; and they did not come into your town before her interference, so I would not expect them to attempt it again."

Someone bitterly shouted, "Those little buggers have been squatting in our houses and stealing our food, and they get to just walk back into the hills?"

"That's not what I'm proposing," I told them as they muttered. "Look—the gimlets speak a language unintelligible to humans, but they still speak a language, and most of them at least understand the common tongue. They're creatures of reason. Why not help them develop a neighboring settlement?"

So many villagers had gathered around by now that I could no longer keep track of the speakers. I only knew by tone and gender that they were not all the same people, but many voices addressing me in a chorus round. "Help them, after their queen destroyed our crops?"

"They could help you establish and harvest new crops to make right what was destroyed. By the same token, you could teach them the secrets of agriculture and have new neighbors to trade with. Instead of dealing with constant raids on merchants coming through the area, you could have new trading partners available to you."

Perhaps inspired by the spiders, I further posited, "They seem skilled in the tanning and crafting of leather, and I saw at least one of them cooking. Another appeared interested in the care of animals. Perhaps, if you gave the gimlets an opportunity to learn mankinds' ways, they would apply themselves to the tasks of living in those ways so readily that they would have no more time or interest to quarrel with you."

"Or," suggested someone crass, "we could obliterate them. Then they'll certainly never be a problem again."

"More like you'll kill the ones you can find and leave a few behind," I told the protester sternly. "And those surviving will grow all the more resentful, and will radicalize their children against you. Another such invasion will be guaranteed."

With a few, somewhat more placated murmurs and still others that remained reluctant, the townsfolk considered this. One spoke up again, saying, "How do we know they won't just take the information we give them and leave us without paying their debt?"

The weight of the scepter somehow all the heavier in my hands in that second, I reminded them all, "Weltyr is the overseer of oaths and contracts. It is a basic standard of decency for all mankinds that an individual be impeccable in their word and commit deeds in line with their actions. Introduce the gimlets to the concept of contracts and the understanding that if one breaks contracts, one cannot be trusted to do business, make trades, or engage in anything else professionally- or socially-motivated."

A few more people seemed amenable to this. Rigan, still skeptical, looked hard at me. "And if they don't abide by the requirements of their contracts?"

I spread my hands.

"Perhaps some will and others won't. Introduce them to the concepts of laws and courts—assuming they don't have such things already. You can either try to introduce them to the ways of mankinds, or you can continue struggling each against the other. Each one trying to eek out separate livings until one of you truly *is* eradicated…and, crafty as they are, I'm not convinced it will be the gimlets."

Contemplative silence draped over the villagers of Soot. Exchanging a few long glances, they all seemed to share variations of the same thoughts; the same awful imaginings.

Erdwud turned to me again.

"I don't suppose you can translate to gimlet, can you?"

"Not without somebody's help," I said. "Luckily, I know just the fellow."

Together, we made our way back to the village in a great procession. Yelp hurried out when we called to him, though he almost ran away when he saw the villagers moving through the darkness. After some explanation of what we wanted, however, his tail wagged and his eyes grew bright. Barking and yipping, the gimlet called his peers out of their many hiding places.

Right then and there in the town square of Soot, before the pile of objects that represented the most precious things in the town, the negotiations began.

There's no point in boring you with the details of all this. Between all the translating and the decision-making, it took until dawn before an agreement was brokered. When it was, however, the results were heartwarming. The gimlets were very eager to learn the ways of mankinds. To them, the concept of a contract seemed the most intriguing way to start.

A treaty was signed, and in it, the gimlets agreed to integrate into various forms of work around Soot in exchange for fair wages after the first year, which would be a year of reparations to pay back the damages along with the costs of their own training. Meanwhile, in exchange for no longer helping themselves to the contents of merchant caravans, the gimlets requested the right to start a settlement on land about ten miles north of Soot. Whether the humans would help them build that settlement remained to be seen, but I suspected, as in every tentative relationship between neighbors in this world, there would be those that would assist and those that would protest. This was just the way things were.

Satisfied, the gimlets at once set about fixing the disarrayed town. While they picked through the remains of the bonfire and golem to see what was salvageable and what was destroyed, the villagers retired to their homes to fulfill the other side of the catalogue—their own precious objects, missing or destroyed. Beds had to be remade, kitchens had to be cleaned, traumatized (and, no doubt, baffled) animals had to be comforted that their disappearing masters had returned.

Throughout all this, I arranged for Erdwud to return to Skythorn with us. Branwen went to fetch the horses while he readied himself. Alone together at last and semi-free to speak, Valeria looked at me.

"What will you do about Strife?"

My eye trailed back over the path to Rigan's house. Soon we stood before the building of the outraged smith, who mopped his brow and sat on his porch looking exhausted from the effort of inventorying his weapons.

"Those bloody gimlets stole all my swords," he lamented.

While I, wholly unsurprised to hear this in the way of those who were accustomed to divine coincidence, went on to ask if we could help him straighten up his place, he shook his head.

"No, no, but thanks for the offer. Something I ought to do myself...or maybe I'll have my grandson come 'round and sort it. It's time I had an apprentice, I think. Be a good opportunity to show him a few basic example pieces...with what's left, anyway. In truth, I had too much sitting around. Good opportunity to go through it all... that armor of yours comes from a few bits I already had sitting around. Your friend see it? What'd he think of it?"

"He's a fellow of few words," I told Rigan, earning a brief glance from hooded Valeria. Pretending not to notice, I took Strife's pieces from her hands and showed them to the old blacksmith. "Now—I'm sure you'll have enough to do for the foreseeable future, and if I'm reading the winds right, Weltyr will not be leading me back to Soot anytime soon...but, maybe if I return for it, or someone returns for it on my behalf, you might take the time to repair this sword and have it ready? I've a few coins now—"

Eyeing the blade and taking its pieces from my hand, he studied the point of the break before looking into my face with a shake of his head.

"Keep your money," he said. "You won me back my house, Paladin. It's the least I owe you. But isn't this your sword from the Order? Thought these never broke...I once saw one said to be a thousand years old. Looked forged the day before."

Heart stinging, unable to look at the pieces of the broken blade, I focused on Rigan's aged face and told him, "It was the will of Weltyr that shattered my Strife... no man can truly know why anything happens in this world."

With a snort and a shake of his head, Rigan agreed, "That's the only thing that really is for certain. All right, Burningsoul...I'll fix your sword. If you're not back by the time my Selectrix takes me to the Hall, I'll see to it that my grandson knows to keep it for you."

"Thank you, Rigan."

Spirit overflowing with emotion, I took one last look at Strife. While the blacksmith stood to go inside, I set my hand upon the cool flat of the blade.

"Good-bye, Strife, old friend...thank you. Weltyr bless you, and whosoever next wields you, if our paths do not cross again. Ah!"

Beset by that awful heart-pain again, I drew my hand away and nodded at Rigan. "Take care of it, and of yourself. Weltyr bless your house."

"And yours," said the old smith, disappearing inside.

The door shut behind him, and I knew that I would not see Strife again.

16

THE DUEL'S APPROACH

WHILE THE JOURNEY was long and tiring, we pushed the horses exchanged at the Dardries' ranch to the limits of their endurance and made excellent time back to Skythorn. Erdwud rode with us, as did the Dardrie boy: the horses still in Skythorn were needed to repair the fields, and at any rate I couldn't fault the family for wanting to keep their steeds close to home in case they needed to take sudden flight. Once bitten twice shy, as a teacher of myself and Elishta-bet used to say sometimes.

Elishta-bet was the subject weighing most urgently on my mind as we headed back to the city. Even as, by night, the tavern-keeper and I took turns regaling our fellow travelers with tales, I could not chase anticipation of the duel from my head.

Zweiding was twenty years older than I was. An orphan, as were we all. He was a powerful warrior with twice my experience—and an actual battlefield veteran, which I, born to peacetimes, was not. Having raided terrorist cells, worked as an officer of the law in Skythorn and trained cadets for years, the Commander responded very well to unexpected battles, let alone planned duels.

And there was me—not having had a full night's sleep in days, journeying all over the face of creation. Missing a sword.

I had no idea what I was going to do…and every time I tried to think of a solution, my mind went in circles. What could I do to best the Commander when I hadn't even a broken weapon? There wouldn't be a blacksmith in all Skythorn open to me before the coming of dawn. Perhaps Sharp would let me borrow his gun when he saw I had returned Erdwud alive and well…now that would have been quite unjust! But I had no other solution.

Father Fortisto—I needed to ask him about the Ring of Roserpine, anyway. Perhaps he might also find me a sword somewhere in the Temple? It was a strange request and somehow absurd, but all the same I felt that somewhere in the sacred halls there had to be something of use to me. There was always Elishta-bet, too: if I saw her before the duel, she might also be tasked with finding a solution.

We arrived in Skythorn around midnight, leaving me approximately four hours to sleep before the duel—and even that, I could not do without delay. There was a reward there, though. It warmed me to see Erdwud reunite with Lively, who sprang up from the armchair by her private room's window to see that the person in the doorway was him. Their joyous celebration attracted the innkeeper, who arrived to tell off the people making so much noise…but, on seeing his friend, Sharp simply joined the ruckus.

Soon Lively had kissed us all and bowed and thanked us hundreds of times. She and her husband promptly retired, and I and my companions did the same.

After laying the wrapped Scepter across the dresser in the corner, I disrobed. Branwen looked shyly over at me, then at the relic. After a few seconds, she asked, "Are you worried I'm going to do something stupid again?"

I laughed just slightly at that, looking over at her and assuring her as I bent to remove my boots, "If you do anything like you did before, it would only be because of Weltyr's command...now that we have the Scepter back, Branwen, I have no quarrel with you."

Satisfied, her hands worrying together, Branwen edged nearer to me and begged to know, "This duel— what are you going to do?"

"I'm not sure. I suppose I'll see what happens."

"You can't just blow off preparing for a fight like this. He could kill you!"

"I'm aware...but I have no choice. I must put my faith in Weltyr."

"Whatever happens," she said, grabbing me by the hand and catching my eye before I could resume undressing, "you have to win, Rorke. You can't die. Seeing you fight that golem for those people, and making peace with the gimlets, and—I love you, Rorke. I'm so sorry I ever betrayed you."

Her eyes were glassy with tears, I was amazed to realize. Softly tutting, I drew Branwen into my arms and caressed her cheek.

"And I love you," I told her. "Will you think me selfish if I love you and Valeria both?"

"Of course," she said with a light laugh, "but I'm very selfish, myself, so it won't stop me. At any rate...I'm very fond of Valeria lately, too. It's my pleasure to love her with you...if—if you'll let me stay with you, Rorke." Her soft hand tightening in mine, Branwen peered uncertainly into my face. "I'm not sure what your plans are once you give the Scepter back to your Church, but—"

"Only to fetch Valeria's ring," I informed her while the door to the room opened. Her eyes widened and I explained, "Before my duel, I intend to speak with Father Fortisto to gain a lead on the ring...then, after my duel and the Scepter's return, I fear I may be severing ties with the Order."

Looking astonished to have walked in on such a conversation, Valeria stood in the open doorway and asked me, "How can you say such a thing so easily? You don't intend to fight it?"

I shook my head, almost frightened to admit aloud that, having divined the sign of my broken sword, I believed it was Weltyr's will that I be ejected from the Order one way or another. "I won't have a choice... either I'll have proved myself unfavored by Weltyr, or I'll humiliate the Commander by defeating him in battle. No matter what happens, I don't think they'll continue with my confirmation."

After peering at me closely, having experienced the change in me even more acutely than had Branwen, Valeria stepped into the room and shut the door behind her. "What happened while we were in Soot, Rorke?"

"I'm not sure," I confessed with a shake of my head. "And what I am sure of...I don't know how to explain."

Branwen and Valeria exchanged a look. No doubt they worried I was going mad, or had at the very least grown incoherent with lack of sleep. Weltyr knows I certainly felt that way at the time...but that is the humbling truth about those humans who consort with the divine. They are exposed to knowledge that, to most, is so utterly without context it cannot help but seem insane. In fact, if anyone had the least of hope of understanding the magnitude of my experience, it was Valeria—but even she had not met the godhead incarnated in any form of Roserpine's.

Mere proximity to the memory of my experience brought upon me such a violent trembling, such a wave of fear, that I felt foolish straightaway. I'd experienced enough fear on that journey to humble a man for eternity! Soon, I hoped, it would be the time for me to build myself back up. Had I not sufficiently been destroyed?

Evidently, no—not quite.

That night was the night of the second strange dream, the bulbous hivemind organ of the spirit-thieves pulsing in the water of its storage chamber like the hideous homunculus of a mad alchemist. The flesh of its hateful body quivered in the shimmering darkness, its thoughts vibrating through the human mind that was, during those hours of slumber, empty of everything but the message it sent.

You are truly skilled, Paladin…and beginning to understand what is really happening. It must be strange to find yourself opposed to your own Order; there is much you do not know about it…and yourself.

A flap of skin opened with a noise like a sigh, the pulses of the hivemind permitting water to lap into the hole only occasionally.

Your god delivers scraps of information, then behaves as if he has satisfied your curiosity…you do not even know what a Wotsung is. You still do not know where you came from. You still do not know what it is the Order believes itself to be fighting for.

A slot opened in the side of the chamber. Fresh water flooded in to raise the level of liquid above the flesh-vent. The entire organ gave a pleasurable shudder, the very membranes rooted in the walls quivering to receive the intake of fluid.

Why, continued that hateful voice, *he did not even tell you the truth about Gundrygia.*

At the sound of her name, I snapped awake to realize I was having another nightmare. Branwen continued sleeping heavily to one side of me; to the other, Valeria stirred. She turned over in the darkness and peered at me tiredly, her eyes puffy with sleep and desperately kissable.

"Are you all right, Rorke?"

"I am—of course, I am."

The pre-dawn morning outside was still crisp. I looked out the window to gauge the hour by the richness of that darkness, then fit my hand to Valeria's warm cheek.

"I'd ought to go to the Temple now."

Nodding, she sat up in the dark as silently as she could. I thought she only meant to give me room, but then she rose and dressed. When I whispered to know what she was doing, she murmured, "I must come with you."

"I'm not sure that you should," I told her, remembering Zweiding's comments about the durrow and El'ryh. "I'd fight better knowing you were there, but—"

"Then I'll be there."

"But the durrow are not well-liked by other members of the Order."

How it saddened me to say! Yet Odile had told me just such a thing from early in our acquaintance. She knew more about my own organization of knights than I myself had ever been permitted to learn while raised among them.

Now I regretted not taking her more seriously; in fact, I felt a complete fool. I could not permit Elishtabet to endure such an impious reproach for something she could not control—something that was, to my mind, entirely unverified and unimportant.

"If I am to spend even part of the rest of my life on the surface, Rorke, I must accept that there are those who detest me. There are also sure to be those who do not. Your makes it worthwhile to me, and—"

Her lips pursed. She fell silent, her hand a fist upon her heart. She remained leaning forward, her gaze upon me, the sheet draping away from her to leave one breast exposed and add tenderness to her plea. My heart ached to see her so worried for me. I knelt, clasping her free hand in both of mine and pressing her knuckles to my lips.

"I'll be safe, Valeria."

"But how are you to duel with no weapon?"

"Weltyr will see to me." At the intensification of her dubious expression, I lowered my voice with a brisk glance at Branwen's back. "It has been told to me specifically, Valeria," I confessed, looking at her in a meaningful way from where I genuflected at her feet.

She absorbed my expression and, after a few seconds, her own changed somehow. It filled with an excitement; an intensification. Bending forward more, the rarely modest durrow forgot her nakedness and braced her hands against the edge of the mattress. "How was it communicated you?"

"The raven informed me," I allotted. "I wish I could tell you more. I can't."

Yet her features sharpened with acute knowledge. She caressed my face with her delicate fingers. "Your hands tell the story in the fierceness of your trembling, my paladin…oh!" She quivered, too, marveling at the very sight of me.

"Are you quite sure?"

"If I wasn't sure, I would be very wrong…or very evil. So, I'm very sure."

"Strife," she whispered at last, understanding.

I nodded, my gaze unable to hold hers. "But I was assured, among other things, that I would find a sword in my time of need. And I don't know how to explain this, but…I feel it. In my heart."

Valeria nodded, her caresses sliding back over my scalp and down my neck. "Yes—I understand, Rorke. The call and assurance of a god within the heart. Many times I have been urged by Roserpine to make a snap decision and trust it will work out, even if success seems unlikely and the decision ill-advised." A faint smile graced her features. "That is the kind of confidence I felt when told to leave El'ryh with you."

Despite myself, I smiled. Kissing her knee, I told her, "Well, that's the confidence I feel when I think of this promise that I'll find a sword at the right moment. I don't really have much choice…I have to believe it will work out well."

"Then you must let me come with you. Pray, ease my mind. Roserpine drives me on to be with you in the same degree of confidence. This assurance that what is being urged is being urged for a reason…it is what I feel right now, when my heart insists that I must go with you. You may need my help, Rorke."

Sighing, I glanced at the back of Branwen's head. Her breathing was softer than it had been when she was actually asleep and I told her, "Don't even think about coming with us."

"Well?" Caught, the high elf turned over to let me

see her frown. "How can I help it, Rorke? I don't like the thought of you going through all this any more than she does."

"If I have too many people with me, it'll look like I'm intending retribution in the case of a loss. I don't want that."

Sighing, shaking her head, the high elf said, "Well, you really do need to have at least one person with you. Anroa forbid something should go wrong...the people at the Temple won't know where to look for your friends, and we'll be stuck back here wondering what happened to you."

"If that's the case, I could have Father Fortisto come tell you...but, I suppose you're right." With a sigh of my own, I patted Valeria once more, rose, and began to dress. "Valeria can come along. If it looks like Zweiding is going to kill me without holding back, perhaps you can intervene."

"I could do it anyway," she said with a crooked smile.

I knew she jested, but I couldn't help a stern reaction.

"No," I said in a firm tone that gave her pause. "If you're to come with me, you must not interfere in any way. Not unless it looks like Zweiding is violating the code of the duel or otherwise striking like he intends to kill. It is vital to my honor that I abide by the standards of duels, and vital to my worship of Weltyr that I abide by the contractual agreements into which I enter. There can be no intercession from you in the actual duel."

Her features once again serious, Valeria fell in line with me.

"Very well, Rorke," she said, searching my face with a sternness of her own. "But if this duel takes a turn against you—"

"Now, Valeria..." With a somewhat wry grin at my

own brash nature, I patted her cheek. "What are the odds of that?"

In part, I joked; but in greater truth I held in my heart a glowing confidence in my future success. To say such things aloud was to invite an ill fate—at the very least to lose friends. After our discussion, Valeria understood the root of my confidence and the importance of the change that had begun within me. Even with that intimate understanding between two loyal servants of the divine, however, there were secret things that could not be expressed.

Before we left, I hovered by the dresser. The Scepter, still in its silk wrapping, lay upon its surface.

This was the object for which I'd journeyed so long. That very same for which I willingly enslaved myself and risked my very life.

Here it sat.

There was something infinitely sorrowful about the thought of submitting it to the Order—not just because it marked the end of my journey, but because it may well have marked the end of my relationship with that very same society of honorable knights into which I once hoped to be inducted.

This was the dream of an entire lifetime—what I'd thought I wanted since being old enough to want. The acclaim and glory that came with being one of Weltyr's anointed paladins was incredible, to say the least. Zweiding might stroll through the streets of Skythorn and, by the time he had traveled twelve blocks, would have been offered several gold ounces' worth of goods and services. Not to mention the praise of women and admiration of children! It was an enviable existence, to be certain.

But my Master had all but informed me that

there were worthier occupations in his name—and that immobile institutions could not contain the full experience of his truths.

To whom do you owe your fealty?

The question returned to me so many times! The answer had been simple at first, but the more I pondered it, the more I found it steeped in complication.

Weltyr was the answer, and the only answer. But since those first raven-eyed glints of memory through the darkness of pre-existence, the Church that clothed and fed and educated me had also taught me that Weltyr's word was only knowable through the outlet of its institutional teachings. I had been educated in an infinite number of examples of men who came forward claiming to know better than the Church.

The result, each time, was the same. Inevitably, a new religious cult would be founded. Time would pass, and the group would either dissolve or grow to a competing faith. Weltyr's word would be woven through all of it, but nothing would be as true as the Church's word.

So I had been taught, at any rate.

But, were it possible to spread Weltyr's faith without the superficial structures of Church or cult, such esoteric truths would resemble those very witchcrafts the Order sought to stamp out. Independent soothsaying and magical prayers were not just considered a danger to oneself when engaged outside of the Church. They were in fact regarded as a greater threat to society. They were gateways to radical thought and to certain alienation from the only divine truth.

And there was I, walking the dark streets of Skythorn with my heathen durrow beloved, about to end my engagement to the Order.

I had grown certain of it. The notion had turned

itself over and over in my mind, transforming from a possibility to an inevitability. I would not back down from the duel, so the consequences would be great one way or another. No matter how I arranged the events in my mind, I could not see Zweiding accepting me into the Order. Not with the duel; and not with Valeria.

She who was foremost among my beloved companions bore the Scepter with me through the city streets. I felt too unclean to touch it then. My acceptance of what was about to happen to me made me somehow forget those parts of my sacred experience wherein my worthiness was assured.

However, no matter how I tried to rationalize the teaching of the Church with what had been told to me, I could not help but fear that I did the wrong thing. Was I mad, or simply stupid? At the gates of the Temple, while Valeria marveled about her from beneath the edges of her hood, I paused before the threshold to say a prayer. The guards at either side of the gate looked respectfully away, paying no mind to myself or my companion.

What did I pray before entering the site of the duel?

That Weltyr might send me a sign—a true sign that it had indeed been he who visited me. That I was right to follow these declarations coming to me from outside the jurisdiction of the Church.

Then, with Valeria at my right hand, I entered the Temple gates for the last time.

The halls were quiet with reverence for a new day, though monks and priests and soldiers of all stations already moved about. Fresh incense sweetened the air and soft prayers filled my heart with longing. This was the home of my childhood, Weltyr, where I first learned to love you! Was I really meant to leave all this behind?

But I chided myself as we mounted the same

staircase Elishta-bet and I had taken to the Rectory Hall. My attachment to the Church was nothing more than that—attachment. Attachment to youth, to nostalgia. It was a longing for the innocent days of my childhood and all the things I once took with absolute ease.

Yet the heart of the man who is visited by God— truly, absolutely, indisputably visited, not pretending he has been visited or merely under the impression by supernatural or hallucinatory forces that he has been visited—is filled with the certainty that he has experienced the truth. One who is so intimate with truth knows that there is no room for attachment to anything mortal in the world...even Weltyr's own organization.

Perhaps this was why I felt a new confidence, a relationship with the past as I had never before experienced, while showing Valeria the halls and paintings and fantastical architecture of my childhood home. A few days before, when I had met Elishta-bet there, I had still felt like a small boy compared to the grandeur of the hallowed tower. Now I experienced a bold new sense of power as I knocked upon Father Fortisto's door and turned the knob at his bright, "Come in!"

"Father," I said, my heart glad to see him. He gasped and hurried up from his seat, crossing around the desk before the door was even fully opened.

"Rorke! Oh, what a frightful morning—I've prayed for days that the duel will go well for you."

"That makes two of us!" With a dark laugh, I embraced the old man, then released him in a gesture toward Valeria. "And this is Valeria, my dearest companion. I wanted you to meet her before the duel. It's she who helped me escape the Nightlands more than any other. Without her safe harbor, I might have spent far longer."

His eyes widening with understanding, Fortisto looked sharply into her face. "A durrow!"

"And a companion sent to me by Weltyr if ever I have known one," I assured him, stepping into the office as he hurried us in and shut the door behind. "Valeria, this is Father Fortisto—a very good man and by far the kindest priest in the Temple."

Amazed to see one of the legendary subterranean elves, Fortisto smiled with the genuine warmth of a loving parent meeting a future daughter-in-law—and a loving priest, meeting a future convert to the sacred paths of Weltyr.

"How wonderful to make your acquaintance, my dear," he told her, gently patting the back of her hand while shaking it with the other. Still not entirely used to the form of greeting, Valeria smiled somewhat weakly and allowed him to manipulate her as he would. "Weltyr bless you for helping our Rorke back aboveground...but I really must admit, if I was worried before, I'm terrified now. Surely you don't want to be here and risk—"

"She insisted," I assured him with a wave of my hand. "I dare not patronize her...where she's from, Valeria is a queen of sorts."

While I winked at Valeria's ghostly smirk, Fortisto's gasp glittered with amazement. "My goodness! Is that so! Well! You do me honor with your presence, Majesty. Have you come aboveground to learn of Weltyr's ways?"

"That does rather seem to be the way things are working out," Valeria admitted with a light laugh, free to push back her hood now that we were in the shut office. For the first time since Adonisius, I witnessed a man who could set eye upon her without lust. Only instant, godly affection.

Fortisto drew out a chair for her and she sat while

continuing, "However, I have lost something most precious to me—something that has brought me to the surface as a consequence. Rorke told me you might be able to help me find it."

"Is that so! Well"—the old man laughed slightly and settled into his seat—"I may be able to lend a bit of advice, but even with the Scepter we could only deliver a general idea of where it was…namely, the Nightlands. It took Rorke quite some time of running about, I'm led to believe, before he got an idea of *where in the Nightlands it might be…and Weltyr knows, we didn't predict its theft by his companions.*"

Fortisto shook his head sadly while leaning back in his seat, but then peered over at me with sudden remembrance. "Ah—how did your search for that one pan out?"

"Far better than I could have hoped," I said, gesturing to the desk. "Valeria?"

At my indication, Valeria opened the fabric of her cloak (a gift from the good people of Soot before we left town) and revealed the silken bundle in her arms. Fortisto's face changed as she rested the package, easily four feet in length, upon his desk.

His eyes widened and his body rocked forward in his seat.

"Go on," I said, "open it. You've been kindest to me of all men here—you deserve to see it before anyone else. Certainly before Zweiding."

Fortisto's faint laugh soon faded. He lowered a hand upon the knot tying the wrapping shut. Hesitation stayed him before he pulled the cord, fright passing through his face as it had through mine that very morning.

Then, with a light tug, he drew the covering back. We both inhaled to gaze upon it; even Valeria exuded a great deference. In the dim light of Fortisto's office, the Scepter's many colorful gems shone like a litany of eyes. Its gold gleamed with the same beauty as the sun rising steadily over Skythorn.

Fortisto pressed his fingers to his lips, eyes filling with tears, and looked as if he considered touching it. After a few seconds, unable to stand his own desire, he draped the silk over the Scepter again with a shake of his head.

"Wonderful," he told me. "Simply wonderful. Oh! Rorke—"

Suddenly exhibiting the energy of a man half his age, Fortisto darted around the desk to kiss my cheeks and embrace me as a son.

"Well done, Rorke," he cried, patting my back. "The Church has been missing this relic for so long! Good show, my boy, how proud I am."

"I owe the success entirely to Weltyr," I told him truthfully. "And I see the wisdom in sending young men out on such tasks, for the simple pursuit of this object has brought me closer to Weltyr than I have ever been before."

"How wonderful." Voice somewhat hushed, Foritsto released me and pressed his hands to his heart. "Ah! I can't describe how pleased I am! Yes, Rorke—and what timing! Perhaps with this they'll overlook your duel with Zweiding."

"Unhappy with me as I expected him to be, is he?"

Looking grim to have broached the subject, Fortisto returned to his seat and reluctantly confessed, "I have it on good authority that he intended to cancel your application to the Order outright…but, for having returned the Scepter, surely you'll be rewarded rather than disciplined."

I wasn't so sure—and, with Valeria to consider, I couldn't imagine being welcomed into the Order and joining those who lived in the Temple. Still, I smiled on. "That is certainly the hope…though, I confess I am still frightened that my relationship with the Order will be forever altered."

Looking empathetic, Fortisto reached across the desk to pat my hand. "All things will organize themselves as Weltyr will have them."

"I know that to be true," I assured him, nodding. "But, however that is, if you might be able to offer us advice concerning the whereabouts of Valeria's ring, we would appreciate the information while we are still welcome here."

"Well, for divination such as this there are two means. There are those questions whose answers we know deep down within our mortal frames, and those questions whose answers may only come by the grace of things outside of ourselves. We must exhaust the questions of the former before consulting the methods of the latter. When you last saw the ring, where was it?"

I leaned forward. "A spirit-thief absconded with it. We watched the creature steal off through a portal—someplace aboveground."

Before mentioning the man who had looked like me, I stopped myself. The dreams of that hateful, pulsing hivemind and the keeper who also bore my voice—were these occurring in the same location as the one we had seen through the portal?

Avoiding the subject of either the dream or the doppelgänger for now, I suggested, "Is it possible that the spirit-thief intended to bring the ring to its originating colony? Its hivemind?"

Looking intrigued by this, Fortisto nodded. "It is,

269

indeed. But what would they want with any ring of yours, Madame?"

"It is no ring of mine," answered Valeria, "but of Roserpine's."

The kindly priest's eyes grew wide. "The Ring of Roserpine—is that true, the very one?" While Valeria nodded, Fortisto laughed in astonishment and teasingly told me, "Well! A good thing we'll be taking the Scepter back...goodness, with the Ring and the Scepter both, you might start getting ideas."

"So where is the hivemind of the spirit-thieves is said to dwell, Father?"

Fortisto shook his head. "No one knows the exact location, though the dwarves of Rhineland are so especially vigilant about spirit-thieves that I think most of us can agree their primary nest is somewhere on the Old Continent."

"Then the dwarves may know where the nest might be?"

"They might! They might, indeed. It certainly would be a worthy path of inquiry...but, of course, dwarves do not look particularly kindly among humans coming to their land. I'm not sure they'd tell you anything if you asked."

I nodded, rising from my seat. "Well, that certainly seems like a place to start. Oh, Father! Talking through such matters with you always orders my mind—I hope I'll have the liberty to visit you after today."

"Fate is certain to none but Weltyr...and even he must read its threads, it's said. The Omniscience of God must be allocated in such a means when the Lord takes on a knowable personage; otherwise, that personage could not maintain integrity. And the divine, knowing so much more than we, permits us to maintain our own integrity; to be the very creatures producing the threads."

Thinking of Valeria's spiders, I smiled.

After some discussion, it was agreed that Father Fortisto would come with us to the site of the duel. He would advocate for the accomplishment represented by the Scepter and argue that it at the very least merited a loaner sword from the Order to fulfill the conditions of my arrangement with Zweiding.

When invited to carry the relic, he recoiled from it as I had. Valeria, therefore, pulled her hood over her face and bore it along the halls of the Temple on behalf of both of us. Orange dawn spilled through the windows, screaming across the floor and crawling up the wall as we made our way out to the training grounds on the far side of the gardens.

The gardens of the Temple were lavish, fit with orchards and edible plants such that in times of a siege the holy site could withstand an assault even if the city had fallen around it. Shimmering bluebirds chirped among the branches and dew glistened on the lips of every flower. Valeria cried with delight to step outside and see the offerings of its colors, its vines. It was almost a good thing that she was forced to keep her hood up to disguise her species; otherwise she might have left it down long enough to blind herself while looking at all the aboveground plants.

The murmur of the growing crowd was audible before we even saw the training grounds beyond the final row of hedges. On the dirt field I counted at least twenty of my fellows, a smattering of trainees, and, of course, Zweiding in his gleaming armor.

Elishta-bet, I noticed as we passed through the hedges, was nowhere to be seen.

Zweiding regarded me coldly but almost respectfully,

his armor gleaming platinum in the soft light draping over the face of the city. "Someone said they saw you riding from town. I was concerned you fled our duel when you came to your senses, but that didn't seem like you."

This faint praise wrapped in insults had been so common during my childhood that I barely noticed it. "Weltyr's call drew me on an errand in his name."

"Bold of you to claim you still work in the name of Weltyr when you would defy the ancient structure of his Church and defend the doings of witchcraft! Perhaps you wish Elishta-bet for your own wife, or perhaps your motivations are even more sinister; either way, you can hardly pretend you are acting in sync with the will of the Lord."

While the crowd shuffled to the sides of the mannequin-lined arena, Fortisto stepped up on my behalf. "It is my belief that he was, in fact, called to Weltyr's business, Zweiding."

The cocky sneer twitched from the face of my opponent. "You of all men would know," the Commander allotted without irony, "but how could you be so sure?"

"Because he has brought proof," said Fortisto, gesturing toward me while looking over his shoulder at Valeria. I extended my hand for the relic she placed in my grasp.

And it felt wrong.

I had accepted the object into my hand without looking away from Zweiding. Now, I stared sharply down at it.

The wrapped Scepter of Weltyr had seemingly grown in length and breadth alike. Indeed, its very shape had changed beneath the cloth that cloaked it.

Silent, all the blood draining from my face amid

a mixture of confusion and sudden understanding, I plucked free the knots of the shroud.

Zweiding, having waited for Fortisto to continue, now looked between me and the parcel I untied with trembling hands. "And what proof is that?"

I could not answer him.

17

EXIGENCE

THE SILK FELL tumbled to the dirt at my feet before it was caught by the wind. Off it billowed, dancing into the sky while Valeria and Fortisto both softly gasped.

A golden sword glittered in my hand, its blade formed of a steel so flawless that it glowed nearly white in the rising light of the sun.

With both hands, I hefted the blade high before me and turned it this way and that. The steel hummed as if severing particles of the very oxygen we breathed— as if tearing at the fabric of reality. Mouth open in astonishment, I supported the blade with one hand to observe the pommel and grip with the other. The great blade's hilt was as studded with glittering gems as had been the Scepter in Fortisto's office.

The priest was as shocked as I. All three of us stood, wide-eyed and open-mouthed as we studied the transfigured object in my hands. Unable to appreciate the stupendous meaning of the spectacle, Zweiding rested an impatient hand upon the pommel of his own blade.

He repeated his question in a tone all the more terse. "What proof has assured you this fool works in the name of Weltyr, Fortisto?"

Naturally unwilling to tear his eyes from the beautiful blade, Fortisto at least recovered his senses enough to answer the question.

"His victory, Zweiding," said the priest softly, finally lifting his gaze to the Commander of the Order. "His victory will be proof that he works in Weltyr's name."

Inhaling sharply, I lifted the flat of the blade and pressed its cool metal to my forehead. My eyes shut, lips moving in prayer. A breeze flowed through my body and spirit, this divine breath washing down from my skull through each one of my limbs.

The promise had been fulfilled. I had received my sign, and my sword.

I had received the manifestation of a greater oath than any I had ever before sworn.

"Let us begin," I urged, lowering the blade and staring down Zweiding. "The sooner we do, the sooner this duel be but an ugly memory."

"For one of us," agreed the Commander, eyes following Valeria as she and Fortisto found a place to stand near the hedges that flanked the field's entrance.

While I stood across from Zweiding and listened to the terms of the duel rattled off to us by a secretary of the Order to whom such responsibilities were allotted, I was amazed to find myself calmer than perhaps I had ever been. Much as I had begun to view my divorce from the order as an inevitability, awareness of my future victory came upon me with the same crystalline cognition. To say I felt confident in my ability to best Zweiding would have been incorrect. Rather, I felt that the victory had been ordained—that it said nothing of my own personal skill, and everything of the grace of the god who had chosen me.

"Weltyr will name the victor of this duel," the secretary told us, having summed up the guidelines by which we were to engage in battle. "When the dust has settled, the winner must abide by the standards of the loser, for that is the will Weltyr has chosen to support. What is your will, challenger?"

"That Zweiding should yield his claim over the hand of Elishta-bet."

"And your will, Commander Zweiding?"

"That this impudent welp should be ejected from the Order, and his rank permanently stripped."

Terms stated, Zweiding and I were sent to back twenty paces.

The secretary made himself scarce and, only when clear at the side of the field, called the fatal word: "Fight!"

A bevy of noise erupted to emphasize how unnaturally quiet the battleground had been. Amid the cheers of the witnesses and the metallic clatter of moving armor, Zweiding charged. I met him head-on, moving not so much by instinct but by the hand of one who knew my body better than I did.

Our swords met.

Across the sparking blades, a wave of surprise altered Zweiding's face. The force of my parry knocked him back some feet, and my charge gave him only a few seconds to recover.

We were both amazed for different reasons as I swung the glittering blade in a blitz the Commander was forced to waste much time and ground parrying. The sword in Zweiding's hands, though possessed by the same unyielding charm reflecting his oath to the Church, rattled as though to warn any lesser blade would have already snapped. He gritted his teeth against the energy rattling through him with each hammering of this new sword of mine through the air, his skull surely ringing as he met each strike with the only defenses he could manage.

"You always were a fighter of reasonable skill," he admitted, dodging a slash only to have his sword nearly knocked from his hands as I swung into another flurry. What a balanced blade! I might have laughed for the pleasure of the fight if he would not have been offended. As it was, he continued on to ask in a tone of consternated appreciation, "But where did you learn to fight like this?"

"Only the blessing of a god can permit a man to win a duel against one such as you, Commander."

With a humorless smirk, he eased up on his sword, then tried to knock my leg out from under me and keep me from another blitz. Before he could get near such a thing, however, I had already followed through on a slice through the air. My blade sank into his pauldron. The metal of the armor gave way like wool, and as the Commander hissed I was amazed to find how easily the sword came away from the wound it had made.

Blood flowed through the gap in Zweiding's armor. The cheers that had begun with the battle had by now faded to shocked murmurs. Face hardened by the pain, Zweiding charged me with incredible strength.

Now it was I who stood at the defense, though the sword that had been, as promised, gifted to me in my most needful hour was strong against the assault. It absorbed every blow with minimum impact, its blade still as unnaturally sharp as it had been when first I set my eye upon it. Moreover, it was so graceful that even with the encumbrance of my armor I felt light as a feather when it came to meeting my opponent strike for strike.

As his blows all came to naught, Zweiding's already reddened face grew hard with frustration. Soon, wrath.

"What nonsense is this," he shouted, beating his blade against mine to drive me back. "You were never so skilled!"

"Your position in the Order and the worldly adulation you receive for it has blinded you to the will of Weltyr," I informed him, knocking his sword from his hands to send it sliding across the dirt. "Perhaps, if you went out into the world again, it would teach you that you know far less than you think you do. Do you yield?"

Teeth bared, Zweiding dashed to reclaim his lost weapon. I let him pick it up and stood while he vented his fury on me, each blow angrier than the last until his arms had begun to shake. Only then did I drive him back to our starting places, his blade unsteady in his hands and soon once again upon the ground between us.

The tip of my gleaming sword pressed against the breastplate through which we both knew it could effortlessly tear.

"Do you yield?"

"I've never lost a battle," he said, ducking down to grab his sword again. "You'll have to kill me."

Driven by fury and dangerous pride, Zweiding swung his blade against my side and did make impact, though Rigan's armor held as I had expected it to. Hoping to end the duel, I sliced toward my opponent's legs.

The shock that blossomed across his features as the blade sliced into his greave to sever the tendons of his leg—it saddened me. How was it that I had been given a blade so deadly only once I asked Weltyr to help me deal more gently with my fellow man?

Perhaps that was why the sword had now arrived. I had proved that my heart's greatest desire was to act not as conqueror in Weltyr's name, but defender of it.

Collapsing to the dirt with a cry of pain, Zweiding released his hold of his sword to tear his armor from his bleeding leg. As a medic hurried forward to see the injury and a few high-ranking Order officers followed suit, the Commander forced himself to hiss, "Very well, damn you, very well! I yield, I yield—the battle and Elishtabet, I yield them both!"

Relief surging through me along with the hollow feeling of victory, I slid the unsheathed weapon into the loop where once hung Strife's scabbard. The Sword of Weltyr gleamed like new, unstained by blood or the dust of the field.

Valeria's fast footsteps drew my attention. I turned just in time to catch her in my arms. Embracing her delicate elf's body to mine, I held her close and kissed her fragrant mouth with a sigh of relief.

"My warrior," she cried with pride, her features as bright with delight as ever I had seen them. "Oh, Burningsoul! Oh, Rorke! How wonderful you are!"

I chuckled, holding her, that regal face once more a wealth of lovely blue grays in the light of the sun. Drawing the hood down just so over her eyes, I told her, "Wonderful, perhaps. A part of the Order, never."

Hissing as the medic probed his wound, Zweiding stared up at me in absolute resentment. Part of me did feel a certain shame—I had beaten him so handily that I experienced a twinge of sympathetic embarrassment, though I was quick to reminded myself it was an embarrassment he would not have endured had he been less heinous a person in his heart of hearts. His ways were not the ways of the All-Father he proclaimed to serve, for the All-Father loved all thinking things upon the planet without regard to their race or creed or magical talent. It was only their disobedience to his will that he did not love…and yet I have heard it said that even the tendency toward rebellion, he admires—for the gods, knowing too much, have no free will of their own. Even the All-Father's True Will is that inevitable force of nature and time that is the sum total of reality.

And it was evident that Zweiding's free will failed to align with my Master's True Will. Therefore, I was the tool of his humbling.

If a man's free will did not align with Weltyr's course for reality, then why should an institution, however old and revered, not be capable of the same straying?

Clarity arose in me. My hand upon the pommel of the sword that was once the Scepter of Weltyr, I told the man being attended to by now more than one medic at my feet, "It pains me to say this, but I cannot join the Order."

"Then you're a coward," spat Zweiding, "and a failure. Forsaking your quest to find the Scepter over a woman! What does this concubine of yours think of that, by the by?"

At Valeria's faint scoff, I drew her behind me and informed my former Commander coldly, "There are truths in this world that may only be found by traveling, and trusting, and risk-taking through time. You took all your risks in the military, Zweiding, and may Weltyr's maiden daughters attend you well in his Hall for it; but, by taking ample advantage of the earthly rewards offered you for this service, you've begun slaving for yourself rather than our Master."

"Fool! The outside world has poisoned your mind. Perhaps you enjoyed your time in the Nightlands a little too much—were you unmanned there in body as well as mind?"

"That's a bitter tone for a duel already decided, and a fine example of why I cannot join the Order. If my time in the Nightlands showed me anything, it is that the durrow are, apart from the values of their society, just like elves; and that elves are just like us. All mankinds are equal in the eyes of God."

A sacred raven crowed merrily from a battlement. I doubt Zweiding took heed of its agreement. "See what traitorous beliefs you've taken on! Next you'll support interbreeding."

I scoffed. "Of course I do." That got a few more sidelong glances than I had expected, and I looked about in surprise. "The Church teaches nothing about such matters."

"But history does," responded Zweiding sharply, gritting his teeth as the wound upon his leg was sutured shut right there on the field. "The Order is the point where the Church meets with secular history. We are the intersection between clergy and *militia*, Burningsoul! It's something you've never understood. You're not a paladin—you're a priest who likes to fight."

I might have had my pride rebuffed by such a remark a mere few days before. Instead, it made me laugh. In so many ways, he was right; and, though I still consider myself a paladin in the name of Weltyr, I have remembered that comment with fondness for all of my days. I can only imagine how enraged Zweiding would be to know such a thing!

"That may be so," I told him, trying to keep my smile under control lest he thought I mocked him, "but you must admit…as priests go, I am a very skilled fighter."

"You really have changed," observed a nearby paladin

with whom I had trained but who I would not consider among my friends or mentors. "Not a boy anymore, eh, Rorke."

"Only a coward. Very well." Zweiding spat from the side of his mouth and into the dirt, his breath hitching as the hooked needle of the medic tugged his flesh shut. "The Order doesn't need those who are too soft-hearted to carry out their duties. How pathetic you are! Lucky for you we're not at war, and luckier still you weren't raised in some rural principality where the primary duty is eradicating heretics."

I had been about to extricate myself from a conversation that I felt could only lead to another, more informal and all the more dangerous fight, but that comment gave me pause. The voice of the hivemind pulsed through my consciousness while I asked, "So it's true? In the Nightlands, I was told a terrible story—one of a durrow settlement destroyed by servants of Weltyr. Have we been truly committing such atrocities for generations?"

""Atrocities!" How weak you sound…and pathetic. Amazing that, after all these years of education, you never puzzled together what it means to defend the faith and wipe away heretical beliefs. The only thing for it is the sword, not words. Pagans will always find ways to justify themselves, but their sound defeat in battle proves Weltyr's will is the only one that's true."

"If Weltyr's will is true, and victory in battle is proof, then how can you say I'm false in my beliefs?"

Valeria's voice was softer than a whisper and most assuredly inaudible from the distance of the other paladins. Some kind of prayer drifted from her mouth while Zweiding told me, "Because your beliefs are not in line with the Church. Are you saying it's a good thing that all these races exist? That false species with false gods were introduced to Urde when the spirit-thieves invaded from whatever hellish location they once called their home?"

Glancing back over my shoulder at softly whispering Valeria, I studied Zweiding more intently and tried not to enjoy his wince too much when the suturing process began on his arm. "What do you mean to say, exactly?"

"You see...you jump to conclusions and leave the Order before the full truth can be disseminated to you. These durrow you so adore—and the elves, and the dwarves, and all of these other races competing with humanity for resources—they were artificially created, Burningsoul! Falsely engineered. Not by Weltyr, but by the spirit-thieves!"

The words of Al-listux swept back to me through time.

You have me and my kind to thank for the love of your life...for your own life, and your so-called 'natural' will.

"But—how could such a thing be possible?"

"Spirit-thieves possess technologies ungodly in design and origin. They hold knowledge that no mortal being should ever be permitted to know, and they worship a demon from beyond the stars."

"To what end, though? Why would the creation of these races assist in anything like what you describe?"

"Because: with so many mankinds, and so many heretics, and with such frequently renewing warfare, we cannot agree on anything. Humankind cannot even agree among itself, let alone elf with human or dwarf with elf! It is not possible for us to become a star-faring planet in such conditions, and the spirit-thieves therefore have no competition when it comes to tightening their control over all the universe."

"What nonsense," I said almost without thinking. "Why should any species desire to control the universe?"

"For resources! That's what the spirit-thieves want more than anything, Burningsoul—fuel for their ships, slaves for their consumption, gold for their sleeping demon-god!"

More aware of Valeria's soft voice than ever before, I turned to see father Fortisto watching nervously from the hedges. He wrang his hands and looked more than once over his shoulder as though to ensure the path remained clear should we need to run...and I had the feeling we would, because I could not let the Commander of Weltyr's Order say such insane things while the other members nodded sagely on, or at the very least listened with close interest.

"Yes, I've heard it said that the spirit-thieves were extraterrestrial demons who migrated to Urde long after its creation...but if that is the case, then I cannot help but suggest this, too, is the will of Weltyr."

Balking, Zweiding demanded, "How can you say such a thing?"

"Because the True Will is too vast to be experienced by mankinds—even the longest-lived elf will never know its full scope. Who is to say that the creation of more races, or even a human loss when at war with the spirit-thieves, does not factor into the longterm aim of this True Will? How are we to judge what is right and wrong when we have not one iota of Weltyr's understanding?"

The Commander's eyes narrowed. "Are you really saying that Weltyr sent the spirit-thieves to us? That all these species and all these false gods are in some way the will of the All-Father?"

I spread my hands. From the corner of my eye, a black dot scuttled across the field. "I suppose I am. Having experienced what I have experienced on my journey for the Scepter, I have come to believe that even the greatest or most loathsome thing that occurs cannot ultimately occur if it interferes with the longterm fulfillment of the Master's will."

"Then I suppose we have nothing more to say to one another," said Zweiding coldly. "Arrest this race-traitor—and that woman, too."

With a scoff, I stepped back against Valeria and set my hand upon my blade. Another insect of some kind crept past. I noticed it was a spider but was much too shocked to fully absorb the implication. "What?"

"Such heretical thoughts cannot be expressed without consequence." While a few of his comrades drew their blades, Zweiding continued. "Rest satisfied in your cell knowing that Elishta-bet will be free from the cold clutches of matrimony with me…and, perhaps, comfortable in the cell next to yours, since without reformation she can never hope to be anything but a witch."

"Valeria," I said as the Order members made their way toward us, "we have to—"

But her voice lifted in a high elvish cry that, upon fading from our ears, revealed like the pulling back of an audible curtain the scuttling of thousands of spider legs. Father Fortisto cried out in horror.

Seconds later a sea of arachnids from all the shadowy corners and dark alleys of Skythorn rushed into the training field in a hideous wave.

A few paladins cried out in fear that was somewhat shocking to me—perhaps it was the first time I saw them as actual, fallible mortals, rather than infallible celebrities. As they hurried back from the skittering onslaught, a pair of massive plane-walking spiders manifested on either side of Zweiding and his medics. All of them cried out in horror, the medical officials hurrying away and leaving the Commander to fend for himself.

"Let's run," said Valeria while Zweiding snatched up his blade. The braver men present all raised arms against the plane-shifting beings while more soldiers, attracted by the sea of spiders rushing past the temple gates, joined the fray and were very soon covered in thousands of the smaller arachnids.

By the time we reached Fortisto, who had found an island of safety upon the large stones lining a flower bed outside the arena, a third alien spider had joined the battle—by the looks of its size, to defend its smaller children.

"The two of you must leave Skythorn at once," advised the old priest, gripping my shoulders while we delayed to try and convince him to leave Temple grounds until the heat was off. "It's not safe for you here anymore—Zweiding will see the both of you arrested, oh, Rorke—"

"But there's no other airport for weeks of riding! Not one with ships that go as far as Rhineland, anyway."

"Then you must flee now and hope you can make it before today's flight departs...once you've left Skythorn, you'll be a wanted man. Surely arrested when you try to return."

My heart sank to think such a thing. Ejected from my own home, and under such sordid circumstances!

But—it was the will of Weltyr. I holstered my sword again and embraced Fortisto.

"May Weltyr grant you many more long, happy years, my friend. I love you as a son loves a father."

When we drew away, Fortisto's eyes were filled with tears.

"Take heed in the streets," he told me, pushing me toward the gates. "Don't look frantic, but neither should you take your time. Oh! Rorke—a true servant of Weltyr if ever I have been blessed to know one. Your name will be remembered forever. God bless you! God bless you! May you be selected for the Hall!"

18

BENEATH SKYTHORN

OUR RETURN TO the inn was tense. Heads ringing with Fortisto's advice, Valeria and I found ourselves hyper-aware of every guard we passed, and the feeling was mutual. With my new sword unmarked by the Order and carried open on my hip without a sheath, I was neither a potential peer nor possible superior, but instead a likely rabble rouser.

Then, there were the citizens. The silver hilt of an Order blade was recognizable to everyone in the city. The blade that was once the gilded Scepter of Weltyr simply marked me as either a man of wealth or of supreme skill in battle, and the general sense of curiosity this drew was worrisome. If asked about us, people would remember.

Yet I could not be made to fully care. My senses were bright and crisp with victory. My heart soared every step, exultant. The sword swung at my side as though to perpetually remind me of Weltyr's favor: of his remaining eye, following me through the city streets.

Impossible as it is to think, a small boy inside me was still afraid I had done something very wrong just then. The image of my old intentions decried me as a blasphemer and false prophet. I had turned away from the Order and quite literally run off with one of the many species to which they were, I discovered, opposed. How many men were confirmed into the Order completely before learning such a fact? How many remained not because they thought it was right or Weltyr's will but because they had no other options left to them by that point?

But Father Fortisto's parting words had taken root far more than any condemnation of Zweiding's. He had lauded me! It was now my impossible task to not feel an excess of pride at being called a true servant of Weltyr by a man who was himself among the most godly I had ever known.

I was resolved, therefore, that I had acted in accordance with Weltyr's will…but all this about the spirit-thieves was far more disturbing.

Though I had been aware that the presence of spirit-thieves on Urde was unnatural by one manner or another, (interplanetary or interdimensional, it made no difference to me then), I had never fully considered what that meant for all the species of mankinds. Why should I? Spirit-thieves were barely even spoken of anymore by the common citizen of Cascadia. Only those who had close dealings with dwarves (or, it would seem, durrow) knew what a danger they presented—and if even one quarter of what Zweiding had told me was true, that danger was greater than I had ever been taught.

The drowned temple with the images of the sleeping

squid-god returned to me. If it was resources they wanted, what use was rousing it from its nightmares? It seemed to me that they only wished to prolong their own existences, and bringing the Sleeper into this reality would certainly not contribute to their own extensive lifespans. I had heard it said the thing drove men mad to look upon—that it devoured worlds and bred infinite offspring which, though lesser than itself, were a thousandfold more horrible than the basest of demons permitted to slip through the cracks of the Wyrd and perpetrate its sins on Urde.

Why, then? What was the will of the spirit-thieves, and, more important, what was the will of my God?

"Do you really think all that was true back there?" As I spoke, Valeria glanced into my face and looked away only before we crossed a certain busy street near the inn. "That business about spirit-thieves producing mankinds other than human."

Though her expression briefly changed, as if she was first shocked I should ask such a thing, I watched her sort out the rationality and, moreover, neutrality of my question. Given a few seconds with it, she suggested, "I, myself, have questioned what was said by the witch woman in Soot. About elves coming from the durrow people rather than the other way around. Rest assured, if anyone remembered such a thing, my people would not let it be forgotten."

I chuckled, thinking of Odile in particular. "No doubt! If such a long span of time has passed that even the durrow have forgotten they were the originators of the elvish peoples, I should think it long enough for aboveground folk with common knowledge to forget the origins of the species. But..."

"But?"

"But for Zweiding to suggest that such a thing could ever be accomplished without the blessing of Weltyr—that is the greater blasphemy."

Her stare bored into me. I turned to see she in fact smiled. Brooding Valeria was so seldom given to such genuine expressions that, taken aback, I laughed even in the chaos of our in-progress flight from Skythorn. "What is it?"

"Nothing," she said, her tone exceptionally fond. Her hand lowered to mine, patting me through the armor. "I love you, Rorke."

Before we stepped into the inn, I caught her and kissed her as I had after the battle. She sighed, patted my chest, and leaned into me even as we parted. Then, stepping into the Mongoose, we straightaway spotted Lively and Erdwud having breakfast with Sharp at a corner table in the presently quiet establishment.

All three looked up; Sharp seemed about to stand before he recognized us. Then, relaxing back down, he expected us to return to our rooms and delivered little more than a casual nod. The friends turned to resume their conversation.

Instead, Valeria and I went straight to them. Sharp's face fell at the prospect of work, but nonetheless he gave us his attention. "What is it then?"

"Don't be so crude." Lively swatted Sharp's hand before beaming to hold Erdwud's. "Thanks to them, my Erdie's all right, and already back to putting on the weight he lost while hidin' in them woods."

Muttering under his breath, Sharp said louder, "Right, well done. What can I do for yous?"

"We'll be checking out today," I said, provoking a sad little noise from Lively. "And, if you could, we need a bit of advice on how to get to the airport quickly...

without attracting attention. It's not a part of the city I've ever seen before."

"Right! You're aiming to leave today, in the blimp headed eastward? Could have mentioned that to me a mite sooner so I could have planned my chambermaid's schedule today."

"Our leaving is a bit short notice."

Arching a brow, Sharp asked, "Do you lot even have tickets?

Valeria and I exchanged a glance. "How much are they?"

He named a price that made my mouth fall open.

"Surely not," I said.

Erdwud, however, swallowed his bite of food and leaned forward, waving dismissively with a napkin still between his thumb and the palm of his hand.

"Don't listen to him," said the rural innkeeper who was, perhaps ironically, the more worldly of the two. "Sharp won't even go near the bloody airport! He's afraid of blimps."

"I'm not bloody afraid, you cock! I just don't cherish the idea of being waylaid by pirates or dying in a fiery crash."

"Pirates! Listen to you. Ten years old…probably secretly wish *The Flying Rhinemaid*'ll drift by and all the lovely lassies will avail themselves of your—"

Lively cleared her throat.

"Right," Erdwud, red-faced and laughing now. "Anyhoo, he's talking about the price for a cabin. The price for an economy ticket is much more reasonable. I've even heard you can give a few copper to the baggage crew and they'll let you ride in the cargo hold, but they don't take responsibility if you're crushed by something, of course."

I tried not to look impatient—but, much as Valeria might have felt through the frequency of her prayer the forthcoming waves of spiders, I could feel the information on our new warrant spreading through the city. When leaving El'ryh we had the benefit of slipping out before anyone knew we were gone. In Skythorn, we were wanted already. Keeping my tone even, I asked, "How much for an economy ticket?"

"Oh, shouldn't be more than two ounce of gold apiece."

"That's good information," I said, nodding. "Will you come by our rooms in a few minutes, Erdwud? I have a few more questions to ask, and I'm afraid we must pack."

"Of course! No problem, no problem at all. What a shame to see you lot move on!"

I could see him wanting to ask where we were headed, but, pressed for time, I smiled at him and said, "Yes, it is a pity in some ways—we've all grown quite attached to you and Lively."

Then, hand in the small of Valeria's back, I steered her toward the stairs and we hurried to our rooms.

Not more than five minutes later the whole party stood together, Indra and Branwen packing while Odile, the self-appointed treasurer of our group, complained, "Why do we keep having to spend all our money!"

"It does us no favors weighing down our hips," answered Valeria while helping me out of my armor, which otherwise made us too obvious as subjects of investigation.

Odile scoffed. "Easy for you to say, Materna. You've never had to worry about money in your life. What if we need it later on down the line?"

"Weltyr has plenty of money," I assured everyone.

"As we require it, more will be allocated to us. For now, we have to trust in him and spend it. Certainly I know no better way to flee our current circumstances and race toward our goal at the same time."

With a hefty sigh of displeasure and a look at the leather sack still sitting on her dresser, Odile snapped, "Fine. But don't come crying to me when our coffers are empty and we need to bribe a guard somewhere. I still can't believe this! Why on Urde did you ever agree to such a stupid duel? And *please!* Don't say it's because of Weltyr."

"I confess that he is the only reason why I do anything, Odile." Sighing and rolling her eyes, Odile fetched the party's purse. "Trust in Weltyr's will was the reason I went agreeably with you two to El'ryh."

"I'm starting to regret that deal," she said, shaking her head while checking through the coins to make sure we had enough. "And I'm really starting to get sick of fleeing from cities…can we make this the last time?"

"If I can help it," I promised her merrily.

Branwen, meanwhile, seemed drawn with concern and paused over the bag she packed, one hand resting against her forehead. I slid my arms around her and asked, "Are you coming with us?"

"I've never been to Rhineland before," she said with reluctance, "or on an airship…but…"

Her lower lip disappeared between her teeth and her eyes lowered to the sword over which the ladies had been given little time to marvel.

"All right," she said, looking up at me seriously. "After all we've been through, and the ways I let you down—I can't stay here worrying about you. But are we really going to make it to the airport before being intercepted? I don't know how fast word travels in Skythorn, but…"

"It's true, I'm concerned about the actual path we're to take. That's why—ah!"

A knock rang out upon the door. Hurrying over, I threw it open to reveal Lively and Erdwud's smiling faces.

"Just in time," I said, my tone still somehow effortlessly carefree. I felt anything but. "Hello, friends! Erdwud, could you explain to us how we would get to the airport?"

I won't bore one with the details, especially because they proved irrelevant. The women hovered about between the rooms, hastily packing, and for a span I swore to be shorter than four minutes we were given a chance to figure out a general route of escape. A difficult task, given how notoriously bad Erdwud was with directions!

Before he had even finished, however, a commotion from the street cut through all the city noise. My companions and I froze, exchanging urgent looks.

Erdwud noticed our expressions belatedly, connected them to the sound, and asked, "What's that going on out there?" just as the door to the tavern blew open.

I and the ladies retreated into the rooms immediately. Erdwud and Lively, exchanging glances, stepped into the doorways and stood as if they were guests of the inn leaning out to find the source of the noise. The clamor of city guards entering the inn was crystal clear around the corner of the upstairs hallway.

"No weapons in the tavern," said Sharp calmly, this immediate reprimand so audacious I would have laughed under another circumstance. "The lot of you will have to let one of my employees check them."

With an audible scoff, whatever captain had led his detail in responded, "We're city guards, you numbskull. Looking for a heretic who's running loose in the city and responsible for an attack on Commander Zweiding's life."

"I don't muck about in religion," was the impeccable innkeeper's response. "I only know the law, and the law says no weapons in my tavern or I can lose my license, and no barging in on private property without a certified warrant in your hand."

"You may not "muck about in religion," but that doesn't change the privileges extended to the Order when dealing with heretics." While I pondered how difficult it would be to put my armor on without making too much noise, I drew the unchristened blade and prepared to make battle.

I ought to have had more faith in Sharp, given the rough area where his tavern was situated.

"Privilege is one thing, but law is another. Bring a beadle around with you or get lost for good."

"I think you need to learn how to speak to—"

A few men gasped beneath the distinct cocking of a dwarvish pistol. Such items were illegal in Skythorn, as I believe I already mentioned: at minimum, he risked a fine and confiscation of the item by brandishing it in our defense. When brandishing at an officer, Sharp most certainly inviting imprisonment. I could only pray he would not see his inn taken from him as a result of this incident. Weltyr bless him, the man the rough around the edges but loyal to those guests whom he was sworn to protect.

"Come back with a beadle and a warrant," said Sharp in a firm tone, "or don't come back at all. Sound reasonable?"

"Oh," answered the captain to the sound of a sword being sheathed, "we'll certainly be back. Don't go anywhere."

With a snarl that his men should remain around the inn and guard the exits in case we tried to leave or someone arrived, the captain stormed from the building. His men filed out after him while Lively and Erdwud relaxed their postures. They turned to us, expressions lined with concern.

"I don't suppose it'd do any good asking what's happened this morning," observed Erdwudwhile the women slung their packs over their shoulders.

I hurried to finish packing my armor and suggested, "The less you know, the less trouble of your own you're likely to be in."

Sharp's footfall upon the stair had me out in the hall again. "You lot need to clear out of here immediately," he warned us, the flintlock still in his hand, "and I'm thinking I might need to do the same. I got something close to good news for you, though."

Soon we were downstairs, all of us crouched around a trap door on the floor of the tavern's cellar. He'd had to push aside a cask of mead to do it, and while Indra sniffed at its contents with a sigh of remorse to leave it untasted, I peered into the darkness below.

"What is this?"

Without so much as a word, Valeria's blue wisp flame appeared in the darkness and illuminated a gray concrete floor far beneath us.

"This," said Sharp, with the first bit of genuine pleasure I had seen him exhibit, "is precisely why I bought this place, and why I cater to the kinds of clientele I do."

"You two really are diametrically opposed," observed Valeria absently, her pale eyes lingering on the mine cart system of some sort established below the building. Darkness expanded from far off, implying a long tunnel sequence about which I'd heard growing up.

"This was a kind of old transport system," I explained while Sharp nodded. "These are all over the city, and off-limits...too dangerous. People live down there, too. As you can imagine, they're not the most savory individuals...then there's rumors of monsters, but probably nothing more than the average slime."

Valeria sat up a bit from her investigation of the darkness. "How far does it go?"

"'Round about forty leagues running northwest, southwest, southeast and northeast, bit like a great 'x' beneath Skythorn. City must have been very small when it were built for it to have served any use!"

"And where are we on that 'x' relative to the airport, friend?"

"We're over here"—he drew a crooked 'x' in the unsavory amount of dust on his cellar floor, pointing with the tip of his finger—"and the airport's about here, but there's only a few places you can cross over between these tunnels. Don't know where precisely they are, since I've just gone north and then only a bit. It's hard to explore. Skythorn guards send patrols through every once in awhile to keep kids from hurtin' themselves, and them aside, you don't want no unsavory sort watching your comings and goings with regularity. But if you go south, and just keep trying to follow them tunnels as far south as south can be, you'll get to the airport. Close to it, anyway—it's collapsed in parts, and other parts have caved out so you can get to the Old City bits. And that *is* dangerous, because you go too far you'll end up in the Nightlands...though I don't suppose you lot care about that."

"Depending on where we end up," Valeria answered, "it could be quite dangerous for us. But thank you, friend, for your advice."

"And thank you for your patronage…Erdwud? I don't suppose I can ask you to watch the tavern 'till the heat is off?"

"No problem at all…Lively's assistant is fixing up the building at home after all that bad business, and I hear we ought to be expecting a few new trainees! I'll let her break 'em in."

While Sharp descended the ladder that extended from the mouth of the trap door to the tunnels blow, I glanced between Lively and her husband.

"Is there any chance"—I addressed the more unassuming of the pair—"you might do us a favor? I'm not convinced that we're going to be able to make the airport in anything approaching a timely fashion if these tunnels are as much a labyrinth as I fear they may be. You'll surely get there sooner aboveground than we will below, or I'd wager as much anyway. Besides—if we're wanted, it might be hard for us to buy seats. Will you take our money and purchase tickets for us?"

While Odile made a little noise of protest that I duly ignored, Lively's expression firmed. The faint furrow of her brow, hinting at nervousness, belied a determined core.

"After what you've done for me and my Erdie," she said, accepting the purse I plucked off Odile's hip and passed over, "the very least I can do for you is this. Where should I meet you?"

"I'm not sure yet—just wait for us outside the airport as casually as you can. We'll find you somehow."

Nodding, Lively bent to kiss her husband. Erdwud's expression, tight with concern, melted somewhat as his wife assured him with a wink, "Don't worry, dear, I'll be back in two shakes. You just watch the bar…if anybody asks, I was woken up by the row and told by the innkeeper

I'd ought to go elsewhere a whiles.

"You just holler if they give you any trouble," said Erdwud, watching his wife hurry back out of the cellar and into the inn proper. Shaking his head in an affectionate way, he looked at me quite knowingly.

"These women," he said with a shake of his head. "It's like finding a field of flowers to discover each one of 'ems made of painted iron. A bit unnerving, really! I think Lively could best me in a fight, you know..."

Soon, one by one, we descended into the ancient tunnel system beneath Skythorn. A mist in his eye, Erdwud called down, "Now, you lot be sure to send word to us that you've made it wherever you're meant to be going...don't want us to worry for the rest of time, do you?"

"We certainly will find some way to let you know," I called up to him while landing upon the old concrete. One by one, my companions had already organized themselves and lit the magical lantern. Now they waved up with me as I called, "Perhaps, if ever you and Lively find yourselves inclined to travel again, you might come see us...wherever we end up."

With that, Erdwud shut us in, and we were left alone beneath the tunnels of Skythorn. By what means Sharp so confidently traversed the dark, I could not guess only to say that he had perhaps practiced the trek on which he embarked so as to flee without drawing attention by torchlight. Whatever his means of departure, it was the last we saw of him. With Branwen at the pack's head and me at the rear to guard from any sneak attack that might have been laid by man or monster, our party of five made our way through the labyrinth beneath Skythorn.

It is here I must make time to pause and describe how grateful I am to have known Indra and Odile.

Today it is patently obvious to me how much I and my family owe to the two who found me in the Nightlands and assisted us through so much of our journey. Were it not for them and their lantern, their familiarity with navigating the darkness, even the simple tools they bore such as compasses and lockpicks, we would have been quite literally lost.

Instead, with the two of them close together in the center of our party, (just behind Valeria, where they could watch the displaced leader of their species and ensure she was in no danger), Odile and Indra navigated the tunnels for us. Amid the occasional soft squeak of a rat, they kept us going in what was roughly the right direction and held the lantern so we could see and avoid the assaults of any dumber beast that happened upon us.

And there were, in fact, things moving in that darkness—things that were not fully discernible and may at times have been human. Whatever they were, brigand or beast, they avoided us and we avoided them.

All except for one particular aggressor.

Although there were points where tunnels crossed with one another and rough passages that connected between them, the main tunnels as the ancients had envisioned them were demarked by the same mine cart-like rail system that had caught my eye from the first. As Sharp had described it, all we needed do was follow those rails through the tunnels in a southwesterly direction. After a certain point we would either run out of exit options or reach the end of the tunnels...but it would be hard to tell which was which.

We had walked for almost an hour. I was beginning to worry because of the airship's noon departure time. Though the duel had been first thing in the morning and we still, by any stretch of imagination, had a fair bit of time still before the ship left, if we became too lost in these tunnels we might end up quite some ways away from our intended destination.

Furthermore, the exits were variable. Sometimes we might pass a set of stone or metal steps that had been installed by a previous owner and neglected by the current one; sometimes, like with Sharp's inn, there might be a ladder up to an emergency exit. Most often, however, any trap doors or diversionary tunnels had long ago been sealed, abandoned, and forgotten.

How were we to know where to exit? What would we find at the end of the tunnels? What would happen if Skythorn guards found us down here and we had to kill a few? What then?

I was so sucked into the miasma of my own thoughts that I hardly even realized we'd been walking in the same direction, without any change of angle or noteworthy landmark, for something in the neighborhood of twenty minutes...at least, that was how long it seemed to us.

Valeria's question broke the tense silence in which we traveled for fear of otherwise attracting bandits. "Have we been going in the same direction for over a mile now?"

"I was just thinking the same thing," I told her, looking back over my shoulder. "Have you noticed, Indra? Odile?"

"Sure, I noticed," said Odile. "I thought it was supposed to be like this."

"But there haven't been any exits," said Branwen. "Not on the ceiling or walls or anything."

Concerned, I asked, "Are we still headed southwest?"

"Hold on"—Indra dug out their compass, tongue poking from the corner of her mouth—"let's see..."

The noise of shock that followed chilled my blood.

"Odile," she said hastily, "look at this!"

Odile took it from her hands and gasped, tone at once drenched in accusatory displeasure. "You ninny! What did you do to this thing?"

"But I didn't do anything," protested Indra, adding tersely while I leaned over their shoulders to see the problem, "and I don't call *you* names, you know, Odile."

The needle of the compass whizzed in rapid circles, indicating nothing.

I was only about to request the device to take a closer look at it when a woman's familiar, cruel-edged cackle echoed through the darkness of the tunnels all around us.

Sword in-hand, I turned to face Gundrygia.

19

THE NEW WOTSUNG

HOW LONG SHE followed us in the fashion of a shadow, I could not possibly say. Even today Gundrygia remains coy about the subject.

I know only this: that I set eyes upon her in that darkened space and knew we were no longer on Urde.

Gritting my teeth, I tried to fathom how much time had passed. The days I had been in her arms had seemed like hours. The minutes in her sepulcher had been near an hour. Perhaps, if Weltyr willed it, there would still be time to make it to the airship. Perhaps, if we could extricate ourselves from this trap, we would escape capture by the Skythorn guards.

Like most traps, this one was lined with the finest of bait. Wilder and lovelier than ever, Gundrygia stood before us in the same furred garb she'd worn when I discovered her; with the same tattoos upon the haughty face that peered through tumbling curls.

"So it's you again, witch." Blade gleaming bright between us in the light of the lantern, I fought back the yearning and subsequent fear that subsumed me to see her. "If you've come for the lantern again, you've made a sore mistake—my friends and I are still making use of it."

"I came for no light, but a flame...for you, Burningsoul."

Scoffing, I lowered the blade somewhat while the enchantress smiled on. "What business have you saying such a thing? What force on Urde could convince me to go of my own will?"

Her lower lip protruding in a pout, Gundrygia drew her furs up from her feet and slunk toward us in the dark.

"Rorke," said Branwen, "be careful."

The elf raised her crossbow. With the wave of a hand and a pink flash of light, Gundrygia sent it skittering across the ground. Branwen cried out and went to claim her much-abused weapon as the witch steadily eyed mine.

"You mean to say you feel no desire for me, Rorke?" Her great green eyes turned toward me in a way almost frightfully girlish while she continued her steady stride toward me. Behind me, Indra and Odile raised their weapons in defense of their queen.

With my companions on-guard for their own sakes, Weltyr's sword was my only defense. Of all things, Gundrygia pressed herself against it when she was near enough. My breath hitched while her slender hand caressed the length of the white blade. Soon those same fingers melted over the hilt and enveloped my hand.

Before I knew what had happened, Gundrygia's body pressed to mine.

The hand folded around my fist guided the sword's razor edge to her cheek.

"Does this body not please you, Paladin Burningsoul?"

"I'm not a paladin in the eyes of the Church anymore, Gundrygia."

"But in the eye of Weltyr, himself—oh, you must be mighty indeed for the All-Father to have selected you as bearer of this. His most powerful weapon."

Her free hand trailed over my chest and down my stomach, which had tightened with anticipation along with the rest of my body. Inhaling once again the rich honey of her supply scent, I brushed my lips across the flyaway strands of her dark curls and, bending lower still, kissed the temple of her forehead. Almost breathless to caress her even now, I dropped my voice to a whisper.

"If you fear the sight of my Master, as I have been informed you do, then surely you must have respect for his power…surely you understand what could happen to you for disobeying his will."

With a soft laugh, Gundrygia gazed into my face and drew another, altogether more haggard exhalation from me with her even lower contact. "Who could disobey the will of the All-Father, Burningsoul? It is the only will in existence, of which we mortals are all simple pawns…our wills cannot help but be expressions of Weltyr's will. Therefore, should you will to come along with me, how could your lovely companions argue that this be anything the will of the divine?"

"We are not called to test," I told her, pushing her away and going on while she gasped to stumble back from me. "We are called to obey. Those slaves that do not obey are doomed to be destroyed by their master. Those that do—"

"Are to be rewarded?"

Lip curling in a vicious sneer, Gundrygia stumbled back further. Her head jutted forward from her shoulders and for a few seconds she looked like an animal baring her teeth.

"Please—ask your durrow friends behind you. Tell them how often the average slave merits reward. How happily you had it in the Nightlands, friend! How coddled and spoiled you were by your own privileged mistress. Yours is not the lot of most who find themselves in bondage in the city of El'ryh."

Remembering the beatings I had witnessed in the streets, or the humiliated and sometimes executed slaves I had seen with Valeria on the way to find Indra and Odile, I agreed with Gundrygia, "Certainly, most slaves suffer. The weak fall to the strong, and though slavery is a woefully inept and cruel basis for an economy, it is typical that the slave should succumb to a master in systems where slavery exists...that is not the fault of Weltyr. These are Nature's laws; and Nature, like the deepest workings of Fate, are aspects of existence to which Weltyr must abide."

"Then how can you bring yourself to serve him happily? How can you bring yourself to serve him at all?"

"Because without Nature's laws and the threads of Fate weaving our reality together, none of this would exist."

Gundrygia's eyes blazed without need for the lantern's light. "And these are my gods, Burningsoul—my only gods. Fate and Nature. See how free I am!"

Regarding her outspread arms, I assured her, "I see only a prisoner. One freed by the grace of Weltyr for a purpose I do not presume to know."

"It was not Weltyr who led you to me! My servants

did that—my own children, from whom I've been kept for ages on end. My own children, created from nothing."

"From Weltyr's blueprint," I corrected her. "Misshapen, gimlets, whatever else you've made—you've produced nothing new. You've only collaged existing works of my Lord. Mangled them into beings most often hostile to mankinds."

"My children would not be near so hostile if mankinds could restrain themselves…if the Church of Weltyr wasn't so bigoted, so spiteful."

"I do not serve the Church," I told her firmly. "I serve Weltyr."

"And you will have nothing to show for it if you persist. Only death awaits you, Burningsoul! Do you wish to be like me? Wish to slumber for millennia with no end in sight?"

"If I serve my master faithfully, I will be brought to the All-Father's Hall of Valor and live eternally."

"And then? When the final battle comes, and the heroes are called from their Hall?"

"Then?"

I looked at her somewhat blankly. She waved at me in disgust.

"Then," she said, "you will be obliged to give yourself up. Then, there will be nothing until there is something. The same something there always is. You will be a slave for eternity."

"All the more incentive to live a right life," I assured her.

"You're a fine one to speak on these matters with such confidence…how you trembled and wept in my arms when I told you all in that grove!" I raised my blade to her, stepping forward now, and she raised a hand to stay me.

"I have already told you more truth than your god ever will, and more clearly. Even now you wield a sword whose name you do not know!"

Faltering somewhat, I asked her, "And you do know it?"

"It has as many names as your All-Father—as many names as I have heard applied against me over my life. Exigence!" The name rang from her in a victorious cry, her hand rolling out from her arm in a gesture toward it. "Exigence, slayer of dragons the world has forgotten! Exigence, born from the heart of need! The weapon that can be wielded only by those who are true slaves to Weltyr's will: the weapon that belongs in the hands of a Wotsung."

"And a Wotsung?"

"A man who could conquer a god—a master among mortals, a king among slaves! The Wotsung line has outstretched through time and now dwells in you, Burningsoul. Here you are, a lord to all, and your heritage has been hidden from you for your whole life! Come with me. I will teach you how much more you're worth. Scurrying about in the tunnels of Skythorn like a rat—this is not what you're meant for!"

Gundrygia's burning eyes seared into mine. Both her arms now outstretched, pleading for my embrace.

"Come with me. Together we can kill my father and I can show you the means of true immortality. Bodily immortality, here and now! Not some vague promise of life eternal in exchange for your enlistment in a future, all the more vicious war. Come with me, Rorke Burningsoul. I will teach you how to become a god!"

Amazingly, I believed that she believed what she was telling me. Such temptations from sorceresses of Gundrygia's ilk might have been base and empty promises to most, but the hope that lit her tone was so bright it almost saddened me. The fear I once felt for Gundrygia dissolved in an instant, her humbling beauty transfiguring from something cruel and dangerous to a hallmark of her true essence.

"You really are afraid of Weltyr," I observed.

Her face changed in an instant despite the gentleness of my own, all her features tightening with disgust.

"I am, too, of course," I continued, lowering Exigence to speak to her as a friend, "but only as the son fears the mystery and power of the father who gave him life, and who is so much mightier than he. Surely, whatever you have done, Weltyr does not think so ill of you that you need fear him like this."

Her hands pressed childishly to her ears. "Ugh! Don't patronize me. I won't hear this nonsense from a slave. If anyone has call to fear Weltyr, it's certainly I. I, who have brought into the world races he did not permit the hand of Time to produce for him. My power is so mighty that he cannot destroy me, but cannot let me live unhindered! Shall I show you, Burningsoul?"

As I lifted Exigence once more, I demanded, "Release us now, Gundrygia, and we will spread your legendary name far and wide. All will know you as the most powerful mortal in the land."

"I care nothing for such acclaim...I only care to bring you with me, Burningsoul." A rat scuttled through the darkness and toward Gundrygia's furs, glowing the same bright pink aura that haloed her head. "If you won't come of your own volition, I'll bring you by force."

The terrible noise of cracking bones echoed through the tunnels. Valeria cried out behind me and began one of her prayers, but I was not convinced that any blessing of Roserpine's could reach us in the space Gundrygia crafted. Only Weltyr's might have pierced such a strange pocket of space-time. Even then, Gundrygia had so much power in the place that I did not want to lean too heavily on the generous intercession of my god.

By the time the rat had emerged into the pink light of Gundrygia's aura, it was twice the size of the largest cat I had seen; as it scrambled between us, it accomplished the stature of small horse; by the time it reached me, it had managed to rise upon its rear legs while, with the elongating limbs of its forelegs, it slashed at me with claws tinged black from a lifetime in tunnels.

Seeing the transformation, Valeria stopped her prayer. I shuddered to think of being faced down with some giant spider for more hideous and violent than a misshapen as a result of her well-intended summoning spell. The rat would suit me just fine. While the squealing, foaming beast slashed at me, I met it with Exigence and its cry rattled through the tunnel.

Branwen, who had been looking in the dark for her crossbow (forever lost in faerieland, I assumed), hurried back to the safety of the light that surrounded my other companions. The overgrown rat's beady eyes followed her movements, its ears and whiskers twitching amid a terrible rolling shudder as it seemed to consider pursuing her into the purview of the lantern. It focused, instead, on gripping my blade with one bleeding hand and reaching forward to grab my head with the other.

Crying out as the abomination made to tear my head from my shoulders, I blindly wrenched the sword from its grasp. Now it was the rat's turn to scream in pain. Exigence's sharp edge effortlessly severed three of its fingers and, to nurse this wound in shock, it released me. I gestured with the tip of the sword at Gundrygia.

"I hope your heart overflows with remorse for the

creature you made conscious only so it might die at the tip of Weltyr's blade."

With a cry, Gundrygia stepped forward, then backpedaled quite a bit as the beast stumbled. I slashed at its hideously contorted muzzle and it howled, its bright yellow fangs now painted with as much blood as they had been foam. Nevertheless, the creature met me again, snapping at me, its tail thrashing wildly in the air.

Exigence met it in the heart. All its motion ceased.

The dead abomination slid off my blade and thudded upon the floor of the tunnel.

"Release us," I commanded Gundrygia.

But the glow about her brightened and her hands raised to meet me. Fire danced at the tips of her fingers, swirling about her palms and wrists and growing wildly between them. As soon as the flame had been contained into a pulsing ball between her hands, she hurled it at my companions.

Acting on instinct, I dove between them and lifted Exigence.

The fireball split in half, its flames dissolving on contact with the truly magical blade. While Gundrygia cried out, I spared no time before I charged her.

Once, in the grove, I had struck her and been haunted by it. This was a different situation altogether. Teeth bared, the witch opened a hand. Her empty palm seemed to swallow the darkness around it. A hard obsidian blade swung forward, pulled from the very absence of light in the tunnel system (or its faerieland duplicate). While Zweiding's blessed steel had suffered immediately beneath the pressure of Exigence, Gundrygia's sword of darkness fared better at absorbing the blows of Weltyr's weapon.

Her body, however, could not absorb the strength of

mine quite so easily. While she was a powerful sorceress and might too have been a fine enough opponent for some fighters, my lifetime of sword-fighting—and, of course, my earlier victory that day—gave me an undeniable advantage over her in matters of physical conflict. She might parry a blow here or there, but she had better luck relying on her nimble frame to avoid my strikes.

While my companions cheered me on and cried out on those rare instances Gundrygia's haphazard fighting style permitted her the unpredictability required to almost wing me with a hack from her blade, I wore her down and began to increasingly catch her in parries. Each meeting of our swords marked a reduction in her strength. Soon her arms trembled when our blades sparked and she, without a chance to so much as think one of those spells of hers, looked pale to think the end was quite possibly near.

"You took such exception before," she panted, a few untamed curls falling across her sweat-beaded face while her arms slowly succumbed beneath my pressure. "In the grove, when you struck me—I felt your shame, no matter how sweet it was to savor the heat of your anger. What makes now any different?"

"Because...now I have given you every chance to release us. Now, you are holding us captive—endangering the women I love. And that, I can never permit."

With a last push, I knocked Gundrygia back and used the recoil to lift Exigence. The blade fell once again against hers with a sharp crack. To my relief, the summoned sword fell from my opponent's hand and dissolved back into the rest of the darkness like smoke or sand. When her lips curled in the genesis of a magical word, I sliced at her, and I do confess—guilt singed my heart to hear her cry as she gripped her cut hand.

Still, dangerous as she was, I could spare no quarter. While she stumbled back beside the metal rail, falling upon the concrete beneath it and pushing herself away with her feet, I advanced. The sword remained between us.

"Rorke!" Gasping to stare down the tip of Exigence's blade, she searched my features desperately and begged, "Be reasonable, now! I'm not really any threat to you, am I?"

"If I kill you now," I asked her, keeping my expression as hard as I could for a woman so beautiful and, even if by her own nature, imperiled, "will we be trapped in this nether-space of yours forever?"

"How could you ask that?"

"Answer my question."

Nostrils flaring, Gundrygia stared defiantly into my face.

"No," she admitted, "you'll be free from here if you kill me. If it's so important that you continue living as a deluded slave, then fine."

Moving quickly, Gundrygia rolled forward upon her knees and once more grasped the blade. My companions gasped while, lifting her chin, the witch guided the tip of the sword to her throat and stared me hard in the eyes.

"Kill the mother of your child, Rorke Burningsoul."

My mind struggled to parse the words once spoken aloud. Lips parting in shock, then tensing, I prodded the blade against her neck and said above her softly hitched breath, "You're lying."

"Not about this," she assured me, maintaining that steady stare into me.

Full of all number of strange emotions, I struggled to find some hint of deception in her face. Indeed, I prayed to find it.

There was defiance there, and feral hostility. But there was no trace of a lie.

I lowered Exigence.

"Rorke!"

Valeria's cry drew my attention away from the witch kneeling before me. Whirling about, blade already raising, I prepared to defend myself against a pair of rat-beasts that thundered along the rails through the tunnels for me—

And, with a rapid chant, Branwen hurled a bolt of lightning as though launching a javelin through the air. Roserpine may have struggled to reach the mockery of space that was Gundrygia's pocket dimension, but the witch herself had claimed Nature to be her very god. I should not have been surprised that it was our druid who counted most just then.

With a bright explosion more rapidly blinding to the durrow than the fireball had been, the druid's lightning danced down the line of the rail and ran through the charging rat-beasts. By the time they tumbled within ten feet of me, both were dead and smoking with the abhorrent stench of roasted meat and burning hair.

I turned back to Gundrygia, but the witch was already some yards away from me.

"How lucky you are to have your little entourage. Where would you be without them, slave?" Glowering at me through the pale moon of her sullen face, Gundrygia gestured to Exigence. "You will throw away ultimate power—destroy yourself—in following the commands of your master. If you don't come with me now, Burningsoul, you'll be exactly as free as Exigence there."

Plagued by the conflicting desires to hold the mother of my child and destroy a threat to my life, I felt only deep sorrow for Gundrygia. I wanted to save her from her own grim fate—or the grim fate to which she bound herself by the decisions she made. By holding in her heart such a fearful loathing for Weltyr.

"So," I suggested to her, sliding Exigence back into its place at my hip, "come with us, instead."

Scoffing, looking totally taken aback by such an idea, Gundrygia demanded, "What do you mean?"

"I mean just that. I mean, come with us. Help us find Valeria's ring."

"Yes," said Valera hurriedly, stepping forward despite the protests of Indra and Odile. "Yes—oh, a child of Rorke's! How pleased I'd be to meet such an angel. What love I feel already to think you the vessel of such life!"

Now looking more sincerely confused—and, perhaps, just a bit angry about the confusion, or a suggestion she possibly perceived as a joke—Gundrygia shook her head.

"How can you be his lover yet say such a thing? You dark elves truly are quite bizarre, aren't you!"

"It's not just them," said Branwen, her hand to her heart, a new urgency in her earnest eyes. "I understand why she would say that. I love Rorke—I'd love any child of his, whether mine or someone else's. Maybe especially someone else's," she added with a wry laugh that Odile dryly echoed.

Smile fading, serious again, Branwen went on to Gundrygia that, "You haven't hurt any of us, and if you had, knowing you're with Rorke's child would change things. Anyway...Rorke obviously cares about you, or he would have already killed you and freed us from this place. Since he cares about you, we do, too. There must be something he sees that's worth loving in you, and I want to know what it is."

"Me, too," said Indra, nodding. "Rorke's such a good-hearted person."

"If he thinks you can be saved from a death at the other end of his sword," Odile agreed, "then I'm willing to give you a chance."

"Please." Valeria stepped just to the edge of the light, her hands clasped before her heart. "Please, Gundrygia—come with us."

I had not expected to receive such commendable help from my companions, but I ought to have believed they would stand by me. Each one of them was a good woman from the first day we met; and though some of them made questionable decisions from time to time, they all had pure hearts and wills unquestionably aligned with my god.

For just a few moments, Gundrygia looked nearly swayed by these good hearts. The warmth that was offered to her would have been alluring to anyone—and to someone like Gundrygia, who had for so long been alone and abandoned in the world, I could not begin to imagine just how deeply she desired to take us up on the offer to join our party of travelers.

Alas, we were not yet a family…and family called to her then, a baleful black voice echoing through the bleak space that mimicked the tunnels beneath Skythorn.

Come home, Gundrygia, commanded the familiar voice, everywhere and nowhere around us. *Come home, daughter. Bring the new Wotsung with you.*

Gundrygia's hopeful face fell, the open expression of marvelous possibilities clamming into a tense, cold mask.

"Yes, Father," she answered it, raising a hand.

Bright light filled the tunnel fast enough to blind even me.

20

ALL ABOARD
THE BATTLE SWAN

WHEN THE WITCH'S light faded from our eyes, we found ourselves on the surface of Urde while busy people passed to and fro around us.

I was in a daze after what I had just learned, and delirious to find myself so abruptly under the sun again. We all looked about ourselves in astonishment—and the durrow, with fear and the quick but ultimately unnoticed snatching up of their hoods—but I, most of all, felt instantaneous relief.

How had we gotten aboveground? Had we gone ourselves, like sleepwalkers in the clutches of some dream? Or had we been in some way teleported by the most powerful magic-user I had ever met?

In either case, I found myself before a familiar face. Lively regarded us as though we had simply walked up to her, and in fact seemed mid-turn as though to address someone who had tapped her on the shoulder.

"Oh," she cried, her face lighting up to see us, "oh, there you lot are! Almost too late—cor! You look like you've seen a ghost, Rorke."

"Only tired, Madame," I told her, patting her shoulder when she briefly embraced me. When we released, Lively drew our purse from her bodice. As Odile took it, I assured our friend, "It's been a long, long day, and looks like it's going to be an even longer one."

"Well, it would have been infinitely longer if you hadn't gotten here when you did. The porter's just made a call for five minutes to launch."

"Did you get the tickets, Lively?"

Beaming, the kind woman plucked five oblong and ornately carved chips from the pocket of her apron. Each bore an intricate design of the airship's logo—in this case, a fragile-necked swan with two marvelously plumed wings outspread—and a small magical sigil that glowed to indicate the tickets' authenticity. She turned them about for us, then passed them over.

"*The Battle Swan*," read Indra, a few locks of white hair falling across her eyes and thereafter pushed back into the mess hidden in her hood. "What a strange name!"

"Swans are vicious," I said, "and some of these airships running today are re-purposed from previous wars…this is just such a one."

Dubious, Odile fit her goggles on and peered up above the gates of the airport. The swollen edge of the dirigible was just visible, shining on the other side of a tarmac heated with the noonday sun. Forced to grimace against the glare even with her welding goggles, the skeptical rogue said, "I don't know…the last time you people were at war was before you were born, Burningsoul. Do we really want to risk riding in a thirty-year-old dirigible?"

"Now you're starting to sound like Sharp," I teased her, adding as I distributed the tickets, "but rest assured, the airships are maintained by dedicated crews. There's very rarely an accident. I've heard it said riding in an airship is safer than riding a horse."

"That may be so, but you lot be careful on your journey." Kissing my cheek, then Branwen's, then the rest of us in turn, Lively pressed the tips of her fingers to her lips and regarded us with glittering eyes. "Oh! I'm getting bleary. Get on with it, now! Pray for me, Master Burningsoul, and I'll pray for you in turn."

"That sounds like a deal to me, Lively. Fare you well! We'll be in touch, we swear."

And then, by Weltyr, we made it aboard the airship.

Perhaps it seems anticlimactic that, given our pursuit, we managed to board the blimp without further problem—but the truth was that the porters were annoyed with our last-minute arrival and barely bothered to glance at the economy class tickets they took from our hands. Actually looking in our faces was out of the question. If there had been any concern that we might be identified, or that the durrow might be singled out due to their species, those evaporated when aboard the airship.

The only trouble was, of course, our weapons—one may imagine I was even less keen to check Exigence than I had been to permit temporary confiscation of Strife—but I was confident none of us would need anything of the sort. Especially not as we entered the airship and saw the happy faces of all the laughing, chatting, bright-eyed, excited passengers.

The *Swan* was an older ship than some of the ones

the Rhineland airports might have boasted, but it was my first and, still to my mind, the most beautiful I've seen. When it was initially remodeled there had been no such thing as an economy class, and as a result the economy passengers were seated in a renovated ballroom. Past gilded scroll-work windows and through the polished arches of doorways, my companions and I found two rows of empty seats. Arranged in threes as they were, we were able to form a merry group by trading seats with an amiable couple who would be getting off at the layover in Estos, the region in the Eastern half of the continent where a few species of orc made their homes alongside some populations of human and wood elf. The thought of this reminded me of Soot and their new gimlet neighbors. How I prayed they would be successful!

And how refreshing it was to talk of mundane things with good, wholesome, god-fearing people who took one look at my durrow companions, assumed correctly that they were nothing more than a species of elf about which they'd never heard, and paid the matter no further mind. After the shock I'd received that morning with Zweiding and the Order's position on mankinds other than human, I had to wonder about nearly everyone I met. Did they, too, harbor some secret impulse against the other species in the world? How could such kneejerk reactions be overcome in any way that mattered? I thought of my own constant rivalry with Grimalkin, who was in his turn quite opposed to humans—the men, at least. Was he aboard the *Swan*? I hoped he was; it seemed now that we owed it to one another to make amends.

When the ship was steady in the clear, blue sky and making its easygoing way over Skythorn, a crew member entered to announce we were free to move about the ship. While the entire room relaxed and people stretched,

Indra and Odile sprang up together. They announced their plans to explore the ship and admire the view— we had all seen, on our way to our seats, the sprawling observation window that permitted passengers to watch clouds beside us and the planet below—and scurried excitedly off to do just that.

Branwen and Valeria, meanwhile, remained. They studied me with some concern.

"How are you, Rorke?" Valeria slid her hand into mine from where she sat between myself and Branwen. Her touch was somehow dizzying. I shut my eyes, aware at once of how exhausted I was.

And aware, too, that somewhere—somewhere north of Rhineland, if she had spoken truth—Gundrygia was with my child.

"I've certainly felt better," I confessed with a dry but not altogether humorless chuckle. "And worse. At least I didn't almost die this time."

"Don't curse it," said Branwen, grinning lightly. "There's still time yet before we find Valeria's ring."

"True...I'd ought not to tempt Oppenhir to challenge Weltyr's will. Ah! But, I must admit—it is a painful and confusing will sometimes."

"That is the way with all gods," said Valeria in gentle agreement, her soft, cool hands working back and forth gently over mine. I sighed at her caresses, leaning toward her, and she took her head in my arms to draw me against her sweet-smelling bosom. There I filled my lungs with tender flesh and drowned my ears in the steady rhythm of her heart. I shut my eyes again as Branwen reached over to trail her fingers down my scalp.

"Do you want to find her?"

The high elf's gentle question was truly a question, unladen with suggestion or reluctance. All the same, I shook my head, saying, "Yes—but there isn't time. Who knows what the spirit-thieves might do with Valeria's ring."

Valeria asked the next question. "And who knows what she might do with your child, Rorke?"

"It's her child, too," I reminded them both, kissing the back of Valeria's hand and straightening back.

While I sat up, a lad with short chestnut hair passed us by. I lowered my voice, at once keenly aware of the other passengers around.

"And she's mad...but I don't know that she's mad enough to hurt her own child. Either way, when next we find her she'll be ready to fight us again. I want to make sure I'm ready for that...and, if that could wait until after she's given birth, moreso the better. I don't like the thought of things turning ugly."

The women exchanged a glance before Valeria, that gentle ambassador of love, asked me in her rich and wonderful voice, "Have you given much thought to fatherhood, Rorke?"

"Only insofar as I find myself frightened by it," I admitted, laughing, "and the question of how I can be what I have never experienced."

"We durrow have no fathers," boasted Valeria with a patient smile, "and we manage all the same to be perfectly fine parents to our daughters."

"Yes, but you at least had mothers. I have no parents except the Church—and now I wonder if I have been regarded as warmly in turn. I don't think so, sadly. But... it doesn't matter."

Again, I lapsed into silence, more given to brooding when I was exhausted. Certainly I was in need of time to fully digest the events of the day, from my acquisition of Exigence on.

Valeria, however, went on. "And if things do come to their worst, Rorke—if you must slay Gundrygia and raise the child without its mother—who will help you?"

I was reluctantly to voice my hopes out loud and hoped the answer showed in my face, but they waited to hear it aloud. I gave it after slight delay, confessing, "Well—if you two find yourselves with me then, I would hope, perhaps—that is—I don't—"

Both women threw back their heads in spates of laughter, sharing a look and rolling their eyes in good humor.

"So bold in matters of sex," teased Valeria softly, her cheeks attractively flushed by her mirth, "yet so shy in love."

"I would not be so shy," I told her in return, staring into her pale eyes in some lovestruck wonder, "if I did not feel it impetuous for me to assume you were willing to leave your duties for me, Materna."

"Haven't I already?"

I opened my mouth, unable to come up with anything resembling a real response, and soon enough shut up again. Smiling, Valeria patted me. She then rose from her seat and announced, "I'm off to find Indra and Odile...aren't you two just famished! Come meet me in that commissary they pointed out to us while we were boarding."

Valeria slipped past Branwen and sauntered up the aisle. The high elf filled her empty seat at my side. Hand sliding into mine, Branwen asked, "What are you going to do with that sword?"

I shook my head. "I don't know. Keep it safe. Gundrygia seemed to think it has some power—what, exactly, I've no idea."

While Branwen lapsed into thought, my hand

tightened around hers. She looked up at me questioningly until I observed warmly, "You came with us."

"I came with *you*," she corrected, pressing against me. Branwen's soft body always able to cause a stir in me, I slid my arm around the small of her back and filled my senses with her marvelous flesh. My head bent over hers as she said, "I'm very fond of Valeria and Indra and Odile after all this, but it's you…you're the one I'm here with."

My mouth sought out hers and she moaned against me, her tongue trailing out to invite the caress of my own. Breaths mingling humidly between us, Branwen's body slid against mine and her hand explored my chest.

"Maybe we'd ought to wait," I breathed into her sensitive ear, kissing it to its high-swept peak. "At least until it's dark…until we won't get caught."

With a chuckle and a randy, crooked grin, Branwen extricated herself from my clutches. "Then I'm going to get something to eat…Valeria's right. I'm starving!"

I laughed slightly, watching her go with what I'm sure was a certain twinkle in my eye. Ah, Branwen!

What a relief to be on good terms with her again—to have finally, fully forgiven her in my heart. Receiving the Scepter—receiving Exigence—had cured me of any remaining ill will I bore her. Now I understood that her betrayal, like all the misfortunes that had befallen me in my life, was part of a very concrete plan that Weltyr had for me. It was not uncommon for even largely secular folk to talk of Weltyr's plan in a general sense, a notion that was expressed often to comfort someone amid grief or another setback.

But now I understood that it was, so far as I could tell, a tangible reality. Weltyr's plan was not some far-flung abstract.

The plan *was* reality: I was living Weltyr's plan, an

expression of his will, and my reclamation of the Scepter had been part of that.

Surely, then, the child conceived by myself and Gundrygia was also part of that.

What was this Wotsung line of which I was a part? What was it that the witch treasured in my seed, and why was it that Weltyr had blessed her, of all the women I had come to love in the past weeks, with the implantation of my first progeny?

Then again...had she received the first? While on my way to the commissary, I passed a pair of parents who smiled as their young daughter nicely entertained her upset brother. The mother, it appeared, was already with child again, and rested a light hand upon her stomach. Children could come quickly enough in concert when it was one woman, but when a man distributed his passion between multiple receptive females, well...suddenly a certain notion presented itself to me, making tangible what was once a distant abstract. It seemed somehow impossible that I should be a father; therefore, the very likely possibility that I had succeeded in inseminating a few of Valeria's durrow friends had not meant anything much to me in the Nightlands. It had just not seemed real.

Now, not just aboveground but flying over it, I knew I had engendered life. My own body had succeeded in passing on some parcel of myself that now grew elsewhere—and, perhaps, not just in Gundrygia.

Not just, either, in Valeria's friends.

Valeria, Branwen, Indra and Odile all sat talking softly in the commissary when I found them crowded around a small table directly near the entrance.

"And here's the lucky man," said Odile, drawing an empty seat from the table adjacent to them and scooting her own over to give me room. "We were just talking about you."

I laughed, sliding into the offered seat. "Good things, I hope."

"Only that you don't know how lucky you have it...some kid was staring at us just now, but he went on through to another compartment."

"If I were a stranger to this table, I have to admit I'd be inclined to stare, too."

The women giggled brightly around me, a choir of angels. Beneath the table, Branwen's boot slid against mine. Clouds and blue sky rolled merrily past the window behind us. Soon enough, a porter came by with the order the women had made.

After, bellies full, we returned to our seats and promptly fell asleep sitting up. Valeria leaned against me, mouth slack, and Branwen against her; in the row ahead of us, Indra and Odile drooled against each other between snores.

I was the last to fall comfortably asleep.

21

IF IT'S NOT ONE THING

VALERIA SHOOK ME awake gently, though when the task proved difficult her motion grew more vigorous. I was amazed to open my eyes only to find the cabin dark and the world outside much the same. Five hours must have passed; maybe more. Blinking through my heady stupor, I asked her to repeat herself and this time had better success at understanding what she'd just said into my ear.

"Branwen's just gone to wait for you in the cargo hold," she whispered, her voice a sultry tone that fired my loins and made me yearn for her greater closeness. "I told her I'd wake you up for her."

"You should come, too."

Laughing softly, Valeria slapped me on the arm. Her velvet lips nuzzling against the ridge of my ear, she told me, "Maybe if you think there's enough room, I'll come next time…for now, I'll let you two take the risk of getting thrown off the airship."

"They'll wait until our next landing," I assured her with a doggish smile, leaning in to exchange a lingering kiss before sliding up from my seat. "Which way is it, now?"

Soon I moved stealthily down the aisles of the *Swan*, past the other, more soundly sleeping passengers. Valeria had directed me to go to the back of the economy compartment and several hallways beyond. Avoiding the porters by hiding momentarily in a latrine, I just barely managed to sneak through to the baggage area where Branwen awaited me.

There, in the dark, my voice a whisper, I called, "Hello?"

"Here," sang Branwen, her pale body reflecting the moonlight pouring through the porthole of a door in the compartment. My desire for her flamed in an instant, though I was still barely awake after such deep and necessary sleep. I would, however, defy any man to look at Branwen's nude body on the offering beneath the moonlight and remain the least bit tired. Her stiff pink nipples and small tuft of gold pubic curls were the only interruptions in the milky flesh that stretched upon a bed she'd made of her clothes and cloak. With these beneath her, outstretched upon a few of the crates the *Swan* was due to transport, she was a veritable Anroa of the Airship. I would have done anything to see her rendered in fresco just then: a portrait to forever seal into the wall of my heart.

Seeing me, her thighs spread slowly open. The display of her body thrilling me, I stripped off my tunic and made quick work of my breeches before enfolding her in my arms. Out mouths connected in the dark, breaths melding while our tongues resumed the interrupted caresses of before. Her hands trailed over my chest and down my stomach once again, this time gripping the staff of passion that ran through me like an all-encompassing fire. I filled my palms with the soft flesh of her breasts, my kisses trailing to her ear and then down over her nipples while she writhed beneath my caresses.

"Oh, Rorke"—her tone of lust was already so desirous that I could only imagine how she had spent the time awaiting me—"yes, oh, please, take me as a reward for your task well-done…oh, Rorke, you saved that girl, and saved us, too, Rorke—oh!"

My head found its way between thighs that tightened amid the rapid lashes of my tongue. Shuddering, moaning, Branwen ground herself against my lips and cupped her breasts in her hands, teasing her nipples while watching me between her legs.

"Yes! Yes, please, Rorke, please—oh, sweet Anroa, I need your cock, Rorke! Fill me with your seed…oh, Rorke!"

Biting her plentiful lower lip with the tips of her white teeth, Branwen wriggled about beneath me and begged, "Give me a baby, Rorke, oh, please, please? I'll carry your child, Rorke, I'll gladly bear your heirs!"

Unwilling or unable to tell her that I suspected she might already be in for just such a task, I stood upright and drew her to the edge of her makeshift bed. Arranging myself between her splayed legs, I bent to press my mouth to hers.

Something fell in the darkness of the baggage compartment.

"What's that," she cried, throwing her hands over herself while I straightened up.

That same something moved quickly, scrambling

from one end of the cargo hold to the other. However quick it was, I was far quicker. Branwen scrambled upright while, stark naked, I held no compunctions about dashing after the spy and catching hold of them. The interloper of our lovemaking cried out, their head lowering while Branwen said a magic word. The car filled with her faerie light, the golden high elf equivalent of the durrow's blue wisp flames. While this magical fire flickered in the center of the car, my vision cleared to find I grasped the spying young man from before in my hands—his head was low, but it was undeniably the same head of hair I'd seen receding down the aisle.

Relieved it was not a porter or someone worse, I nonetheless scoffed as I asked, "Like sneaking about, do you?"

"Let me go," protested the lad, his voice high and somehow familiar while he struggled to yank his arm from my grip. "Let me—"

An explosion whistled through the air. The airship rocked violently and the intruder tumbled against me. Our eyes locked.

Just as I recognized Elishta-bet, her hair cut short and her soft Temple garments exchanged for a boyish wardrobe to hide her identity, someone a few compartments back from us screamed, "Pirates!"

Branwen sighed and bent for her clothes.

"Guess we'd better get dressed," she said. "See that sword of yours anywhere around here, Rorke?"

ABOUT THE AUTHOR

Regina Watts is the penname of a woman who certainly is not also M. F. Sullivan, founder and flagship author of Painted Blind Publishing. From her cozy home a few universes away from this one, Watts transmits stories to Sullivan that are then transcribed and published. Her available titles range from transgressive erotica to psychedelic fiction to horror to romance. Be sure to sign up for her mailing list at hrhdegenetrix.com!

ABOUT THE PUBLISHER

Painted Blind Publishing and its erotic imprint, Painted Blue Publishing, are the brainchild of author and devoted editor to Regina Watts, M. F. Sullivan. Founded in 2015 while Sullivan resided in Tucson, PBP is a house dedicated to bringing readers the finest in consciousness-expanding fiction. Be sure to check out the wide variety of essays available for free at paintedblindpublishing.com to learn more about the company, Watts, and Sullivan.

OTHER PAPERBACK WORKS
FROM PAINTED BLIND PUBLISHING

REGINA WATTS

INDUSTRIAL DIVINITY (2020)

WILD GIRL RUNNING (2020)

DOTTIE FOR YOU SEASON 1 (2021)

SEDUCED BY SABINE (TBD)

M. F. SULLIVAN

DELILAH, MY WOMAN (2015)

THE LIGHTNING STENOGRAPHY DEVICE (2017)

THE DISGRACED MARTYR TRILOGY (2019-2020)